PRAISE F

"A classic concept – a built wo......................................ld – a setting fo............. imagi.....tive adventure ...*elix* is the very D.................................. discovery ...."
Stephen Baxter on *Helix*

"Essentially a romp – a gloriously old-fashioned slice of science fiction... What gives the novel a unique spin is its intertwining parallel plots. It's smart, fun, page-turning stuff, with an engaging cast and plenty of twists... A hugely entertaining read."
SFX Magazine on *Helix*

"Equal parts adventure, drama and wonder. Sometimes they work alone, providing a raw dose of science fiction. Other times, Brown uses them in concert to spin an irresistible blend that pulls the narrative along almost faster than you can keep up. However it's served, *Helix* is a delightful read and is an excellent reminder of why we read science fiction: it's fun!"
SF Signal on *Helix*

"A thoughtful, provocative book that sets up a bigger story than it has a chance to tell... A surprisingly calm and fluid read, gracefully skimming over the years with the same detachment displayed by its immortal protagonist. If my regret is that this book was not longer, it is a very good book indeed."
Pornokitsch on *The Kings of Eternity*

"A novel about discovery: about the discovery of other worlds and other species only – I repeat only – insofar as it is about the discovery of love, and one another... A charmingly timeless tale, lithe, powerful and tremendously affecting."
The Speculative Scotsman on *The Kings of Eternity*

"So very fast as to speed past, and feisty enough to excite... Sets the scene for a strange world wherein anything and everything science-fictional can happen."
Tor.com on *Weird Space: The Devil's Nebula*

"Spot-on... It delivers a good story, introduces the premise
of the setting and the threats and dangers posed within it,
but also works well as a stand-alone... With Eric Brown
already signed up for another book, I know that it'll
be a series worth following."
Walker of Worlds on *Weird Space: The Devil's Nebula*

"Brown's spectacular creativity creates a constantly
compelling read... a memorable addition to the genre."
Kirkus Reviews

"Brown concentrates on stunning landscapes and in the
way he conveys the conflicting points of view between races...
No matter how familiar each character becomes, they
continue to appear completely alien when viewed
through the opposing set of eyes."
Interzone

"There is always something strikingly probable about
the futures that Eric Brown writes... No matter how dark
the future that Eric Brown imagines, the hope of redemption is
always present. No matter how alien the world he
describes, there is always something hauntingly familiar
about the situations that unfold there."
Tony Ballantyne

"Eric Brown joins the ranks of Graham Joyce, Christopher Priest
and Robert Holdstock as a master fabulist."
Paul di Filippo

"SF infused with a cosmopolitan and literary sensibility...
accomplished and affecting."
Paul J. McAuley

"Eric Brown is *the* name to watch in SF."
Peter F. Hamilton

ALSO BY ERIC BROWN

Novels
Weird Space: The Devil's Nebula
The Kings of Eternity
Guardians of the Phoenix
Xenopath
Necropath
Cosmopath
Kéthani
Helix
New York Dreams
New York Blues
New York Nights
Penumbra
Engineman
Meridian Days

Novellas
Starship Summer
Starship Fall
Starship Winter
Revenge
The Extraordinary Voyage of Jules Verne
Approaching Omega
A Writer's Life

Collections
The Angels of Life and Death
Ghost Writing
Threshold Shift
The Fall of Tartarus
Deep Future
Parallax View (with Keith Brooke)
Blue Shifting
The Time-Lapsed Man

As Editor
The Mammoth Book of New Jules Verne Adventures
(with Mike Ashley)

First published 2012 by Solaris
an imprint of Rebellion Publishing Ltd,
Riverside House, Osney Mead,
Oxford, OX2 0ES, UK

www.solarisbooks.com

ISBN: 978 1 78108 047 4

10 9 8 7 6 5 4 3 2 1

A CIP catalogue record for this book is available from the
British Library.

Designed & typeset by Rebellion Publishing

Printed and bound by CPI Group (UK) Ltd, Croydon, CR0 4YY

ERIC BROWN

HELIX

WARS

SOLARIS

For Phillip Vine, Patrick Mahon,
and Mark Chitty

– Champions all –

with thanks

One /// Descent

I

AFTER THE ROW with Maria, which left him feeling sick and wishing he could retroactively edit his words, Ellis strapped himself into the shuttle's couch and prepared to take off from Carrelliville spaceport.

For the next thirty minutes he lost himself in the anaesthetic of routine, running through the pre-flight systems check with his controller in the terminal tower. Soon, thankfully, he would be leaving New Earth and heading for D'rayni, seven worlds further along this circuit of the Helix.

"You're ready to go, Jeff. Initiate in ten, nine..."

Ellis handed over to the smartcore, and seconds later the main drive ignited and the shuttle eased itself from the gantry. He closed his eyes as the pressure forced him back into the couch. The shuttle rose slowly, then gained speed, and in his mind's eye he saw Maria's pursed expression of barely suppressed hatred.

He opened his eyes and concentrated on the view.

He'd piloted shuttles for almost ten years now, and he knew he would never cease to feel the thrill of taking off and looking down on the misty green expanse of New Earth and its neighbouring worlds curving away beneath him.

He wondered what it must have been like for shuttle pilots back on Old Earth, over a thousand years ago. The thought of inhabiting a single planet, a spherical world floating alone in space, was a concept he understood intellectually but found hard to envisage.

On the Helix, things were very different.

The vast curving length of the fourth circuit looped away before him. Directly below, New Earth was an expanse of green parks dotted with small cities and townships, linked by arterial roads and monorails. In the distance, the blue expanse of the sea separated New Earth from the next barrel-shaped world along the chain. Beyond that was the next world, as yet uninhabited, an even hazier stretch of verdure separated from its neighbour by yet another sea. And so it went, world after sea after world, on and on – ten thousand of them in total, wound around the light of the G-type sun.

As a child he'd continually called the circuits 'tiers'. But, as his father had never tired of telling him, how could you have a 'tier' in a continuous spiral? One tier phased into another, and who was to say when one tier became the next? He smiled at the memory of his father's exasperation when trying to drum the concept into him. He'd finally cut the bottom from a plastic bottle and placed it over a lighted candle; then he'd wound a length of plastic-coated wire around the bulbous bottle in a creditable facsimile of the Helix.

"This is the Helix," his father had said. "Now do you see? There are no tiers or levels as such, just one continuous spiral: four circuits below the sun, and four above, from circuit one at the top down to circuit eight at the bottom. It's lazy to call these circuits 'tiers,' though that's what a lot of people do call them."

And to better illustrate the place where humankind now lived, his father had meticulously painted tiny sections of the wire blue and green, to denote the many worlds and seas that were laced on the spiral like rotating beads on a thread. "Not that this is to scale," Ellis senior had pointed out. "There are thousands of worlds on the Helix, and only a few hundred on this."

But Ellis had finally understood, and began questioning his father about the Helix, its construction and provenance, right up until his death twenty years ago, when Jeff had been fifteen.

His father – an administrator in local government – had never lived to see his only child join the Peacekeepers as a pilot. He would have been proud, curious as he was about the Helix and frustrated by the humdrum nature of his own chosen profession.

Ten thousand worlds, Ellis thought to himself now in wonder. *And six thousand of them inhabited by as many alien species.*

Most of those species were off-limits to the more technologically advanced races of the Helix, the Mahkan and the Jantisars and others who had attained spaceflight alongside humankind. The Builders, in their wisdom, had proscribed contact between the less developed races and those more advanced: the former had to find their own way on the long path of species evolution, with no influence from outside forces.

Ellis had come into contact with around a dozen alien races, but for the most part – with one exception – that contact had been fleeting and visual only. The exception was when he'd come to the aid of a Mahkanian vessel stranded between the circuits three years ago, an event which had led to the frequent reunions with the alien engineer whose life he'd saved that day.

And his contact with the Mahkanian had made him even more curious about the thousands of other races which dwelled on the Helix. He realised that he was probably just as frustrated in his own profession as his father had been in his.

His thoughts were interrupted by a soft tap on the door between the cockpit and the passenger lounge. The hatch opened and a small faced peeked through.

"Jeff! I thought it was you – saw you through the viewscreen when we were crossing the tarmac. Mind if I join you?"

His heart skipped and he tried to wipe the grin from his face. In the company of Abi Ajemba he was a schoolboy again.

He gestured to the vacant co-pilot's couch and she slipped into it. She was about five feet tall, as slim as a twelve-year-old schoolboy, and as black as a ripe nightfruit. She'd once told him that her forebears, way back, had hailed from a country in Africa called Ghana. She was in her early thirties, but looked much younger.

"Had to get away from Doc Travers back there. Boring? Arrogant?" She laughed.

"I'll try not to bore you too much, then."

"'Sif you could do that," she said with a shy smile, and looked through the side panel at New Earth passing far below.

He had first met her five years ago while ferrying peacekeeping officials around the Helix, and for some reason they'd hit it off.

Conversation flowed with Abi; they had things in common – strict, conservative fathers, and a curiosity about the world their kind had left behind.

Now she glanced at him, smiling. "Still dreaming about Old Earth?"

"Not so much these days. That said... you know, it's never far away."

"I wish we had more history files," Abi said. "Just more information about the place."

So much had been lost when the colony ship crash-landed on the lowest circuit of the Helix over two hundred years ago. As well as losing a thousand colonists in the impact, countless com-caches and files had been destroyed, irretrievable information about all aspects of the planet they had left. Fortunately, the ship's vast cache of deep-frozen animal embryos had survived the impact, enabling the colony to populate New Earth with many of the species that had once roamed Old Earth.

Abi screwed her lips into a tight loop. "And I'll tell you what's so difficult. Not only not knowing what Earth was like way back – but not knowing what became of it."

He wanted to reach out and take the tiny woman's hand, but stopped himself. He was more than just platonically attracted to her, but as ever found himself reluctant to escalate the terms of their relationship.

She went on, hugging herself. "I mean, what happened on Old Earth? Did the rest of humanity die out? Do they still exist – and if so, then in what conditions?"

He looked at her. "You feel guilty?"

She laughed and playfully jabbed his upper arm. "Of course not. Guilt's your thing, Jeff. Not mine!"

He had confided this to her during one of their post-flight drinks in the terminal bar. He'd got a little drunk and found himself admitting that his default emotion these days – and, if he were to be truthful with himself, in the past too – was guilt. Guilt at not being at his father's bedside when he died; guilt at the thought that he was living a good life here on the Helix while, for all he knew, the remnants of humankind were scraping an existence on an Earth barely able to sustain life. And guilt, he'd finished drunkenly, at the state of his marriage.

And Abi had reached out and taken his hand, raised it to her lips and kissed it.

Then the guilt had kicked in again and he'd withdrawn his hand, made excuses and fled.

"Just curious," she said now. "I want to know what's happening on Old Earth. Whether humanity survived, and in what condition. I mean, it was a hell of a long time ago. Humanity might have recovered, prospered."

"Or we... they... might have perished."

She fell silent, watching him, and he busied himself needlessly with the controls.

At last she said, "You're an odd person, Jeff Ellis. Why all this pessimism?"

He shook his head. He was often surprised at other people's assessment of him. He did not think of himself as a pessimist.

She said, "We've known each other... how long, now?"

"Five years, a little more?"

"Five years, three months and two days, to be precise."

He looked at her, surprised.

"I was thinking about you the other day, thinking back... It's a long time." She paused, then said, "And you know, in all that time you've never mentioned Ben. Or rather you have, once, when you were drunk."

Something closed up in his chest, tightened around the knot of pain in there. He said, "I don't recall that."

She reached out and touched his hand, her fingers hot. "You were very, very drunk, Jeff. Otherwise, I would never have known."

He had no desire to talk about his son, to Abi or to anyone. He'd never even discussed with Maria what had happened that day.

Abi's hand still connected them, warming. The seconds ticked by as they raced above the surface of New Earth. Her thumb moved across the back of his hand, stroking with an insistent, urgent rhythm.

She said, "Things still bad with Maria?"

He swallowed, made himself look at her. He nodded, and wondered if, with that single gesture, he was enabling a course of events which would eventually cause him to feel an even greater burden of guilt.

She almost whispered, "Just to say, I'm always there, Jeff. You know where I am if you need someone, okay?"

He looked away, stared through the viewscreen, at once apprehensive but, he had to admit, also excited. He nodded for a long time, until he realised that the action must look foolish, and forced himself to smile and reply, "Thanks. Yes. I know where you are."

He wondered if, once the flight was over and they returned to Carrelliville, he would be able to go through with it and call on Abi... or if he'd attempt yet again to make things better with Maria, for all the good that would do.

She stretched, and with that simple gesture broke the tension in the cabin. He glanced at her chest, at the outline of her small breasts beneath the red material of her Peacekeepers' uniform, and then looked away quickly as she said, "I'm looking forward to getting some furlough. I seem to have been doing nothing but work for the past month."

"Busy time?" he said for want of anything better to say.

"When I'm not on a routine field trip, and there have been plenty of those these days, I'm sitting in front of a com making reports that no one will ever read. The files are shunted up to head office, where some fat-cat bureaucrat will ignore whatever recommendations I've made."

"Tough. Ever thought of quitting?"

She grinned. "What? And miss travelling the Helix, seeing planets I'd never normally see, meeting bizarre and exotic life-forms? You kidding? I might gripe, but allow a girl a little gripe time, okay?"

He smiled.

"You know what?" she said. "I don't know how most of the people dirtside can bear it. I mean, to see all the worlds stacked up there, swirling away above their heads, and know that they'll never visit them. Must be so frustrating."

"You're lucky."

"And you too, Mr Shuttle Pilot."

He shrugged. "I'm no more than a glorified taxi driver. I ferry VIPs like you all over the place, and then I end up in a dull terminal building... That's if I'm even allowed off the shuttle."

She cocked her head, regarding him. "Maybe one day I'll be able to get you along as my aide."

He laughed. "Well, if you could..."

"I'll consider it a mission, Jeff. Of course, chances are it'd be an overnight stay..."

He felt himself colouring and he covered his embarrassment with, "And today? D'rayni? I've heard it's not that pleasant: cold, icy, ugly..."

"I've never been there before. This is a contact follow-up mission. The D'rayni are pre-spaceflight, but five years ago they contacted us. We made an initial peacekeeping mission to D'rayni then, letting them know who we are, what we're doing here."

"Do you know if the D'rayni recall their arrival on the Helix?"

She shook her head. "It happened over five thousand years ago, Jeff. They were stone age-equivalent. They had a lot of nature-god myths, but evolved out of them. And just a few years ago they learned the truth, from us, for the first time."

He smiled. "Some responsibility you have."

"And I'm very aware of that responsibility every minute of every day."

"What's the world like geographically?"

"Mountainous, oxygen-rich, and heavy in metals, which is how the D'rayni succeeded with such a rapid industrial revolution. Had their world been one along – Phandra, which is metal-light – they would still be hunter-gatherers, or at least pre-industrial."

"What do they look like?"

"Squat, thuggish-looking humanoids. Quite threatening the first time you set eyes on them, but as gentle as lambs."

"They sound interesting."

She nodded. "They petitioned to expand their territory down-spiral – or at least asked our original peacekeeping mission if they might occupy an uninhabited neighbouring world. Of course we said we'd consult the Builders."

"Even though the Builders have been incommunicado for almost two hundred years..."

She smiled. "The D'rayni don't know that. The line we're taking is that expansion is frowned upon, as who knows when any neighbouring world might be needed."

Ellis was silent for a time, then said, "I wonder why the Builders clammed up after their initial contact with us?"

She shrugged her slight shoulders. "Who knows. They're a law unto themselves. They're almost…"

He glanced at her. "Go on. Almost?"

"I was going to say almost godlike."

He laughed. "Don't tell me that you're a cultist!"

She feigned to punch him. "No way. I'm a hardened rationalist, and you know that. But it's easy to see the Builders' superior science as supernatural."

There had been a fad, a few years ago among the youth of Carrelliville and beyond, which promulgated the belief that the Builders were deities who not only brought ailing species to the Helix, but had created them in the first place. The notion had soon been quashed, though Ellis knew that some people privately harboured not dissimilar beliefs.

Abi said, "Doesn't your wife work for the Builder Liaison Team?"

He nodded. "She's a doctor. Every few months they make a field-trip to the coast and tap on the side of the Builders' ziggurat."

"A pretty sophisticated tap, by all accounts."

"Okay, the Liaison Team analyses microwaves and radio waves emanating from the ziggurat, or some such."

"What's her take on the Builders' silence?"

Ellis stared through the viewscreen, seeing Maria turn away from him, reluctant to discuss the Liaison Team's work. "She's tight-lipped about the whole affair. Official secrets and so on." He fell silent and Abi, watching him with her big brown eyes, nodded her understanding.

After a while he said, "Doesn't it make your job more difficult? I mean, with the Builders giving nothing away?"

"It does and it doesn't. In one way it gives us latitude, allows us to make our own decisions, based on what we think the Builders would desire. In another, it makes us realise that we have to be very, very careful when we make those decisions. It's humbling, in a way." She smiled at him. "As is the whole thing about being the Builders' representatives. I mean, our race screwed up the running of our own planet to the point where we had to leave Earth in order to survive. And then the Builders in their infinite wisdom set us up as Peacekeepers. In a way, it doesn't make sense."

"Who are we to fathom the motives of the Builders?"

"Exactly."

He pointed through the viewscreen. "Look."

Abi peered down, her shaveskull head touching his shoulder. "Beautiful," she said.

He magnified the image, and the string of worlds sprang into view, a string of blue and green strips sequencing along the chain. Much of the circuit below was covered in cloud, but here and there great sweeps of land showed through, veined by rivers and marked by great mountain ranges mantled with snow.

Abi said, "How long before touchdown?"

Ellis glanced at the chronometer. "Just over two hours."

She sighed. "I really should go and compare notes with Dr Travers before we land."

"I sense a 'but' coming."

"But I'd rather be here, chatting with you."

"Good. Then leave the good doctor to his own devices. If you'd like a coffee..." He gestured to the unit. "And if you're making one, I wouldn't say no."

They drank hot rich coffee and for the next hour chatted about nothing in particular, and Ellis relished the ease with which he could trade smalltalk with Abi. Any conversation these days with Maria was forced, and more often than not escalated into an argument. The only occasions when they didn't argue was when Ellis forestalled his wife's acrimony by terminating the conversation and walking away – a tactic which only served to infuriate Maria even more.

He blinked, irritated at himself for thinking about his wife while Abi was speaking. "I'm sorry?"

"I was just saying," she said, pointing through the viewscreen, "what's that?"

He looked down, following the direction of her small forefinger.

Mountain and ravines showed through a rent in the cloud, marked by the brilliant white of snow peaks and glacial flows.

"I don't see..." he began.

"To the right."

He made out what looked like a blur of dirty cloud, but when he increased the magnification he could see that the pewter-grey pall was a drift of smoke. Through it, colourful against the monochrome grey and white of mountain rock and snow, orange flame flickered.

"What's happening down there?" she said.

"Can't make it out for the cloud cover."

The cloud parted briefly, and he glimpsed a small town or village. Dwellings were wrecked, some burnt out and charred, others still burning.

"Natural, or hostile?" she asked.

"Impossible to tell."

Seconds later they had left the conflagration in their wake.

He tapped at his com-console and routed the images of the burning township to the console screen. They watched again in silence.

"I'll send this back to New Earth," he said, "and see what they make of it."

He squirted the package back to headquarters, then brought up a schematic of the fourth circuit on the screen. The shuttle's position appeared as a flashing dot, passing over a world labelled *Phandra*.

"The world is positioned between D'rayni and Sporell," Abi said. "It's non-industrial, its civilisation comparable to Earth circa 1200, or thereabouts. But very, very different."

He looked at her. "How so?"

"The Phandrans are tiny humanoids, around a metre tall on average."

He couldn't help the dig: "Like you, then?"

"Very funny. Not like me at all. Among them, I'd be a giant. They're elfin, and... sensitive."

"Sensitive?"

"That's their official designation on our files," she said. "It means they have a certain telepathic, or empathetic, capability. They were brought to the Helix over fifteen thousand years ago, but interestingly they retained the knowledge of where they came from, their origins. That's rare: among the races brought here so long ago, creation myths supplant the truth, especially among pre-industrial peoples who have limited means of recording history."

"But not among the Phandrans? How come?"

She shrugged her narrow shoulders. "Some ethnographers have postulated that it's to do with their 'sensitivity' – that it's some kind of race memory, handed down from generation to generation. Another odd thing about them is their longevity – or rather their lack of. They live for an average of just twenty New Earth years."

"Strange." He would read up on these people when he returned to Carrelliville. "How is it, if they're pre-industrial, that we've had any contact with them at all?"

She looked at him. "You must have heard of what happened to Friday Olembe?"

He opened his mouth in a silent 'Ah' of understanding. "Of course. That's where he washed up."

"A hundred and ninety years ago, when Carrelliville was established and Olembe was getting itchy feet. He didn't want to join the nascent Peacekeepers, so he set off in his own ship to explore."

Ellis had read – first as a child in an old story book, and then in a more detailed account years later – that Olembe's shuttle had suffered a mechanical failure and he'd ditched into the sea between Phandra and D'rayni. He washed ashore, badly injured, only to be found and nursed back to health by the elfin humanoids.

Days later a rescue mission had been mounted from New Earth, and further contact between humans and Phandrans had been inevitable.

"But since then?" Ellis asked.

"I think the last contact was around fifty years ago, a routine follow up mission to ensure all was well on Phandra. The contact was limited, and brief."

They flew on in silence for a while, and he considered Abi and what she'd said earlier. Two or three times in the past year he'd thought about leaving Maria, but always he'd shied away from walking out. Three years ago, after their son's death, he'd gone through a painful period of intermingled grief and a strange sense of liberation – because a part of him knew that now he had no reason to stay with the woman who, since the birth of their son, had withdrawn into herself and treated him with cold contempt.

In the months after Ben's death, however, they'd come a little closer, and the thought of leaving her had filled him with yet more guilt.

But now... Now, three years later, they'd weathered their grief and the idea of leaving Maria filled him with an odd surge of hope.

He reached out and laid a hand over hers, his white flesh eclipsing her black, and he was about to say that he'd very much like to see her next week when the communicating hatch flew open.

He didn't have time to withdraw his hand before Dr Travers inserted his leonine head and stared at them, his gaze lingering on their intertwined fingers.

Ellis quickly removed his hand.

The doctor said, "I was wondering, when you've quite finished your tryst in here, if you'd care to discuss work, Ajemba?"

Abi gave Ellis a dazzling smile, then said to Travers, "I was just on my way, Doctor." She slipped from the couch. "See you later, Jeff."

He smiled at her, aware of the thumping of his heart and his burning face.

2

As THE HATCH clicked shut behind her, Ellis glanced through the viewscreen. What he saw made him sit up and reach out to magnify the view.

The stark geography presented an arabesque of mountain ridges, and winding through them a wide track. It was not the track that was of interest, however, but what was progressing along it at a snail's pace.

He counted a dozen small black shapes, alien in design but even so recognisable as military vehicles, bristling with gun barrels of various gauges.

So what was a caravan of tanks, he asked himself, doing in the high sierra of a pre-industrial civilisation?

He recalled the burning township and belatedly made the connection.

He opened communications to the lounge. "I think you'd better get in here, Abi, Doctor Travers."

The shuttle bucked in the thermals as the mountains raced by beneath. Abi appeared at the hatch, holding onto the sides as the shuttle pitched back and forth. She steadied herself, staggered to the co-pilot's couch, and fell into it.

Travers appeared in the hatch behind her, gripping the frame and looking displeased at the summons. "Well?"

Ellis pointed at the military convoy on the viewscreen. "I thought Phandra was pre-industrial, Abi?" He stared at her as she bit at her bottom lip. He went on, "I think we have the cause of the destruction back there."

Travers moved from the hatch and braced himself between the couches, staring at the image of the crawling tanks.

Abi explained about the burning township they'd seen earlier. Travers said, "Okay. Right. We have this cached, I take it? Let's get out of here and beam it to New Earth."

Ellis nodded. "I've already –" he began.

He never finished the sentence.

Something exploded to the right of the shuttle. He saw an actinic flash which lingered on his retina. The shuttle pitched as if swatted by a giant hand and his ears rang with the deafening cannonade of the explosion. Before he could take evasive action, a missile struck the shuttle. He heard a crunch to his rear and the craft lifted twenty metres as if rammed from below.

Ellis read the com-screen before him: system failure. An alarm blared, shrill and insistent, filling the cabin and deafening him.

"What is it?" Abi yelled.

"Com's down," Ellis said.

"Can't you control this thing?" Travers shouted.

Ellis didn't waste his breath replying. A peak loomed a couple of hundred metres before them. He leaned back, pulling the column towards him, and the spire of rock flashed beneath the shuttle with metres to spare. Abi sobbed, pulling herself into a foetal ball on the couch.

"What's happening, Ellis?" Travers called out.

"Limited manoeuvrability, even on manual," he said. "I'm going for an emergency landing."

But not in the mountains, he thought. That would be suicide. If he could maintain the shuttle on an even keel, leave the mountains in their wake and find a plain... He recalled the view of the terrain from earlier, how the mountain range petered out to the west, the very direction in which they were heading.

"Travers, there's a couch behind you. Strap yourself in."

The doctor crawled across the cabin and hauled himself into the seat. Abi reached across the gap and squeezed Ellis's thigh, the gesture more desperate than affectionate. She smiled at him, quickly, and he felt a sudden welling of indescribable sadness.

The shuttle was not responding. He tried to ease the craft to the right, to put more space between themselves and a nearby mountain peak, but the lateral control was compromised. The shuttle flew on, as straight as an arrow, missing the peak by fifty metres.

A vast valley opened out before them and Ellis saw that they had left the snow behind and entered a region where vegetation grew – strange trees with tall, thick boles and a tangle of cloud-like foliage that intermeshed with that of their neighbours to create a canopy kilometres wide.

He laughed aloud at the idea of dying in paradise.

"What?" Abi asked with desperation.

He glanced at her. "I'm sorry," he managed. "I just wanted to say..."

He wanted to say that he would very much like to kiss her, but, before he could articulate the phrase, the shuttle sliced through the haywire tangle of alien foliage and a split-second later impacted with the ground. The cabin was torn apart and something struck Ellis in the chest. He had time to wonder, with surreal curiosity, if he'd suffered a heart attack, and then blackness consumed him.

Two /// Death in Paradise

1

He opened his eyes.

His first reaction was amazement that he was still alive, his second that he must have suffered severe injuries. If the impact hadn't killed him, then surely his injuries would…

He blinked. Where was the shuttle? He expected to see the wreckage of the cockpit all around him, expected to find himself entangled – embedded, even – in its torn and twisted metal. But he was lying on his back on something very soft and staring up into a mellow twilight. The scene above him was so idyllic that he could only smile in wonder. The sun was going down over distant jagged peaks. The fiery orange ball set the cloud cover ablaze and ignited a silver filigree mist high above his head. Then he knew what the spun silver was: the cloud-like foliage of the trees he'd seen while descending.

He tried to move, to roll onto his side. Instantly, pain attacked him with a thousand talons. He caught his breath, not daring to let it out. He fell onto his back, the wind expelled painfully from his lungs, and lay panting. He must have passed out; the next thing he knew he was staring through the gaps in the silver foliage at the twinkling points of distant stars.

He drew a breath without causing his ribs to explode. "Abi?" he called.

He willed her to respond. A silence greeted his call – no, not silence: wind soughed through the forest canopy, and somewhere far off an animal, or bird, called a low, achingly poignant, oboe tremolo.

"Abi!" he shouted again, with increasing desperation. He wanted to hug the tiny woman to him.

His vision faded a few moments later and he passed out again.

It was daybreak when he next came to his senses.

He stared up, shocked. Maria was standing over him, staring down. Her face was a mask of undisguised contempt. He tried to reach out to her, wanting nothing but her comforting embrace. His stretching hand fell well short.

"How dare you?" she shouted.

He blinked, and realised that he was crying. Tears flooded his eyes, distorting Maria's image. "I'm sorry?"

"I wanted you more than just someone who'd give me a son!" she cried. "How dare you accuse me of such selfishness?"

Had he ever made such an accusation – or was it his guilty conscience, conjuring this apparition?

He tried to recall the content or their last – their final? – argument. Something about the fact that she would not be at home when he returned. She would be on a fifteen-day field-trip to the coast, working with her team at the Builders' ziggurat.

"And no doubt you'll be spending all your free time with Director Stewart?"

Her icy gaze had frightened him with its intensity. "And what do you mean by that?"

"I've seen how he looks at you. That party we attended –"

She cut him off: "Dan's a good friend. Nothing more. We're colleagues, we share theories, ideas."

"As if that's all you share."

She had lashed out then, slapped him across the face, and left him standing in the lounge while she stormed from the house. Later Ellis had made his way to Carrelliville spaceport, feeling sick at his stupidity and wishing he could go back and un-say what he'd said.

He blinked, and Maria was gone.

"Abi!" he called out again, sobbing.

The day warmed. The sun shone through the gossamer foliage. A distant bird gave a sad, prolonged call.

He raised a hand to his face and felt his flesh. It moved like slit blubber beneath his finger-tips, and when he lifted his hand away he saw dried blood. His face had been lacerated in the impact, had suffered a dozen cuts. He smiled, then laughed. Well, he'd never been all that handsome.

What about his limbs?

Both arms appeared to function reasonably well, though they too had been sliced here and there.

He moved his right leg, bending it, and he felt no pain. But when he tried to move his left leg, bring it up to mirror his left, a vicious stabbing pain lanced up his femur. The material of his right legging was ripped, blood-soaked. He decided not to look too closely at the wound beneath the fabric.

"Abi! Abi, answer me! Travers!"

He moved his head, squinted. To his left he made out a sward of red grass embroidered with a million tiny, polychromatic blooms. He really was, he thought, in paradise.

He turned his head the other way and saw, for the first time, what was left of the shuttle.

Only its nose cone had survived, buried in the loam of this alien world. Beyond the cone, in a long trail that receded into the distance and defied his vision, was a confetti of metallic fragments. How the hell, he wondered, had he survived the crash-landing?

He closed his eyes, opened them, and stared at something twenty metres away. "Abi?"

She was lying on her back, but something about her posture told him that she could not be alive. Her right leg was twisted, bent back on itself. Her red Peacekeepers' uniform was slit like a Chinese lantern.

He moaned to himself and determined to reach her remains. He wanted to straighten her twisted leg. It was undignified, the way death had dealt with her posture. She was a beautiful woman, and it was not fair.

He would... he would reach her, rearrange her leg, set her head straight, and kiss those lips for the first and last time.

He propped himself up on his elbows, trying to ignore the pain. He might not be able to walk, but he could drag himself along, backwards, towards where Abi lay. He set off, digging his elbows into the soft loam, humping himself along, stopping for frequent deep breaths when the effort and the pain became too much.

Fifteen minutes later, soaked with sweat and shaking with the exertion, he reached Abi.

He sat up beside her, staring at her remains. Something had scored a deep incision across her torso, opening her up from shoulder to pelvis, revealing the bloody slick surfaces of her internal organs. Her right leg was bent at the knee, so that the toe of her boot was inserted into the space between her thighs.

Ellis wept as he reached out and, gritting his teeth against the pain, took hold of her heel and pulled. He straightened her leg, and in doing so it came away at the knee, held together now only by the thin material of her slacks. Weeping, he set her right leg parallel with her left, and then straightened her head.

He face was unmarked, perfect. She seemed at peace, her eyes open and staring up at the beautiful canopy above them.

He reached out and closed her eyes, and then, with difficulty, leaned forward and kissed her lips.

Exhausted, he fell onto his back beside her and passed out.

When he came to his senses, much later, the sun was directly overhead. He could not bring himself to look at Abi's body, preferring to recall her in the shuttle when he had been so close to agreeing to visit her back at Carrelliville. She had been small and perfect then, and wonderfully alive.

He stared past Abi, towards the wreckage, and wondered if the com had managed to emit a distress signal, if right now a rescue team was on its way. Or had the com malfunction prevented the activation of the signal? There was no way of knowing, until the team turned up, or failed to.

Among the wreckage he saw Dr Travers' body. A fragment of the shuttle's superstructure had sliced his torso and opened up his chest like a clamshell. Ellis looked away, gagging.

He lay back and thought through the last few minutes of their descent. He told himself that there had been nothing he could have done to prevent the crash-landing, but even so he felt the first stirrings of guilt.

He had a sudden vision of Abi laughing and telling him that guilt was *his* thing.

It was not his fault that Abi and Travers were dead, but the fault of whoever was responsible for the razing of the Phandran township; the operators of the military vehicles he had seen winding their way up the mountain track.

What had Abi said about the Phandrans? That they were a pre-industrial, peace-loving people? So it was unlikely that they were responsible for the attack on the township and his shuttle. But the thought of an invader from another world was almost as impossible to contemplate.

He felt a sudden stab of anger at the unknown assailants, followed by a sense of incredulity. In the two hundred years humankind had dwelled on the Helix, peace had reigned. No race had thought it necessary to attack another. Now, that had changed. Now, for whatever reasons, an alien race had set about another.

He shook his head at his reaction: he wanted to smash to pieces whoever had done this, annihilate the people responsible.

So much for reasoned pacifism, he thought.

He was distracted by the sound of something buzzing nearby. When he turned his head he saw a tiny tornado of flies – or their Phandran equivalent – swarming over Abi's body. They landed, invading her, and he wept and propelled himself away.

Later, exhausted, he passed out again.

2

This time when he came to his senses he was aware of another sound. It seemed to be close by, and he wondered how he had failed to notice it earlier.

The soft plash and play of flowing water.

Suddenly he realised how thirsty he was. He raised himself and looked around. Directly behind him, glinting between the boles of two trees, he made out a stream. He drew a deep breath and dragged himself towards it, grimacing with the effort.

It took an age for him to reach the stream's bank, but when he finally lowered his head to the silver water and drank, the relief was worth the effort. He laughed aloud at the sensation of the cold cut of the liquid down his parched throat. Water had never, ever, tasted so wonderful.

He drank his fill and lay back on the bank, warmed luxuriously by a patch of sunlight. There had been rations aboard the shuttle, but how to find them among all the mangled wreckage? It would be an impossible task. Better, he thought, to seek fruit or other food in the forest.

But how to tell if they were poisonous?

He sat up carefully and looked around. Bushes grew nearby, and on them hung clusters of pale pink berries. He propelled himself away from the stream towards the bushes, and ten minutes later arrived, exhausted, before the shrub. The berries looked tantalising, mouth-watering – too good to be true. And when he tasted one, tentatively, he instantly spat it out, and then the tainted saliva that remained. If taste denoted poison, then the bitter berries were surely toxic.

A few metres beyond the bush he saw a low shrub bearing a hundred golden globes. He shuffled towards it and plucked a fruit – the size of a pear and similarly shaped. It smelled ripe and sweet, and he took a small bite. The soft flesh flooded his mouth with nectar, and he reasoned that a fruit so wonderfully tasty could surely not be poisonous. He ate one, then another and another, then lay down beneath the bush and closed his eyes against a wave of pain from his leg.

Seconds later he heard something move in the undergrowth beyond the shuttle's wreckage.

He sat up, startled, and stared across the sward.

His first thought was that the military responsible for bringing the shuttle down had, finally, traced him. It was a measure of his mental confusion that until now he had not thought of getting away from the site of the crash. But how to do that, with an injured leg and cracked or broken ribs?

He dragged himself into the cover of the golden-fruit bush and peered out.

Something moved among the still steaming wreckage. He expected to see an invader, or a Phandran, but what he saw, shuffling its way through the debris, was certainly no elfin native. Was this the invader, then? He stared, trying to make sense of the thing. It resembled a cross between an overgrown seed-pod and a giant crimson caterpillar, three metres long, with an open-ended orifice surrounded by what looked like tendril feelers that quested across the ground as it pulled itself along.

Only when it emerged from behind a smoking engine cowling did Ellis see that its back end was connected to a long stalk or vine. He followed the course of the vine and traced it back to the trunk of a gossamer-cloud tree. The vine coiled around the trunk and vanished into the foliage.

He wondered why the pod had descended from the tree, and what it was doing probing through the wreckage.

Absently he plucked another golden fruit and ate it as he watched.

Five minutes later, his question was answered.

The shuffling pod approached Abi's body. At first Ellis assumed it would caress the corpse with its tendrils in the same way it had felt all other obstacles in its path, before moving around them. But not this time.

The pod's orifice opened slowly, a rheumy sphincter strung with drools of saliva like harp-strings. The pod shuffled forward and, as Ellis watched with mounting revulsion, eased first Abi's feet into its maw, then her legs.

He wanted to cry out, distract the creature so that it would leave Abi in peace. But he quelled the impulse, fearful of the thing's attention.

He watched as, little by little, the pod drew Abi into its maw like a snake ingesting a rat. Ten minutes later Abi's head disappeared through the orifice, which slowly closed. She was now encapsulated within the pod as if it were a body bag.

As he stared, the tendril that connected the pod to the tree tightened, and the pod was dragged slowly backwards along the ground. Minutes later the pod bearing Abi's mortal remains tilted upright and was drawn into the tree-top. There the pod hung, spinning slowly, as its digestive juices set about breaking down Abi's flesh.

He saw movement beneath the tree. Yet another pod was moving through the wreckage, approaching Travers' shattered corpse.

He heard a sound to his right and turned in alarm.

Five metres away, a pod was shuffling towards him. He swore out loud and backed towards the stream. The pod changed its course, fractionally, to compensate for its prey's evasion, and came towards him with stoic, unhurried persistence.

He looked around for a branch with which to club the thing, but saw none. Very well, then; he would lash out with his feet when it came within range. He was moving as fast as he was able, towards the stream, but the pod was shuffling a little faster. He wondered if he would make it to the water before the pod reached him. Then, he thought with sudden relief, he would pitch himself into the river and, despite the pain, swim downstream and evade the vegetable monster.

The pod was a couple of metres from his trailing feet, its crimson tentacles questing blindly after him. He wondered how it had detected him, and with what senses it now charted his progress.

A metre from the river, a thought struck him. What if the water, mid-stream, was not deep enough to allow him to swim, and he was in effect stranded there? He wondered if the pod would come in after him.

As if sensing his intentions, the pod reacted.

Something lashed out at him from the wrinkled skin on the upper side of its orifice. Ellis had time to see a flash of crimson tentacle – then cried aloud as it stung his lower leg. He looked down. A small hole showed in the material of his jumpsuit.

Alarmingly, the pod had ceased its remorseless shuffling.

It was waiting.

He took a breath, attempting to quell his fright, and dug his elbows into the ground. He tried to drag himself backwards, away from the patient pod. He felt as if all his strength had left him. Numbness crept up his body, radiating from the pod's sting. Seconds later he was unable to move his arms and he collapsed onto his back.

At least, staring up into the gossamer cloud of the trees, he would be spared the sight of the pod's hungry approach. He hoped he would be unconscious before it swallowed him whole.

He realised he was weeping: the one physical ability he could perform. What a stupid, stupid way to die. He wondered if the authorities would ever find his body, a scatter of desiccated bones spat out across the meadow's floor when the pod-tree had sucked out all his goodness.

He wanted to cry out when something touched his booted feet. He felt his legs rise, as if cushioned on something soft and warm. Slowly, the pod drew him into its maw. He lolled this way and that, paralysed, unable to do a thing to prevent himself from being swallowed alive.

He felt a sudden resentment at the thought of how Maria might take the news of his death. There was something almost dignified about dying in a shuttle accident, at least when compared with being eaten whole by an ambulatory vegetable. In time, Maria would see the funny side of his end, would comment scathingly at dinner parties...

The spongy lips of the creature's mouth had reached his chest now. He felt a circle of wet warmth around his upper torso. He closed his eyes and wept as the monstrous lips sucked themselves around his neck and head like oversize slugs.

He felt the skin of the pod constrict around his body. He was rapidly losing sensation in his limbs now, for which he was thankful. Perhaps he would be totally insensate when the digestive juices got to work. He opened his eyes, but all he could see was the puckered skin of the pod's interior, tight across his face, glowing crimson with filtered sunlight.

He moaned as the pod moved, dragging him across the ground towards its parent tree. On the way he hit rocks and bits of wreckage, but whatever had paralysed him had also anaesthetised him to the blows.

Minutes later the pod came to a halt, and he was tipped slowly until he was hanging upside-down. Then, slowly, he was hauled high into the tree-tops, spinning lazily as he went.

At last the ascent came to a halt, and the spinning worked itself out until the only movement was a gentle, side-to-side rocking in the breeze.

He was still weeping, minutes later, when unconsciousness came.

THREE /// SOPHAN

I

THEY WERE HAVING trouble with the sea bordering an unnamed world, three along from Kranda's homeworld of Mahkana.

She stood on the edge of the cliff and stared out across the storm-tossed ocean. The Mahkan monitoring agency had reported severe storms lasting almost thirty days, storms which should not have happened and which if they continued were in danger of eroding parts of the world's western coastline. The agency had brought in a team of meteorologists, and then climatologists, in a bid to solve the problem, but they had reported that the storm's cause was neither meteorological nor climatological. As a last resort, Kranda's engineers had been called in to assist.

There was an almost surreal contrast between the condition of the sea, a whipped-up frenzy of troughs and peaks, and the clement weather which prevailed along the coastline. At her back, the monotonously flat plain stretched away for thousands of kilometres, above which a blue sky was unmarked by the slightest cloud. The sky over the sea was clear, too, which made the raging waves below all the more odd.

She knew the ocean's activity, which initial observers had termed a storm, was nothing of the kind. Storms were the result of weather conditions, and conditions along the coast were fine. The activity of the waves, the surging plunge of grey ocean, was the manifestation of a more fundamental problem. Kranda had her theories, but she was keeping quiet about them until she knew a little more about the situation. There were those in her team, beneath her, who would be eager to capitalise on her slightest error or misjudgement.

Kranda had recently made the transition from male to female, and was still adjusting to the metabolic and mental changes this entailed. She was still negotiating the subtle changes in relationship between herself and the members of her team; it didn't help that some of her closest rivals had undergone male-female transformation at around the same time. There was too much rivalry, even hostility, in the air at the moment, and there were times when Kranda wished she could just walk away from it all and return to her homeworld.

But that was the cowardly residue of male hormones lingering in her system, she knew. The period immediately after transition was always like this, with old ways of thought and feeling laying their treacherous palimpsest over her new psychological persona. In time, male equivocation and uncertainty would fade, usurped by female certitude and strength.

She could already feel the hormonal aggression at work within her. She had been overly critical of a clerk's report the other day, and had questioned a colleague's finding in a way she would never had done as a male. Also, her thoughts of late had been turning with nostalgia and poignancy to her childhood, specifically to the five years of her girlhood, and the long coyti hunts she had undertaken with her hive-mother. She loved the life of an engineer, but always, immediately after undergoing the male-female transition, she longed for the mountains of her homeworld, the familiarity of the hunt, the simple, more aggressive ways of her old female life.

As she stared out to sea, she detected movement other than the chaotic surge of the waves. Something as grey as the ocean emerged from the morass, a streamlined craft that for a second resembled a teardrop flung from the highest wave-crest. Then the vehicle gained solidity as it approached, and running lights and a delta viewscreen became visible. Kranda glanced at her chronometer and smiled to herself: just on time.

The submersible flier banked over the cliffs and came to rest beside her own craft, easing itself down with a sigh of ramrod stanchions. Kranda watched it settle and then crossed the veldt towards the craft, marked along its length with the intertwined lettering of the Mahkan Engineering Corps.

A dropchute fell from its belly and one by one the crew of five emerged.

Three of her team were female, two male. Two of the women had recently made the transition, or *hayanor*, and were consequently testing the boundaries of their new-found aggression, resenting Kranda's superiority and letting her know about it. To make matters worse, one of the men had recently experienced *hayanor* in reverse, after five years of womanhood. His resentment smouldered, though of course he no longer had the psychological wherewithal to voice his objections to Kranda's leadership.

The management of her team was often fraught at the best of times, but even more so after multiple *hayanors*.

The men hung back, conversing in low tones. Their sergeant, the woman Farini and Kranda's greatest rival, stepped forward and presented her softscreen.

"Well?" Kranda asked.

"Read my report," Farini said, unable even to look Kranda in the eye.

Kranda looked past the grey-snouted Farini to one of the men and said, "Glaran, with me, please." Glaran had been male now for over four years, and was suitably docile. She gestured to her ship and he followed her. Over her shoulder, she said to Farini, "Take a break. We'll convene for a meal at noon."

She sat down on the steps of her flier, gesturing Glaran to sit beside her. Of her team, the small male was her favourite, and while she tried to discourage sexual congress between her team members, she had felt strong urges towards Glaran soon after emerging from her *hayanor*. It did not help matters, she admitted to herself, that Glaran was also a favourite of Farini.

She indicated the softscreen. "Well, was I right, Glaran?"

He smiled. "Of course. We knew you would be. Farini too, although she wouldn't admit as much."

"She'll calm down. I don't have time to read all this, so if you could précis..."

The small male looked uncomfortable. "Shouldn't you be asking Farini?"

"Are you questioning my judgement?"

Glaran bridled. "Of course not!"

"Very well then, a précis..."

Glaran said, "The technical co-ordinates are in the report, Sen-Kranda," he said, using her official title as team leader. "On the sea bottom we discovered evidence of disturbance. Initial analysis suggested accidental tectonic slippage, which has resulted in something... *leaking*, perhaps, from the hub."

"Or, as I suggested, a disequilibrium of pressure, Glaran. If there's been a breach on the sea-bed, which there obviously has, then that might explain the surge."

Glaran nodded tentatively. "That might explain the storm activity, Sen-Kranda. We did detect thermal activity issuing from the vent."

She smiled. "It's always nice to be right, Glaran." She reached out and touched his knee. He looked away. "And it's also quite pleasing to know that the Builders are not infallible, hm?"

He looked at her, startled at her near-blasphemy. "Sen-Kranda..."

"I'm joking, Glaran," she said, then, "Did Farini say anything? I mean, did she have an alternative theory?"

"She wouldn't venture an alternative explanation, Sen-Kranda. As I said, she knew you were right."

She looked up. "And here she is. On the warpath, by the look on her face."

Farini strode up to the pair and stared at them. "Must I report you for unprofessionalism?"

"Meaning?"

"You should be discussing these matters with me, as team sergeant, after all."

Kranda, reasonably, indicated the softscreen. "But I did attempt to," she pointed out. "As I recall, you advised me to consult the 'screen. As you seemed unwilling to give me an immediate verbal report, I sought one from your deputy." She glanced at Glaran. "That will be all."

When he'd hurried away, Kranda stood and faced Farini. "Let's talk this over like fellow professionals, hm? Glaran reported the finding of tectonic slippage. I diagnose depressurisation. What do you think?"

Mollified, Farini blinked and said, "Yes, that is the most likely explanation."

They walked away from the ship, turned and paced back again, discussing the slippage and what they should do about it. The rest of her team looked on, perhaps expecting a fistfight. That, Kranda knew, would not happen: she had defused Farini's anger for the time being.

Five minutes later they were about to return to the others when Farini stopped in mid-sentence, screwing her eyes up as she stared at something flying low over the veldt.

A vast Engineering Corps interworld ship was lumbering towards them. Seconds after it came into view, the dull drone of its engines rumbled over them like thunder.

At first Kranda thought that it was in transit past them, on some mission to a neighbouring world. But the behemoth slowed, eased itself to the ground, and touched down on a hundred flexing stanchions a hundred metres away. The heat of its engines swept across the veldt in a wave, causing Kranda and Farini to turn away and shield their faces.

When she next looked, a ramp was unfolding from the ship's flank and a Mahkan officer was striding out, flanked by two officials. In her trim crimson uniform, and towering over her underlings, the woman looked imposingly impressive.

She crossed to Kranda, who wondered what the hell an Engineering Corps high-up was doing here. The storm was a minor inconvenience in the scheme of things, hardly something that should have merited such attention.

The woman stopped before Kranda and Farini. "Sen-Kranda'vahkan, I am Major Lan'malan. If we could have a few words, alone?" She indicated the cliff-top spur where earlier Kranda had stared out over the ocean.

The major told her aides to remain where they were and led Kranda across to the cliff-top.

She went over her last few decisions, wondering if she might have done something wrong, made some catastrophic error of judgement...

"Don't worry, Sen-Kranda," said Major Lan'malan, sensing her unease, "I am not here to reprimand you. Quite the opposite, in fact. The quality of your work has been brought to our notice – even before you underwent *hayanor*. Now that you have undergone the transition... I am here to offer you promotion."

"Promotion?" Kranda stared at the major. "You came all the way here in an interworld vessel to offer me promotion?"

The major smiled. "Don't allow yourself such delusions of grandeur, Sen-Kranda. My ship was on its way to the neighbouring world." She indicated the ocean. "Yankari-Darani retired last term, and left an absence in the ranks, and as there is work to do on Helix 4721... we could think of no one better to whom we might offer the post." The major hesitated. "You will accept, of course?"

Kranda was taken aback. "Of course. Yes. By all means." She laughed. "This is all a little sudden... When do I start?"

The major laughed. "Your human friends have a saying, do they not? Something along the lines of, there is no time like now? Well, if you would care to pilot your flier aboard the *Fighting Coyti*..."

Kranda gestured. "But the project here...?"

"You have an able sergeant, I take it? Allow her to take command. You will be appointed Yankari..." Yankari, Kranda thought, a rank above Sen!

"I will brief you as we fly," Major Lan'malan said.

2

"YOU WILL BE a member of my team working on a project which will last a year," the major said, "and you will report directly to me."

They were speeding over the ocean which, until mere minutes ago, had been Kranda's principal concern. It was an odd feeling to know that the problem of the surging ocean far below need not now bother her in the slightest. She was being taken away from such mundane matters as sub-basal depressurisations...

But what might she be working on, as part of the major's team?

They stood in the major's palatial suite aboard the *Fighting Coyti*, drinks in hand, looking down through a viewport at the raging sea.

"And what might that project be, Major?" she asked.

Lan'malan smiled. She indicated the landmass ahead, a world four beyond their homeworld. Like the world they were leaving, this one was uninhabited.

As they crossed the coastline, Kranda stared out over a very different terrain to the one at their backs. Rolling, forested hills extended to the far horizon, the arboreal vegetation deep green with occasional, very odd outgrowths, spear-like plants which grew to a height of three hundred metres and terminated in a crown of lethal-looking spikes.

"Welcome to Helix 4721," the major said.

Kranda smiled to herself. Odd to think that Mahkana, too, had been designated with a number before the Builders brought her people to the Helix, over eight thousand years ago.

"And the problem?"

"Oh, Yankari-Kranda, there is no problem, as such."

"In that case… routine maintenance?"

The major inclined her head. "Routine maintenance," she said. "You will head a team with jurisdiction over the dozen subterranean access points." She handed Kranda a softscreen. "Their positions are detailed in the notes, which I'd like you to assimilate before you meet your team. It is midday at the latitude which is our destination. I will show you around the base-site, and later I'll introduce you to your team."

The major glanced at her. "You look a little… disappointed, Yankari-Kranda?"

Kranda smiled. "Not at all, Major. I'm honoured to be part of your team."

Lan'malan smiled. "All of us aboard this ship have had to start somewhere, Yankari-Kranda. I began as a lowly clerk, would you believe? I was in charge, for ten years, of softscreen data-storage – and you cannot imagine how dull a job that was. It wasn't until I reached thirty that I was promoted to field duties, and even then they were menial."

The major was right – she had no reason to be disappointed. She might be on nothing but routine inspection duty now, but she had been promoted and she was working aboard a premier interworld vessel under a highly respected Engineering Corps Major. She would put her head down, work hard, and in time would come the better postings.

She considered what Lan'malan had said. "May I ask when the access points were last inspected, Major?"

"To my knowledge, ten years ago, Yankari-Kranda. Ah," she went on. "We are approaching the base-site."

Ten years, Kranda said to herself as the ship decelerated with a loud diminuendo of main drives. The average inspection cycle of subterranean access points was twenty-five years, so why now?

The *Fighting Coyti* came down in a jungle clearing as wide as a city plaza. The comparison was apt, given that the clearing was surrounded by what looked like a makeshift city of bubble domes and inflated access tunnels. As Kranda stared out, she realised that there must be hundreds – make that thousands – of people down there, going about their business with little regard for the landing of the leviathan amongst them. The arrival of an interworld ship in any city on Mahkana would have been cause of much curiosity, and crowds would have gathered to watch it land. Here it went unremarked, just another arrival amid hundreds. Kranda saw fleets of fliers and flitters coming and going, and ground-effect vehicles beetling along makeshift tracks heading into the jungle.

If this was an uninhabited world, undergoing routine maintenance, then why the overkill of personnel? She had worked on other maintenance projects which had employed just tens of Engineering staff.

And that was another thing, she thought. The crowds out there didn't belong just to the Engineering Corps. As the interworld ship settled, she made out the uniforms of at least half a dozen different Mahkan scientific teams. Climatologists, geologists, biologists... among others she didn't recognise.

"Come on," the major said. "I'll give you that guided tour I promised."

They left the major's suite and made their way through the ship. Personnel passed them, saluting the major and glancing curiously at Kranda.

The air of this world was thick, humid, and the heat hit them like a warm, wet cloth. The major smiled at Kranda's reaction. "It does take some getting used to," she said. "Don't exert yourself. Take big, deep breaths."

The midday sunlight beat down mercilessly. Kranda felt like sitting down and drinking pints of ice-cold water. Instead the major was leading her down a corrugated plastic road rolled out across the clearing. The road branched off, leading to various domes and dwellings.

"Admin and supplies," the major said. "There's the recreation block, sleeping quarters for when you're back in town, canteen, emergency hospital. There's a city plan somewhere among the softscreen's files. It'll all become a little less confusing when you've been here a while."

The major indicated a red plastic walkway which led to a diaphanous dome. "And most importantly, the bar...." She glanced at her chronometer. "Your team's due in any time now. You can get to know them over a drink."

The dome was split-level, its upper deck looking out over the spectacular jungle. Lan'malan led the way to the second level and they found a table near the curving inner membrane.

They ordered refreshing qeer-wine – "As good as you'll get anywhere on Mahkana," the major said – and strips of pickled vegetable, a speciality of Kranda's home canton.

Kranda looked out over the makeshift city and the hectic activity. "I'm impressed," she said, taking a long drink. "I've never seen anything quite like it. And you say it's all in aid of routine inspection?"

The major gave her an appraising glance. "And what else might it be in aid of?"

"I don't know. I'm mystified. An inspection of subterranean access points happens every twenty-five years. But you said they were last inspected ten years ago."

"That's what the records show." The major snapped a vegetable stick between big teeth.

"And… if you don't mind my saying… the personal attention of a major, the conducted tour… it's all highly unusual."

Lan'malan smiled. "I can answer the last quite candidly. I like to get to know the people I appoint, the members of my team. It's all very well reading personality reports compiled by others, accessing psych profiles of my team members – but there's nothing like one-to-one contact to really get to know people. Does that answer your question?"

Kranda smiled. "I think it does," she said.

"As for your earlier observations, I agree." The major waved beyond the walls of the dome. "All this is… highly unusual, Yankari-Kranda. This does seem to me to be overkill." She leaned forward. "But would you believe that I'm as much in the dark about it as you are?"

Kranda opened her mouth, intending to say that she found that hard to believe, but stopped herself. That would be tantamount to accusing the major of lying… And though it was hard to believe that someone so high up might be in the dark, something in her manner convinced Kranda that she was telling the truth.

Kranda sipped her ice-cold wine. "But you must have your suspicions?" she said.

"I have, and I approached my superiors with them last week."

"And?"

"And they were tight-lipped, to say the least." Lan'malan gestured with a vegetable stick, before popping it between her teeth and crunching. "They gave nothing away."

"And those suspicions?"

"When I first arrived here, I thought something major had occurred, some catastrophic cross-disciplinary breakdown – the malfunction of an entire world, right up from its engineering base to its eco-system. But when I looked closely… I realised that everything was functioning as it should be. It was a perfectly working world. So, why the presence of specialists in every scientific discipline here? Care to guess?"

Kranda thought about it. "Okay, how about this: expansion? We've come to some kind of agreement with the humans and we're expanding onto this world. It's not that far from our respective homeworld, and…"

She trailed off when she caught sight of the major's expression. Lan'malan shook her head. "We don't need to expand, Yankari-Kranda. Mahkana is hardly bursting at the seams."

"So…"

Major Lan'malan was smiling, showing her big lower incisors. "I have a hunch, Yankari-Kranda. No more. I might be wrong…" She sipped her wine, reflecting, and then said, "What might account for all this sudden activity, centred on one world? Why the inspection, across all the disciplines?" She paused – and at that second, Kranda's wrist-com chimed.

She frowned at the interruption. She accessed the call, intending to tell whoever it was that they should call back later. She assumed it would be one of her old team, Farini or one of the other women, with some procedural question or other.

She was surprised, and a little shocked, to see the face of her hive-mother's valet, Khell, staring up out of the tiny screen.

Kranda looked at the major. "Would you excuse me a moment?"

The major gestured, and Kranda rose and moved around the dome to a quiet area. "What is it?" she asked, panicked. "Is –"

"Marran is well," Khell reassured her. "But she must see you."

"Immediately?" Kranda was taken aback. "What's wrong?" Illness in the family, or an accident?

"Your *Sophan*," the valet whispered.

"*Sophan*," Kranda echoed. "What has happened?"

"You need to return, right away. Marran has more information."

Kranda nodded. "Tell Marran that I will set off immediately."

She cut the connection and returned to where the major was patiently waiting.

"Is everything well?" Lan'malan said. "You look as if you've seen your grand-hive-mother's ghost."

"I must return to Mahkan," she said, only then fully realising what this meant. "On a matter of *Sophan*."

Major Lan'malan listened solicitously as Kranda explained, then nodded her understanding. "It is a matter of *Sophan*, Yankari-Kranda, and that surpasses all else. Nothing stands in the way of honour." She smiled. "My theory as to what is happening here will have to wait."

Kranda felt ambivalent about that. She knew she had to leave, but at the same time she so much wanted to stay. She said, "You will hold this post open for me?"

The major smiled. "Of course," she said.

Kranda felt a weight of relief. "It might be over very quickly," she said. "Then again, depending on exactly what it might entail."

"I fully understand, Yankari-Kranda. Come, I'll show you back to the interworld ship."

3

It was almost one Mahkana day later when Kranda piloted her flier over the familiar coastline of her homeworld and headed for the central mountains.

She had not been home since undergoing her last *hayanor*, fifty days ago. He – as she had been then – had fallen ill while on a routine supervisory field-trip to an arctic world on the eighth circuit, and had requested immediate leave. Rather than seek hospitalisation, and ease his *hayanor* with the drugs that were so common these days, he had elected to undergo the process of transition in the old-fashioned way, as was expected of his hive-tribe, and see out the change using only the old tried and tested herbal medicines. He had set off with a family servant, with the traditional furs of *hayanor* to protect him from the bitter cold, and trekked into the mountains. There he had found the family cave, built a fire, and waited.

Hayanor occurred approximately every five years, and he had quite forgotten the pain of the last transition. Now it leapt upon him like a wild animal, taking his breath away with its savagery, and for three days Kranda had suffered the physical agony of change and the accompanying mental fever-dream, ministered by the loyal servant and soothed by the foul-tasting elixirs made from ground herbs. More than once during the process Kranda had wished he/she'd taken the easier option of hospitalisation.

Then, miraculously, on the dawn of the third day, with the sun climbing over the southern mountain range and shining directly in through the mouth of the cave, the pain had passed and Kranda was female.

She had felt whole again, and strong, and it seemed that the man she had been for five years had been a shallow, weak alter ego, and the period of maleness a time of half-life she was glad she had overcome.

Now she smiled at the recollection of her *hayanor* and steered her flier over the mountain pass leading to the cave. She made out a dark trail of footprints through the snow, and wished the Mahkan who was undergoing *hayanor* now the best of transitions.

As she flew on, the ice-grey mountain ranges of her homeland brought back a slew of nostalgic memories which intensified when her hive-mother's manse came into view.

It was an architecturally ingenious series of castle-like fortifications erected in and around the mountain's natural crags and fissures. In certain places it was hard to tell where the cliff-face ended and buildings began, and the few facades that could be seen – with illuminated slit-windows shining in the twilight – gave a false impression of the manse's true dimensions. The dwelling extended far back into the mountain itself, over a hundred rooms chiselled by Kranda's forbears from the hard heart of the rock.

She brought the flier down in a cantilevered courtyard surrounded by frost-trees, iron-hard growths that protected the entrance to the manse with a tangled thicket of deadly thorns.

A servant, lagged to twice his usual dimensions against the cold, stood beneath the archway between the frost-trees with a torch to guide her way.

Kranda shut down her ship and hurried to the exit.

The cold smote her face with the audacious familiarity of an old, rambunctious friend. She steeled herself and strode to where the servant waited, hopping from foot to foot.

He greeted her with the familial honorific, "Yah-Kranda," and hurried before her, his torch lighting the way through the enfilade of frost-trees to the massive arched timber entrance of the manse.

Once inside, warmth fragranced with summer-flower oils replaced the bitter cold, and Kranda shed her cloak and strode after the servant to the main hall.

Her hive-mother waited on a chair like a throne positioned before a blazing fire. The open fire was an anachronism, of course, a tradition kept alive like much else in and about the manse. This was her hive-mother's way: in tradition she found comfort, a link to the distant past on a world far away from this one.

Her valet, Khell, a shrunken oldster in his male phase, perched upon a high-stool at her side.

Kranda knelt and kissed her hive-mother's hand. "Marran," she murmured. She noticed grey hairs sprouting between her mother's facial scales, which themselves had faded from brown to fawn – all signs of advancing age.

Marran said, "You look well, Kranda'vahkan. Congratulations on the promotion."

"You know?" Kranda asked, surprised.

"There is little I don't know, Kranda. What else have I to do with my time, sequestered up here, but observe the progress of my daughters, all... But guess how many, Kranda."

Kranda smiled. Her hive-mother was astoundingly fertile, even in her sixtieth year. "Fifty?" Kranda guessed.

"Fifty? More like seventy, you scabbed coyti! Seventy. And of all of my offspring, you have done me proudest."

"And now *Sophan*," Kranda said, bringing her mother back to the reason for her presence.

A servant hurried in with big goblets of mulled juice; Kranda's favourite, which she had not tasted since her last *hayanor*.

Marran indicated a seat opposite her, and Kranda eased herself into the padded cushions. Khell handed Marran a softscreen, which she in turn passed on to Kranda.

The image on the screen was stilled, showing an aerial view of an unfamiliar landscape.

Marran was saying, "I have informants in many places, in this case a clerk in the Observation Corps. He keeps me abreast of the Sporelli situation."

"I've heard rumours."

"I can tell you for certain that rumours of invasion are true. The *skath*" – she almost spat the word; skath were vermin which lived in the manse walls – "have invaded Phandra. The casualties, so I'm told, are high."

"Have moves been instituted to halt the slaughter?" she asked.

"You know what the human peacekeepers are like, Kranda, and our ruling council are little better these days, since Jekeri's hive gained ascendency. Who knows how it will end."

"But... *Sophan*?" Kranda reminded her.

Marran indicated the softscreen on Kranda's lap with a palsied claw. "Touch the screen to set it into motion."

She did so. The screen showed a mountain vale with strange, white-blossomed trees and scarlet grassland. She increased the magnification, and the view zoomed in. She made out, between the trees, a tangle of burnt-out wreckage.

"A human shuttle..." she said, fearful.

Marran turned her hand in acknowledgement. "The shuttle came down – was brought down by Sporelli fire – two days ago. Our observers noted the infringement and contacted the human peacekeepers, and it was from them that Darvian learned the identity of the pilot and his crew."

Kranda said, "Jeff Ellis?"

"Darvian knew of Ellis, and your *Sophan*, and contacted me."

Kranda stared at the wreckage. "But there is no way Ellis could have survived this..."

Marran gestured. "Scroll to the next image. Magnify to its utmost resolution. Observe the shape at the bottom of the screen."

Kranda scrolled, with shaking fingers, and made out what might have been a human figure lying beside a silver stream.

"Now scroll to the next image," Marran said. "See, the figure has moved. This image is one hour later. The evidence is that the figure, the human figure, was alive at this point."

Kranda looked up and asked, "But is the figure Ellis?"

"It wears the blue uniform of a shuttle pilot," Marran said. "According to the human authorities, he was not accompanied that day by a co-pilot."

With increasing apprehension, Kranda scrolled to the next image. It showed the same scene, but there was no sign of the human figure.

"What might have happened to him?" she asked.

"We cannot tell. Cloud cover obscured the next dozen or so satellite images. When the cloud cleared – scroll on, Kranda – we see only a team of Phandran natives harvesting some local growth."

Kranda scrolled, taking in all the images captured by the satellite. The later ones showed the tiny figures of a dozen natives and some kind of cart hauled by an ugly, bloated creature.

Kranda scrolled back to the image showing the human figure – Jeff Ellis – and stilled it. She looked up. "The natives might have found him, or know what happened to him."

Marran inclined her head. "That is one possibility, yes, Kranda."

Sophan, she thought. Debt of honour.

"I must travel to Phandra immediately."

Her hive-mother pulled back her top lip in an affirmative grimace which also signalled her pleasure. "I knew that no daughter of mine would baulk at such a thought, despite the dangers involved."

"The Sporelli?" Kranda asked.

"They are advancing across the face of Phandra. We suspect their destination is D'rayni, a world rich in metals, which their own world lacks. Along the way they show the hapless Phandrans no mercy."

"I will have to be armed, and well-protected."

Marran said, "I have acquired a varnika, and a complement of weapons."

She stared at her hive-mother. Was there no limit to her ingenuity? "A varnika?"

"I know hive-mother Shaar, over in the neighbouring canton, and her daughter is Director of Builder artefacts."

With a varnika, Kranda thought, I will be invincible.

She would find Jeff Ellis, and save him, and in doing so would discharge her *Sophan*.

She stood. "My love and respects, Marran. I will leave for Phandra without delay."

She knelt and kissed her mother's hand, then stood and strode from the room.

4

KRANDA EASED HER flier from the courtyard and instructed the computer to chart a course along the fourth circuit to the world of Phandra.

"And when we approach Sporell and Phandra," she said, "establish a visual and aural shield."

Sophan.

She thought back to the time, four years ago...

It should have been a routine flight, but a mechanical error had almost cost Kranda her – or rather his – life.

He'd been returning from a world on the second circuit and looking forward to a period of leave. His attention had been on the future, and a holiday in the glacier fields of his homeworld, when the meteor hit his ship and his com-system shrieked a system failure alert and advised immediate evacuation.

He had attempted to escape his failing ship, and might have successfully done so had the impact with the meteor not ripped a hole through the escape hatch, taken out the store of vacuum-suits, and allowed the air to escape at an alarming rate.

Only the fact that, quite by chance, a human shuttle had been in the vicinity had saved his life. The human Jeff Ellis had matched his shuttle's flight-path to that of the stricken Mahkan flier, left his ship with spare breathing apparatus, and made his way across the intervening vacuum, inserting himself through the meteor impact gash and dragging Kranda to safety.

Only later had the human shuttle pilot admitted his gut-wrenching fear at the thought of the operation; to his credit, he had carried it out as if he'd performed the same actions every day of his life.

Over the next few years Kranda and Ellis had met up occasionally, and their meetings had served to dispel Kranda's prejudices against humankind. Kranda's people were a proud warrior race, originally hailing from a world thousands of light years away from the Helix, a planet whose conditions had been harsh, inimical. In order to survive and prosper, a collectively brutal regime had been necessary: the Mahkan were, like all other races, a product of their environment.

That brutalist regime had been tempered somewhat after their transfer to the Helix, where life was easier, and where the Builders, a thousand years ago, had honoured her people with the mantle of Engineers. But even so, her people were genetically predisposed to bellicosity – so it was little wonder that when the human race became Peacekeepers and the Mahkan found themselves working alongside this puny, effete race to the betterment of the Helix, Mahkan prejudice against the feeble simian species came to the fore.

And then Jeff Ellis had saved his life, and Kranda had looked past his people's prejudices – the humans were, after all, merely the products of their own Earthly environment – and come to see in this example of the human race a being who, while physically weak and sharing none of the Mahkan's strengths, lived by admirable codes of honour and a clear morality.

She had never told Ellis about the code of *Sophan*, the debt of honour incurred when he had saved Kranda's life.

Now, she was determined to discharge that debt of honour.

If, of course, Jeff Ellis were still alive.

The flier burst through the cloud cover shrouding her world. She stared out at the arc of worlds, scintillating in the dazzling sunlight far below, and set course for Phandra ten worlds further along the circuit.

Four /// Calla's Destiny

CALLA'S FATHER, WHO had been a Diviner, once told her that she was destined for great things. She would, he said, travel far and accomplish much.

Now she was old, and though she had travelled the length and breadth of her world, Phandra, and accomplished everything that she could as a Healer, she had in her heart expected something *more*. She had gone through her life wondering what it might be, this great thing; she had resisted petitioning other Diviners and seeking her destiny. What would happen would happen. But as the years passed, she began to wonder if all her father had meant was that she would travel the face of Phandra and heal thousands of her people.

She had less than one year of life remaining, and she still harboured the hope that this great thing might happen.

She rose early that morning, as always, and bathed in the stream that tumbled down the mountainside beside her hut. The water was ice cold, and concentrated her thoughts. Today she was due to go into the village of Yan and conduct her monthly healing sessions with whoever sought her services.

And then next year, in the season of honey-fruit, she would make a final journey to the Retreat of Verlaine and for the last two weeks of her life take to her bed, surrounded by Elders and acolytes, and slowly, painlessly, die.

Hers would have been an exemplary life, a life spent in the service of others, healing her fellow Phandrans, for she had inherited her mother's talent for Healing and none of her father's for Divining.

And when she had passed from this life, she would join her parents, and their parents, and everyone else who had ever lived on Phandra – and, who could tell, on the Helix and beyond as well – in the reality which underpinned this reality.

The realm of Fahlaine.

Her last duty before leaving her little hut and setting off for Yan was to feed the birds that gathered every dawn and awaited their handful of seed. She stepped from the hut, clutching the seed, and expected to be deluged in a twittering, feathered storm.

But this morning the birds did not come. She stood, almost stunned, and stared into the clear blue sky. There were no birds, no ice-hawks, redwings, or night-pippins in the air or perched in the yahn-trees.

She waited, then called out and whistled, but still they did not come.

This she took as an omen.

With heavy heart she returned to her hut, packed her bag with the medicaments of her trade, donned the red robe of her calling and set off down the rocky path to Yan.

She moved slowly, picking her way with care over the rocks which, over the years, her footsteps and those of Healers before her had worn to rounded smoothness.

She was troubled by the absence of birds, and no matter how hard she tried to fathom their non-arrival, she could think of no satisfactory explanation.

She was a third of the way to Yan, with the sun rising over the mountain peak and warming her back, when she felt the pain in her head. She stopped dead in her tracks and touched her temple. The vicarious pain of another throbbed in her forebrain like a migraine. A boy, no more than four seasons old, was approaching along the path. His thoughts, addled with pain, were a confusion of horror, fright and disbelief. She hurried onwards, anxious to find the boy and treat him and learn of the catastrophe that had befallen him and, if his desperate thoughts were to be credited, the rest of his village.

He came into view five minutes later. He was no longer climbing the path, but had collapsed beside the same stream that, higher up the hillside, surged past her hut. She hurried down to the stricken child, damping out the distress of his thoughts and his pulsing pain.

She stifled a cry when she reached him and saw the severity of his wounds. He was on his belly, attempting to crawl to the stream and slake his thirst. She turned him over, weeping as she did so, and saw the bloody hole in his chest. It was a miracle he had managed to drag himself this far from the village. With each ragged breath he took, more blood pulsed from his wound and stained his jerkin.

She touched his forehead, working to ease the pain, and he smiled up at her. "Healer," he whispered.

She murmured consolatory platitudes, for that was all she could manage now. He would die, in minutes, and the only blessing was that he would now die without pain.

He was trying to speak, to tell her what had happened, but she whispered for him to rest and opened her mind to his, briefly.

She withdrew, catching her breath, having seen enough in just three brief seconds.

Someone had attacked the village of Sharah, half a day beyond Yan, on the main track to Verlaine. She had discerned fleeting images of otherworldly vehicles, *mechanical* things, and creatures in black uniforms firing weapons into dwelling huts.

She soothed the boy, and his breathing came easily. Five minutes later his eyes fluttered shut and he died.

She laid him out on the path, decorating his chest with a garland of blue fahrl flowers, and spoke the words of Leaving above his small body.

She stood, shouldered her bag, and hurried on down the path.

Soon she came to the village of Yan and found that other wounded Phandrans had sought refuge there, with tales of violence and destruction. She ministered to the needs of the injured, treating everything from bullet wounds to burns, and from the dozen men, women and children she treated she managed to piece together a fragmented scenario of what had taken place at the village of Sharah that morning.

At dawn, without warning, a flying craft had descended from the sky and six blue-skinned men in black uniforms had jumped out. In minutes, they had collected together all the elders in the village, and one of the aliens, speaking a corrupt form of Phandran, had interrogated the cowering old folk. The blue men wanted to know where the humans were. She knew the word – humans were another, technological, race of beings who dwelled upon the Helix. But the invaders' request made no sense; the elders knew nothing of the whereabouts of any humans, and told their tormentors this... and their admission provoked terrible rage.

An invader shot an elder at point-blank range, and another turned a device that spat flame and torched a hut. Inside were Phandrans, who died a terrible death, and still the alien soldiers questioned the elders, and then other men and women, demanding to know the whereabouts of the humans and threatening everyone with death if they did not speak.

Many villagers managed to flee the violence, but many did not, and the heads of those who had escaped rang with the cries of the dying as the soldiers wrought their senseless carnage.

Calla moved from injured man to maimed woman, from sobbing child to terrified infant, and did what she could to ease their pain and heal their wounds, and when she had learned all she could about what had happened, she damped their thoughts, allowed their nightmares no further place in her head.

When she had done all she could for the dozen survivors, she knew what she had to do next.

She repacked her bag, lodged it on her shoulder and hurried from the village, ignoring the pleas of the elders to think twice before approaching the village of Sharah.

She hurried down the path, probing ahead for straggling survivors, and for the minds of the men from another world. She encountered only blissful mind-silence at odds with her memories of the pain she had left behind.

She came to the village of Sharah at noon, as the bright sunlight cast sharp shadows among a scene of utter destruction. Not a single hut or dwelling had escaped the attention of the aliens. Twists of smoke rose in the clear air. The dead lay where they had fallen, pierced by bullets, scorched by fire. She moved among them in a daze, arranging limbs, closing eyes, showing a respect to the dead that the aliens had failed to show them while they lived.

She wept, less for the dead – for they had passed on to the realm of Fahlaine – but for the souls of the people who had done this.

How reduced they must be, to be able to commit such violence; how ignorant of the sanctity of life.

She had once seen a yahn-gatherer, in a fit of drunken jealousy, strike a work-mate, and that had been shocking enough.

Phandrans were a pacific people: many millennia ago the Builders had saved her kind, and ever since, the Phandrans had lived by the principles of their saviours, respecting the sanctity of life, eschewing the way of violence.

She had heard that not all the races of the Helix lived by these tenets, but the knowledge had always been abstract, intellectual. Now she had ample evidence of it.

But what did it mean? Why had the aliens come to her world, in search of humans?

Had the Diviners seen this? Of course they had, she reasoned, for the Diviners saw everything. So they had foreseen this, and decided to keep the knowledge to themselves, in their wisdom – for they knew the course of future events and understood the pattern of this arbitrary violence in the grander scheme of things.

Still, it seemed inexplicably cruel to her. Couldn't they have warned the villagers, told them to be elsewhere this morning?

But who was she to question the motivations of the Diviners?

She was startled by a sudden noise. She looked up, expecting to see an alien flier descending from the heavens to finish the business begun that morning. Instead, on the loop of track above the village, she saw two green-robed Elders rising on the back of a rurl.

They paused, staring down at her with serene dignity.

She raised a hand in a forlorn wave.

They called down to her, "Calla-vahn-villa?"

"That is I," she said.

"Approach, Healer," the older of the Elders said.

She looked around the carnage, feeling a sweep of sadness return, and moved from the village. She walked up the path that led, eventually, to the track which made its way to the Retreat of Verlaine.

She stood before the great wrinkled head of the rurl, which regarded her with its tiny, rheumy eyes, and stared up at the pair of Elders.

They were males, and wore their great age in the sallowness and in the folds of their skin, almost as wrinkled as the rurl they rode.

"I did what little I could," she said. "I treated those survivors who made their way to Yan, but no one survived here."

The oldest Elder inclined his venerable head and said, "You did what you could, Calla-vahn-villa. You obeyed your calling. Now you will come with us."

She squinted up at them, silhouettes against the noon-day sun. "To where?"

"The Retreat of Verlaine," they said as one.

She showed her surprise. "May I ask who has summoned me, Elders?"

"Diviner Tomar," said one, "on a matter of the utmost importance. Now please, climb up and join us and we will be upon our way."

She did as she was instructed, climbed up the scaled leg of the rurl and straddled its broad back. The creature set off, lumbering along the track, and Calla fell to wondering just what Diviner Tomar might want with her.

2

A DAY LATER, with frequent stops upon the way, they arrived at the Retreat of Verlaine.

She visited the Retreat twice a year, but it still struck her anew with its soaring majesty. Built into the very summit of Phandra's highest mountain by the very first generation of settlers on Phandra, according to her father it was a replica of the greatest of all Retreats on the Phandran homeworld, five hundred light years away towards the rim of the galaxy. Its lower ramparts nestled in the gulfs and fissures of the mountain, while its towers and belvederes soared above the mountain's craggy peaks. It was the seminary where as a child, after leaving her parents, she had been trained; it was like home to her.

The rurl laboured up the switchback road that rose from the valley, and each bend of the road brought her closer to the vast timber door, fully a hundred times her height, set into the cliff-face.

It was almost sunset by the time the rurl eased its bulk around the final bend and halted before the gate.

She took her leave of the Elders and approached the tiny picket gate set into the timbers. As ever, the tiny door opened before she reached it, and she stepped through.

A nervous acolyte greeted her and led the way up the winding staircase to the central corridor. She had expected to be left in one of the waiting rooms outside the Diviners' chamber, but the acolyte twittered "This way, this way..." and led her from the front of the Retreat and through the mountain itself towards the Council chamber.

The acolyte left her before they reached the Council corridor, and Calla pushed through the small door before her, stepped into the dimly-lit corridor, and approached the great door.

She paused before it and stared in wonder. Twice her height and just as broad, it was fashioned from ancient silverwood and even in the half-light of the corridor gave off a lambent lustre, a vitality she knew had lasted for over fifteen millennia, for the door had been brought all the way from their ancestral homeworld.

Every Diviner and Healer, with death approaching, was allowed to lay a hand upon the door which, over the thousands and thousands of years on New Phandra, and for countless aeons on Old Phandra, had accepted the touch of every dying Healer. This ritual would commence the Healer's final week of life.

She wondered if this was why she had been brought to the Retreat; perhaps she had miscalculated, and did not have a year to live, but much less. But why then had Diviner Tomar summoned her? That was not established practice.

She reached out and placed her hand flat against the warm wood. She closed her eyes, gasping, and felt the cumulative touch of the myriad others who had laid hands on the sacred timbers before her.

At her touch, the door swung open, and, trembling, she stepped through.

The door, hallowed as it was, gave no clue as to the dimensions of the room beyond. The Council chamber was five thousand paces long and half as broad, lined along its length with timber pews said to have been brought from Old Phandra along with the silverwood door. Draped hangings, representing every family on New Phandra, covered the walls on each side, and at the far end, diminished in the perspective, was the Southern Window.

It blazed with the light of the setting sun, filling the chamber with a million polychromatic patterns like a kaleidoscope made gargantuan

She knew the protocol of a summoning to the Council chamber. She was to walk half its length, towards the circular reception area, and there wait for Diviner Tomar to beckon her the rest of the way.

She set off, her light footsteps whispering over the polished stone. She stared ahead, her breath tremulous, and drank in the details of the sacred chamber, the ranked pews, the ancient hangings, and the coloured glass window.

Ten minutes later she came to the pews in the reception area and took her seat.

From here she could just make out the distant circular arrangement of padded benches in the Council area at the foot of the Southern Window. Seated on the benches were two figures, one large and one small. They were too far away for her to detect the flow of their thoughts, and she had to rely on visual clues only. She knew that the man on the left was a Diviner, for he wore the green robes of his calling and, even seated, was stooped with great age. She thought she recognised, from his posture, Diviner Tomar. But the second figure...

Her breath caught as she realised, with a start, that the second figure was an alien.

He or she was twice the size of Diviner Tomar, and garbed from head to foot in red. The figure was bending towards Tomar, and seemed to be speaking in lowered tones to the venerable Diviner.

She wondered if this audience had anything to do with the arrival of the violent aliens.

And she wondered again why she had been summoned here.

3

SHE WAITED A further hour, every minute filled with the miracle of her presence here, and then realised that the audience between the Diviner and the off-worlder was drawing to a close.

The tall alien stood, and reached out and touched Diviner Tomar's hand. They spoke again, and the alien turned and walked away from the Council area, striding down the central aisle towards her. She held her breath, then released it in a rush. Soon, within minutes, the alien would pass within metres of her. She had never before set eyes on a being from another world – the closest she had come to doing so had been the previous morning, when she had beheld images of the aliens in the minds of those she healed.

But now the tall alien was striding towards her.

A minute later he was within hailing distance, and Calla stared in wonder.

What struck her initially was his ugliness. She was accustomed to Phandran skin the shade of snow-flowers, with hardly a variation in tone, but this creature's flesh was as dark as midnight, contrasting with his red one-piece uniform. He had the usual complement of facial features, but his nose was disproportionately huge. He possessed, also, an air of confidence she had never beheld in a fellow Phandran – but most striking of all was the total absence of mind-noise.

She could not help probing as he approached, but it was as if pure emptiness existed within his skull. She gasped, wondering at this being. Never before had she encountered a living, sentient creature

– or, come to that, a non-sentient creature – without a cerebral signature. What kind of being was this that possessed none?

He strode towards Calla, looked upon her without expression, and swept on past.

A locus of emptiness, as vacant as a yahn-tree...

Minutes later she became aware of a soft voice, calling her. She looked up. In the distance, surrounded by bright sunlight, was the diminutive figure of Diviner Tomar. "Calla-vahn-villa," he said. "Please, this way."

She stood and hurried towards the light.

Diviner Tomar was as old as herself, but men of their species aged more quickly than women. The years had scored deep runnels in the pale flesh of his thin face, and his cheeks were sunken. Vitality, however, burned in his eyes, betokening the intellect still at work beneath the whitening hair.

She probed towards him, but the Diviner was well practised at keeping his thoughts and emotions from the prying minds of others.

He gestured for her to be seated on a padded bench, and hardly believing where she was, she sat opposite Diviner Tomar.

"You are no doubt wondering why I summoned you here, Calla?"

"That, and many other questions beside," she said. "Why the arrival of the aliens, and why was their violence not foreseen, and who was the tall being, who has manifest life and yet does not possess a cerebral signature?"

Tomar smiled. "We foresaw the invasion of the Sporelli from the neighbouring world to our east," he said, "and we foresaw their violence. It is all, Calla, a part of a much vaster picture."

"But the violence they –"

He raised a hand. "The violence belongs to the Sporelli, and affects us only physically."

"But the suffering..."

"You know that all life is suffering, Calla, until the end. And before you say that the suffering could be avoided, I will say that you are right; but to what end? Our dead are now in Fahlaine, and the perpetrators of evil must look into their souls and regret."

She bowed her head. "I understand that, Diviner. I was too close to the suffering, when I went among the injured and dying."

"That is the burden of the Healer," he said.

She looked up. "But the aliens, the Sporelli? What do they want with us?"

"They are passing through, bent on invading our western neighbours, the D'rayni. On the way they will use us, take our finest Healers and Diviners for their own ends."

Calla opened her mouth in sudden understanding. "Ah... so that is why you summoned me? To warn me, yes?"

Tomar smiled. "No. The Sporelli will take who they want; it is divined, and will be so, and there is little we can do to prevent what is divined."

She inclined her head in understanding. "And the tall man, the man without a cerebral signature?"

Tomar said, "He was... advising me, Calla, and I, for my part, was advising him."

"About the violence of the blue men?"

"That, and many other things, yes," he said.

She said, with sudden realisation, "He was one of the humans sought by the invading aliens, yes?"

Tomar shook his head. "No, Calla, he was not who they were seeking."

She shook her head, confused.

Tomar sat back in his seat, regarding her. A minute elapsed, and a slight smile played on his thin lips. He said at last, "Your father was Diviner Ehrl-vahn-villa, your mother Healer Caro-vahn-villa."

She frowned, wondering at this sudden turn in the conversation. "Yes."

"You issue from the finest stock. Your father was my supervisor, I his acolyte. He was a fine man. He told you, once, when you were very small, that you were destined to achieve greatness and travel far."

She smiled. "He said this, yes. But he was mistaken, Diviner Tomar. I am almost ten years old, and close to the end of my days."

He said, staring at her, "He was not mistaken, Calla-vahn-villa. You are destined for greatness, and you will travel far."

Her heartbeat thudded through her and a hot wave passed over her face. She sat back and shook her head. "I will?" she managed.

"Details are vague, especially concerning events ten days and more from now. But even so, we have divined, the Council and I, that momentous incidents will play themselves out in your presence."

She inclined her head, attempting to take this shattering news with dignity. She had anticipated a final year like all the others, serving the people, travelling the nearby valleys... and now this.

She said, "And events within those ten days, Diviner?"

"You will be called upon to heal, but to heal not a Phandran but a human." He swept on, before she could question him. "He will be arriving here very soon, and will be badly injured, and poisoned also. But your ministrations will save his life."

"They will?" she whispered.

"More, you will then leave the Retreat with the human, and travel to the western coast. There it is foreseen that you will be parted – but you will be reunited again. Calla, you will suffer much hardship in the days that lie ahead, and pain, but you will persevere through all the pain and hardship, alone and with the human, and you will travel far... And through helping the human, Calla, your actions will bring peace to our world."

Her head was spinning. "Travel far, to where...?"

"To another world on the Helix," he said.

"Another world?"

"And there our foresight grows dim," Tomar admitted, "though we can discern, dimly, the many wonders that lie beyond. But now, Calla, you must repair to the Healing Garden and prepare for the coming of the human. He will be suffering broken bones, and lacerations, and gan-fruit poisoning."

"Diviner Tomar," she said at last, "I am honoured."

The Venerable Diviner reached out and took her hand. "And I, too, am honoured to know one whose destiny is so great," he said. "Now go."

In a daze Calla stood and made her way up through the many levels and galleries of the Retreat until she came to the Healing Garden, bathed in the last golden light of the setting sun.

And there she prepared herself to nurse her patient.

FIVE /// THE HEALING GARDEN

I

ELLIS CAME TO his senses and, for the second time since the crash-landing, was amazed to find himself alive.

The pod was spinning again, and rocking from side to side, and he sensed that he was being lowered to the ground. He opened his eyes, but all he could see was the red-tinted interior of the pod's membrane.

He tried to move, to struggle, but he was still paralysed.

He allowed himself a flash of hope. This, surely, was not what the tree had planned – if such could be ascribed to a non-sentient plant? He should have hung up there, surely, until wholly digested. So what was happening now?

He heard what he thought were voices far below, and felt a renewed surge of hope.

Had a human rescue mission located the shuttle, and somehow worked out what had happened to him?

However unlikely that scenario might be, he could not deny that there were people down there attempting to rescue him.

They were not human voices, however. He strained to hear, and made out high chittering calls between two or more individuals. Seconds later the to and fro motion of the pod ceased, and his head hit the ground softly. Through the flesh of the pod he made out a shadow – the form of a small humanoid – as it grasped the pod, lowered it the rest of the way to the ground, and then knelt to hack at the connecting stalk with what might have been a machete.

He tried to cry out and sit up, but could achieve neither.

He was left there for what seemed an age. He listened intently. He heard movement around the clearing: the susurrus of footsteps through the crimson grass, the soft call of voices, and a regular chop-chopping sound as the pods were harvested.

It came to him that he might survive, that – no longer connected to the tree – the pod's digestive juices might be unable to do their work. Soon the paralysis might wear off and he'd be free.

Maybe an hour later he made out approaching footsteps. Two individuals, chattering together in their piping tongue, took hold of each end of his pod and lifted.

They exclaimed – perhaps in surprise at the weight of the pod – and staggered under their burden across the clearing. He found himself being swung through the air. He landed with a thud on something soft, and shortly after felt another pod land beside him.

He tried to move, but to no avail. He was still locked in frustrating paralysis which, as the minutes elapsed, he began to fear might be more than temporary.

Ten minutes later the sound of the chopping ceased and he heard the sound of voices approach the place where the pods were stacked. He wondered if the native workers were standing by, admiring the piled pods and congratulating themselves on their magnificent haul.

Were they meat-gatherers? Was this a harvest wrested from the pod-trees and consumed as a delicacy by nearby villagers? He considered their surprise when they opened his pod to find an alien within.

Seconds later he heard a shout and the piled pods shook and juddered. He had been placed aboard a cart or some such, and now they were setting off.

The movement as they progressed – the tilt suggesting that they were travelling downhill – was somnolent, lulling, and Ellis found himself drifting off.

He came awake, startled by a cry, some time later.

His instinct was to sit up, and he attempted to do so, but the skin of the pod had shrivelled and cocooned him tight. He moved his arms with difficulty and brought his right hand up to his face to scratch at the encrusted blood on his cheek.

Only then did he realise that he had moved. The pod's anaesthetic had worn off, and he felt a surge of relief at the thought that he had survived the alien poison.

The cry which had awoken him came again.

The native harvesters were communicating among themselves with some degree of consternation, their voices even shriller than normal.

Ellis heard a low rumble, which grew as he listened, then cut out abruptly. The natives ceased their twittering and fell silent.

He heard something creak, ahead of the cart, and then a metallic slam. Boots approached the cart – more than one set – accompanied by harsh, guttural conversation.

He found himself holding his breath.

The boots halted before the cart and a gravelly voice called out what sounded like, "Krayak gah."

The natives on the cart responded with silence.

"Gah, rankah. Krayak!"

The pod's skin was desiccated. He raised a hand and prodded a hole through the thin vegetable matter before his face.

He adjusted his position minimally, not wanting to attract the attention of whoever had apprehended the cart, and peered out. He was stacked with other pods on a flat-bed drawn by what looked like a shell-less turtle. A slight being, pale and elfin-thin, with a pelt of silver hair, sat upon the beast's neck. Others of its kind – Phandrans, obviously – squatted behind it on the turtle's humped back.

Before the beast stood an alien in a black military uniform. He appeared human, but for the slight blue cast of his features. Six other soldiers, positioned behind their leader, carried bulky weapons held across their chests. Ellis made his breathing shallow.

Their commander spoke again, a barked order, but it was obvious that the Phandrans did not understand.

The alien stepped forward and gestured towards the cart and its cargo of pods, then pointed to the ground. His meaning was obvious: deliver a pod for my inspection.

Ellis felt his stomach clench. He judged there were around a dozen pods stacked on the cart – two of which contained human remains, and his own. If the alien commander should find any one of them...

Belatedly the Phandrans atop the turtle-beast moved to obey. Two of their number rose from the turtle's hump and skipped nimbly onto the cart. They bent towards the closest pod to hand – which happened to be the one in which Ellis lay – and took hold of either end. In doing so, the membrane where Ellis had poked a hole split even further and he found himself staring into the startled visage of a Phandran – an albino angel, as he came to think of them later.

With a gesture he hoped might be universal, he raised a finger to his lips and held it there.

After a second of bewilderment, the Phandran piped something to its neighbour and they moved to take hold of the pod next to Ellis. They lifted, grunting with effort, and eased the pod over the side of the cart and carried it to the feet of the alien commander.

The alien reached down and, with the tip of its weapon, ripped the skin of the pod to reveal the corpse of a deer-like animal, striped red and black.

The commander, not satisfied, repeated his command and gestured towards the cart. The Phandran duo returned, clambered aboard the cart, and selected another pod. Ellis closed his eyes, praying that it was not one containing either Abi or Travers.

They dropped the pod at the feet of the alien and retreated. Heart pounding, Ellis peered through the rent in the membrane, hardly daring to breathe.

The alien reached out and prodded the pod with the snout of his rifle, worked a hole in the membrane, and ripped it open. He stood back suddenly, as if in alarm, and Ellis feared he'd found human remains.

Only then, seconds later, did the stench of putrefying meat reach his nostrils. The rotting corpse of some six-legged beast lay at the commander's feet.

One of his minions barked a comment which was not to the commander's liking. As quick as lightning, the commander turned, levelled his rifle, and fired. A blue beam drilled a hole in the centre of his chest. The commander barked an order and the remaining soldiers retreated hurriedly to their troop-carrier parked further down the track. He moved to the body, stared down at it with contempt, then rolled it into the ditch with his boot.

Ellis swallowed and realised that he was shaking uncontrollably.

The commander turned to the Phandrans and snapped in its ugly tongue: "Garak sen. Kayag-na!"

He turned on his heel and marched back to the carrier, and a minute later the vehicle started up and accelerated towards the cart. Only swift action by the turtle-handler, and somewhat slower footwork from the beast, prevented a collision. The carrier swept by, its commander staring at the Phandrans imperiously from the high cab.

Ellis closed his eyes and released a long breath.

Only when the roar of the carrier's engine died to a distant murmur did the Phandrans resume their onward journey. A minute later three of their number jumped from the turtle's hump and landed on the cart beside Ellis's pod.

Cautiously, like frightened children, they approached him.

Ellis sat up, aware that the pod-tree's toxin had not only anaesthetised him but had acted as an analgesic. The pain in his ribs and leg had abated to no more than a dull ache.

The Phandrans backed off quickly. They dropped into squats at the front of the flat-bed, staring at him in amazement.

They turned and called to their colleagues, and the turtle drew to a halt. Seconds later all six Phandrans were crouching before him, swapping comments and swift, bird-like gestures. If the biology of these aliens correlated at all with that of humankind, then these creatures before him appeared to be male; at any rate, they were flat-chested and slim-hipped.

One of the Phandrans returned to the turtle-beast and the journey resumed.

Ellis looked beyond the staring aliens and took in the countryside. They were passing through a broad valley made idyllic with the spun-silver clouds of a million gossamer trees. The sun slanted down from above distant mountains, warming him.

An alien, the individual who had discovered Ellis, knelt before him and held out his hand, palm down. As Ellis watched, the Phandran moved his palm through the air until his slim fingers collided with a pod and his lips made a silent plosive.

Ellis smiled, suddenly understanding. "Yes. Yes, that's right. I was aboard a shuttle. We... we were shot down by..." He gestured over his shoulder to the alien military.

The Phandrans laughed among themselves, obviously finding the sound of his deep voice a source of amusement.

The Phandran spoke, a series of high piping notes, and Ellis smiled his incomprehension. It looked at its fellows, and then they withdrew to their positions on the turtle's hump, casting him curious glances from time to time as they proceeded down the narrow track between the gossamer trees.

Ellis lay back in his pod and closed his eyes, and within seconds he was dozing.

2

He was shaken awake abruptly. He cried out and sat up, alarmed.

The speed of his movement startled the Phandran, who backed off with a look of fear on its angelic face. Ellis reached out in a placatory gesture. "I'm sorry. I didn't mean to frighten you. I was dreaming."

In his dream he was confronted by an alien in a sable uniform and a visor, and when the being lifted its visor he saw that the face beneath belonged to his wife.

The turtle had halted in the shade of a low, spreading tree – not a gossamer tree, he was glad to note – whose gnarled branches bore round yellow fruit which glowed like lanterns in the descending twilight.

The other Phandrans were seated in a circle beneath the tree, eating. The native before him gestured to Ellis, then indicated the group. The alien appeared young, with a long scar running down its right check from its eye to the side of its mouth. It hopped down from the cart, then gestured for Ellis to do the same.

He smiled. "Well, that's very kind of you. I'll do my best, but you'll have to forgive my lack of mobility."

However, when he sat up and swung his legs from the pod, he found that the ache in his right leg was manageable; even his ribs no longer throbbed. He would have to recommend the analgesic properties of the pods when he returned to New Earth. However the hell he might manage that small task...

He climbed down from the flat-bed, the alien taking his hand as he stood, swaying. He smiled and withdrew his hand. He'd known the Phandrans were tiny, but only when he was standing next to this one did he realise quite how small they were: the alien barely reached his ribcage.

He took a deep breath and moved carefully away from the cart, surprised at the lack of pain. He felt like an invalid, walking for the first time after weeks of convalescence. The scar-faced Phandran danced attendance all the way, reaching out a hand when Ellis stumbled or swayed.

He stepped into the shade of the yellow-fruit tree. Although it accommodated the aliens with headroom to spare, he had to duck beneath its drooping branches. The Phandrans shuffled around to make room for him.

They were eating what looked like flat-bread, each of them dipping it into a communal bowl of bright orange paste. Ellis was handed an oval of bread, and he broke off a chunk and scooped up the slurry. He ate hungrily – having had nothing to eat but the golden-fruit hours ago – and found the paste to be sweet at first, and then hot, and not unpleasant.

The Phandran who had escorted him to the tree now scooped a small cup into the paste, took an oval of bread, and retreated to the turtle. It sat on its hump, eating, from time to time looking up and down the track.

The alien next to Ellis saw him looking and touched his arm. In explanation, the Phandran placed a thumb and forefinger below and above its right eye and moved its head back and forth in a scanning motion.

Ellis nodded. "A lookout. Good idea. I just hope..." he began, then shook his head and smiled. He had been about to say that he hoped no harm would come of his rescuers if the invaders discovered him – but what was the point when they obviously didn't understand a word he was saying?

The Phandran seated across from him, whose lined face marked him as the oldest of the group, raised a small hand to attract Ellis's attention. He spoke a few piping words and indicated the loam before him.

As Ellis watched, the alien drew a symbol in the soil.

It consisted of two big curves, like grammatical brackets, one nestling in the other. Ellis stared at it in mystification for long seconds, and only then did he smile in understanding.

The two curves were the Helix – or as much of the structure as was observable from the surface of Phandra. These people, he reminded himself, were pre-industrial, and though some of their number must comprehend the notion of the Helix in its entirety, he guessed that these relatively uneducated agricultural workers, his saviours, did not.

He nodded, and then the alien drew a series of rectangular blocks on the lower curve to represent the individual worlds and the seas between them.

The alien paused, then bent forward and indicated a central block. He looked up at Ellis and said what sounded like, "Fahn'ra."

Ellis nodded. "Phandra. Yes, I understand. Your world." He indicated the central section. "Fahn'ra."

The alien bent forward again and pointed to the adjacent section or world. "Zzprell!" he spat. With marching fingers he moved his hands from Zzprell to Fahn'ra.

Ellis understood. "Sporell," he said under his breath. "Yes, of course. The invaders are from Sporell."

A chorus of piping greeted his words, and the oldster gained his attention again. "Zzprell!" he said. "Sharray! Kay!"

And the alien raised a hand to its chest and thumped, then mimed falling backwards and lying still.

Ellis looked around the group and nodded. "Yes, I understand. The Sporelli, they invaded Phandra, killing many of your people." He made what he hoped was a sympathetic face. "I'm sorry. Of course you can't understand." He shook his head. "There's nothing much I can say, other than once the Peacekeepers find out..." He stopped there and looked around at their staring, childlike faces, and had an idea.

He pointed to the lower curved line. "Fahn'ra," he said. He reached out and drew more barrel-shaped worlds on the lower curve, and indicated the sixth one along from Phandra. "New Earth."

Now for the tricky bit. With his finger he traced the descent of an object, and said, "Olembe."

He recalled the other alien's hand gesture to imitate a shuttle. He flattened his hand and planed it from New Earth to Phandra. He crashed his hand upon Phandra and said, "Olembe."

He pointed to himself. "Ellis. Olembe." He pointed to world six along from Phandra. "New Earth."

He looked around the group. To his dismay, they looked uncomprehending.

"Ellis," he said, putting his hand to his chest. "Olembe. New Earth. We are human."

To his surprise, this had a galvanising effect on the group. They sat up, staring at each other, and a rapid chatter broke out.

"Whoma, whoma!" said the oldster.

Another said, "Olmb!" And planed his hand through the air, crashing it into the sea next to Phandra.

They turned to him and said, in concert, "Whoma! Olmb!"

"Olmb, yes. *Olembe*. He was one of the First Four. The first humans to set foot on the Helix. That was two hundred years ago. They went through much hardship, much suffering. They were six to begin with, but two of their number died when their ship crash-landed. They were on the lowest, ice-bound circuit, and had to make their way up to a more temperate circuit."

He fell silent, not because he realised the futility of trying to convey these concepts to aliens who didn't have his language, but because for some reason he found himself choking up, his eyes filling, as he spoke of the exploits of his forbears.

He smiled at the Phandrans. "Anyway, yes. I am human. Olembe was human. And when my people get to know what the Sporell are doing here, we'll take measures."

Only when he said this did he wonder what the Peacekeepers might do to halt the advance of the Sporelli. In the one hundred and ninety years that the Peacekeepers had been in existence, never had they had to intervene in a military conflict. They were militarily equipped, had a small army, but it was only ever employed in a monitoring capacity. The humans, along with most every other race on the Helix, lived by pacific ideals. How to confront an army bent on a flagrant invasion of a peaceful neighbouring world, bent on death and destruction?

The aliens were packing up their bowls preparatory to resuming the journey. The oldster pointed to the cart and Ellis climbed to his feet.

He had – notwithstanding his injuries – been well until that point. But as soon as he stood, his head swirled, his vision blurred, and he felt a sickening nausea rise in his chest. It was like, he thought later, having consumed too much alcohol and realising the fact only when attempting to stand.

His stomach clenched in pain. He fell to his knees and vomited, regurgitating first all the bread and paste the Phandrans had served him, and then chunks of the golden fruit he'd eaten much earlier.

He braced himself on all fours, head hanging, drenched in sweat, as a glorious relief passed through him. He laughed and tried to say that he rather thought the bread and paste hadn't agreed... Then he was retching again, and brought up more golden-apple pulp.

He spat, feeling better, and crawled away from the spreading pool of vomit. He sat up, taking deep breaths and hoping the sickness was over.

He smiled an apology to the alien, but the Phandra was paying him no heed.

Instead, he was crouching over the slick of vomit, staring at it with an odd intensity. He looked up, at another Phandran, and barked urgently, "Gan – yer-ahn! Gan!"

As Ellis stared, baffled, the scar-faced alien took off and raced into the forest. The others conferred in hurried lowered tones, occasionally looking back at Ellis.

A minute later the Phandran returned, holding something, and passed it to the oldster.

Ellis stared at the golden fruit as the oldster held it out to him. The alien pointed to his own mouth in obvious enquiry. "*Did you eat a fruit like this?*"

Ellis nodded.

A cry went up from one of the aliens, and another gripped the arm of its mate.

Oh, hell, Ellis thought, *what have I done?*

The oldster snapped something at the scarred alien, who raced back into the forest. The oldster took Ellis's arm and escorted him to the cart. He gestured for Ellis to lie down, and Ellis climbed back onto the flat-bed. Feeling more than anxious, he lay back. He wanted to tell the Phandrans that he was feeling fine now... but his little knowledge of poisonous plants was enough to tell him that there was often a period of wellbeing following the initial sickness.

The scar-faced alien hurried back clutching, Ellis saw with wry amusement, a handful of the bitter pink berries he'd first discarded as possibly harmful.

The oldster passed them to Ellis and gestured that he should eat them.

Obviously an antidote, he thought as he crammed the berries into his mouth, chewed and swallowed. The taste was truly terrible, bitter and dry, and it was all he could do to swallow them quickly and stop himself from throwing them up immediately.

The oldster leaned over him, a hand on his shoulder, and mouthed a string of sibilant, reassuring words. The Phandran pulled an empty pod skin over Ellis, leaving only his face uncovered.

Seconds later the cart juddered, lurched, and they were under way again.

Ellis lay on his back, staring at the succession of high wispy clouds interspersed with the foliage of the gossamer trees with their pendent pods bearing who knew what gruesome cargo. He smiled as he realised how lucky he had been that the aliens had happened along when they did.

They had, he realised, saved his life twice over now.

If, of course, the pink berries had done their job of counteracting the poison of the golden-apples.

As the cart juddered along, he turned his thoughts to wondering how he might escape from Phandra.

Even assuming the shuttle's emergency beacon was working and had managed to relay the fact of the crash-landing to the authorities back on New Earth, they would have to mount an expedition in order to locate him. Which, given the Sporelli invasion, might be no easy task.

In effect, he was stranded on the world for the indefinite future.

Treading, he thought, in the steps of my illustrious forbear.

It had ended happily for Olembe, he recalled. On his return to New Earth he had written about his adventures and lived to a ripe old age in a villa beside the eastern sea.

Which, Ellis thought as the cart swayed from side to side and a clenching pain gripped his stomach again, would suit me just fine.

He shot up into a sitting position and vomited over the side of the flat-bed, a mess of golden apple and pink berries. He was surprised that he had any more of the poisonous apples inside him. How many had he eaten? Three, four? Had they expanded in his gut?

This time, following the sickness, there was no accompanying relief from the nausea. Worse, his head thumped with a sharp, insistent migraine.

He lay back, groaning.

The oldster was at his side, staring down at him. He spoke, a string of soft, feathery words, but Ellis could only smile and shake his head and clutch the alien's tiny, bird-boned hand.

Seconds later pain lanced through his gut and throbbed within his skull. He wanted to void the toxins from his system, but it appeared that he had ejected as much of the golden apple as was coming out. He dry-retched, weeping at the pain and gripping the oldster's hand.

Some time later the old Phandran, accompanied by another, dragged Ellis into a sitting position and made him eat more of the bitter pink berries, helped down this time with a draft of ice-cold water which made him feel slightly better.

He slept, and when he came to his senses, much later, he saw that the sun was sinking behind the distant mountains.

He was experiencing another period of remission, as he felt not quite as bad as earlier. Still at death's door – he managed to smile at the thought – but not quite over the threshold.

Two Phandrans squatted beside him, pointing at something. He followed the direction of their gestures and wondered if what he saw, high up on the mountain-side, was a hallucination.

Fairy towers, belvederes with slit windows, a zigzag approach road up the precipitous incline. It looked like something from a fantasy holo-drama, its make-believe splendour enhanced by the tangerine and silver lamination of the setting sun.

He smiled. "Journey's end?" he asked.

The oldster spoke, softly.

"Don't understand a word," he said feebly, "but thank you anyway. Without you... without..."

He passed out again.

3

HE HAD ONLY a partial memory of what happened over the course of the next few hours.

He recalled fragments of the climb to the castle, the zigzag track with one particular steep drop that fell for five hundred metres as the cart turned a sharp corner. He recalled the Phandrans shouting to each other and pointing. He had roused himself from his stupor long enough to look at what had excited them: far away, kilometres across a flat valley bottom, he made out the tiny vehicles of the invading army; he heard the retort of their weapons and, seconds later, saw small puffs of smoke as villages or towns were destroyed.

He'd passed out again, and some time later awoke to see the façade of the castle rearing up before the minuscule cart. As he lay on his back, staring into the air, his view of the wall was almost vertiginous. The edifice had been chiselled from the very face of the cliff itself, and seemed to rise forever, ending in a succession of towers with, high above in the twilight, the loop of the Helix's third or fifth circuit – he was unable to tell which – catching the last light of the sun.

Then they were rattling over a stone road and entering a vast airy space the size of a cathedral which was merely the entrance hall to this magnificent edifice.

After that his memory misfired. He had sequential recollections of being lifted gently from the cart, of his saviours coming to him one after the other and mouthing soft words of farewell before he was carried rapidly off. He recalled glimpses of pink marbled corridors, helical stairways, and long cloisters. But interspersed with these images of the castle's interior, he recalled scattered glimpses of paradisiacal gardens and flamboyant flowers, of darting birds and droning insects, and periods where he was left by himself in these strange places before being borne away again. At one point he was in a narrow chamber, on a hard stone bench, surrounded by a dozen Phandrans in red and green robes who stared down at him while murmuring amongst themselves.

He passed out, and when he came to his senses he was once again outside.

The nausea had passed, thankfully. He no longer felt the urge to vomit, and the headaches had passed too. As if to compensate for his partial recovery, he could feel an increased pain in his ribs and right leg.

He was propped up in a bed, and he was indeed in a garden. He was alone in a clearing of short crimson grass fringed by tall, slender trees with drooping frond-like branches. Flowers of every shape and colour grew amid the trees, and the air was filled with birdsong. He stared up into the air, looking for the next circuit of the Helix. He was on the roof of the castle.

A silver bird darted towards him and inserted its long curved beak into a tangerine trumpet bloom growing nearby. It hovered with the aid of two pairs of wings, and Ellis could only stare at it in amazement.

He looked down at his body for the first time since waking. He was naked; his flightsuit had been removed, and something placed over his ribs – not so much a bandage as an amber substance which felt wet on his chest and yet glistened like shell, which nevertheless allowed his chest to rise and fall with every breath. His right leg was similarly encased. The flesh of his arms and legs was patched with ugly red sores, and he wondered if these were the result of the pod's acidic digestive juices.

Across his loins – suggesting that modesty was not solely a human affectation – a length of white material had been placed.

He considered the blue aliens, wondering why they had invaded this peaceful world, and if the authorities back on New Earth were aware of the violation.

He returned his attention to the bird. It had supped its fill of the bloom, and he expected it to fly off to the next one. Instead, and before he could react, it darted towards him, slipped its beak between his lips, and squirted honeyed fluid into his mouth. He had no choice but to swallow, shocked, and watched as the bird darted off and vanished into the trees.

He wondered if the fluid was a sedative, for minutes later he began to feel lethargic. He smiled to himself at the strangeness of this world, then closed his heavy eyes and slept.

A sound awoke him. He sat up. The sun was high above. Birds called in the clearing, and the air pulsed with the drone of insects. The sound that had drawn him from sleep, however, was neither that of birds nor of insects.

He looked to his left, and through a stand of frond trees saw the distant wall of a building, and an archway set into it. Great double doors were in the process of being hauled open, and through the entrance stepped a procession of Phandrans.

Perhaps two dozen slight, robed aliens passed from the castle and crossed the garden. As he watched, they parted, a dozen to each side, and formed what he took to be a guard of honour.

He looked through the arch, and watched as two figures appeared and walked sedately through the honour guard. One was an old man, garbed in a long green robe, hunched over and walking with the aid of a staff, his silver hair threadbare. Beside him was a young girl, perhaps twelve years old, in a red robe. She was slight and elfin-pretty, her face fine-boned as if crafted from delicate china. What struck him most, though, were her cobalt blue eyes, bright and piercing.

Only then did he become aware of other Phandrans on the periphery of the clearing. There were around twenty of these shy, elusive creatures, hiding behind the trees and peeking out at... not him, he realised... but at the advancing duo, the ancient man and the girl-child. It was as if the watchers were awed, entranced.

He recalled, with a stab of sadness, what Abi had told him before the crash-landing: that Phandrans lived on average for only twenty New Earth years, and he realised with incredulity that, for all the disparity of their apparent ages, the girl could not be that much younger than the old man.

The pair stopped at the foot of the bed and stared at him without expression. He recalled something else that Abi had told him – that the Phandrans were empathetic. He wondered if they were able to read his alien thoughts.

At length the pair turned their gaze from him and spoke together in hushed tones, their breath-like words hardly reaching him.

Minutes elapsed before they moved again. The old man turned and hobbled slowly from the garden, taking the honour guard with him. At the door he turned and called out, and as if by magic the circumspect watchers slipped from their hiding places behind the trees and drained in silence from the garden.

Within a minute, when the timber door had closed finally, Ellis and the girl were quite alone.

She approached the side of the bed, drew up a high stool fashioned from polished wood, and seated herself with grace, carefully drawing the folds of her robe around her.

She looked upon him in silence, and Ellis was struck by her ethereal, other-worldly air. More than any of the others, she made him think of an angel.

She sat with her slim hands enfolded together in her lap, the slightest smile on her alien lips.

He said, "I would like to thank you, your people, for what you have done for me. I know you can't understand my words, but perhaps you can... can somehow *sense* my gratitude."

The girl appeared deep in thought, staring down at her folded hands. Then she looked up at him.

"We helped you because we are a civilised race, and..." She relapsed into thought again. "...and we could do nothing but help a fellow sentient."

He smiled, then laughed aloud in amazement. Her words were the softest, slightest emanations of sound imaginable.

"You speak my language!"

Her facial expression did not react as a human's would; she seemed impassive, dwelling in some inner, cerebral realm. In his current frame of mind, it gave her the calm piety of a saint.

She digested his words, considered them, and at length made her response.

"Some of my people, numbering only in our hundreds, were schooled by the Elders who were schooled by the Elders who tended Olembe. From him we learned your language, and much more. We learned of humans, of the Peacekeepers. We have much for which to be grateful to Olembe."

He wanted to reach out and take her hand. "The story is still told, on our world, New Earth, of the kindness the Phandrans showed Olembe. Now, we have reason to give thanks again."

She turned her right hand in a modest gesture. "Thanks are not necessary for actions which, in the circumstances, are the only ones possible."

"Even so..."

She was silent for a while, regarding him. In normal circumstances, if the person watching him had been human, he might have felt uncomfortable. The odd thing was that, in this girl-child's watchful presence, he felt entirely at ease.

"You were near death when the yahn-fahrs brought you in. You had eaten gan-fruit, which are poisonous. They saved your life in giving you ker-berries. Without them, you would have died within hours."

"They also saved my life when they cut me from the pod-tree."

"They are yahn-fahrs. They harvest the yahn-pods every twelve-day. The meat within is considered a delicacy among some of my kind." She turned her hand again. "Also, the yahn-pod had burned you. But your skin is healing now."

He smiled. "Thank you."

"You arrived here five days ago –"

"Five days?" he said. "Five? I thought I'd been here a day, two at the most."

"Five days, and our world turns more slowly than your own. So perhaps ten of your days elapsed while you have been in our care. You were unconscious for much of the time, and you were beset by nightmares and hallucinations."

"I can't remember anything," he admitted.

"You are mending well, now. You will live."

He said, "I am Ellis. Jeff Ellis."

She inclined her head. "And I am Calla-vahn-villa," she said. "You may call me Calla. I am a Healer."

"We call people of your profession doctors," he said.

Again the calm turn of the right hand. "Healing," she breathed, "is not my profession. I was born to heal, like my mother and her mother before her. It is a... a calling. It is what I was destined to do. Just as I was destined to minister to your needs."

He stared at her. "Destined?"

"I was told by Diviner Tomar that I was to help you, and by helping you as my people helped Olembe, many generations ago, my actions will bring peace to Phandra and to the Helix."

He laughed to himself, then fell silent. Who was he, having benefited from the succour of her people, to call her beliefs superstitious nonsense? He had the urge to question, to gently chide her beliefs. But all he said was, "And how might your helping me bring about that peace, Calla?"

No facial reaction at all, just the turn of her palm. "*That* I am not wise enough, nor privileged enough, to know."

She slipped from the stool in one fluid, graceful movement, and drew her robes about her.

He reached out, his hand falling short. "One minute. Please, don't go. Can you stay and talk? There is much I would like to know about you and your people, about what is happening to your world."

She stared at him; long seconds elapsed. At length she resumed her seat. "You are still ill, and must rest, but I can talk for a little while longer, yes."

He nodded, smiled, and considered his words. "My people believe that you, the Phandrans, are able to read the minds of others. This is an ability humans do not posses, and find hard to understand."

She considered his words, staring down at her alabaster hands. She looked up, into his eyes. "We cannot read minds, so much as feel emotions, intentions. This I do not think is the same as reading thoughts, exactly. Certain amongst us are able to sense the moods of others, the dominant emotions. From these we can extrapolate intent."

He paused, then asked, "And are you able to do this with members of an alien species?"

Her cobalt eyes fixed him with an unreadable expression. "Your emotions, moods, are there, like fish in a river... observable. However, you are alien, you are formed by influences I have no hope of understanding. So many of your moods and emotions are... are fish unidentifiable to me." Her lips twitched in what might have been a smile.

"Many of my emotions? But not all?"

She considered his words. "I can understand your pain, your grief. But your other emotions – these will take more time for me to understand, Jeff Ellis."

He was cheered, then, by something inherent in her words: that they would have more time together.

She made to leave again. She slipped from the stool and gathered her robes. "Now sleep. You are tired, and you grieve for your colleague, the woman named Abi."

"Abi..." he said, wondering how she had learned her name. "And her remains?"

"My people have taken the bodies of your colleagues and interred them with respect."

He stared at her as she turned and sedately walked away.

"One more thing," he called after her.

She stopped and turned to face him.

"How old are you?" he asked.

She considered her reply, and, when it came, he was shocked. "I am almost twenty of your years," she said, and swept from the clearing.

Twenty, he thought when she had gone. *Twenty*...

But how could that be? If her kind lived only to be twenty, and the old man who had accompanied her was approaching the end of his life... then Calla, at twenty, must be at the end of her allotted span, too?

But how could that be, when she had the appearance of a girl barely out of childhood?

4

HE HEALED QUICKLY over the course of the next few days.

Phandra turned slowly on its lateral axis, so that a day lasted for approximately two New Earth days. It was a regime to which his body clock could not adjust, and he soon found himself out of synch with the phases of night and day, sleeping during the daylight hours and often awake through the long hours of darkness – though the night was never fully dark in the Healing Garden. Many of the trees bore fruit that glowed, and floating insects carried their own luminescent night-lamps.

Calla attended to him three or four times a day, and often during the night. She changed the strange amber dressing on his chest and leg twice a day, simply laying a hand on the shell-like carapace. At her touch it flowed from his body, and from an amphora she poured on more of the caramel-like liquid. It flowed over his chest and leg and solidified rapidly as Calla shaped it with her tiny hands.

He asked her what it was called one morning, and she said a word in her own language which he did not catch, and went on to say that in its own way it was sentient, and that she could communicate with it. Shortly after, Ellis slept, smiling in wonderment at his situation.

The next time he awoke, Calla informed him that he should leave the bed and walk with her.

She helped him upright, and he swung from the bed and took a tentative step, expecting to feel pain in his leg and chest. To his surprise he experienced neither. He felt fully healed, renewed, and laughed aloud at the transformation.

"For one day and one night, Jeff," Calla informed him as they strolled around the garden, "you will eat well and exercise, in preparation for the journey ahead."

He stopped walking and looked at her. "The journey?"

She looked up at him. "Come," she said, and led him from the garden, through the arched doorway and into the castle.

They passed down a long corridor furnished with rugs and carvings of Phandran animals, to a room positioned in the façade of the castle. "This is my chamber, Jeff."

The room was long and low, and he had to stoop to avoid the thick timber beams that supported the ceiling. Sunlight flooded in through an arched window at the far end of the room, its dusty light illuminating a cosy area of tapestries and rugs and old sofas.

He moved to the window and stared out, drawing a breath in wonder. They were so high up that a cart, making its way around the switchback path he'd come up days ago, looked like a tiny beetle. Beyond, a vast plain of crimson grassland stretched for as far as the eye could see, with mountains on either side diminishing in perspective. The plain was dotted with gossamer-tree forests, giving the scene an ethereal quality, and quicksilver rivers threaded the wide valley beneath the setting sun.

"Jeff, here," she called from behind him.

She was sitting at a small table, poring over what looked like a barrel mounted on gimbals. He joined her, sitting on the floor beside the table, and saw that the barrel was the representation of her world.

She turned it, and mountains and valleys, great plateaus and lakes, passed beneath her childlike fingers.

She stopped the barrel and pointed. "This, here, is the western range, or the Mountains of Haedra as we know them." She pointed to the western extremity of the mountain range, where it petered out into a vast plain, or rather a plateau, still high above the level of the sea. "We are here, at the Retreat of Verlaine, perhaps a thousand..." She paused to translate the distance into a measurement he would comprehend. "Perhaps six hundred of your kilometres from the sea."

"How do you know...?" he began.

She smiled, and said simply, "I calculated from your knowledge of distances. Of course, my estimation is only an approximation."

He paused, then said, "And what else are you able to read of my thoughts?"

"Your thoughts? Very little. They are still alien to me. But I can discern images, moods." She turned her hand. "It is inexact, and hard to explain in your language."

He smiled. "You do very well."

She returned her attention to the barrel-world. "We are here," she said, her finger-tips resting on a bluff overlooking a vast plain. "Here, ten kilometres across the plain, is the town of Trahng. In the early hours of the morning, we will leave here and make our way to Trahng."

"Together? You are coming with me?"

She looked up at him, piercing him with her cobalt eyes. "Of course. This is a journey we must make together."

He smiled, warmed by the thought.

She continued, "We are going to the coast, to the western sea. There you will take passage on a boat destined for the world of D'rayni. From there, you will be able to contact your people on New Earth, and inform them of what is happening here on Phandra."

"You have contact with the D'rayni?"

"We have limited trade links. They are more technologically advanced than ourselves, but we trade foodstuffs and woven materials and such like."

She turned the barrel absently, the world of Phandra spinning beneath her fingers.

After a period of reflection, he said, "Why have the Sporelli invaded Phandra?"

She rose and paced across the room, to a cabinet where she poured a thick brown liquid into two tiny goblets. She returned and passed him one, saying, "Drink this. It will give you strength."

He raised the glass to his lips and sipped. The liquid was sweet, fruity, and it tingled on his palate.

Calla said, "We are merely an obstacle to be overcome. The Sporelli have no need or desire to quell the Phandran race or occupy our world."

"In that case?"

She sipped her drink, her tongue-tip showing as she dabbed a bead of liquid from her lower lip. She said softly, "The Sporelli are crossing Phandra in order to reach D'rayni. That world is rich in metals, in other things they can mine from the ground. Their world, Sporell, does not have an abundance of these materials. For their advancement, they must have these things."

"How do you know this?"

"My people have had contact with them, with their minds."

"And on their way, the Sporelli raze your villages, kill your people."

"They are a cruel people, Jeff, or they have cruel leaders; perhaps the latter. Perhaps the average Sporelli is as... humane... as you or I."

"Maybe. But the ones I saw seemed... vicious."

Calla went on, "I thought, when the invasion continued, that the Builders might do something to halt the Sporelli. However, minds wiser than mine informed me otherwise: they said that for whatever reasons the Builders would not intervene."

"When I return," he said, "I will tell my people what is happening here. Our peacekeeping forces will do all within their powers to halt the Sporelli. The Builders are no longer corporeal, Calla. They live now in a virtual realm." Her face showed no comprehension, so he rephrased: "They live lives of the spirit, as it were, no longer physical. Also, they no longer communicate with us as they once did, two hundred years ago when we first arrived here. It's as if we have been left to our own devices to do the best we can."

He paused, then said, "You knew I was coming, Calla. You said, earlier, that by helping me you would bring peace to your world."

"The Diviners tell of this. I knew little of my destiny until Diviner Tomar told me that through my actions the times of trouble on Phandra would be ended and the halcyon days would be resumed."

He smiled, then laughed. "I hope you're right, Calla." He considered the thought which had vexed him the night before.

"Tomar is old," he said. "But I understood that your people live to the age of twenty New Earth years, and you told me that you are twenty years old."

"And you wonder why I am not as... as manifestly aged as Tomar? Why..." – she traced the fine line of her cheek – "why I do not have fissured skin and sunken eyes?"

He smiled. "You are twenty, old for a Phandran, and yet you appear so young."

"The male and female of our kind age at different rates," she said. "That is, the female of the species is... how to explain? ...more physically able until the age of around twenty years... Or ten of our own years. We can conceive, bear children, until we are almost as old as I am. But after that, the decline is rapid."

He felt something constrict his throat, and he nodded. He stared at her beauty, and wondered how little time the woman before him might have to live.

She said, as if divining the drift of his thoughts, "In one Phandran year, I will move from this phase of existence."

Her words rocked him, and the sweet liquid that coated his palate tasted suddenly cloying. At last he said, "And you will move on to...?"

She smiled, and he wondered at her sudden utilisation of this very human expression. Days ago, at their first meeting, her face had been a blank slate, as it were, her expressions neutral, indecipherable; now, as if learning from him, she employed smiles and frowns, shrugs and gestures that made communication between much easier.

"I will move on to a realm very much like that one you describe the Builders as inhabiting," she said.

He was about to say that the Builders now dwelled in a virtual realm of their own technological making, but stopped himself. Who was he to gainsay her beliefs? And, for that matter, how did he know that the Builders' virtuality was materially based?

Calla drained her goblet, and Ellis found himself hoping that this did not denote an end to their meeting. He said, "You have been a Healer all your adult life?"

She inclined her head. "Since I was three of our years," she said. "A Healer, a... you would call them counsellors. I have helped others of my kind, both physically and psychologically."

"And do Healers... mate, Calla? Do you have children?"

She trilled a laugh at this. "Of course not. I chose, at an early age, to devote myself solely to Healing."

He looked down, at the intricate inlay of the polished table. "And you have never regretted your decision, never felt *alone*?"

She smiled again. "But I am never alone, Jeff! My life is rich beyond your imagining. My contact with my kind surpasses any intimacy you and your kind would understand."

He felt humbled, then, before the wisdom of this apparent girl-child, who was nothing of the sort, but an elderly, wise member of a race he would be mistaken to assume was anything at all like his own.

She looked up at him. "In the journey ahead, Jeff, you can tell me of your own relationships, yes? You will find that talking will help considerably."

He nodded, staring into the eyes of this strange alien woman, and he could not help but feel that he was a child in the company of someone incomparably wiser than himself.

"It is late, and you must rest. I will wake you before sunrise, and we will set off for Trahng." She rose to her feet, and paused before saying, "It will be a journey beset by danger, Jeff Ellis, but I know we will be enriched by the experience."

She reached out and squeezed his giant's hand. Dismissed, he left the chamber and made his way back to the Healing Garden.

Six /// The Yahn-Gatherers

I

FROM HIGH ORBIT, with her magnified viewscreen, Kranda watched the progress of the Sporelli army. They were traversing the world of Phandra from coast to coast, having crossed the intervening ocean from their own world aboard a combination of battleships and fliers. Now, convoys of tanks, troop-carriers and rocket-launchers flying the red and white striped Sporelli flag were perhaps halfway across the world, *en route* to their destination of D'rayni. A vanguard of fliers led the way, while the following military wrought havoc on the innocent population of Phandra, indiscriminately torching towns and villages. From her orbital vantage point, Kranda saw no reason for the Sporelli to be inflicting such punishment: the Phandrans put up no resistance to the invasion. They were a peaceable people with neither the wherewithal nor the inclination to commit violence. They were merely supremely unlucky to occupy the world they did, coming between the Sporelli and their goal, the metal-rich world of D'rayni.

She was tempted, with the weapons she possessed, to mete out a little justice on the invading army, but resisted the urge. There was always the danger that hubris would get the better of her and she'd fall victim to a lucky shot from Sporelli artillery. She could not endanger her duty to Jeff Ellis: saving him was the priority now.

If, that was, Jeff Ellis were still alive.

She instructed her flier to shield itself, then slipped into a lower orbit and overflew the mountains that reminded her so much of her homeworld. In minutes, the serried, iron-grey mountain range was in her wake and she was decelerating over high crimson meadowland and the curious cloud-headed trees. She allowed the flier to follow the pre-set co-ordinates and came at last to the valley where Jeff Ellis's shuttle had been brought down.

She hovered over the area, ensuring that it was free of both Phandrans and the invading Sporelli.

The ugly burned-out wreckage of the shuttle still occupied the great furrow it had ploughed through the meadow. Kranda eased her flier down between two cloud trees and cut the engines. She sat for a time, staring out at the mangled wreckage of the human shuttle.

Such ugliness amid such beauty...

She stood and drew her varnika from its peg on the bulkhead. The exo-skeleton hung in her grip like the bones of a filleted primate, a collection of matt black spars and struts which belied its incredible power. She laid it on the deck and stepped into the foot-shaped pads. The effect was instantaneous: it flowed up the back of her legs, up her back and over her head, enclosing her rib-cage and arms in its shackle of spars. She braced herself for the pain of the occipital cut, as the varnika accessed her sensorium. She had only ever worn a varnika once before, in routine training, and this was the bit she least liked: the needle-sharp incision at the base of her skull. It came, taking her breath, and she felt its insidious tendrils crawl through her neural pathways like some alien form of migraine. Then the pain was over and the varnika was part of her – or, perhaps, she was part of the varnika.

She was forever in awe of Builder technology – from the macro, the incredible construct of the Helix itself, to the micro, the various devices the Builders had bequeathed the Engineers and the exo-skeletons that augmented both strength and perceptions to supra-normal degrees.

Mahkans of her acquaintance believed that some essence of the Builders still dwelled in the smartcores of the varnikas, but Kranda didn't hold with such irrational nonsense. The exo-skeletons were simply a form of technology so far ahead of what her people could conceive that it seemed like magic.

With a simple thought she commanded the varnika to shield itself, then strode to the reflective surface of the bulkhead and stared at where she should have been. All she saw, if she stared hard, was the very vague, fuzzy outline of herself. To the casual observer, not looking for her, she was invisible.

She broke out a pair of weapons from stores, clipped them to the spars of her forearms, and left the flier. She strode towards the wreckage of the shuttle, then stopped and looked back. She saw a grove of cloud-trees, an expanse of red grass... and only if she increased her visual magnification and squinted at where her flier was could she make out its squat shape. She was satisfied that it would be safe from casual observation.

She hurried towards the river where the satellite image had last shown the figure of Jeff Ellis. She exerted little effort – no more than she might if she were strolling – yet the effect was exponential: it was as if she had given her body the command to run. She covered the fifty metres between the cloud-tree and the stream in less than three seconds.

She knelt and examined the silver water of the river, and then the grass on its bank. She made out shallow impressions in the turf, marking – she surmised – where Ellis had dragged himself along. Did this indicate, then, that he had been injured and unable to walk?

She followed the trail. The indentations left the stream and approached a small bush bearing red berries, then moved from there to a shrub of golden fruit. Then the indents became deeper scuff marks, as if for some reason Ellis had propelled himself with more urgency away from the bushes and back towards the stream.

But what had become of the human? Had he pitched himself in the river, hoping to swim downstream away from the wreckage, assuming that sooner or later Sporelli troops would investigate the shuttle they had brought down?

It made sense. It was what she would have done, in his situation.

She moved back to the wreckage and examined the halved cockpit. She made out a generous spray of dried blood, but no bodies. According to information cached in the smartcore of her varnika, Ellis had been ferrying two peacekeeping diplomats to D'rayni, a man and a woman. If they had perished in the crash, then the Sporelli might have taken their bodies for reasons known only to themselves. If they had survived, then like Ellis, there was no evidence to suggest where they might be now.

According to her varnika, the cloud-trees were harvested from time to time, and animals taken from their ambulatory pods. A team of yahn-gatherers had been in the vicinity not long after the crash, according to the satellite images. So perhaps...

She walked towards the closest cloud-tree, stood beneath its spreading white foliage and looked up. Twirling in the slight breeze was a pod, and she was surprised at its size. She had expected something much smaller.

She began to wonder.

Ellis had been injured, and on his back, and at one point had been propelling himself away from something...

Could he have been taken by one of the cloud-tree pods? According to her varnika, they were carnivorous.

But surely he could have fought it off, kicked out in self-defence... always assuming, of course, that he was not too badly injured.

She moved from tree to tree in the area, staring up at the hanging pods. They all appeared to be empty, and she made out tendrils from which the pods had evidently been cut, which stood to reason. The yahn-gatherers had been here just three days ago, harvesting the captive meat.

Was it conceivable, she thought, that Ellis had been captured by a cloud-tree pod, then harvested by a yahn-gathering team?

It was a possibility worth investigating.

The priority now was to find the local yahn-gatherers.

She would gain high ground – the bluff a few hundred metres to the north of the glade – and assess the lie of the land. From there she might make out tracks, habitation.

She was heading for the outcropping of balding rocks when she heard the unmistakable sound of a flier's engines. She ducked behind the bole of a cloud-tree, even though the precaution, protected as she was by the varnika's shield, was unnecessary.

A Sporelli flier landed in the glade fifty metres away. She watched as a hatch in its side folded open and a dozen black-uniformed Sporelli soldiers filed out.

2

SHE CROUCHED BEHIND the tree and watched the troops deploy themselves around the cloud-tree grove, a sick feeling in her stomach as she anticipated their stumbling across her ship. Six of their number stood guard while the remaining six picked over the wreckage, poking through the shattered metal debris with the snouts of their carbines. Her ship was situated behind their flier, and fortunately the Sporelli showed no inclination to move in that direction.

A tall, attenuated, grey-haired Sporelli officer strode down the ramp from the ship. He approached the shuttle, kicking aside fragments of debris with a look of distaste on his lean, pale blue face. He looked up from a scorched fragment of bucket seat and snapped something to the nearest soldier.

Kranda instructed her varnika to increase its amplification and initiate a translation.

The soldier approached the officer and saluted. He spoke in the guttural, grating Sporelli tongue. The translation sounded in Kranda's ear-piece. "As I reported yesterday, Commander. Nothing."

The commander replied, "You do realise that we are not looking for whole corpses, Sergeant? The remains might very well be shredded. Humans, after all, are physically feeble."

"Yes, sir. But there are no remains of any kind. Plenty of dried blood, but no body parts."

The commander looked up, staring into the distance, and more to himself said, "In that case, what happened to the pilot and crew?"

"I'll continue searching, sir."

"Very well – and make it thorough."

The commander strode back and forth, occasionally kicking at scraps of wreckage. He glanced at his wrist-chronometer, then looked up at the sound of an approaching vehicle and moved from the grove to a narrow track.

An open-topped ground-effect vehicle drove up and braked in front of the commander, a hundred metres from Kranda. She instructed her varnika to magnify the image, and the scene jumped, became clearer. An overfed soldier climbed from the car, crossed to the officer, and saluted.

They exchanged words, and when the varnika failed to translate, Kranda thought: *What's the problem.*

"*Proximity issues,*" the voice sounded in her ear-piece.

"You can't increase the gain?"

Negative.

"So in other words, I'll have to get closer?"

Affirmative.

She glanced around the grove. The closest Sporelli soldier was ten metres away, searching through the wreckage. Even though she knew that she was perfectly safe, concealed in the varnika's visual baffle, she still felt terribly vulnerable when she stepped from behind the tree and crossed the crimson grass towards the Sporelli officers. She expected to hear a shout at any second, followed by gunfire.

She moved carefully, aware that her steps were tamping down small areas of red grass. Only the most astute observer would notice the disturbance, but even so she approached the Sporelli soldiers on their blindside. When she was three metres away, she crouched behind a bush of golden-fruit and listened.

"...no chance of surviving the crash, but then why no bodies?" the portly soldier was saying.

The commander looked back at the grove, his gaze lingering on the cloud-trees. Kranda wondered if he had made the same connection as she had.

He said, "I read somewhere, before we invaded this fairyland, that the natives harvested the pods of these trees. I want you to locate the nearest village and question the harvesters, using all means necessary to extract the required information. If one or more of the humans survived, then I want him found."

"I have the guran ready, sir."

"Very good."

"The only problem being, if we do find a survivor and use the guran, then the human might not survive."

The commander turned an imperious gaze on his subordinate officer. "And why is that a problem, Sergeant?"

"Well, if the Peacekeepers find out what we did to one of their…"

"As if that matters!" the commander retorted.

The portly sergeant snapped off a salute. "Very good, sir."

"Very well. Take three of my men and question the locals."

The soldier saluted again. He moved to the grove and spoke to the Sporelli troops, then returned to the vehicle with three of them and accelerated down the track.

Minutes later the commander called out, ordering his men to return to the flier, and followed them up the ramp. Kranda watched it take off with a thunderous roar, gain height and swing away over the cloud-trees.

There was only one course of action to take now: follow the soldiers in the car. If they did learn from the locals what had happened to Jeff Ellis, then she wanted to be there.

She rose and ran after the vehicle, amazed at the speed with which the varnika was carrying her. Within seconds she had caught up with the speeding car and was compelled to slow down in its dusty wake so as not to overtake.

As she followed the car along the winding track, she considered the guran the sergeant had mentioned; evidently some device of torture which they intended using on any survivor of the shuttle crash.

Half a kilometre away, nestled into the side a rolling hill, a cluster of conical huts appeared. Tethered in a central clearing were three of the big beasts of burden Kranda had seen on the satellite images.

The Sporelli car braked on the track before the thatched huts. The fat sergeant climbed out and, drawing a pistol, climbed the incline followed by the other Sporelli troops.

Kranda recalled the commander's instructions. "*Question the harvesters, using all means necessary to extract the required information.*"

At the sound of the engine, Phandrans had begun to drift from their huts. They huddled together in twos and threes, reminding her forcefully of frightened children: they were tiny. Even the tallest amongst them would barely reach her upper thigh. The Sporelli's brutal invasion of these people was even more barbaric in light of their size, though she told herself that this was hardly relevant. Any coercion against another race was a violation of the Builders' ethos of non-violence.

So the Builders created a force tasked with keeping the peace – which was all very well if they *succeeded* in keeping the peace; but what about when war broke out? The Builders' ethos had to be contravened, in certain circumstances. For example, how did one deal with a race of merciless invaders like the Sporelli?

The overweight soldier approached the gaggle of Phandrans and spoke, haltingly, in their language.

Kranda's varnika translated, "A human ship crash-landed in a yahn-tree plantation east of here. We have reason to believe that there were survivors. Do you know anything about the humans who were aboard the crashed ship?"

Phandran children stared with big eyes at the Sporelli, clinging to their parents' rudimentary smocks. If the adult Phandrans appeared small, then their children were minuscule. The smallest infant, a babe in arms, would have nestled in Kranda's palm with room to spare.

A male Phandran stepped forward, evidently an elder, judging by the nexus of wrinkles around his thin-lipped mouth. He looked up and spoke hesitantly to the towering Sporelli soldier.

"There were no survivors of the terrible accident," he said. "We found two bodies, and we interred them with all due ceremony."

They found two bodies, Kranda thought. So Jeff Ellis, who had been alive at the time the aerial image was taken, had managed to flee the area.

The soldier stared at the oldster with ill-disguised contempt. "Show me the graves."

With an open-handed gesture the Phandran indicated the hillside. He led the way, followed by the soldier and his troops. The rest of the Phandrans brought up the rear. Kranda followed at a safe distance.

They crested the rise and came to a small glade on the far side of the rise. Kranda made out two dozen small mounds in the short red grass, each one marked by a bush of red berries. She noted that the two nearest graves were considerably longer than the others.

The elderly Phandran gestured. "They are there."

The soldier moved down the hillside and paused at the first grave. He turned and looked up, shielding his eyes from the sun. "Dig them up."

A fluting murmur passed through the gathered Phandrans. Their spokesman said, "This would be disrespectful, and against our ways."

"I said, dig them up!"

The Phandran turned and murmured to his people, and a young man ran off. He returned a minute later with a wooden spade.

The oldster took it and approached the first grave. With reluctance manifest in his every movement, he leaned forward and dug the spade into the soft loam. A few strokes were all it took to dislodge the earth and reveal the red fabric of a Peacekeeper's uniform.

"Give it to me!" the soldier snarled, grabbing the spade and attacking the grave.

He shortly had the corpse uncovered from head to foot. Kranda caught sight of a shattered ribcage.

The soldier moved on to the second grave and began digging, soon uncovering another human corpse.

The Phandrans looked on with ill-concealed horror at the Sporelli defilement.

"Two Peacekeepers," the soldier said. "So... where is the pilot?"

The old Phandran looked mystified. "The pilot?"

"The human who piloted the shuttle. He would be wearing a blue uniform. Where is the third human?"

The oldster turned his palm. "But there was no third human. Just these two, and they were dead. We interred them, as is our way."

"You're lying! There was a pilot. Where is he?"

The oldster remained gazing evenly at his interrogator. "But I assure you, there was no third human. No... pilot, as you say."

The Sporelli soldier snarled something untranslatable. He turned and snapped an order to one of his men, who hurried down the hillside and approached the car.

He returned bearing a device that looked like a skullcap.

The guran, Kranda thought.

How could she stand by and watch the Sporelli torture a Phandran, when it was within her ability to kill all four invaders here and now and save an innocent life? She would have no compunction about exterminating the soldiers – Builder ethos against taking life notwithstanding – but knew that she had to be very careful. It was all very well saving one or two lives now by taking out these thugs, but, when the Sporelli learned of their deaths, then retribution against the Phandrans might be terrible and disproportionate.

The fat soldier took the guran and approached the oldster, who eyed the skullcap with manifest unease.

"You will tell me now where the pilot is, or I will be compelled to use this. A guran. It will be painful, but it will make you tell the truth. Now, which is it to be?"

The oldster held the Sporelli's gaze. "There was no human pilot. We found two bodies, no more."

The sergeant reached out, lightning fast, and grabbed the Phandran's collar. He forced the man to his knees, to the audible consternation of his watching fellows. Several of them turned away, weeping.

Kranda watched, promising herself that if the Phandran died, then she would – in the near future – execute the pot-bellied soldier.

The Sporelli dropped the skullcap onto the Phandran's head where it sat lopsidedly, three sizes too big. "The controls!" he called to one of his men, who passed him a hand-held device inset with studs.

"Now, where is the pilot?" the soldier demanded.

The Phandran stared at him. "There was no pilot," he said.

The soldier's finger hovered over a stud. "If you don't tell the truth, you will live to regret it. Have you ever experienced pain, Phandran?"

The oldster remained tight-lipped, staring up at his tormentor.

"Because this will be painful beyond imagining! Now, the pilot?"

"There was no pilot," the Phandran said again, slowly, emphasizing every world.

"Very well," the Sporelli said, "but I did warn you..."

The thin, blue forefinger came down on a stud. The Phandran oldster grimaced and moaned in pain.

"The pilot?" demanded the soldier. He jabbed the stud again.

The oldster, on his knees, spasmed and fell face down on the grass.

A Phandran woman rushed forward and dropped to her knees beside the oldster. She reached out, feeling for a pulse, then let forth a high, anguished keening.

The soldier looked across to his men and, much to Kranda's disgust, smiled. "Even weaker," he said, "than humans."

He climbed to the top of the hill and looked down on the village. He called out to one of his men, pointing. "Bring me that rope."

The Phandrans had gathered together in the grave-hollow, holding each other in terror as the soldier returned with the rope. The fat Sporelli took it and turned to survey the natives. "You," he said, selecting a male Phandran whose face bore a deep scar running from temple to jaw.

The man stepped forward with a lack of apparent fear, and Kranda vowed that she would not stand by and watch this Phandran die too.

"Here!" ordered the Sporelli.

Obediently the Phandran climbed the hillside and paused before the soldier.

The Sporelli looked around, found what he was seeking, and gestured towards a nearby cloud-tree. Kranda closed her eyes briefly, knowing what was about to happen.

"Follow me!"

The soldier led the way from the grave hollow and across to the cloud-tree. He slung the rope over a low branch. The Phandran stood by, watching what the Sporelli was doing with apparent ignorance. The soldier took his time in fashioning a noose from the end of the rope.

Kranda noticed the other troops; they were nudging each other and smirking like schoolboys.

"Come here!"

The Phandran stepped forward. The soldier looped the noose around the Phandran's neck, then adjusted it as if he were fussily attending to the knot of a necktie. Something about the Phandran's docility, as he stood and allowed this to happen, fuelled Kranda's rage.

"We have an old custom on Sporell," said the soldier. "It's called hanging. It was very popular at one time, though less so these days.

We've developed finer means of punishing criminals. Still, as they say, the old ways are often the most efficacious."

He tugged on the rope, jarring the Phandran's head to one side and causing him to choke.

"Now, for the very last time – what happened to the pilot?"

On tip-toes, his neck stretched, the Phandran managed a strangled, "I... don't... know."

"Where is the pilot!" the soldier yelled.

"There was no... pilot..."

Down in the hollow, the villagers looked on with horror.

The sergeant, frustrated beyond endurance, yanked the rope and the Phandran shot into the air, letting out a strangled scream.

Kranda moved.

She stepped behind the dangling alien and reached up, taking a handful of smock at the top of the Phandran's spine. She lifted, taking the small man's negligible weight, easing the bite of the rope.

At the same time she leaned forward and whispered, hearing the varnika translate her words a moment later. "Do not be alarmed. Act dead. Close your eyes and act dead!"

The Phandran started with surprise, then slumped as instructed.

The gathered Phandrans moaned as one, some turning away while others held each other and wept.

One of the watching Sporelli troops laughed and called out, "Weak as *groi* [untranslatable]."

The soldier spat in disgust and released his grip on the rope. Kranda allowed the Phandran to drop to the ground, where he played dead.

"What now, sir?" one of the troops asked.

The fat soldier looked down at the gaggle of cowed Phandrans. "Perhaps the bastards are telling the truth," he said in Sporelli, then addressed the Phandrans in their own language. "I'll give you one last chance – what happened to the human pilot? Tell me now, and be spared the fate of your fellow."

A young female Phandran stepped forward, ineffably elfin and graceful. "Kill me first, before the others. Then kill us all, one by one, if you gain pleasure from doing so. For I tell you this – we do not know where the human pilot is, so believe our words when we tell you."

Another fairy-like alien stepped forward, "And then kill me..."

"And me," said another.

"And then me..."

"And me..."

"And me..."

Kranda was to recall this moment for many years, this show of astounding bravery in the face of such brutality, as one by one the Phandran villagers stepped forward and offered themselves for sacrifice.

Soon all the villagers had stepped forward, including the children, and stared up at the Sporelli quintet with unwavering intensity.

"So... what're we going to do," asked one of the soldiers, "string them all up?"

Enraged, the sergeant stared at the gathered aliens, considered his words, then said, "I will give you until sunrise tomorrow to consider your future. I will be back, and if you still withhold the information" – he spat on the ground at their feet – "then I will personally kill you one by one." And as if for emphasis, with each word he spoke, he patted the butt of his holstered pistol.

Then he turned away and marched down the hillside, followed by his men. Kranda watched him climb into the car. The engine roared and the car shot off down the track, trailing a cloud of dust.

At the foot of the tree, the 'hanged' Phandran was sitting upright, much to the astonishment of his fellows. He pulled the noose from his neck and looked around quizzically for his saviour.

Kranda approached and knelt, commanding her varnika to deactivate its visual shield.

Her sudden appearance, as if from nowhere, caused cries of consternation from the adults and whimpers from the children. They stepped back, staring in bewilderment, then with increasing bravery edged forward, staring at her all the while.

Kranda helped the hanged Phandran to his feet. Even kneeling, she still towered over the little alien.

She said, "Do not be alarmed. I am Kranda, a Mahkan, from another world on the Helix. My people are the Engineers, and we attend to the smooth running of the Helix."

They gathered around her, one or two of the younger ones even plucking up the courage to reach out and touch her strange, scaled skin. She must have appeared as a hideous giant to these people.

"You saved my life," said the hanged Phandran.

"And I would have saved your friend, too, if it had been possible. But understand, had I acted against the Sporelli, then others of their kind would have visited your village and sought revenge."

The Phandran said, "As it is, they will still come at sunrise and expect an answer to their question."

"Your show of collective bravery shamed the tyrants, but I think it would be wise to relocate your village. Here, by the track, you are vulnerable to passing Sporelli." She gestured to the high hills and distant mountains. "I would advise that you leave the area and seek the refuge of the foothills."

They conferred amongst themselves, and then the scar-faced Phandran said, "We will do that. But first, a question. Why are you here, Mahkan – to fight the Sporelli?"

She smiled. "The Sporelli will pay for their transgressions, but I cannot exact punishment alone. I have come simply to find a friend, a friend who once saved my life. On my world we observe *Sophan*, which means a debt to another that must be repaid. I owe this brave man my life, and he is in danger now. It is my duty to rescue him." She looked around the staring group. "The man I seek is the human pilot, and it is a great pity that you do not know what became of him."

She sensed a stirring among the Phandrans; they whispered to each other, exchanged inscrutable glances. The scar-faced Phandran stepped forward and said, "Kranda, but we do know where the pilot is."

She stared at the man, considering the villagers' collective bravery in light of this information. She gestured towards the grave-hollow, where one of their people lay dead. "But he gave up his life so that my friend might remain free..."

"To have told the Sporelli the whereabouts of the human," said the scar-faced alien, "would have been dishonourable. Better death than the shame of dishonour. Frear has gone to another place, Mahkan, to a life beyond this life."

She said, "And the human?"

"We found the human in a yahn-pod. He was injured, but alive. We took him on our cart, but he fell violently ill, for he had eaten poison berries by mistake. We gave him ker-fruit, the only antidote to the poison, and transported him to the Retreat at Verlaine."

"But he lives?" Kranda asked, heart pounding.

The alien hesitated. "We do not know. He was very ill when we last saw him, and few survive such poisoning, even with the administration of ker-fruit. But your friend is human, so perhaps it will be different with him. At any rate, the Healers at the Retreat will do their very best to save him."

"And where is this Retreat of Verlaine?" she asked.

The Phandran pointed along the track. "Five days rurl-ride to the west," he said. "You will approach a steep mountain to your left, and high upon it, fashioned from the very pinnacle of the mountain itself, you will behold the Retreat. If he lives, then the human will be there."

Kranda reached out and took the Phandran's hand. "I promise that my people will act to stop the Sporelli violence."

"Their actions," said the scar-faced alien, "are inexplicable to us."

Before she left their village, she urged the Phandrans to take to the hills and not return until the Sporelli had left the area. Then she activated her varnika – smiling at the gasp that went up from the diminutive aliens – and left their village at speed.

She returned to the cloud-tree grove and boarded her flier. In short order, she powered up the engines, lifted the ship and set off in the direction of the Retreat of Verlaine.

SEVEN /// LEAVING VERLAINE

I

THEY LEFT THE Retreat of Verlaine well before dawn and took a yahn-cart to the town of Trahng. An honour guard saw them off from the castle, two lines of Phandrans bearing lamps in the darkness. Calla dispensed with her red robe and wore instead simple brown leggings, a jerkin of the same colour, and a dull grey cloak.

This time he did not make his bed among stacked pods bearing the carcasses of hapless forest creatures. The cart was piled with skins, under which he buried himself and attempted to catch up on his interrupted sleep. Calla lay at the far end of the flat-bed, staring up at the stars.

He awoke as the sun was coming up over the mountains and the stars were being washed from the dawn sky.

Calla had bread and fruit ready for him, and icy water, and they sat side by side on the furs and ate while travelling across the gossamer-tree plain he had seen from Calla's room the day before. He watched her, seated upright and moving with the loll of the plodding turtle-beast. She stared ahead, her expression impassive.

For the most part they passed through countryside familiar from his earlier journey on the yahn-cart: fairytale glades of gossamer-trees set amid meadows of crimson grass. From time to time they passed villages, scant collections of two-storey timber buildings raised on stilts, beneath which domesticated animals lived. If the Sporelli had passed this way, there was no sign of their desecration.

At one point he asked, "If the Sporelli are bent on invading D'rayni, then they will be ahead of us by now, on the western coast?"

The Healer inclined her head in assent. "Yes."

"Then isn't it rash of us to be heading towards the very same coast?"

She smiled at him, her serene head rocking this way and that with the motion of the cart. At last she said, "The Sporelli forces are massed two hundred kilometres north along the coast, near the town of Pahran. There is a harbour there, and from there they will mount their invasion of D'rayni."

He thought about it. "And when we reach the coast?"

"There we will part company. But we will be reunited again, or so say the Diviners."

They fell silent, and Ellis watched the countryside passing serenely by. He saw yahn-gatherers at work, climbing the gossamer-trees with coiled ropes over their shoulders; when they reached the pods, they attached ropes to them, hacked at the stalks, then lowered the pods to the ground.

"Calla?"

She turned her calm face to him. "Yes?"

"I've been thinking about our relative lifespans. Your people live for an average of twenty New Earth years, my own race for almost one hundred." He shook his head. "I often feel cheated that our time is so short, when there is so much to experience, so many worlds to see. And I'm likely to live for a hundred years – five times as long as your people." He stopped abruptly, silenced by her amused expression.

"Are you trying to say, Jeff, 'are you not crushed by the knowledge of the short span that is your destiny'?"

He grunted. "Yes, if not quite so eloquently."

She shrugged – another gesture she had picked up from him – and said, "I am aware only of the richness of my life. We live as long as we live. It seems sufficient to me. Think on this, that the race known as the Garl, who dwell five worlds along from D'rayni, live for almost *five hundred* of your years."

"I've heard of the Garl," he said.

"They are, like my people, pre-technological. They are nomads, and from time to time a lone wanderer has fetched up on our shore with many wondrous tales to tell of his exploits."

Ellis smiled as he imagined the encounter between the fire-fly Phandrans and the aged Garl.

"Do they know of their history?" he asked. "Are they aware that millennia ago their ancestors dwelled on a world far away from the Helix?" It was a question which fascinated him – how the various races of the Helix viewed the past: whether they were aware of the immense translocation perpetrated by the Builders, or if in their ignorance they had dreamed up creation-myths to account for their presence here?

She smiled at him. "According to a Garl wanderer I met, the Helix is a limb of their god, on which we all dwell like parasites."

Ellis laughed. "Did you tell him what you believed, Calla?"

She tipped her head to the side, regarding him. "And what might that have achieved? Originally, many millennia ago before the Builders brought us here, my people thought their planet a fruit on a jall-tree, the life-tree, planted by a... by the Universal Gardener. But, do you not see, that this explanation is just as valid as that which you know as the truth?"

He smiled and fell silent as the turtle-beast plodded somnolently along the track.

A while later, when the sun had climbed and was directly overhead, he stirred himself to ask, "Are you curious about the original world of the Phandrans? What kind of people you were that the Builders thought it necessary to bring you here?"

She considered his questions for a while, then said, "Personally, no. But I do know that certain thinkers among my kind have thought deeply on these matters."

"And?"

She shrugged with grace. "And they have arrived at the conclusion that whatever reasons the Builders had for saving us from ourselves on our original world, they have no relevance to the beings we have become. This happened almost eight thousand of our years ago – fifteen thousand of your years. Whatever bellicose or self-annihilating race we might have been then, we are no longer. We have evolved, become better. We are now, I think, as the Builders desired us to be: one with our world, one with the life-force that governs the Helix."

He absorbed that, and said, "And you, personally, have no curiosity as to the world your people left behind?"

She shook her head. "No, Jeff, I have not." She was watching him. "And you? Are you curious about the world you call Earth, the home of the human race?"

"Not a day goes by when I don't think about Old Earth," he said. "We left there relatively recently, Calla. We settled here just two hundred years ago, though the ship that brought us here took a thousand years to do so." He shrugged. "So, one thousand two hundred years ago the Builders brought us here, and my people were divided: the many millions who remained on Earth, a planet whose various nations were at war with each other, a planet rapidly running out of natural resources – and the three thousand colonists who settled New Earth. I often wonder what became of Old Earth – if humanity survived, and if so, how. Or if they perished, if indeed we were saved from the violent end the Builders foresaw."

She shook her head. "But what can such curiosity achieve?"

"I don't know," he said honestly. "Perhaps that's one thing that separates our races, Calla – curiosity. We've always been curious, inquisitive. It can be our undoing, and our making."

She said, "Perhaps it is why the Builders made you Peacekeepers, Jeff? Because you are so close to the terrible past that resulted in your arrival here? You can still recall, as a race, what befalls a world when it is at war with itself. And you have no wish to see that happen again. The Builders, in their wisdom, divined this, and bequeathed you a singular destiny."

"I've never really thought about it like that before," he admitted. "But to be honest, your assessment smacks too much of a manifest spiritual destiny to my materialistic mind."

She laughed. "You will learn the truth one day, perhaps, Jeff."

He said, staring at a silver stream twinkling along parallel to the track, "One day, I would like to return to Old Earth, to see what became of the people left behind."

She stared at him. "One day, Jeff, you might just do that."

She glanced up suddenly. He looked along the track, following the direction of her intent gaze – and made out a shape in the distance.

An animal, he thought – a long-necked, long-legged creature that galloped with an oddly somnolent, almost negligent grace. It resolved, became more than just an indistinct blur: it was a golden-pelted creature not dissimilar to a terrestrial giraffe, not that Ellis had ever seen anything but archive film of such a strange animal.

And riding on the back of the giraffe-analogue was a tiny jockey.

Calla stood and stared ahead as the rider drew alongside the cart and shouted down to her.

She replied with urgency, and the rider heeled its mount and steered it off the track and through the gossamer trees. On the hump of the turtle, the yahn-gatherers were chattering amongst themselves with apparent agitation.

"What is it?" he asked.

"Up ahead, at Trahng," Calla said. "A platoon of Sporelli infantry arrived this morning and set up a blockade around the sail-rail station."

"The sail-rail...?"

"Where we were due to catch the coast-bound train," she explained. "It is as if they knew about our imminent arrival."

"Would that be possible?"

She shrugged. "I don't know. I'd like to think not, but..."

"What do we do?"

She ignored the question, climbed over the skins and conferred with the yahn-gatherers.

Minutes later she returned and said, "There is a station ten kilometres west of Trahng, and the sail-rail train stops there. Of course, the Sporelli might have soldiers stationed there too, or aboard the train. We will find that out in due course. I have asked that we bypass Trahng. We will arrive at Karralan in approximately three hours."

Thirty minutes later they came to a fork in the road. The driver urged the turtle-beast down the track to the left. Ellis asked, "And if the Sporelli do know of our rendezvous with the train?"

Calla's expression was a study in concentration. "If that is so, and they have troops around the station or aboard the train, then we will proceed to the coast by some alternative manner."

He lay back and stared at the looping wisp of the Helix high above.

He considered Maria, and how she might be reacting to the news of his non-arrival on D'rayni. He liked to think that, despite the state of their relationship, she would be more than a little concerned.

He recalled an incident over a year ago when Maria had been involved in a mono-rail accident on the coast. They'd been going through a particularly rough period, when their every attempt at conversation ended in a row. But when Ellis found out about the crash, his first reaction had been one of shock and concern. He'd rushed to the hospital to find that she'd suffered merely a broken arm, and it had been symptomatic of their relationship that within fifteen minutes, after a jibe from Maria about his thoughtlessness in not bringing her a change of clothing, they had found themselves locked in antagonistic silence.

He told himself that, despite her animosity towards him, Maria would be worried – and he felt a sudden rush of guilt that, all things considered, and despite the danger he was in, he was almost enjoying the role of being a fugitive on an alien world.

He sat up and looked at Calla; she was sitting cross-legged on a pile of furs at the front of the flat-bed, staring serenely ahead.

He said her name.

She turned her head and smiled at him. "Yes?"

"You said we were boarding a train at Karralan? But I thought you didn't possess technology on Phandra?"

Her smile widened. "We don't. Not mechanical technology as you know it, utilising metals and such. The train is a *sail-rail* train, constructed from timber. You will see soon enough."

"I'm intrigued."

"A network of tracks link all the populous areas of Phandra, and some under-populated areas, too. The tracks are over eight thousand years old, or rather the infrastructure dates back that far. The timber itself is being constantly renewed. It is a never-ending task."

She fell silent, staring at the fields that had replaced the gossamer-trees. A patchwork of red and yellow stretched up a hillside to their right, and workers toiled at harvesting large black fruits from rows of low shrubs. He contrasted the agriculture here to that back on New Earth, where every process in the farming industry, from planting to harvesting, was conducted by mechanical drones.

He realised that this was how farmers must have worked in the fields of Old Earth, millennia ago.

A while later, Calla turned to him. "Jeff, look."

She gestured ahead. A great timber construction crossed the fields before them, with regularly spaced v-shaped stanchions bearing three tracks, a central one in the valley of the v and two upper parallel tracks supported by each arm.

"The sail-rail track from Trahng to the sea," Calla said.

Ellis laughed. "Why... it's *vast*, Calla. What kinds of vessel runs along a track so big?"

She smiled. "A train more like a ship." She frowned prettily. "I think you called them *galleons*."

The cart approached the track and, instead of passing beneath it, turned left along a dirt-track running parallel with the giant timber construction. Ellis looked up. The two higher rails were thirty metres overhead, and spaced twenty metres apart.

"Not far now, Jeff," Calla said. "In fact, look: the town of Karralan."

He followed the gentle curve of the track as it diminished in perspective, and made out a blur of buildings in the mid-distance. Calla gestured him to ride lower in the flat-bed and to pull the furs around him, and minutes later he saw why. Peering from beneath the skins, he saw other carts join the track, along with a file of pedestrians, all heading for the distant town.

Fifteen minutes later he heard a faint susurrus, which grew as they approached, and peering out he saw a crowd of Phandrans in what looked like a market place. Ahead, a warped two-storey timber building stood at the far end of a cobbled square. Calla whispered to him, "The sail-rail station."

As he watched, the oldster leapt down from the back of the rurl and disappeared into the crowd. He returned minutes later and spoke with Calla.

"Good news," she told Ellis. "The Sporelli do not have the station under surveillance. The train is due in shortly. We have someone aboard who will apprise us of the situation, whether or not Sporelli troops are riding on the train. If so, then it would be impossible to take the train, and it will be a long, slow journey from here to the coast." She gestured to the furs. "Now, cover yourself and be patient."

She climbed down from the cart and approached the station, a tiny figure jostled by the crowd that surged before the timber building. Ellis pulled a silver fur over his head and closed his eyes.

The piping chatter of the crowd was muffled now, along with the bellows of animals being led towards the station. It was hot beneath the furs, and while he hadn't much noticed their aroma while riding on top of the animal skins, buried beneath them he was soon aware of their musky stench. He breathed shallowly and willed the train to arrive soon.

What felt like a long time later, the chatter of the crowd increased as if in anticipation. Minutes later he heard a distant creak and grind, then a high-pitched squeal that lasted an age. At last the piercing note ceased, and with it the creak of timbers, and he guessed that the train had drawn into the station.

Curious, he peered out from beneath the furs. His view was limited, but he made out the station's façade, and rising above it to a height of thirty metres the train's crimson and silver sails, bellying like over-filled shirt-fronts. He smiled to himself. From interplanetary shuttle, he thought, to farm cart, to this, a timber sail-rail vessel like a galleon of Old Earth.

The cart shook, and he felt someone climbing aboard. He heard voices, and shortly afterwards Calla drew the fur aside and peered in at him.

She was smiling. "The Sporelli are not onboard the train. We are safe to board." She shook her head. "But I don't understand. Their soldiers surrounded the station at Trahng, as if they knew we were due to arrive, and before the train set off they searched it – but they did not bother to ride the train, nor to send troops here, to Karralan."

He looked at her. "You don't suspect a trick?"

She bit her bottom lip and shook her head. "I don't know, Jeff. But we must be very careful. Now, cover yourself again while we board the train."

He pulled the skins over him and heard Calla call an instruction to the oldster.

The cart juddered into motion and rolled forward slowly, edging through the crowd.

Five minutes later the flat-bed tipped. He rolled beneath the furs. The oldster called out, urging the turtle to greater effort, and slowly the cart moved forward and upwards. A ramp, Ellis thought. The flat-bed levelled out again, and he peered out.

They were on a broad timber deck, busy with the to and fro of passengers boarding the train. He felt pressure beside him, as Calla lay down and lifted a fur. "Be ready to climb down. Very soon I will escort you through the ship to a cabin I have booked."

She lowered the fur, and he waited for the signal from Calla. A few minutes later, it came. The fur was yanked aside and Calla gestured Ellis to follow her.

The deck was quieter now, and keeping the bulk of the cart between himself and the passengers still boarding, he followed Calla through a tiny timber door and along a wonderfully warped and twisted corridor that ran the length of the ship.

In due course they arrived before another small door. Calla unlocked it with a great wooden key and Ellis had to duck to gain admittance.

Head bent to avoid dangerously low beams, he followed her across to a window-seat at the far end of the chamber. A small mullioned window overlooked the rails curving off into the distance.

"The largest room aboard the train," Calla said. "I am afraid it is still rather cramped for someone of your size."

The chamber was hung with tapestries and spread with woven rugs. Not one surface – wall, floor or ceiling – was set square with another, and the predominant odour was that of old wood and polish. He had the feeling of having been sent back in time, exiled from all the reassuring comforts of modernity he was accustomed to on New Earth. This was almost medieval.

He curled himself onto the window-seat before the thick glass window. Calla said. "You must be hungry. I will bring food for us. Bolt the door when I leave, and open it only when I knock like this." And with her tiny knuckles she rapped five times on the window frame.

While she was gone the galleon creaked and strained, and he heard a distant cheer. Almost imperceptibly the train began to move. He pressed his face against the flawed glass and made out the gargantuan timber beams that crossed the width of the train above him, terminating in great greased wooden wheels which turned on the tracks to either side.

The train gained momentum and, with much creaking and groaning, pulled from the station. He watched the quaint timber buildings flash by, the crowds of locals waving off loved ones, and within minutes they were racing along the track through open fields. As their speed increased, the walls of the room flexed and buckled, setting up a rhythmic creak that counterpointed the constant thrum of the wheels on the tracks high above.

Calla returned five minutes later with a tray of food, and they sat side by side on the window-seat and ate.

EIGHT /// AT THE BUILDERS' ZIGGURAT

I

MARIA SAT AT a table in the plaza of her hotel overlooking the tourist resort that had grown up around the Builders' ziggurat.

She was due to meet Dan Stewart at noon, and, as ever, before they spent any time together, she experienced both excitement and guilt; excitement for obvious reasons... but guilt? It was, she told herself, ridiculous. Things had never been as bad between her and Jeff as they were now, not even during the bitter recriminations that followed Ben's death three years ago. They lived, to all intents, separate lives. They rarely spoke, and then only to synchronise their busy time-tables. They shared the lakeside house, but were rarely in it together – Maria made sure of that. So why, then, the nagging guilt? Maria blamed her parents, and more specifically her father; the grandson of an Orthodox Greek whose morality he had tried to pass on, with limited success, to his daughter. If he could have seen her now, cheating on her husband, he would have reduced her to tears with just a few words.

She swore, cursing as much her weakness as her father's posthumous influence over her, and tried to push the guilt aside and concentrate on the days ahead. She had more reason than ever today to anticipate their meeting. She had been seeing Dan Stewart, head of the Builder Liaison team, for over a year now, attracted to him initially because he was everything that Jeff was not. Tall and blond where Jeff was stocky and dark; talkative and emotionally forthcoming where Jeff was taciturn and inhibited. And, importantly, highly intelligent while Jeff was, to put it kindly, intellectually dull. At first Maria had wondered if she was attracted to Dan only because he was so different from Jeff; then she came to appreciate the differences as important attributes in themselves, and by that time, even though she did wonder occasionally if she were no more than an adventurous fling for the high-flying Director, she was in love with him.

Over the past few months she had come to believe that her sentiments were reciprocated. Dan told her that he loved her, and at their last meeting she had steeled herself and issued an ultimatum. If he really did love her, she said, would he leave his wife for her?

He had greeted her words with silence, stroking her hair as they lay in bed in the aftermath of love-making. "I've never claimed," he'd said, "not to love my wife."

"But you say you love me. If you really did, you'd leave her."

"That would... destroy her."

She told herself that he was being melodramatic, or was she trying to convince herself of this in order to minimise her guilt?

"So you're happy to go on like this, sneaking off for clandestine weekends, when we could have a fulfilling life together?"

He looked away, his blue eyes unreadable. "No, I'm not happy doing it like this. I'd like to spend more time with you... but at the same time I don't want to hurt Sabine."

She didn't know whether to be cheered at this example of his humanity, or enraged. And then the niggling doubt began: did he really love her as he claimed, or was she merely the source of physical relief which his marriage failed to provide?

He'd moved his hand from her cheek and slipped two fingers between her legs. Despite herself, she opened up to him.

Afterwards, he had stroked her hair and murmured, "I love you, Maria. I'll... I'll tell Sabine. I have a week off in a little over a month. Let's go away somewhere together to celebrate, okay?"

He had suggested the resort complex near the Builders' ziggurat because it was a tacky tourist site which members of their team would be unlikely to frequent; and while it was not the most romantic of destinations, Maria would have been happy to take a week alone with Dan Stewart *anywhere*, even on the ice-fields of the first circuit.

2

SHE LOOKED AT her wrist-com. It was not yet eleven: she had another hour before Dan was due in. She'd arrived late last night and had not had time to do the tourist trek.

She left the hotel plaza and crossed one of the many walkways that meandered over the greensward connecting the complex of hotels to the ziggurat and adjacent visitors' centre. Beyond, partially embedded in grassy mounds, was the wreck of the Agstarnian ship which had followed the First Four from the eighth circuit. As a child she had read about the First Four, and seen holo-films of their exploits, and she recalled her first sight of the wreckage, and the ziggurat, at the age of nine. She had been almost breathless with the wonder of it, the stuff of myth made physical. She had come to the coast with her parents, and had gratified their expectations with unbidden tears when she stepped towards the ziggurat where Hendry, Kaluchek, and the Agstarnian Ehrin had first encountered the Builders, channelled through their team-mate Carrelli.

Even now she felt a constriction in her throat as she stepped into the shadow of the rearing bronze ziggurat. She wondered how much this emotion was a genuine response to what the building represented, or a reaction to the memory of the innocent girl she had been all those years ago.

She took her place in the line of tourists snaking towards the arched entrance of the ziggurat. She made out a couple of tall, reptilian Mahkan, the Helix's engineers, their bearing severe and military, almost hostile. Next to them were three Jantisars, the thick-set, porcine creatures from a frozen world on the seventh circuit. There was even a gaggle of tiny Agstarnians which Hendry, in his famous account of his arrival here, had referred to as lemur-like, whereas Friday Olembe had called them rats. They were, she thought, a little like both.

They passed through the entrance and into a vast chamber, which she recalled from Hendry's account as the largest walled space he had ever experienced. She looked up, as he had done two hundred years ago, and experienced an odd, vertiginous dizziness as she took in the myriad galleries rising inside the soaring tower.

But most remarkable of all, she thought, was the great bronze oval that occupied the centre of the chamber. As if drawn like pilgrims, the tourists – and Maria with them – moved *en masse* towards the oval.

She paused before it, staring at its lambent perfection.

She heard a gasp from someone to her right, and turned as a human tourist pointed in awed silence.

Maria didn't know whether to be horrified at the tackiness of what was taking place, as four ghostly blue-uniformed figures and an Agstarnian stepped from around the side of the oval and stood before the tourists, or swept up in the sense of wonder at what the scene represented.

She recognised the figures as Joe Hendry – her husband's childhood hero – Sissy Kaluchek, Friday Olembe the truculent Nigerian engineer, and Gina Carrelli, the puppet and mouthpiece of the Builders, the woman who had vanished mysteriously, shortly after the founding of the city that was to be named after her. Alongside them was the Agstarnian, Ehrin.

Maria forgot her adult cynicism, and just stared.

The ghostly holographic figure of Gina Carrelli stepped forward and spoke in barely-accented English. "After weeks of travelling, from the inhospitable ice-bound eighth circuit – or, as we called it then, the first circuit – enduring many travails and hardship along the way, we arrived at last at the ziggurat of the Builders. And this is what they, the Builders, had to say…"

Maria was nine again, and gripping the hand of her father, as she listened to the pronouncement of the Builders speaking through the medium of Gina Carrelli, the Italian psychologist the Builders had been 'employing' over the years to facilitate humankind's passage to the Helix.

"Over thousands of millennia," she said, "the ancient race known as the Builders have been working to save the many otherwise doomed races that occupy the galaxy..."

Maria hung on every word, as the Builders – through Carrelli – explained to Hendry and the others just why they had been brought here, to the Helix. It was as if Maria was hearing this for the first time and experiencing vicariously Hendry, Kaluchek and Olembe's wonder as they took in her words.

The speech lasted perhaps fifteen minutes, after which the figures faded and the watching tourists came back to their senses; they smiled and laughed, and exclaimed amongst themselves. It was, Maria thought, like they'd just witnessed a particularly wondrous magician's act.

As Maria moved away from the group and strolled around the bronze oval, then took her leave of the ziggurat and crossed the greensward towards the crash-landed starship, she considered the irony of what she had just heard.

For a decade after humankind settled on New Earth, the Builders had kept up constant communications with the humans' appointed leaders. Together they had set up the Peacekeepers and established the complex ground-rules and protocols governing the politically delicate matter of maintaining harmony between so many alien races. Then, almost ten years to the day after humanity's first encounter with the enigmatic Builders, the aliens had announced that they had told humanity all they needed to know, and were retreating into the virtual quiescence they had maintained for millennia. Despite protests, led by Hendry himself, the Builders had been incommunicado from that day forward, leaving humankind to the task of peacekeeping as best they were able.

Ever since then there had been a Builder Liaison team attempting to re-establish contact with the aliens, wherever they might be residing now. Director Dan Stewart was the team's current head. It was, he had often told Maria, a thankless task, not made easier by the fact that the whereabouts of the Builders was unknown. All the team had to go on were the artefacts the Builders had left behind, and the transcriptions of the initial communications between them and the early human settlers.

Maria approached the black Agstarnian ship and stared up at its fractured superstructure. The ship, crewed by members of the Agstarnian totalitarian Church, had followed Hendry's vessel from their planet with the intention of destroying both the human devils and the apostate Agstarnian Ehrin, who had helped the humans escape from the Church's custody.

She walked up the grassy mound to the ship's buckled nose-cone. Beneath its jutting prow she saw a gaggle of Agstarnians, a couple of families with tiny children who tumbled playfully around the mound, oblivious to their parents' intent focus on their guide.

Maria moved towards the group, along with a dozen humans, and listened in as the guide spoke first in Agstarnian, and then in English. She was finishing her spiel: "...and as we know, the Church in effect met its nemesis here on that momentous day. Friday Olembe, in the golden ship, crossed the sea and shot it down before it could wreak further damage on the ziggurat or, indeed, murder Hendry and his colleagues... Weeks later, the Builders ensured that the rule of the Church came to an effective end on Agstarn when they banished the clouds that had cloaked that world for millennia and allowed the populace for the first time to behold the wonder of the Helix's circuits..."

Maria gazed back at the rearing ziggurat and considered the drama played out here two centuries ago.

One of the younger Agstarnians piped up in its own language, and the guide smiled and replied with a string of high whistles. She looked above the heads of the aliens and addressed the gathered humans. "She asked, what became of Ehrin and his mate, Sereth? Well, as some of you might know, they returned to Agstarn and married, and Ehrin managed the family airship company. Sereth rose to be an influential politician on her world, and oversaw the uneasy transition from the Church's draconian rule to that of a freely elected governing council..."

The Agstarnians chattered excitedly amongst themselves, and Maria left the group and strolled down the incline. She glanced at her wrist-com. It was almost noon. She hurried across the greensward to the hotel plaza to keep her date with Dan.

3

IN THE EVENT, he was over an hour late.

He contacted her just after twelve, and for a terrible second, as his face appeared on her wrist-com, she thought he'd called to cancel their holiday. "Dan?"

"Look, I'm sorry. I'm still in Carrelliville. Something's come up."

"Sabine?"

He shook his head. "No. Work." He hesitated. "Look, I'll tell you when I get there, okay? I should be with you in an hour. I'm sorry about this, Maria, but I couldn't get away."

She smiled. "I understand. Can't wait to see you. Love you."

"See you soon," he said, and cut the connection.

She sat back in her seat and sipped her ice-cold mango juice. Dan had appeared harassed, and had not reciprocated her avowal of love. She wondered if he were telling the truth. Perhaps he hadn't yet told his wife about her, and couldn't find an excuse to get away. She told herself she was being paranoid. If that were the case, then he would simply have called her to cancel the vacation, not tell her that he was delayed.

She decided to order lunch, and while eating a light salad with local bran bread, she watched the vast, spinnaker-like shapes of the Sails – as they had come to be known – disport themselves in the thermals over the ocean. They were great rectangular membranes, an animal life-form which remained perpetually airborne above this ocean and the neighbouring world inhabited by the sentient, frog-like Ho-lah-lee. It was the Sails which had transported Hendry, Kaluchek, Carrelli and the alien Ehrin across the sea to this world as they attempted to evade the Agstarnian's black ship. In the collective consciousness of humankind, the floating Sails had come to represent the epitome of altruism, and Maria never saw one of their kind, whether in the flesh or as an image, without experiencing a resurgence of hope.

A couple with a young boy were eating lunch on the next table. They appeared to be in their thirties, the woman a tall, well-groomed blonde, the man an equally well-presented executive type. The boy was around seven... Ben's age, had he survived.

She looked away, attempting to squash the demon of grief back into its box.

The boy resembled his father, chunky and dark. Just as Ben had looked like Jeff... She had joked to Jeff that, as Ben had taken after him in looks, then it was to be hoped that he'd inherited her intelligence. And Jeff had always taken it in good part, to begin with. In the later years, as their relationship after Ben's death entered a deep freeze, he'd come to resent her constant barbs at his lack of education.

She flinched, inwardly, at the thought of what she'd said when they had last parted.

She finished her lunch, ordered another juice and read a magazine for half an hour.

"You look miles away, darling."

"Oh!" Disoriented, she stood quickly, too quickly, managing to knock over her glass in the process, and clung to him. The feel of him in her arms, solid and substantial, banished the guilt and the grief.

"Hey, what's wrong...?"

"Just glad to see you. Oh, look...!" She picked up the glass, tried to mop up the spilled mango juice. He wrested the glass from her grip and whispered, "A waiter will see to that. Come on, let's get a drink. I need one."

He took her hand and led her into the hotel. They took the elevator to the penthouse bar and sat at a window seat, gazing out at the expanse of greensward and the glittering blue ocean. Not that they had eyes for the view.

"Maria, forgive me. Something came up at the last minute and I couldn't get away. And I couldn't leave it with Gonzalez."

She took his hand and smiled at him. "Care to tell me, or is it another secret?" she asked, when all she really wanted to know was how it had gone with Sabine.

Their drinks arrived, a whisky and soda for Dan, a lager for her. As he sipped his drink, she watched him, enjoying the play of his lips, the twinkle in his eye. He was in his early forties, but looked younger. He was tall and fair and of Nordic stock – his great-great-great grandfather had been a geneticist, one of a hundred Swedes chosen to leave the Earth aboard the starship *Lovelock*.

Dan was into jogging – one of their shared passions that had brought them closer together a year back, when she had joined his team on a field-trip as in-house medic. She'd arranged to bump into him accidentally-on-purpose a couple of times while out running, and had suggested they meet every other day to help each other along... and a week later one form of physical exercise had turned to another.

And that was all it had been for Maria, at first. Casual, no-ties sex with a handsome man after too long without it. Then, as the months elapsed and their trysts increased, she soon realised that Dan meant much more to her than a desire to work off her sexual frustration.

"I..." he began, then amended it to, "I mean, *we* discovered something today."

She laughed. "That sounds... what's the word... portentous?"

He smiled. "I suppose it does. And it is. Look, this goes no further than the two of us, right?"

She crossed her heart. "And hope to die."

"You know how we've suspected the Mahkan of... if not being directly in contact with the Builders, then not being truthful about the fact of their whereabouts."

"I've seen you snarl at the very mention of the Mahkan," she said. "So?"

"So something came up this morning that suggests we're right." He took a drink. "We have someone working with the Mahkan engineers, liaising with them. Between you and me, he's a spy, working on a certain soft Mahkan we think might be willing to divulge more than her superiors would like."

Maria frowned. "Not sure I like the sound of that."

He shrugged, as much to say, *That's the way of the world...* "Anyway, Governor Reynolds had word from the spook and summoned me to his office this morning. The upshot is that our Mahkan contact more or less confirmed what we suspected."

Maria sat up. "That the Mahkan are in contact with the Builders?"

But Dan was shaking his head. "No – but they do know where this... this so-called virtual realm they're inhabiting is situated."

"One of the polar worlds, right? Stands to reason that it'd be somewhere well out of the way."

Dan drew a frustrated breath. "That's just it. Although our tame Mahkan confirmed that the Builders' whereabouts was known, she didn't know exactly where." He shook his head. "It's so damned frustrating! I'm this close – *this* close" – he squeezed his thumb and forefinger together – "from making the biggest breakthrough for a couple of centuries and it all depends on some lowly spook and his tame Mahkan contact. Reynolds wouldn't give me much more than that. 'Security reasons,' he said." He swore. "Christ, if only we knew where the bastards were... then at least we might know what measures to consider in order to contact them."

She took a sip of lager, watching him, and said playfully, "But... have you ever considered that the Builders haven't contacted us because they don't want to establish contact? Because there's no *need* to renew contact?"

He laughed, but without much humour. "Often. I have nightmares about it. But" – he smiled at her – "and this might sound arrogant... but I'm less concerned about the motives of the Builders than I am about the need for us, the human race, to establish contact."

She reached out and twirled a finger in his blond locks. "It'd certainly be a feather in your cap, Dan."

"Of course it would, but I'm truly not thinking about what it would mean to me, Maria. The bigger picture is that for the first time in a couple of hundred years we'd be in contact again with perhaps the most powerful race that has ever existed in the galaxy. Hell, you don't know how difficult it is attempting to monitor the Helix and maintain peace among the races – despite the best teachings of the Builders. The Peacekeepers would give an arm and a leg just to ask for the Builders' occasional advice."

"Seriously, Dan, why don't the Builders realise this and contact us?"

"You want my opinion? They see being incommunicado as a ploy to strengthen us. They placed us in a position of trust, all those years ago, and they want to see us prosper through our own efforts. A crude analogy is a parent who lets his kid climb a tree without…" Suddenly, his face crumpled. "Oh, Maria… Hell, that was crass of me." He reached out and drew her to him. "I'm sorry. I wasn't thinking…"

She smiled at him, more touched by his contrition than hurt by his unheeding words. "Dan, it's okay. I know you didn't mean… I get what you're saying. The Builders want us to stand on our own two feet, right?"

He took her hand and squeezed. "Something like that. At any rate, they want us to learn by our mistakes… even if some of those mistakes might prove costly."

He reached out and, with the back of his hand, stroked her cheek. A silence came between them, broken a little later by his whispered, "Bed?"

She kissed his fingers. "Yes, please."

4

THEY MADE LOVE in the penthouse bedroom overlooking the ocean.

As ever with Dan it was both cathartic and tender; it was both a giving and a taking. He knew how to give her pleasure and, she liked to think – confirmed by his reaction – she knew how to give it in turn. She couldn't help contrast this with what she'd experienced with Jeff, who'd worshipped the temple of her body like a fumbling, amateur acolyte, but had never learned how to give her real pleasure. She smiled at how he'd used those very words early in their relationship, 'I worship the temple of your body...' and how, innocent as she was, she'd found his naivety endearing.

They lay entwined as the sun set, and Maria traced a line down the centre of his chest and asked, "Sabine?"

She looked into his eyes as he replied, without a beat, "I... I told her about us."

Maria swallowed, nervous. "And? How... how did she take it?"

"Badly. Very badly. She..." He sat up and pulled her to him, pressing her head to his shoulder. She could not see his expression when he said, "I told her that I'd met someone, someone who meant a lot to me and who I wanted to be with. I didn't mention your name. She asked... but..." He shrugged, jogging her head. "I just thought she didn't need to know."

"What did she say?"

He sighed. "Christ, it was awful. I... I don't like hurting people, especially someone I once loved and who I still feel a lot for. To see her like that, to see what my words did to here... how they *reduced* her."

She had an awful presentiment that he was about to tell her that he'd capitulated, backed down, and told Sabine that he was not going to leave.

He said, "She pleaded with me, begged me to stay."

Her throat felt suddenly parched. She managed to say, "And?"

"And... we came to an arrangement. She suggested it, not me. She said I could see you whenever I wanted, but that I must remain with her."

She sat up quickly, trying to suppress the tears. "And you agreed to *that*?"

He smiled, drew her to him and cupped her face in his hands. "Of course not. I love you. I want you. The agreement we reached was that I'd spend a week every month with Sabine, and the rest with you..."

She looked into his eyes. "And she agreed?" she asked.

He nodded. "I gave her an ultimatum – it was either that, or I would walk out and never see her again. She relented."

She swallowed, nodded. "Okay..." she murmured.

He said, "But that's just a start, Maria. It won't work out, of course. Sabine will resent you, resent the time I spend away... and given time, given her anger, that will work to my advantage." He stroked her cheek. "Be patient, Maria, and we'll soon be together for good, okay?"

She nodded, not liking the side of Dan Stewart he was exhibiting here; the manipulator, the schemer who set people against each other and eventually got what he wanted. She'd seen him employ similar tactics with his team.

She silenced her doubts, told herself she was being disloyal to someone who had only ever shown her love and honesty.

They made love again, and later, as he slept, she lay on her back and stared out through the floor-to-ceiling window at the silent Sails, floating serenely in the light of the setting sun.

Nine /// Capture

I

THE SAIL-RAIL train passed through swathes of agricultural land that extended across the broad plain between the mountain ranges, and Ellis found the view fascinating. Though he had visited over a dozen worlds as a shuttle pilot, his schedules had been so tight that he'd seen little of the various worlds he'd visited. Now, for the first time in years, he experienced a sense of freedom – ironic considering the fact that he was imprisoned in a small room aboard a hurtling train, on the run from the Sporelli.

"For perhaps a hundred kilometres," Calla said, "the land is like this. All farmland. This area produces much of the food that feeds the planet. We have only a small population; little more than a million souls. Many work the land. Then there are fisher-folk, and a few who work in industry, mainly with timber."

"A million? That seems a lot compared to the population of New Earth. Of course, we've only been here for two hundred years." He smiled as he recalled the bi-centenary celebrations four years ago; he'd taken Ben to the fair in Carrelliville.

"How many humans live on New Earth?" Calla asked.

"A little over three hundred thousand," he said. "Half of those in the capital, Carrelliville, and the remaining fifty thousand in a dozen townships scattered across the world."

"Were you born in Carrelliville?"

"I'm from a small town on the coast, called Hendry. Named after one of the First Four, Joseph Hendry. He retired to the coast in his seventies, when there were only a few A-frames there."

He recalled how he'd perched on his grandfather's knee in the main square and gazed across at the A-frame where the famous Joe Hendry and his wife Sissy Kaluchek had ended their days, and his grandfather had told Jeff about the time, as a five-year-old, he'd actually met the famous Hendry.

Calla was watching him. "You have good memories of growing up there."

He looked into her cobalt eyes, and wondered if she were reading his mind, or rather his emotions. Oddly, the thought did not bother him at all.

"Very good memories. I had a wonderful childhood. I was brought up by my father; he was a good man, if a little strict. My mother died when I was young – I can hardly recall her. My father used to read me the books about the Settling written by Olembe and Kaluchek. I loved the adventure story about the *Lovelock*'s crash-landing and the trek from the lowest circuit to what was to become New Earth."

She laid a gentle hand on his. "And now, Jeff, you are on an adventure of your own."

Memories of growing up in Hendry always fetched up against his first meeting with Maria Ellenopoulis, the bittersweet recollection of his initial infatuation, his love for her, soured in retrospect by what had happened to that love.

Calla's hand was still on his, her touch as light as that of a resting butterfly. She said, almost under her breath, "You can talk about that, too, Jeff."

He squeezed her hand. "Thank you, but..." If she were reading his emotions, then she would know full well that he did not want to recollect the pain. "So tell me about your childhood."

She smiled. "My father was a Diviner, my mother a Healer. It was inevitable, I suppose, that I should inherit one of their talents." She paused, her gaze miles away.

She went on, "We lived in a manse in the high-plateau town of Hansa. I went to a local school from the age of one to three, and then, when my abilities manifested themselves, I moved on to the seminary at Verlaine. I have been based nearby ever since."

"Based?" he said. "But you travel around your world?"

She inclined her head. "My work is peripatetic. I think I must have criss-crossed my world a dozen times or more."

"That's far more than I've ever travelled on New Earth. There are places there I've never visited."

"But your duties take you to worlds I can only dream of visiting," she said.

He explained about the frustration of seeing only the spaceports and their surroundings. "But here I am again, talking about myself. I want to know about you, your work."

She shrugged her slender shoulders modestly. "I lead what you might think of as a monotonous life, travelling from town to village to town, healing people, settling disputes."

"I would have thought that a people as pacific as the Phandra have few disputes."

"There are always disputes, petty squabbles, differences of opinion about how to go about things. In these cases I get to know the people, to read their characters, divine their motivations, and then use the knowledge to suggest a resolution that best suits all parties."

"It must be a wonderful gift."

She smiled. "I know, intellectually, that it is. Yet, as I have always had it... We have a saying, among my kind. Now, let me see if I can translate it." She paused a second or two, frowning, then said. "We say, 'familiarity can lead to apathy.' Well, I hope that doesn't apply to me."

He smiled. "I'd never accuse you of apathy."

He stared into her eyes, wondering if she were reading his emotions, his feelings.

She turned quickly to the mullioned window and said, "We are almost at the plateau's edge. In one hour, maybe two, towards sunset, we will arrive at the junction town of Lamala. It is one of the most beautiful places on all Phandra, clinging to the lip of the escarpment and overlooking the lower plains and the distant coastline. And it is most beautiful of all when the sun is setting. When we arrive, Jeff, we will leave the room and go to a small deck directly above, and watch the sun sink into the ocean, yes?"

"That sounds wonderful."

"But first, I will fetch supper."

He took the precaution of bolting the door behind her, and opening it minutes later when her five insistent knocks sounded. She hurried into the room, bearing a hessian bag, and crossed to the window.

"I met an Elder in the refectory, Jeff. He had news from the interior."

"News? Bad news, I take it?"

He sat down on an ancient sofa, sinking back so that his knees projected into the air. She joined him. "The Sporelli are rounding up Healers and Diviners and taking them from this world. So far they have arrested over a hundred of my kind."

He shook his head. "Why? What do they want with...?"

"The Elder says that they will force the Healers to mend the casualties from the imminent conflict with the D'rayni." She bit her lower lip. "And the Elder reported that the Sporelli have agents in Mayalahn."

He repeated the word. "So?"

"Mayalahn is where the sail-rail terminates on the coast. It will be the end of our journey. The Elder says the Sporelli will check everyone who alights from the train."

He rubbed his jaw, feeling the beginnings of a prickly beard. "And how will I get off the train undetected?"

She took his hand and led him across to the window seat. "Open the window," she ordered.

He clumsily worked at a stiff wooden catch, and finally it came free. The small window panel swung outwards. "Now look out," Calla said.

He stuck his head through the narrow gap, thinking he would be hard pressed to force his shoulders through the opening.

He peered down at the grassland speeding by thirty metres beneath the ship. "A long way down."

"The plan was to wait until the train had emptied. The Elders had arranged for a ladder to be placed against the stern of the train. You would climb down to a covered wagon which would take you to a boat in the harbour."

"And now?"

"A change of plan," she said. "The Elders have arranged for the train to be delayed. Before we reach Mayalahn, a stretch of track will be found to be in bad repair and the train will halt. Once we have stopped, we will make our escape."

"You'll come with me to the coast?"

She nodded. "But there we must say goodbye, and I will make my way inland, to the central mountains and relative safety."

"You'll be in danger?"

"Wherever I go, I will be in danger."

"Then make the crossing to D'rayni with me," he urged. "And after that…" What was he saying? That Calla could come with him to New Earth? The idea was ludicrous, if appealing.

She smiled, reached out and touched his cheek. "Then I would perhaps be in greater danger, a Phandran on the world the Sporelli are intent on invading."

"I'm sorry."

She smiled. "Don't be, Jeff. I am doing this, helping you, because it is the right thing to do, for you, for me, and for my people."

She opened the bag. "Now, I have brought red bread and garl cheese, a local delicacy, and white wine from the region where I was born. We will eat, and then watch the sun go down as the train arrives at Lamala."

2

THEY LEFT THE cabin and Calla led the way up a narrow, twisting staircase. Ellis squeezed uncomfortably between the timber planks, climbing the tiny treads as he would a ladder. They emerged onto a small, high deck with a view over the rails curving ahead towards the setting sun on the horizon.

"Oh. I expected the sails to be up," he said. The masts and rigging were bare, the sails furled.

"They are only used on the plains," Calla explained. "For the past twenty kilometres we have been travelling down a slight incline towards the escarpment's edge."

"Freewheeling," he said.

Calla leaned against the low rail, staring ahead, and he sat down on the deck and admired the view.

The sun was going down to their left, a molten globe spreading its orange light across the horizon. Directly ahead, Ellis made out a string of lights. "Lamala?" he asked.

"The junction town. From there, the track branches three ways – north, south, and straight ahead to the coast. We will arrive shortly."

"It's beautiful," he said. The air was warm, heavy with a spicy, floral fragrance.

Calla watched him as he inhaled. She said, "This region produces a number of spices used in cooking. The predominant scent is the yander tree. We are passing through a plantation now."

Far below and to either side, he made out orderly rows of tall trees hung with a dark ribbon-like fruit.

The sight provoked a sudden bitter memory. Maria's father had been a fruit farmer: the regimented rows of trees brought back memories of a particular vacation spent looking after the farm one summer, during which he and Maria had argued, seriously, for the first time.

He realised that Calla was watching him in the twilight, her large eyes catching the last light of the sun. She said softly, "You humans, you are a strange people."

He smiled. "Met many of us, have you?"

"Just you, Jeff."

"And you deduce collective strangeness from a sample of one?" he said.

"I know you well enough to know – vicariously, I admit – several of your acquaintances, friends, lovers."

He stared at her. He murmured, "Like who?"

"Your father; your friend, Michael, a fellow pilot. And Maria..."

He did not know whether to feel violated at her ability. He looked away, at the approaching string of lights on the lip of the escarpment.

She said, "You are strange in that you show only a certain aspect of yourselves to each other. You keep parts of yourself hidden, as it were. To your father, you exhibited only what you thought he would see as your strengths, and you kept your emotions to yourself. To Michael, your best friend, again you show only your masculine attributes; you speak of nothing but your work, and sport; never your feelings."

She was silent for a period, and he guessed what was coming. At last she said, "Perhaps this is one of the reasons your relationship with Maria is... problematic. You do not know how to share your emotions, how to open out your divided self and share with her. Perhaps the fault is that you do not fully know yourself; and how can you really share with someone a self who is not wholly known?"

He shook his head. "By that reckoning, all human relationships are doomed to failure."

She was watching him. "Perhaps too much is expected from certain bondings? It seems strange, to me, that human society requires a pairing of the sexes that should last for years."

He laughed. "And on Phandra? How do you do it?"

"Men and women come together briefly to propagate, and for the most part they lead separate lives. We are more open, emotionally, with each other." She waved a hand. "But it is impossible to compare our races. Different biological drives govern us. We are a short-lived people; our children are independent far sooner than human offspring. We do not need to attend to their needs for more than two of your years. Whereas humans..."

He closed his eyes, trying not to think about Ben.

He said, "I loved Maria so much when we met, and for the first few years. We seemed to have so much in common; it seemed to work. I was so damned happy, Calla... and then we had a son."

He stopped, then forced himself to continue, "It was shortly after Ben's birth that Maria withdrew into herself, away from me. She accused me of not talking to her, of not sharing emotions. As far as I was concerned, I was the same as I'd always been. It was painful, watching her grow ever more distant, resentful of my very presence, finding fault with everything I did, everything I *was*. I thought that she'd got what she'd wanted from me when Ben was born. I was surplus to requirements. And then..."

She reached out and touched his hand. "I know," she whispered. "I know what happened."

He let the silence stretch as the train thrummed over the triple tracks and the warm, fragrant headwind blew in their faces.

"What happened brought us together for a while, for a year perhaps. Then something happened in here." He tapped his head. "And I saw that with Ben no longer there... then I was suddenly free. You can't imagine the sense of liberation I felt, and at the same time the guilt."

"But you remained together."

He nodded. "Maria wanted another child. I... I couldn't, I just couldn't." He looked at the elfin, alien woman and said, "And I don't know whether that was because I feared the pain of having another child and running the risk of... of suffering loss again, or whether I was just using this as an excuse to deny Maria, to force a separation."

"And you never spoke with her about this."

He shook his head. "No, I couldn't. That is, I told her that I didn't want another child, but not why."

"And that is where the issue remains, unresolved, with the two of you mutually resentful."

"And the stupid thing is that I know she's seeing someone else, and I feel..." He stopped, staring down at her hand on his. "I feel angry and jealous and... and I just wish things were like they'd been nine, ten years ago."

After a while, Calla said, "And you have never told this to anyone before now?"

He shook his head. "No. No, of course not."

"And you feel better now for having done so?"

He looked up at her and smiled. "Perhaps. I don't know."

She nodded slowly, and was silent for a time, contemplating. "Jeff," she said at last, "you have admitted your failings, your mistakes. You have shown insight and honesty. You know what you should do, for both Maria and yourself."

He looked at her. "Do I?"

"Be as open with Maria as you have been with me. Your relationship with her will either end, or be repaired. I suspect that she has been just as guarded with you, and perhaps your opening up with provoke a similar honesty on her part. But the important thing is that you should talk, admit your weaknesses to each other."

He smiled. "That's a difficult thing for some of us humans to do, Calla."

"I know, but it is important for your own peace of mind that the situation with Maria is resolved, and resolution will come only with candid dialogue."

He reached out, and the silver pelt of her head felt like velvet.

He felt buoyed at some release she had effected in him. He said, "If I get back to New Earth, Calla, I promise I will do just that."

She looked up at him. "Not if," she said, "when."

He nodded. "When," he said.

She pulled away from him. "Look," she said. "We have arrived at Lamala."

The sail-rail train lumbered towards the string of lights that stretched along the edge of the escarpment. A huddle of timber buildings came into view, a town so chaotic to Ellis's sense of architectural order that it appeared less planned from the street up than dropped from a great height. The three-storey buildings leaned against each other drunkenly, their eaves attempting to meet over narrow alleys and streets. To his amazement the sail-rail track cut straight through the jumble. The train slowed and inched its way past gas-lighted windows and the twisted gable ends of warped wooden terraces. He could have reached out and plucked the weeds growing from the overhanging gutters.

Minutes later the train came to the escarpment and lurched forward alarmingly. Slowly, brakes screeching with the effort of keeping the bloated galleon from hurtling down the incline, they rolled into the station, its warped timbers enclosing them on either side. Ellis stared ahead at the jumble of buildings and alleys which tumbled to the plain far below.

"We will be here for a short while," Calla said, "and will set off again in the early hours."

He peered down at the teeming platform. "No sign of Sporelli troops."

"They will be waiting at Mayalahn station," she said. "By which time we will have left the train and will be well on our way."

They returned below decks to their cabin and Calla suggested they take the opportunity to sleep. Curtained cupboards doubled as beds, far too cramped for Ellis to sleep in with comfort. He dragged a straw mattress onto the floorboards and lay down, watching as Calla slipped into her bed-cupboard and drew the curtain after her.

He listened to the noises from outside as the train was loaded, and stared through the mullioned window at the stars. He considered what Calla had elicited from him, and what she had told him, and the fact that she had so little time left before she passed from this life.

That night, sleep was a long time coming.

3

HE AWOKE TO pitch blackness and the sound of someone rapping on timber.

He sat up, attempting to adjust his vision to the darkness. He sensed Calla brush past him and approach the door. She pulled it open, and he had to shield his eyes from the sudden dazzle. His first thought was that they had been discovered and that this was a Sporelli raiding party.

Then he heard Calla speaking in her breathy tongue, and a similar reply from someone carrying a lamp.

She approached Ellis and knelt, while the bearer of the lamp remained on the threshold. Ellis made out an old Phandran, presumably the Elder Calla had spoken to the evening before.

Now she said, "There has been another change of plan. The Elder has been speaking to passengers who had boarded at Lamala. They reported increased Sporelli activity in the area where my people were due to damage the track."

"So what do we do now?"

"The Elder says that when the train reaches the coastal plain, it will slow down while the sails are hoisted. This is our only chance..."

He stared at her in the half-light. "To do what?"

She hesitated, then said, "To jump from the train."

"Jump?" He recalled the drop from the window and shook his head. "We'd kill ourselves."

He felt her hand clutching his arm. "The Elder says that the train will come almost to a stop. His cabin is directly below ours, and much closer to the ground. We will go there now."

She fetched her travelling bag from the bed-recess, and Ellis quickly pulled on his boots. Seconds later they were hurrying through the cramped, twisting corridors, following the bobbing lamp, and squeezing down a staircase that corkscrewed into the bowels of the train.

They came to a cabin similar in dimensions to their own. The Elder ushered them within and crossed to a mullioned window. Ellis opened it and peered out. The drop was around five metres – enough for an ill-judged jump to break an ankle, or worse.

For the next hour he and Calla sat on the window-seat, the window open in readiness, and waited.

"And when we leave the train?" he asked at one point.

"We will make our way through fields to a canal," she said. "There I will ask a bargee to take us to the coast."

"Won't I prove something of a disincentive for them to help?" A giant alien, he thought, the like of which they had never seen before.

"Not when I have explained the situation, and told them you are working for the Phandrans, against the Sporelli."

He looked through the window. Shadowed land raced by below, and the greased wheels hummed on the tracks. "When we leave the train, how far will we be from the coast?"

"Perhaps fifty kilometres, a little more. It will take us a day or so to get there."

The Elder spoke to Calla, and she relayed his words. "We are approaching the plain. See, the land is levelling and we are slowing."

He nodded, apprehensive. Overhead the brakes squealed and the train slowed still further. The Elder spoke, and Calla said, "He wishes us speed and safety. Now climb out, Jeff."

The train was still travelling at speed, despite having slowed considerably. He opened the window as far as it would go, then climbed out feet first. It was a tight squeeze, and he skinned his back on the frame as he forced his way out. His boots found a ledge a metre below the window opening. He turned and, standing upright, felt for a hand-hold. His fingers encountered a gap in the timbers. He held on and edged his way along the ledge to allow Calla room to climb out.

She hopped onto the sill, making his exit seem clumsy, then turned lithely, lowered herself and found the ledge on which he was standing. She edged her way along and joined him, peering down.

He said, "It's still a long drop. I think I can climb down. You?"

Lips nipped between teeth, she peered down and nodded.

He made out hand- and foot-holds in the sheer face of the timber: flanges, bosses, gaps between planks and jutting ledges.

"Okay, slowly does it..."

He lowered himself so that he was kneeling on the ledge, then peered down for the nearest foot-hold. A couple of metres down and to his right was a protruding boss. He lowered his right leg towards it, found purchase with his boot, and held onto the ledge with outstretched arms. He found hand-holds, looked down and made out a projecting ledge. Carefully he eased himself down. Like this, descending carefully little by little, he descended the vertical face.

At one point he looked up to see Calla nimbly coming after him, and he smiled to himself at her agility.

They were still travelling at speed, though slowing down all the time. He looked up and made out the tiny shapes of Phandrans, silhouetted against the stars, in the rigging high above. The crew were unfurling the sails.

Calla lowered herself so that she was standing beside him on a ledge, her face pressed to the timbers. If she felt at all apprehensive, her calm expression gave nothing away. She stared at him with big eyes and smiled unexpectedly, and the odd juxtaposition of such a warming smile in such a dangerous situation made him want to reach out and hug her.

He looked down. Grassland spun by below, a couple of metres from his feet. He turned himself around so that he had his back to the timbers. "On the count of three, I'm jumping." He hesitated, waiting for the train to slow even further. When it failed to do so – in fact, when it seemed to him that it was gaining speed, he said, "Okay. One, two, three!"

He leaped, and a second later impacted with the ground. His thighs hit his chest, winding him, and he tumbled head over heels and came to rest on his back. Gasping, he rolled over and pulled himself onto all fours, taking great breaths to replace the air punched from his lungs.

He looked up, saw the dark bulk of the train, sails billowing, racing away into the darkness.

"Calla!" he called out in alarm.

A tiny shape ran across the grass towards him. She knelt and reached out, her expression all concern in the starlight. "Jeff, are you injured?"

"I'm... I'm fine. Winded. That's... that's all. I'll be fine." A minute later he managed a laugh. "You?"

"I am well." She smiled at him. "I was worried that you had seriously injured yourself. You cried out when you hit the ground."

"A little unaccustomed to jumping from moving Phandran trains, that's all."

She pulled her bag from her shoulders, pulled out a small flagon and passed it to him. "Water," she said.

He drank thirstily and returned the flask, watching as she raised it to her lips and sipped.

She wiped her mouth with the back of her hand and looked into the night sky. "We have one hour until dawn," she said. "By then, we should have reached the canal and found a boat. Are you ready?"

They walked from beneath the sail-rail track through waist-high grass, and minutes later came to a tended field. He made out row after row of fruit trees similar to the ones he'd seen from the train earlier.

Side by side they walked down an avenue between the trees; at one point Calla reached up and plucked a fruit, long and stringy like a runner bean, which she urged him to eat. "This is excellent energy food," she said, chewing on the fruit she had plucked for herself. He took a bite, scowling at its peppery taste which soon became a rich sweetness as he chewed.

Fifteen minutes later they came to the canal.

Calla laid a hand on his arm and pointed to a silvery glimmer between the trees up ahead.

They approached the water with caution, Calla leading the way. When she reached the last tree she knelt behind its trunk. Ellis joined her.

Starlight glimmered on the stretch of water before them. He heard a grunt. In the distance, dim shadows in the darkness, he made out a team of animals trudging along the path beside the canal.

"What the hell?" he began.

"Shurgs," she said.

Rhinoceroses, he thought, as the six animals came into view. They were squat and solid, with powerful shoulders and short thick legs, but there the resemblance to the terrestrial animal ended. Shurgs were brown-furred, with pointed heads more like badgers, and they gave high-pitched grunts with every laboured step.

Behind them, moving serenely along the surface of the canal, was a wide, low-sided barge.

"Stay here," Calla said, and stepped out from behind the tree.

The barge drew alongside. Ellis saw the figure of a Phandran seated in the prow, holding a set of reins with which he controlled the shurgs.

Calla stepped forward and spoke to the bargee, who ordered the animals to halt. They spoke hurriedly, and a minute later Calla returned.

"Good news. We are just thirty kilometres from Mayalahn."

"He's agreed to give us a ride?"

"She. Of course she has. I am a Healer, after all. Also, one of her shurgs is sick."

As they hurried towards the boat, he stared at her. "You heal animals, too?"

"Naturally. Aren't we all, really, animals?"

They edged past the foul-smelling shurgs and reached the boat. The barge woman stared at him with an unreadable expression, eyes wide. They climbed onto the running board and stepped onto the deck. There, curled behind the seated woman, was the odiferous bulk of a shurg, moaning with what sounded to Ellis very much like self-pity.

Calla gestured to piled bales stacked along the length of the boat. "Rest, Jeff, while I attend to the shurg. I will join you presently."

Ellis climbed onto the bales, finding them more comfortable than the palliasse back on the train. He fashioned a nest for himself, more like an armchair than a bed, and watched Calla as she lay hands on the panting shurg and murmured soothing words.

Ten minutes later she rose to her feet, spoke to the bargee, then climbed onto the bales beside him.

"It's okay?" he asked.

"It is old, and has painful joints. But I have soothed the pain and it will be fine when it has rested for a while."

He looked at her. "It must be a wonderful gift to possess, the power of healing."

She inclined her head. "What better, Jeff? To aid others, to see their relief, their joy."

"You're a selfless person, Calla."

She laughed. "I am not selfless. I was destined to be a Healer, to help others. What other course could my life have taken, if I were destined?"

He thought about it. "You are a peaceful people. Has there ever been conflict on your world? Wars? Political disputes?"

"No wars, in many thousands of years. Disputes? There are differences of opinion, yes, but we negotiate such disputes. Never do we come to physical violence. But with humans it is different, yes?"

"Well, there have been no major conflicts in the two hundred years we've been on the Helix," he said. "Some have a theory that the Builders, when they chose us as Peacekeepers, somehow... altered us, changed us – genetically reprogrammed us away from violence. I don't believe it. And anyway, even if it were true, it hasn't entirely worked. There is still violence among my kind. I've seen fights between individuals, groups. These are swiftly and harshly dealt with, though." He coloured when he recalled the odd occasion when he'd felt the urge to strike out at Maria, and hoped Calla did not pick up on the recollection.

She said, "The Builders are all-powerful. Olembe told my people that. He knew Carrelli, who was a hand-servant of the Builders."

He looked at her in the starlight. "Some say that she was a Builder herself, made corporeal. She helped to guide the colonists to New Earth."

"And then?" she asked.

"And then she disappeared one day, a few years later. Some say she was absorbed back into the Builders' gestalt virtual mind."

Calla was silent for a while, staring along the length of the canal. She said at last, "And yet, a paradox: if the Builders are so powerful, and peace-loving, then why do they allow such races as the Sporelli to invade my world, to kill my people?"

He shook his head. "I don't know, Calla. Perhaps in bringing us here they have discharged their duty, saved us once, as far as they are concerned, and are now leaving us to our own devices, to learn by our own mistakes, as we grow collectively into adulthood."

She smiled at him. "In that case, Jeff, some races have a long way to go."

He almost asked her, then, if she were referring to the Sporelli, or to the human race.

To the west the sky was lightening. Calla led him from the stacked bales to a small cabin amidships, where she said they would be safer when approaching the busy port of Mayalahn.

He slept then, and woke with a start from dreams of New Earth: he was on a small boat on the river that bisected Carrelliville, with a woman who was not Maria but a small, gentle girl whose smile illuminated the day.

He was disoriented when he woke and lay blinking at the cabin's low ceiling. Awareness of where he was came flooding in. He looked around for Calla.

She was seated across from him, staring out at the passing fields.

"How long have I been asleep?"

"Two hours. We are almost at Mayalahn. Are you hungry?"

"Famished." He watched her as she dug into her bag and produced cheese and half a bottle of the sweet white wine. He recalled his dream, the details elusive now, and realised that the woman in the boat with him had been Calla. He was overcome with sadness at the thought that soon they would be parted.

"How will you get back to Verlaine?" he asked as he ate.

"I will wait for a day in Mayalahn," she said, "and then hire a cart to take me back to Verlaine. The journey should take six days."

He stared across at her. "I'll be thinking of you," he said, "and what you've done for me."

In due course the fields gave way to scattered buildings on either side, small farms and villages, and then the sprawling outer margins of the port town. Gaunt timber residences alternated with square parks planted with single gossamer-trees, and beyond, through the interstices between the buildings, he made out the sail-rail track.

He felt a knot of apprehension form in his stomach. The next phase of his escape would soon be under way, this time without the person who had made the journey so pleasant.

He moved across to her. In silence they stared out at the passing town.

Minutes later he was paying no attention to what was outside, but watching Calla's calm, beautiful face, when she drew a sudden, sharp breath, her expression shocked.

His heart skipped. "What?"

He followed her gaze through the narrow window.

Something very alien and at odds with the timber architecture of the town stood between two rickety buildings. At first he thought it was the model of an outsized beetle, the jet black chitin of its dome glistening in the sunlight. Then he saw that it was a Sporelli military vehicle, its armoured carapace bristling with weapons.

"And there is another!" Calla pointed along a boulevard flanking the canal. Another black Sporelli vehicle stood guard, a bulky troop-carrier similar to the one he'd seen in the mountains.

"There are no citizens about," she whispered. "The place is deserted."

His mouth was dry as he asked, "What do we do?"

She bit her bottom lip, thinking. "Remain here," she ordered. "I will go ahead and try to find out what is happening."

She slipped from the cabin. Ellis stared through the window as the barge edged along the canal. More Sporelli vehicles came into view, and dozens of soldiers. They wore uniforms as black as their tanks and carried bulky rifles held at the ready as if they were suspecting trouble.

The barge slowed and came to a halt. To the left was a square framed on three sides by timber buildings; the obligatory gossamer-tree took pride of place in the centre of the square, which – like the rest of the town – was eerily deserted.

As he looked out, three troop-carriers rumbled into the square and halted. Dozens of soldiers spilled from the vehicles and jogged towards the canal.

Seconds later Calla returned, looking worried.

"They are on the banks of the canal," she reported. "They are watching the boats as they pass one by one."

"They surely don't know about us?"

She shook her head. "I don't know."

"Are they boarding the barges and searching?"

"No, just... just watching them."

He kept to himself the thought that they might have heat-sensitive apparatus with which they were scanning the boats for stowaways. The Sporelli were technologically advanced, though how advanced he didn't know.

Calla moved to the swing door, opened it a slit, and looked out. Ellis joined her. Ahead, an arched bridge spanned the river, and on its apex stood three figures.

Calla gasped something in her own language.

The trio comprised two tall Sporelli and, between them, a diminutive, green-robed Phandran.

"A Diviner!" she gasped. "The Sporelli must have apprehended Janyl, the Elder, when he left the train, and the captive Diviner informed them of what he knew about us."

She stared through the entrance, then closed her eyes. She appeared to be in a trance.

Seconds later she opened her eyes and turned to him. "You must not think less of my kind for what the Diviner has done," she said. "The Sporelli have threatened him. They have arrested his family and threatened to kill his daughters, one by one, if he does not comply with their wishes. He is in an impossible position."

"I detest no one right now but the Sporelli," he assured her. "Calla... stay here. I'll leave the boat, lead them away from you."

She smiled at him, reached up and touched his cheek. "They know we are together, Jeff, on this barge. There is no need to place yourself in any more danger."

"We can't just give up. Even running would be better than –"

"Run where, Jeff? There is nowhere to run to."

The barge advanced slowly. The trio on the bridge were around twenty metres away. To either side of the canal, Sporelli troops were gathering.

A few minutes later the barge came to a halt. He heard a shouted command in the harsh language of the Sporelli.

The barge shook and rocked, and footsteps sounded on the timber decks. The door flew open. Ellis held Calla to him, staring through the opening at the soldier who stood there, watching them without expression. He was breathing heavily, as if scared himself, and gave off a sour body odour.

He gestured with his rifle. Ellis squeezed Calla's hand and urged her forward.

The soldier backed off as they emerged from the cabin. Ellis blinked in the bright daylight, looking around at the silent enfilade of black-uniformed troops lining the canal, their weapons trained on him and Calla.

He looked up, at the trio on the bridge above them. The small Diviner had closed his eyes and hung his head, shamed by his actions. Ellis thought reassurance at the Phandran, hoping the Diviner would detect that he bore him no ill-will or resentment.

He glanced at the Sporelli flanking the Diviner, expecting to see triumph on their faces. All he saw were two blank, pale blue faces, staring at him impassively.

He and Calla stepped from the barge onto the cobbled quayside. The barge woman had been ushered off ahead of them, protesting to the Sporelli soldier.

One of the troops on the bridge called out a single, sharp command, and the soldier raised the butt of his weapon and brought it down on her skull. The woman staggered and fell.

The commander on the bridge called out again. With mounting incredulity and the realisation that he could do nothing to prevent what he knew was about to happen, Ellis watched as the soldier lowered his weapon, directed the barrel at the sobbing Phandran on the ground, and pulled the trigger.

Calla cried out and buried her face against Ellis's chest.

He could only stare at what had become of the woman's head.

He looked away, gripping Calla as she wept, and felt a creeping numbness steal over his senses.

He looked back at the soldier who had murdered the Phandran, and something the Sporelli did then – a gesture that struck Ellis as even more callous than the execution – provoked him to act. The soldier frowned with disgust at a splash of brain adhering to the toe of his boot, casually extended his leg towards the twitching corpse, and wiped his boot on the woman's dress.

Ellis cried out and dived at the Sporelli. Behind him, Calla sobbed his name, but he was already upon the soldier and threw a punch at his face. The soldier looked incredulous, staring at Ellis as he tripped backwards and fell to the cobbles beside the bargee's corpse.

Another soldier stepped forward, raised his rifle, and struck Ellis in the face with its butt. Within seconds, he was surrounded by a dozen Sporelli, and his only regret as the blows rained down on him was that his impetuous action had parted him from Calla.

Then the solid haft of a rifle crashed against his temple and he fell to the ground unconscious.

TEN /// VENGEANCE

I

KRANDA BROUGHT HER flier down beside the looping road that wound its way up to the Retreat of Verlaine, then strode down the ramp and stared up at the mountain redoubt.

In many ways it reminded her of her family manse back on Mahkan, merging with and springing from the very rock of the mountain. The Phandran example, however, was more elaborate than her mother's functional abode. Here they had added towering belvederes and turrets which extended beyond the summit of the mountain, and carved arcane symbols into the cliff-face, circular mandalas and something that looked very much like the Helix.

And this was the place to which Jeff Ellis had been brought. The possibility that he was still up there, recovering from both his injuries and the poisoning, was almost too much to hope for. Kranda thought that it would be better to prepare herself for the worst: that either Ellis's injuries or the alien toxins had taken his life.

She moved to the edge of the road and stared down at the plain far below. There was no sign of Sporelli activity, either on the ground or in the air. She drew a breath, looked up at the ethereal Retreat, then began the winding ascent, jogging at first and then, as she hit her stride, sprinting up the switch-back road.

In a matter of minutes she was standing before the vast arched entrance of the Retreat. A timber door loomed over her, and set into its ancient timber was a tiny door that barely reached to her waist.

She deactivated her varnika's shield and was casting about for a bell-pull, or some other means of summons, when the hatch opened and a small Phandran face peered out.

"Mahkan," the figure said, her varnika translating the words with barely a delay, "you are expected. Please, enter."

She was relieved to find that they did not expect her to squeeze through the hatch. The vast door swung open minimally, allowing her to enter. She found herself in a great foyer which dwarfed the dozen or so red-robed Phandrans there to witness her arrival.

"You were expecting me? The yahn-gatherers got word to you?" But even as she spoke the words, she knew that that would have been impossible. She had covered, in her flier and on foot, perhaps fifty kilometres in a matter of fifteen minutes. The yahn-gatherers could not have communicated with the Retreat so rapidly.

"We will explain," said a red-robed Phandran. "Please, if you would care to follow me."

The Phandran was walking away, leading her across the foyer. They climbed a narrow staircase which twisted up past several floors and which came eventually to a wide corridor leading towards the front of the Retreat. The beamed ceiling was twice the height of a Phandran, but Kranda had to duck awkwardly as she followed the alien.

They came to a small door and she was forced to bend almost double in order to enter the long, low room which stretched for fifty metres. The entire far wall comprised a great window which looked out over the valley and the looping road she had climbed.

The Phandran gestured to a couch, which Kranda folded herself into with little room on either side. Four Phandrans might have occupied the couch; not for the first time since arriving on this world, she felt gigantic and clumsy beside these fairy folk.

The Phandran took a seat opposite her.

"I came here..." Kranda began.

The Phandran gestured. "We know why you came, Kranda'vahkan; and your arrival here was forecast."

She smiled uneasily. "By whom?"

"By our Elders, our Diviners."

She tilted her head and stared at the smooth, lined face of the old Phandran. "So your people can look into the future..." She was unable to keep a touch of scepticism from her words.

"The human, Jeff Ellis, is no longer here. Yesterday we sent him, with one of our people, to the coastal town of Mayalahn."

Kranda sat back, almost laughing with relief. She felt emotion constrict her throat as she said, "So he's alive?"

The Elder inclined his head. "He came here with injuries from a shuttle accident, and with poisoning. My colleague nursed him back to full health. Yesterday he was deemed fit enough to travel."

Kranda closed her eyes briefly. She considered the Sporelli's cruelty earlier, and contrasted it with the altruism showed by the Phandran people. She said, "If you can tell me where I might find Jeff Ellis, I will take him from Phandra to his homeworld, New Earth."

"On that point there is news both good and bad. We sent him on a sail-rail boat with a colleague named Calla; however, the Sporelli learned of this and necessitated a change of plan."

"Which was?"

"He and Calla left the train between stations, some point after the town of Lamala, and proceeded to the coastal town of Mayalahn by means of canal barge. At present they should be somewhere upon that journey; I wish I could be more specific."

Kranda said, "And what of the Sporelli? Have your Diviners looked ahead and assessed the success of their aggression?"

The Elder turned a tiny hand. "Their destiny is that of all aggressors: what they might gain in material possessions from their acts accrues only spiritual loss."

Which tells me, Kranda thought wryly, *absolutely nothing.*

The Elder said, "The scourge of the Sporelli is like a storm that will, in time, play itself out."

Kranda smiled. "Thank you for saving Jeff Ellis," she said. "Without you..."

The Phandran stood and drew a device on small wheels towards where Kranda sat. It appeared to be a wooden representation of their world, a barrel on an axis which the Elder now rotated. He pointed to a marked range of mountains and said, "We are here. This, here, is the sail-rail station at Trahng. Here is the coast, and the town of Mayalahn, their destination. It was our plan to have the human travel to D'rayni, where he might achieve communications with his people."

She stood and moved to the door. There she paused and turned to the Elder. "One more thing," she said, "you said that the Sporelli found out about Jeff Ellis and Calla's plans to take the sail-rail train?"

The Phandran said in barely a whisper, "The Sporelli arrested several Elders, among them Diviners, and... and applied certain pressures. The Diviner in question would have gladly died rather than divulge information concerning the human, but the Sporelli threatened his family." The Phandran gestured with a small hand. "Also, the fact that the Diviner *knew* that the human would successfully elude the Sporelli made his apparent weakness acceptable."

"So the chances are that Jeff is in Sporelli custody?"

The Phandran inclined his head. "That is so."

Kranda spat, "The Sporelli are truly evil."

The Phandran reached up and laid a small hand on Kranda's gigantic claw. "We do not believe in evil, just *hran* [untranslatable]. Perhaps you would say, 'the consequence of unthinking and unfeeling actions'?"

"Perhaps we might," Kranda smiled. She thanked the Phandran once again and took her leave.

2

SHE BROUGHT THE flier down in a field beside the sail-rail track, ten kilometres beyond the town of Lamala.

Hovering at an elevation of fifteen metres for the past three hours, she had followed the course of the sail-rail track west and scanned the margin of farmland directly beneath the track, searching for some evidence of where Ellis and Calla might have alighted.

Despite the Elders' prognostic assurance that all would be well, Kranda half-expected to find their broken bodies in the fields beneath the tracks. How might they have managed to alight from a speeding sail-rail train, she asked herself, other than by jumping?

Now she left her flier and crossed to the track. There, directly below the lower central rail, was an indentation in the loam, and another a few metres further on.

She knelt and examined the impact point, the scuffed earth that told of a body's impact. She scanned the immediate area and made out small footprints leading from the far impact point to this one. And to the right, leading off between rows of tall bushes, were the joined tracks of both small and larger footprints.

Kranda took off and sprinted through the serried crops, and minutes later came to the broad, serene waters of a canal.

So Ellis and Calla had reached this far, at least, without being apprehended by the Sporelli.

She returned to her flier and eased it into the air high above the fields. She followed the line of the canal as it arrowed west, scanning for any sign of the Sporelli. She had confidence in her flier's shielding technology, and in the Sporelli's inability to detect it... but it would not hurt to be a little circumspect. She had come so far, had almost located Ellis and the Phandran, and it would be stupid of her now to risk everything through lack of vigilance.

Ahead, she made out the crude timber architecture of the coastal town. She judged she was around three kilometres from its sprawling outskirts, which was near enough for safety's sake. There was a good chance that Mayalahn, a town on the coast opposite the world the Sporelli intended to conquer, would be crawling with invading troops.

She brought the flier down in a fallow field half a kilometre from the canal, intending to proceed into the town on foot.

She ran from her ship and crossed the farmland to the canal, then followed it through the outskirts of town. She proceeded with caution along the narrow alleys and streets that flanked the water. The last thing she wanted was to collide with a hapless Phandran; the impact, at speed, could be fatal to the tiny, bird-boned natives. She slowed when she came across locals going about their daily business, and slipped past them, swift and silent. She found herself holding her breath as she did so, amazed despite herself at the miracle of the varnika.

The timber buildings became taller and more densely packed. She was coming to the commercial heart of the town now, a noisy hubbub of commerce, where traders unloaded carts of goods and barges deposited their cargoes.

She arrived at a cobbled square beside the canal and halted. Ahead was a Sporelli tank, and beside that, a troop-carrier. Perhaps twenty black-uniformed soldiers were stationed strategically around the square. A crowd of Phandrans had gathered at the far side, staring silently at the troops. Kranda eased herself behind a timber pillar and stared out.

The crowd appeared mute with shock or fear, and at the same time she detected an undercurrent of anger. She wondered if some atrocity had taken place close by... and her suspicions were heightened when she made out, on the cobbles beside the canal, a small group of locals. She increased her varnika's visual magnification. The Phandrans were scrubbing the cobbles, sluicing what might have been blood into the still waters of the canal. From time to time they looked up at the Sporelli troops watching the clean-up operation impassively, and Kranda made out fear and resentment in their eyes.

To her right, a group of Phandrans stood watching and occasionally exchanging comments. She increased her auditory gain and listened. Seconds later, the translation came through.

"...a good woman, worked the barges all her life."

"Didn't deserve an end like that."

"The Sporelli!" an oldster spat.

"But what was the alien doing aboard her barge?" another asked.

She listened to them, and another group nearby, for fifteen minutes, and pieced together a likely scenario. An alien – Jeff Ellis? – had been found by the Sporelli aboard a barge and arrested, and the Sporelli had made an example of the bargee in the square, summarily executing her for harbouring the alien.

Which put an entirely different complexion on Kranda's mission, now.

She controlled her anger, her impulse to seek retribution on the nearest Sporelli soldier.

And yet...

Perhaps that might be one way to find out what she wanted.

She moved around the square, heart hammering at her proximity to the enemy, and scanned the troops.

She saw one slip off down an alley, unfasten the front of his trousers, and relieve himself against the wall. Kranda followed him. She paused in the entrance to the alley, assessing the likelihood of being observed, then moved towards the soldier.

As fast as lightning she grabbed the Sporelli, clamping a hand over his mouth and fastening her left arm around his torso, binding his arms. She was surprised by how puny and weak the soldier was. She lifted him off the ground and whispered, "You struggle, you die..." and heard her varnika translate her into the Sporelli's guttural tongue.

The soldier fell limp in her grip, his eyes above her claw bulging with terror.

She took off at speed, carrying the Sporelli through the deserted backstreets towards where she had left the flier.

ELEVEN /// EASY TARGETS

I

ELLIS SAT UP, then raised a hand to his forehead, which throbbed with a seismic headache.

He had no idea how long he'd been unconscious. He was in a large timber room, empty but for himself and the chain shackling his right leg, snaking away across the packed earth floor and through a slit in the timber panelling. A window without glass, at Phandran head height, looked out onto a deepening twilight.

He stood up, wincing at the pain lancing through his skull, and when it abated slightly he shuffled across to the window.

The timber shack rested on a hillside surrounded by sere countryside. A Sporelli beetle-tank stood outside the shack, and half a dozen soldiers sat on the vehicle, cleaning their weapons and chatting. They might have been human reservists on a training exercise.

He crossed the shack to the opposite wall and placed his eye to a gap in the planks. There was another vehicle stationed outside, a troop-carrier, and the chain that shackled his leg continued across the sandy ground and vanished into the vehicle. Escape, it seemed, was impossible.

He considered the dead bargee, and then Calla. The Sporelli had shown themselves to be casually brutal, but he reassured himself that Calla would have been spared the fate of the bargee. She was a Healer, after all, and hadn't she told him that the Sporelli were rounding up Healers and Diviners to aid them in the war effort?

At the far end of the shack was a low door, but the chain didn't allow him to reach it. He had little doubt that the Sporelli had that angle covered, too.

He returned to his original position against the timber wall and sat down. He thought back – how many days now? – to the morning he'd taken off from Carrelliville spaceport, his row with Maria and the sour taste it had left with him. Well, he'd had other things to occupy his mind since then, but it was odd that even now, *in extremis*, his thoughts should return to Maria, and maddening that he should experience the pain their row had caused all over again.

He listened to the sound of the Sporelli troops talking amongst themselves, the growls and occasional bark of what might have been laughter. He reasoned that, if they wanted him dead, then they would have despatched him by now. Why imprison him, if they intended to execute him somewhere down the line?

Unless, of course, their plan was to question him and then perform the *coup de grace*.

He closed his eyes and thought of Carrelliville, and specifically the Oasis Bar beside the lake and the beers they served there. Hell, what he'd give for just one long draft of ice cold beer now.

If he got away from here, he promised himself, then one of the first things he'd do on arriving back on New Earth would be to stand a round with his friends from the spaceport.

He heard a sound from the end of the shack.

The door swung open and a soldier peered in at him. The Sporelli knelt and rolled a cylindrical canister across the floor. Ellis backed up against the wall, fearing a grenade, then laughed with relief as he realised that the canister contained water. He stopped it with his boot and picked it up. The soldier watched him, then retreated and closed the door.

Ellis opened the canister and sniffed. He poured a drop of the liquid onto his palm and sniffed again. Water, as far as he could tell. He raised his palm to his lips and slurped. It tasted wonderful, cool and sharp. He raised the canister and drank, reasoning that if the Sporelli wished to kill him they would have used a bullet rather than poisoned water.

He set the canister aside and tested the iron cuff around his leg. It was a tight fit, and there was no way he might pull his foot free. He tried, even so, but succeeded only in abrading his ankle. He gave up, sat back, and poured a little precious water over his face and rubbed briskly.

An hour elapsed, then two, and he could not help but dwell on what the Sporelli might have in store for him. The sun went down and darkness descended, and the only source of light was the meagre illumination of the distant stars seen through the window.

Would he be taken back to Sporelli and paraded before their media as the abject human captured during their army's glorious advance across Phandra? Would he then be handed over to some neutral world, or imprisoned by the Sporelli as a spy?

As the night elapsed and he became ever more tired, his exhausted mind played out increasingly pessimistic scenarios. He must have fallen asleep at some point, as he dreamed of being reunited with Calla, only to find that they were being led towards a compound where a firing squad was waiting.

He sat up suddenly, crying out loud. He leaned against the wall, panting in the aftermath of a nightmare. He had dreamed he'd been chased by a gossamer-tree pod, and had backed away only to find himself chained to the ground.

The window showed a patch of dawn sky. He drank the remainder of the water, which served only to make him aware of how hungry he was. He stood up wearily and crossed to the window, intending to locate the soldier who had provided him with the water and mime his need for food.

The tank was a threatening shape in the dawn light, and around it he made out the bivouacked shapes of sleeping soldiers. He moved to the other side of the shack and peered through the gap in the timbers. The troop-carrier was still there, but there was no sign of its complement of soldiers.

He sat down again, reasoning that surely he would be moved from here sooner rather than later. He was keeping two military vehicles and more than a dozen troops tied down, when they might have been better employed invading D'rayni. He smiled at the thought; at least his capture was achieving that small thing.

He closed his eyes and dozed, then came awake suddenly some

time later. The sound of an engine broke the silence. He stood up and shuffled to the window. The troops were struggling from their bivouacs as a military vehicle – a sleek roadster this time, in the sable livery of the invading army – swept up the hillside and braked between the tank and the shack.

A small, rotund soldier climbed from the roadster, eliciting smart salutes from the hastily assembled troops. He strode across to the shack accompanied by an aide carrying an ominous-looking black bag.

Ellis resumed his position against the wall and tried to look disinterested.

So this is what it came down to, he thought; he had been kept captive until the torture squad arrived.

The door creaked open and the squat, imperious soldier stepped through, followed by his aide.

The leading Sporelli looked to be about forty by human standards, round-faced and dead-eyed. A soldier through and through, exercising the dreams of a life-time in the subjugation of a powerless, defenceless world.

His aide advanced, knelt beside Ellis and opened the black bag. Ellis watched, trying not to let his curiosity show, as the soldier withdrew what looked like a safety helmet used by skyball players.

He was determined not to show his fear, not to back away and give the bastards the slightest cause to despise him any further.

The kneeling soldier reached to place the cap on Ellis's head. Ellis moved away, backed into the corner. The soldier simply followed him, reached out and roughly pulled the skullcap over his head. Then he pulled a com-device from an inner pocket and glanced at the screen.

Ellis knew that there was no way to avoid whatever was about to happen, and it was all he could do not to let his fear show. He turned his head and stared at the fat soldier, attempting to communicate his hatred.

The soldier operating the skullcap turned and spoke. The fat Sporelli nodded and stepped forward.

He peered down his nose at Ellis and began speaking. As he listened to the impassioned flow, Ellis gained the impression that the soldier had rehearsed the speech and was relishing being able at last to deliver his patriotic, self-justifying diatribe.

He looked up at the soldier and, when the latter ceased his address, he gathered a mouthful of saliva and spat. The gob of phlegm fell short of its untended target, the sergeant's face, and adhered to his greatcoat. The soldier winced, stared at Ellis with murder in his eyes, and snapped an order to his aide.

The soldier tapped something on the hand-held com, and instantly two things happened.

Ellis felt a firestorm blaze through his cranium – and at the same time a deafening explosion sounded outside the shack.

The blast rocked the building, knocking the fat Sporelli off his feet. Ellis rolled over, snatching the skullcap from his head. No sooner had the echo of the first blast died away than there was another explosion, even louder, coming from the other side of the building. He heard a hail of debris pepper the timbers, and then a cacophony of agonised yells issuing from the Sporelli troops outside. He staggered to his feet and lurched towards the window. The beetle-tank was a twisted, smoking tangle of wreckage; one Sporelli soldier was a flaming puppet dancing in agony; others lay scattered across the ground, ripped limb from limb. He reeled away from the window, retching.

The Sporelli aide ran to the door, drawing his pistol. He yanked open the door and was about to dash out when he gave a sudden cry, and Ellis saw daylight through a bloody, fist-sized hole in the soldier's back. He staggered and fell backwards, his pistol skittering across the floor and fetching up a metre from where Ellis cowered.

He curled in the corner, dazed by events. Certainly this was not the work of the Phandrans, a peaceable people who did not possess the capability to mount such an attack. Who, then? The human Peacekeepers? But they would never commit an all-out assault, such a bloody and violent attack, merely to effect the rescue of a shuttle pilot.

A blur of motion appeared at the door, a sudden whirlwind that deceived the eye and tricked the mind. One second it was on the threshold, the next within the shack. Then the blur vanished completely and Ellis wondered if his eyes had been playing tricks.

Then, as if by magic, a figure manifested itself before the cowering Sporelli soldier.

"Kranda...?" Ellis said incredulously.

The Mahkan was staring down at the overweight soldier, lips

drawn back in a snarl. Kranda spoke, a string of flowing Mahkan, and Ellis was bemused to hear harsh Sporelli words fill the air.

He saw movement through the open door. A wounded soldier was staggering towards the shack, drawing a pistol as he came. He paused in the doorway, sagging against the jamb, and was raising his weapon when Ellis acted.

Looking back, he told himself that he'd had no idea he was about to do what he did then: it was a reflexive act committed without conscious thought. He reached for the pistol on the floor, snatched it up and fired just as the Sporelli soldier was about to take aim at Kranda.

The pistol kicked in Ellis's hand, its power shocking him.

The soldier fell to his knees, clutching frantically at the sudden tumble of innards slopping from the hole in his uniform. He swayed for a second, and then fell on his face. Ellis looked away, a terrible cold weight in his gut.

The Makhan fired. Ellis watched the fat Sporelli soldier fall to the floor, the top of his head spinning away across the room and clattering against the far wall.

Kranda turned and stared at the Sporelli soldier lying face-down in the doorway, then turned to Ellis.

"You have done it again," the Mahkan said.

"What?" Ellis said, still shocked.

"Saved my life."

Kranda aimed the weapon at the chain beside Ellis's foot, fired and shattered the links, then grabbed his arm. "Now swiftly. We have little time."

A second later, Kranda was rendered invisible.

Choking, Ellis stepped over the corpse of the soldier he had killed – *he had killed!* – and followed Kranda from the shack.

2

THEY EMERGED INTO dazzling sunlight. Ellis felt Kranda's grip, painful on his wrist, and stared at where the Mahkan should have been. All he saw was a vague, Mahkan-shaped outline, and beyond it the distant grassland and trees.

They ran towards a Sporelli roadster – the very same one the fat soldier had arrived in – dodging between the burned and lacerated corpses of half a dozen troops. He looked away but couldn't avoid the stench of burning meat that filled the air. All the while he saw in his mind's eye the look of incredulity on the face of the soldier he had killed, the appalled realisation that he was going to die.

They reached the car and Kranda let go of his arm. The door on the driver's side opened as if by itself and Kranda called, "Get in!"

He jumped into the passenger seat and Kranda fired the engine. As the roadster raced away, Ellis looked back at the carnage. Around twenty soldiers lay dead and dying. The tank and the troop carrier were burning lustily, sending great billows of oily smoke high into the bright blue sky.

He was startled as Kranda appeared, suddenly, in the driver's seat beside him.

Back at the shack Kranda had seemed bulkier than he recalled from previous meetings – and now he knew why. The Mahkan's body and limbs were contained in the struts and spars of an exo-skeleton, a carbon cage which moved with a fluidity alien to Ellis's understanding.

Quite aside from the exo-skeleton, there was something else very different about Kranda compared to the last time they'd met. The

Mahkan's scaled reptilian tegument had been a dull charcoal grey, but now Kranda's skin had the burnished, copper complexion of lubricated leather.

Kranda glanced at him as they sped away from the shack and into the wooded hills at speed, pulling back a long top lip to reveal a fierce set of upper teeth. "Since our last meeting, I have undergone *hayanor*."

Ellis stared at the alien. "You're female now?"

The exhibition of teeth again. "How to explain *that*," Kranda said, inclining her head back towards the carnage they were fleeing, "other than as the result of female strength of body and will?"

Ellis realised he was shaking. "The Kranda I knew, you wouldn't have...?"

Kranda gripped the steering column and accelerated along the forest track, the Sporelli vehicle's excellent suspension compensating for the rough terrain. "I would have been driven to save you, my friend, for I was honour-bound to do something to effect your escape. But, as a male, I might have been more... careful as to the means I employed."

Ellis said, "You killed..." He floundered, considering what the Mahkan had just done on his behalf.

"I did what I had to do in order to rescue you."

"Even if that that meant the deaths of twenty Sporelli?"

"Don't start your specious human preaching, Jeff. The Sporelli invaded a peaceable people, and right now they are bombarding another. I do not hold to the humans' – or the Builders' – liberal ethos of the sanctity of all life. Also," she went on, "I have personally witnessed the depravity of the Sporelli."

"But you said as a Mahkan male you would have gone about it differently?"

The Mahkan flicked him a lizard-like glance. "And so I would. But the difference of approach would be in terms of spending more time calculating the attack so as to minimise not Sporelli casualties, but the danger to myself. Mahkan, in their male phase, are famously... circumspect."

"While females...?"

"Are impulsive, headstrong. We get the job done with the minimum degree of procrastination."

Despite himself, Ellis smiled. "But even so," he found himself saying, "was all the killing necessary?"

The Mahkan turned her cold gaze on Ellis. "Do you realise," she said, "what the Sporelli sergeant was about to do to you?"

The skullcap, he thought.

Kranda went on, "The guran would have scoured your mind. I suspect they wanted to know why you had come to Phandra, whether you knew of their intentions and were an advance party. Whatever. The end result of being subjected to that device would be that the Sporelli would have a record of your last few days – and you would have ended up brain dead."

Ellis closed his eyes, and when he opened them again, Kranda was watching him in silence.

She said, "I only wish I had been more alert in the final few seconds. I am honestly sorry that my inattention resulted in your taking the Sporelli's life. As much as I fail to comprehend your aversion to killing, I believe you hold the ethos with sincerity."

"The Sporelli troops could not, individually, be held accountable for the actions of their commanding officers," he said.

Kranda hissed with what Ellis thought was disgust. "And now you sound just like your pusillanimous Peacekeepers! As soon as each and every Sporelli soldier donned the uniform and invaded a peaceable world, they surrendered peacetime rights of safe conduct and subscribed to the ethos of war: kill or be killed. And for your information, the soldier I killed in the shack was the very one who used the guran on an innocent Phandran villager. I swore to avenge his death, and I am pleased to say that I succeeded."

They drove on in silence for a time.

Ellis contrasted this aspect of Kranda's character with that of the Kranda he had last met a couple of years ago. In his male manifestation he had been coolly philosophical, gentle of mien: the Kranda beside him now might have been another Mahkan entirely.

He said, "Did New Earth know of your mission here?"

Kranda hissed again. "What? The Peacekeepers? Had we approached your governors, they would have sat upon my request for a few days, discussing the ramifications of my actions, and by now you would be dead."

Ellis closed his eyes, but all he saw was the dying expression of the Sporelli soldier. He opened them again and stared ahead at the track rising through the trees.

"How did you find me?"

"A Mahkan ship charted your shuttle through Phandran airspace, and reported when it vanished."

"You located the wreckage."

"And from there it was a matter of diligent investigation to follow your route across the face of Phandra."

"I was travelling with a woman called Calla, a Phandran Healer. Do you know what became...?"

"Not specifically. As with all Healers, and other Phandrans of special abilities, she will have been taken into Sporelli custody. She will be shipped from here, whether to Sporell itself or to the battlefront at D'rayni, I do not know."

Ellis was silent for a while, thinking about the tiny Phandran who had healed his wounds and accompanied him so selflessly. He recalled her fatalism, and hoped it would help her to accept the hardships she was suffering now.

He said quietly, "The debt of honour you felt towards me, Kranda, I have to the Healer called Calla. If there is any way in which I might help her..."

The Mahkan turned her reptilian visage to regard him. "I understand, and sympathise." She paused, then went on, "When I return to Mahkan, I will do my best to locate the Healers taken from this world. Perhaps my people might be able to take action there, too."

It was a small sop to his conscience, but, Ellis reasoned, better than nothing.

"If you could inform me if and when you learn anything."

"I will do that, my friend."

"And now?" Ellis asked. "How do you propose we leave this world?"

Kranda pulled back her lips to show both sets of teeth. It was a gesture Kranda had developed to mimic a human smile, but as such it fell well short of the intended effect. "First, we have to evade the Sporelli," she said.

"They know where we are?"

Kranda glanced at a series of alpha-numerics sequencing along the spar of her left forearm. "They have had a ground-effect vehicle on our trail for the past three minutes. Hence my speed."

Ellis turned in his seat and looked back along the track. It snaked tortuously through the forest, intervening trees obscuring the view. He hoped that the Sporelli were following only by car, and not by flier. From the air they would be an easy target.

"A ground-effect vehicle, nothing else?"

"Not as yet, Jeff. But I think it will only be a matter of time before they have a flier in the vicinity."

"How far are they behind us?"

Kranda glanced at her read-out. "Approximately half a kilometre, and holding steady." She glanced at Ellis. "But do not worry yourself." She patted the ugly weapon on her lap. "If they draw any closer, I will simply stop the car and ambush them."

"Great," Ellis said. He glanced at the Mahkan. "And just where are we going?"

Kranda pointed ahead. "See that hilltop? By the time we arrive there in exactly thirteen minutes, according to my varnika" – she tapped the spars of her exo-skeleton – "we will be safe."

"We have a saying back on New Earth," he said. "Unlucky thirteen."

Kranda hissed. "Spare me your superstitions, human!"

Ellis was about to ask why they would be safe on reaching the hilltop when he heard something loud in the air high above. He looked up. The sable shape of a flier appeared in the strip of blue sky between the treetops.

"What did I say about unlucky thirteen?" he muttered.

3

THE MISSILE STRUCK the track just ahead of the roadster, and only swift evasive action from Kranda saved them. She swerved around the explosion, and Ellis covered his head and ducked.

"Their intent now is certainly to kill us," Kranda said, "not capture."

"And I wonder why?" Ellis glanced up. The flier was keeping pace. "We're sitting ducks!"

Kranda glanced at him. "That makes no sense at all."

"I'm sorry. Old human term. Means, approximately, we're dead if we don't do something."

"Understood."

Without warning Kranda swerved the roadster from the track and bucketed it through the forest.

"And I didn't mean slam us at speed into a tree, Kranda!"

She braked before the vehicle did just that.

"This is as far as we go in this, Jeff. The rest of the way is on foot."

Ellis leapt from the roadster and followed Kranda through the forest. For a second they halted, at the Mahkan's behest, and listened. The vehicle in pursuit sped past the point where Kranda had left the road.

He looked up. He could hear the deep thrum of the flier's jets high above, but the craft was hidden by the tree cover.

"This way," Kranda said.

She took off, not employing her exo-skeleton to power her flight, for Ellis's sake, but even so running much faster than him. Ellis struggled to keep her in sight, aware that tiredness and lack of food was contributing to his exhaustion. Ahead Kranda paused beside a moss-covered gossamer-tree. As soon as Ellis drew alongside, the Mahkan took off.

He took a deep breath and set off again. He wanted to shout at Kranda to stop and rest, but it was all he could do to conserve his energy in order to keep on running.

At least now the forest floor was tending to incline upwards, which suggested they were climbing towards Kranda's hilltop.

The gradient increased until they were forced in places to scrabble on all fours up rocky outcroppings. He could still hear the thrum of the flier's engines high overhead as the Sporelli searched for them.

Kranda had come to a halt, much to Ellis's relief. The Mahkan was standing on the summit of a small knoll, looking like a heroic war statue with her rifle lodged on her hip as she swept her gaze across the forest.

"What?" Ellis panted. "What is it?"

"Foot soldiers," she said. "Following."

"Just... just what we need!" He braced his hands on his thighs and breathed deeply, wondering if his feebleness was due to the poison from the gossamer-tree pod lingering in his system.

"Keep climbing," Kranda said. "When you get to the last of the tree-line, stop in its cover. I'll be back."

"Where the hell are you going?" Ellis said. Kranda vanished. He heard the sound of her footsteps as she retraced her steps through the forest. He swore, hoping that the crazed Mahkan knew what she was doing. If she went and got herself killed now...

He looked up the incline. The rocky prominence was half a kilometre away, dark against the blue sky. There was a little open ground between him and the last of the tree-cover, but he could skirt it and keep himself hidden behind the trees. He climbed, heading through the forest. Once he paused to listen, but there was no sound of the Sporelli flier.

He continued, wishing Kranda were back with him.

Seconds later he heard the first explosion, and a distant Sporelli cry. Kranda, doing her dirty work.

He stopped again, exhausted, and peered up through the trees at the hilltop. The knob of rock was stark and bald. Not for the first time, he wondered at Kranda's insistence that they make it their destination.

He climbed, frequently on all fours, slipping and sliding as tiredness got the better of him. At one point he paused to regain his breath, bracing himself against a tree-trunk. He looked around and saw, fifty metres to his left across the scree-covered incline, the dark shape of a Sporelli soldier, legs braced against the gradient. As he watched, paralysed, the Sporelli raised his rifle and aimed directly at him.

He started as he heard the detonation of Kranda's rifle. Fifty metres away the Sporelli soldier dissolved into an atomised cloud of bodily fluids. Three further explosions sounded and for a brief second Ellis found himself pitying the Sporelli troops. What supernatural being must they think themselves up against? An invisible force that appeared from nowhere and slaughtered at will...

He set off again, and felt something grip his arm and almost lift him up the gradient. He glanced to his right. All he could make out, where Kranda should have been, was a crazily fractured scene of forest and sky.

"Why... why the summit?" he panted.

"Save your breath!" Kranda said.

They came to the last of the trees. Ahead stretched a rocky incline denuded of vegetation. If the Sporelli stood any chance of killing them, then this is where it would happen.

This fact had clearly occurred to Kranda, too, for a second later she barked, "Don't struggle. Just relax."

Ellis felt strong hands enfold him and he was lifted suddenly from his feet. He tried not to cry out in alarm as he was whisked up the hillside. He felt his cheeks forced against his skull as if he were undergoing g-force pressure. His vision was a blur. One second he was standing under the last of the tree-cover, and the next Kranda had deposited him on the far side of the summit.

Ellis looked around, searching for a cave entrance.

"Where the hell...?" he almost wept.

He heard the thrum of distant engines, drawing closer, and when he looked up he saw the shape of the approaching Sporelli flier.

"I thought you said..." he began.

"Human," said the Mahkan testily, "please cease your whinging."

Ellis made out a blur of movement beside him, and heard the crack of Kranda's rifle.

Up above, the Sporelli flier disintegrated into a rapidly plummeting fireball.

He looked down on the surrounding forest. He made out the small figures of Sporelli troops on a dozen sides, closing in.

He began to feel rather exposed.

"Kranda?" he said.

"Look!" the Mahkan said, pointing.

He looked into the sky, but saw nothing. Seconds later he felt a blast of intense heat against his face and a hail of grit sand-blasted his exposed skin. He made to turn away, but Kranda grabbed his arm and hauled him towards the source of the heat. One second the rocky surface of the hillside was underfoot, and the next he was stumbling up the sloping grid of an invisible ramp.

The next thing he knew he was aboard a vessel and stumbling along silver corridors. The sensory anomaly was disconcerting as his brain attempted to catch up with his vision. They came to a triangular flight-deck and Kranda thrust him into the co-pilot's seat.

"Strap yourself in, Jeff. This is no human toy we're talking about here. This is Mahkan engineering."

He heard an explosion and thought the Sporelli had scored a direct hit. But Kranda was laughing.

"The neutron drive, kicking in."

Then Ellis was smeared against the padded couch, his cry stopped in his throat. Through the delta viewscreen he saw the cloud cover, and an instant later they had punched through it and were streaking away from Phandra.

He closed his eyes and thought of the Oasis Bar and ice cold beers.

Then he thought of Calla, imprisoned somewhere down there, and his stomach turned sickeningly.

"Next stop: New Earth," Kranda said.

TWELVE /// HER FUTURE, FROM NOW ON...

I

MARIA LAY ON her back, buoyed by the salt-rich New Earth ocean, and stared into the sky. She made out the tiny speck of a shuttle approaching the third circuit high above, and realised that she hadn't given her husband a thought for the past few days. In fact, she hadn't given any aspect of her old life much consideration. Even the grief that stabbed her whenever she thought of Ben was diminished here, in the company of Dan Stewart.

It was great to be away from the day-to-day demands of ministering to the healthcare of the liaison team. She had nothing to think about but the blissful present and the near-future, the time when she and Dan would be together for good and wouldn't have to sneak off on these stolen, clandestine trysts.

A Sail wafted above the ocean and for a moment became a paper-thin ellipse as it turned sideways-on. There was something soothing in its stately, floating progression from sea to land; it rose on a thermal, presenting its entire face to the watchers below as if putting on a show especially for their benefit. She wondered what it might be like to hitch a ride across the ocean, as Hendry and the others had done two hundred years ago.

"Maria! Drink?"

Dan was standing on the beach, holding up a long glass. She swam to the shore until her knees butted the fine sand, then fought the sea and stood.

Dan watched her stride from the waves and smiled. "Venus," he said appreciatively.

"Wasn't she blonde?" Maria asked.

"Maybe, but not as beautiful."

"Flatterer!" she laughed, flicking water at him. She took her ice-cold lager and settled beside him in the shade of a parasol.

"I was thinking about what you said the other day," she said. "About the Mahkan."

"What did I say?"

"You were telling me about our spy and the tame Mahkan," she said. "It made me wonder why they're so hostile towards us."

He shrugged. "You've got to understand their mind-set, Maria. They're a strange race. Bellicose, at least historically. Their homeworld was apparently a savage, dog-eat-dog place. They transported something of that across the light years, culturally and genetically. And that bellicosity has been tempered only a little by the influence of the Builders." He grunted a laugh. "I have a theory: the Builders only gave the job of engineers to the Mahkan to keep them out of trouble. That might not be strictly true, of course – they're damned fine engineers into the bargain."

"But are they hostile to all races, or just us humans in particular?"

"Probably all, but specifically us because they see the human race as inherently weak. Also – and this is supposition – they resent our role as Peacekeepers. Probably think they could do a better job."

He propped himself up on an elbow and looked at her. "You said Jeff once saved…"

She pulled a face, irritated by the mention of her husband. "Hard though it is to believe, he did once save a Mahkan's life."

Dan smiled. "That doesn't quite square with the picture of him you've painted. Dull, apathetic, lazy…"

"That's just around me," she said. "Anyway, he said it was pure luck he was in the vicinity of the stricken Mahkan craft at the time. All he had to do was match velocities and get from his ship to the Mahkan's."

"That all? Simple. A cake walk." Dan laughed. "You don't get to be a shuttle pilot, running missions between the worlds, if you're an apathetic dullard."

She sat up, frowning as she tried to find the right words in reply. "It's hard to explain. The character he presents to me and to the world is quiet, introverted. He rarely expresses an opinion, or tells me what he's feeling or thinking."

"Was he always like that? Surely not in the early days?"

She reflected. "I think he was. And... and that might have been one of the things that attracted me to him. He was strong, silent. Still waters run deep, kind of thing. But it soon became maddening. And then after what happened to Ben..."

"Some couples find themselves drawn closer together after such a tragedy."

"And others find themselves split apart," she said. "I suppose we became a little closer immediately after the accident, but then..." She shook her head. "Jeff wouldn't talk about what had happened, how he was feeling. He... it was as if he was unable to grieve, as if he just bottled it all up inside him."

He reached out and took her hand. "That must have been hard for you."

She gave him a smile. "It was hell. All I wanted to do was talk, find some... some catharsis, some comfort from him, and he was like a stone. Ungiving."

"It was his way of coping, Maria. Some men are like that."

"It was... selfish, Dan. Insular. He didn't for one moment think about me, about what I needed, what I was going through."

He squeezed her hand. "Did you try to get him to speak about what he was feeling?"

"Hundreds of times, until I realised the futility of it. He just didn't empathise with me. He's... he's one of the most unsympathetic men I've ever met." She looked up and smiled. "But then he doesn't even look into himself, think about what he's feeling. He's one of the least self-analytical people I've ever known, too."

Dan laughed. "He must have some good points?"

"Give me a few days," she said, "and I might think of one."

Impulsively she straddled Dan and pressed her crotch against him, feeling his erection hard against her pubic bone. "Anyway, less of him..."

He smiled, pulled her face down to his, and kissed her.

They returned to their room, made love for the rest of the afternoon, then ate at an outdoor restaurant in the tourist complex next to the sea.

Later, as the sun was going down, Dan led her from the restaurant and along a sea-front walkway. There was a sense of purpose in his stride. "Where are you taking me Dan?"

"Indulge me, Maria."

She laughed. "Don't I always?"

"I hope you won't find this boring..."

She knew what was coming. She'd seen him eyeing a softscreen ad in the foyer of the hotel earlier. A learned Mahkan engineer-academic was giving an informal talk at the resort that evening, entitled, unimaginatively enough, Helix Engineers. It was not normally, to say the least, something she would find remotely entertaining.

But seeing that Dan was interested...

"Boring?" I spent ten years with Jeff, she thought... "Of course not. Let's go along."

The venue of the talk was a community dome which occupied a hill beyond the Builders' ziggurat. Around a hundred people, humans and aliens alike, sat patiently in the auditorium as the resort's Director of Operations introduced the Mahkan, Dr Lien'vyrran.

Maria and Dan took their seats. She found his hand and squeezed.

The engineer, almost three metres tall, dominated the stage as she rose and moved to the dais. "Ladies and gentlemen," she said in the gravelly English, "I am delighted to be here tonight. My talk today will focus on the rudimentary aspects of my people's work as engineers of the Helix..."

Her voice droned on. Maria sank deeper into her seat and closed her eyes. Minutes later she was asleep.

2

THE FOLLOWING AFTERNOON they were enjoying a drink in the hotel's penthouse bar when Dan's wrist-com chimed.

He swore. "This had better be good..." He accessed the call. "Yes?"

From across the table, Maria made out the face of Dan's PA, a young man named Chen Li. She heard him say, "...apologise for the interruption. We're trying to locate Dr Ellenopoulis..."

Dan frowned. "And what on earth makes you think...?" he began.

Chen Li went on, "We've been trying to contact Dr Ellenopoulis directly, but her own com seems to be switched off. I was wondering if you knew of her whereabouts?"

Dan said gruffly, "I am not in the habit of keeping tabs on every member of my team during their vacations, Chen."

"No, sir, of course not..." But something in the PA's tone suggested that he knew about Dan and Maria.

"Who needs to speak to her?" Dan asked.

"Someone from the Governor's office, sir. They said it's high priority."

High priority, she thought. But who might want to contact her from the Governor's office?

Dan said, "Well, I suggest you get back to them and suggest they try her com-code again, Chen."

"Very good, sir. I'll do that." Chen cut the connection.

Dan looked across the table at her. "What was all that about? Any idea who – ?"

She shook her head. "I can't begin to imagine..." She tapped the activation code into her wrist-com. "But we'll soon find out."

"Another drink?" he said.

"No. No, let's go for a walk along the coast. You okay with that?"

"Fine. Come on."

They left the hotel and took the littoral walkway, Maria wondering why she was nervous at the thought of the call from the Governor's office.

As ever, the day was warm and sunny. The beach was dotted with holiday-makers, their children splashing in the sea. A dozen Sails were putting on a spectacular aerial display, a synchronised series of swirls and arabesques.

Maria's wrist-com chimed.

"Yes? Dr Maria Ellenopoulis here."

A young woman's face stared up at her from the tiny screen. "Dr Ellenopoulis, I have a priority call for you. One moment while I put you through to Director Reynolds' deputy."

She looked at Dan. "Reynolds' deputy? What the hell?"

A second later the stern face of a middle-aged woman stared out at her. "Dr Ellenopoulis?"

"Speaking."

The woman's eyes flicked beyond Maria, and she said, "Dr Ellenopoulis, I suggest you sit down."

"What is it? What's wrong?"

She experienced a feeling of unreality as Dan steered her to a nearby bench and sat her down. She didn't know why she was feeling like this. With the man she loved by her side, no news could possibly harm her.

The woman said, "I am sorry to have to report that your husband's shuttle came down, in hostile circumstances, on the world of Phandra. This happened over a week ago, but we have only just been cleared by security to report the incident."

She shook her head. "*Came down?*"

The woman smiled in an attempt at sympathy. "Your husband's shuttle crash-landed, Dr Ellenopoulis."

She felt Dan's arm tighten around her shoulders, but at the same time he seemed to be a million miles away.

"And... and Jeff? My husband?"

"We are unable to ascertain at the moment the exact status of the pilot or passengers."

Maria wanted to say, "I don't want you to ascertain his exact status, you bitch. Just tell me if he's alive or dead."

The woman went on, "Of course we are monitoring the situation and will be in contact just as soon as we find out anything more definite."

Maria nodded in silence and cut the connection.

Dan massaged her neck. "I'm sorry."

Maria stared into the distance, across the ocean, and tried to assess her feelings. Jeff had crash-landed in his shuttle... what were the chances of his surviving that? Very low? Nil?

In all likelihood, Jeff was dead – and how did she feel about that?

Dan said, "I'll drive you back to Carrelliville."

She surprised herself by saying, "No!" She shook her head and smiled at him. "No. I mean, there's nothing I can do there, is there? I'd rather be here, with you."

"If you're sure."

"Sure I'm sure. Come on, let's walk."

Later, back at the hotel, they had an early dinner and returned to their room. Dan was quiet, considerate, obviously concerned for her. She led him across to the bed and kissed him, slowly at first, and then with mounting passion. They made love savagely, unlike all the previous times, and she wondered if she were doing this to prove something.

She said, as they lay in the sweaty aftermath of their exertions, "I love you, Dan. I love you more than anything. You matter to me more than..." She stopped herself, then went on. "More than anything."

Later still, as Dan slept, she slipped from the bed and padded across to the window. She sat on the window-seat and stared out across the ocean, glittering in the ring-light.

In all likelihood, her husband was dead, killed horribly in a shuttle accident, not long after they had parted so bitterly.

She looked into her heart, and tried to find the stirrings of grief there. But it was as if her quotient of that emotion had been used up, spent on the death of her son, and there was none left for the man she had come, over the years, to despise.

And, she wondered, if he had managed to survive the crash-landing? What then?

She returned to bed and held Dan to her.

She knew what she would do if Jeff had survived and returned to New Earth: she would confront him with the truth, tell him that she had found someone else, someone she loved very much, and that their marriage was over.

Her future, from now on, was with Dan Stewart.

Thirteen /// To D'rayni

I

CALLA STILL HAD the shocking image of the executed barge woman lodged in her head, many hours after the event. She knew that it would be a memory that would stay with her until the end of her days: the image of the Sporelli soldier casually aiming his weapon, firing at the innocent woman, and then cynically wiping the toe of his boot – smeared with the woman's brains – on her smock.

Calla had been one with the woman in the seconds leading up to her death, sensing her disbelief and sudden shock at what was about to happen. And then sudden emptiness, as the bargee's consciousness fled to another place, to Fahlaine.

Then Jeff Ellis had acted, and attacked the Sporelli soldier, and Calla had found what happened then almost as shocking as the woman's death, as the soldiers attacked him with their rifles and he'd fallen to the cobbles.

The Sporelli had bundled her from the square, slung her in the back of a waiting truck with other Phandran Healers, and driven her away at speed.

For the duration of the journey, which lasted for hours until sunset, she told herself that their parting had been foretold, and she reminded herself of what Diviner Tomar had told her – that she and Ellis would at some point be reunited. She would go through much hardship, both mental and physical, but she would overcome it. It was a comforting, reassuring thought, as night fell and the truck rattled and bounced over an uneven track.

Until now she had been aware only of her own thoughts as she went through the events of the past few hours. She registered the presence of other Phandrans peripherally, other Healers rounded up like her, but she worked at keeping her thoughts calm, telling herself that she would survive what was to follow, that her safety and eventual reunion with Jeff Ellis was assured. Now, however, she sensed distress in the mind of one of her fellow Healers, a young boy just a year out of the seminary.

She turned to him in the half-light of the truck. "Try not to be afraid," she said. "The Sporelli will not harm us."

In the twilight, she saw the boy's brave smile.

Another Healer, a shadowy figure at the front of the truck, said, "How do you know that? They've killed hundreds of us so far, thousands for all I know."

She turned to the voice, registered the despair in his mind. He had witnessed the murder of someone who just days ago he had healed. She said, "They have killed many of our kind, but they want us, Healers, to tend to their injured. Therefore they will not harm us."

"And when we've tended to their injured, and they have no further use for us? What then?"

"Then eventually... Fahlaine awaits us," she said.

The boy stared at her. "I sense... Diviner Tomar, he told you that you would overcome suffering and travel far," he whispered.

She smiled at him. "Your ability is powerful," she said, "for one so young."

Someone else said, "I sense that you and... and an alien, a *human*... Your destinies are linked, or so you've been told."

This occasioned excitement among the half a dozen Phandrans in the back of the truck. "Tell us more..."

So she told them what Diviner Tomar had told her about the human, Jeff Ellis, and how she would travel to another world on the Helix, and she was gratified that her account served to increase the morale of her fellow prisoners.

Dawn was slicing long bloody gashes across the horizon when the truck stopped and a Sporelli soldier shouted at them to climb out. They were on the coast, with the ocean a calm pewter vastness. She shuffled away from the truck with her fellow Phandrans. A flat compound stretched away for kilometres, encompassed by a tall wire fence. A hundred black ground vehicles came and went from the compound. Columns of soldiers marched up the ramps of waiting fliers, which then rose into the air and lumbered low across the ocean towards D'rayni.

A soldier shouted at the Phandrans in their own language, "Move! Get into the flier!" and gestured with his rifle towards a hunched, black shape which squatted on the tarmac like an overgrown insect.

Calla sent a probe towards the soldier, but met only the resistance of an alien mind. She sensed something almost corresponding to emotions, but they were of a shape and colour wholly unfamiliar to her, and his thoughts were as unreadable as a foreign language.

They hurried towards the vehicle and the young Healer trotted alongside Calla and found her hand. She squeezed reassuringly and sought to transmit tranquil thoughts.

They climbed a ramp into the belly of the flier and found a dozen other Healers squatting there in silence. She sat on the floor with her back against cold metal, gripped the boy's hand and worked to muffle her thoughts. Around her, the other more experienced Healers were doing the same. In such a confined space, the presence of a dozen Healers, and their attendant mind-noise, could prove discomfiting.

The flier made a low grumbling noise which grew in volume. The vehicle shook and rattled, then lurched as it left the ground. Several Phandrans cried out in alarm, and Calla found herself holding onto the boy with her right hand and, with her left, gripping a spar affixed to the wall as the flier tipped alarmingly and banked out over the sea.

Through a strip window in the back of the flier she watched the coastline of Phandra, and the distant jagged mountains of the interior, grow ever more distant.

She wondered if she would ever set eyes on her homeworld again. Diviner Tomar had not mentioned that.

2

SOON THE THIN, distant filament of Phandra's coastline was lost to sight and Calla felt a cold weight lodge itself in her stomach.

She found herself thinking about the human, Jeff Ellis, and their time together.

Had she been told, beforehand, that she would come to know an alien so well, would come to feel kinship and even affection for someone so different from her and her kind, then she would have been disbelieving. She had found the human very strange at first, the product of an environment she had no hope of understanding, his emotions alien to her. And then, as the days passed and she tended him around the clock, his emotions became a little less alien, a little more comprehensible.

There was a contradiction at his heart, though, and one she found hard to comprehend. She read his anger, the latent aggression that lived just beneath the surface of his psyche – which to her and her kind was an unknown emotion. However, as she came to know him better, she came also to appreciate his innate gentleness. He abhorred violence, knew it to be a sickness that not only injured the victims but also corrupted the perpetrator.

She had looked into his psyche, come to understand his grief, and how that grief had soured his relationship with his mate; and she had spoken to him, tentatively, as to what he might do about that, if he ever had the chance.

She wondered if it were these experiences that were responsible for all his anger.

Towards the end of their time together, she had found herself feeling closer to Jeff Ellis, an alien, than she had to any other living being. And she had come to a strange understanding: that, despite their differences, Phandran and human were very much alike. She wondered also if the same was true of her people and the Sporelli.

The flier carried her across the sea to D'rayni, and she comforted herself with the thought of her predicted reunion with Jeff Ellis. As they climbed, the cold became intense.

Hours later she glanced through the strip window and saw that they had left the ocean far behind. They were flying over an iron-grey land now, and snow flurried from a leaden sky. So this was D'rayni, home to a rough, squat people she had only ever heard Phandran sea-traders talk about: they were a people toughened by their severe environment, she had heard, ugly of body and even uglier of mind.

She huddled next to the young boy, and an older woman to her left, and gained warmth from their bodies.

Later she managed, despite her uncomfortable position seated against the wall, to snatch a little sleep.

She was awoken some time later by a startling sound.

She came upright with a cry, yanked from dreams of childhood, riding on the back of a somnolent rurl with her father. The other Phandrans in the darkened hold were crying out in alarm too, and the flier lurched like a toy boat in a torrential river. Something exploded close by, and through a sidescreen she saw a bright orange flash.

Were the D'rayni attempting to repel the invaders, she wondered, or was this some kind of atmospheric storm unknown on her world?

The flier tilted, and through the slit screen she made out a stretch of flat land far below. Down there, tiny against the featureless grey plain, she made out a line of military machines. From time to time they spat fire, which then exploded around the Sporelli flier.

They were under fire from D'rayni ground forces.

She closed her eyes and said to herself, "I survive hardships both physical and mental, and I will be reunited with the human, Jeff Ellis."

The barrage seemed to last for an age, though she knew that perhaps only minutes had elapsed. Then they passed through the turmoil and into a sudden calm, which seemed almost silent at first and then was filled by the droning of the flier's engines.

An hour passed, and at last the flier lost height. Calla peered through the sidescreen and made out a severe, ice-bound landscape, patched with forest here and there, but for the most part bare and rocky. As she watched, the lights of a town came into view, forlorn in the surrounding greyness.

The flier landed and the Phandran prisoners braced themselves collectively for the ordeal which awaited them. After long minutes of silence the rear hatch clattered open and the ramp banged down onto stone. A guttural Sporelli ordered them out, and wearily they climbed to their feet and shuffled down the ramp.

They were in a compound surrounded by a wall which was topped by two lines of bright blue light. The flier stood before an ugly, rectangular building with barred windows set along its length. She wondered if this was to be their prison, for the time being, until they were transferred to the battle-front. Or was this the battle-front?

A guard shouted at them to move into the building. Calla led the way inside, still gripping the young boy's hand.

The dimly lit interior was bare but for a brazier situated in the middle of the floor. They hurried over to it and huddled round, warming frozen limbs and fingers.

Behind them, the door clanked shut and was locked.

Calla moved away from the others and walked around the building, inspecting the barred windows. An icy wind blew in, and all she could see was the surrounding grey wall topped by the bright blue lines of light.

She was in a prison in a cold and distant land – and yet Diviner Tomar had reassured her that she would be reunited, at some point, with Jeff Ellis.

At the moment, that was very hard to believe.

She returned to her fellow Healers huddling around the brazier.

3

NOTHING HAPPENED FOR an hour, and the waiting was the worst part of the ordeal.

The bone-aching cold seemed to increase, despite the brazier. They huddled in a seated circle around the fluted iron dome, first attempting to warm their fronts, and then turning to warm their backs. At one point the door at the far end of the room opened. They looked up together. A Sporelli soldier slipped in, locked the door behind him, and stood to attention, pointedly ignoring the prisoners.

A little later, a woman climbed to her feet and approached the alien. She appeared ridiculously small as she stood before him, peering up at his impassive blue face.

She spoke a few words in Phandran, then supplemented them by raising her fingers to her mouth repeatedly in the gesture for food. The guard snapped something at her. The woman spoke again, and again brought her small fingers to her lips.

At this, the guard lashed out, backhanding the woman across the face. She cried out and reeled away. Calla was on her feet, rushing over to the woman and escorting her back to the brazier. She laid the woman on the ground and inspected her face: the blow might not have been a terribly forceful one, but Phandran bones were delicate. The woman's jaw was broken.

Calla closed her eyes and touched the woman's face, and, joined by another Healer who took the injured woman's hand, murmured a Healing litany. Calla sent the woman into a deep sleep, the better to ease the pain and aid the healing process.

An hour later the door opened again and a Sporelli soldier entered carrying two large flagons of icy water and a bucket filled with coarse grey bread.

They ate hungrily. For all that the bread was rough and tasteless, and the water brackish, Calla was grateful for the meagre sustenance.

Later, as they sat round the brazier which now seemed to produce little or no heat, the first of her fellows fell sick. The young boy she had comforted on the flight here groaned and rolled over, emptying the contents of his stomach across the floor. A minute later an old man did the same. Calla felt her own belly cramp, but fought the pain. She suspected the water was responsible, though the bread might have harboured bacteria just as harmful.

Those Phandrans not stricken aided the others, sent them into deep sleeps, and worked to quell the grumbling in their own bellies.

She was sleeping, a while later, when the door crashed open and a dozen Sporelli soldiers burst into the prison. Calla sat up, disoriented, and saw that the soldiers were carrying stretchers.

Four injured Sporelli were ferried across to the brazier and set down on the floor, and one of the stretcher-bearers snapped a command to the staring Phandrans.

Calla approached the closest injured soldier and winced at what she saw.

The Sporelli was naked from the waist up, and his stomach had been bound tight in a bandage now soaked in blood, suggesting that the wound was still open underneath. Calla looked up at the nearest soldier and said, "We are Healers, not surgeons…"

More Sporelli entered the prison, these bearing medical supplies which they deposited next to their injured comrades. Clearly none among them were qualified to treat the wounded. She wondered if they had come under surprise attack nearby and she and her fellow Healers were the only immediate option.

She organised the Healers, dividing them into teams of three or four to treat each Sporelli soldier. She had performed simple surgery before, and so had two other older Phandrans, and the three of them treated the worst injuries as best they were able with unfamiliar Sporelli equipment.

The soldiers were young, and as Calla worked she reminded herself that despite what these people had done on her world, she had a duty towards her injured charges.

She and two other healers worked on the soldier with the lacerated stomach. They replaced the innards that had spilled, stitched the muscle and then the flesh, doing their best to clean the wound. The soldier had lost a lot of blood, and there was nothing they could do about that, but after their ministrations he was in a better condition than before. There was, she thought, a possibility that he might live.

She sent him to sleep and did her best to soothe his pain. It did not help that he was alien, that she could not enter his mind and effect more radical care. Had he been Phandran, she would have melded with him, given him some of her own strength, and he would have stood a greater chance of pulling through.

The three other soldiers were not as severely injured, suffering bullet wounds to limbs. Her fellows treated the injuries with a combination of Phandran healing techniques and Sporelli medical equipment, and the chances were that they would survive.

Calla stood and approached a watching soldier, aware of what had happened to the previous Phandran who had dared to address a Sporelli. She gestured to the brazier, and asked if there was any way – for the sake of the injured troops – that they might increase the heat.

She had no illusion that the soldier might understand her words, but the meaning behind them was obvious, she hoped.

The Sporelli turned away and spoke one of his fellows, who hurried from the room.

Fifteen minutes later the brazier gurgled, and heat radiated from its ugly flutes. The warmth cocooned the sorry group, and her fellow Healers murmured their thanks to Calla.

She sat cross-legged beside her injured charge and laid a hand lightly on his chest, closing her eyes and concentrating on the life-force flowing through the alien.

A short while later she was surprised to hear a single, spoken phrase. "Thank you..."

She opened her eyes in surprise. The soldier was looking up at her. She said, "You speak our language?"

"I am a... translator," he replied in badly accented Phandran.

"Rest," she told him, "and you will be well."

He made a facial gesture similar to the one Jeff Ellis had used, a quick lifting of the lips to denote pleasure. A smile, Jeff had called it.

She said at length, "Why have your people invaded my world and this one?"

The soldier blinked, then said, "Because... our leader said it was our destiny. We were sent here to bring liberation to D'rayni. The people here... they live under..." – he searched for the word – "harsh conditions. They are impoverished, often starving. Under the rule of our leader, they would live better lives."

She inclined her head, and said softly, "Is that why the D'rayni attacked you?" and she gestured at his injured comrades.

He stared up at her. "They were mistaken. They were acting on orders from leaders who did not know the truth – that we came to liberate them. Their leaders... they want only to retain power."

She considered his words, and wondered how much the soldier knew about the truth of his situation. "And why did your people invade my world?"

"We did not invade Phandra," he said, "we merely crossed it in order to reach D'rayni."

"You killed many of my people, innocent villagers, men, women and children. I saw the carnage with my own eyes."

"Then... we must have met opposition, and fought to save ourselves."

She felt despair open like a pit within her. "We did not oppose your invasion," she said. "We did not fight you. We are a peaceable people." She paused, then said, "Some of your soldiers were looking for an alien from another world, and in order to find him you threatened my people, and killed them."

"I know nothing of this. I only know what our leader told us, that we are here to help the people of D'rayni, and that in time we will rule the world and make it as successful as our own."

Calla murmured, more to herself than to the deluded soldier, "I pity you."

An hour elapsed, and then the door opened once again and three Sporelli strode into the prison. They spoke briefly to the guard, who led them across to the injured troops. Calla watched as the trio examined the injured men with unfamiliar instruments and strange devices, and she wondered if these people were Sporelli medics; Healers, in their own way.

They spoke among themselves, then looked at the Phandran Healers.

At her side, the soldier murmured to Calla, "They are… surprised at the level of your… success."

Calla inclined her head. "We treat everyone with the same degree of care, even people who have invaded our land, and killed innocent men, women and children."

One of the Sporelli medics barked an order, and the guards lifted the stretchers and carried the injured soldiers from the building. Calla's charge smiled at her and lifted a hand briefly in farewell, and she inclined her head and watched as they carried him away.

The door was locked behind them, and the lone guard stood by the door, clutching his rifle and watching the Phandrans with what might have been new respect.

Calla returned to ministering to the needs of the sick among her own people.

FOURTEEN /// CONFRONTATION

ELLIS STOOD BEFORE the picture window of his A-frame and stared out at the waters of the Great Western Lake. He had a beer in his hand, the house behind him was silent and empty, and he found it hard to believe that just two days ago he'd been fleeing the Sporelli on Phandra.

He drained his beer and moved through the house. Despite its familiarity, it felt like a stage-set, his possessions taking on an unreal quality in light of recent experiences.

On the coffee table in the lounge he came across a holo-cube of Maria and himself, taken on holiday shortly after they'd met: it showed a younger version of himself, and a beautiful, raven-haired woman in her early twenties. He touched the surface, and the younger version of himself laughed at something Maria had said, back then, and smiled out at Ellis. Maria had pulled him to her and planted a big wet kiss on his lips, telling him how much she loved him. He touched the cube again, stopping it. The image froze, showing them locked in intimacy. Sickened, he touched it again, allowing it to play on, and only when the scene panned away from them and across the sea did he freeze the image. He had placed the holo-cube in a drawer, out of sight, more than once over the past year, but Maria had always retrieved it – as if, he thought, taunting him with this reminder of how things once were. Now he left it where it was on the coffee table, no longer playing the game by allowing her to see how much the images hurt.

He recalled what Calla had said on Phandra about his relationship with his wife.

Maria would be back tomorrow. Two days ago she had left a message on the com-system, saying that there had been 'complications' at her end. He wondered what 'complications' might be a euphemism for, and tried to banish images of his wife and Dan Stewart from his mind's eye.

When she did get back, he decided, he would confront her, admit his failings and tell her that things must change.

He came to the bedroom and leaned in the doorway. Maria had never been the tidiest of people – she mocked his penchant for order and organisation as proof of his anal-retentive tendencies – and a collection of her clothing was strewn across the bed and the polished wooden floor like the debris of a whirlwind. He tried to recollect the last time they had actually shared the bed: a month ago, maybe longer, when their routines had accidentally intersected – and they had last made love perhaps six months earlier, a loveless coming together dictated by the degree of his need and her reluctant willingness to accede. He could not help contrasting the state of their relationship with how it had been in the early days, and he closed his eyes in sudden pain and pushed himself away from the door-frame.

He crossed to the kitchen, fetched another beer from the cooler and stepped out onto the veranda.

It was midday on a beautiful summer Saturday, and pleasure boats were out in force on the glittering surface of the lake. He watched them idly for a while, polychromatic slivers riding the wind that blew across the lake. Earlier that day he'd called Michael, a friend and colleague from the shuttle service, only to find that he'd left on a routine flight to Agstarn and would be away for six days.

This was his first free time since arriving back on New Earth. For two days he'd undergone endless debriefings and medical checks. The former had been exhaustive, conducted by a grim-faced government official who seemed to take the line that, until proved otherwise, the crash-landing on Phandra had been Ellis's fault. Only with his detailed description of the subsequent events, and his recounting of the Sporelli invasion, did the official's manner relax, as if Ellis's first-hand account of the aggression tallied with government intelligence.

When the official dismissed him, Ellis had remained in his seat and asked, "I'd like to know just what the authorities intend to do about the situation on Phandra."

The official had busied himself with his com-screen, not even looking at Ellis. "The situation is still in its... formative stages, let's say. We have a council meeting in a couple of days, and we'll discuss your account along with the little intelligence we have gathered thus far." The official had looked up. "Is there anything else, Mr Ellis?"

He had half a mind to ask why the council had not convened an extraordinary meeting, in light of the unparalleled events on Phandra, but had known the official would merely stonewall him.

The gears of government, and the even larger gears of the peacekeeping force, ground slowly. Nothing he could say would urge them to precipitate action.

By comparison to the debriefing, the medical examination had been rapid. An hour after feeding Ellis through the body-scanner, the medic had said, "For a man whose ribs were broken in three places, and who'd suffered a fractured femur, you're in remarkable condition. Those fairy Healers sure know a trick or two."

Only then, after the debriefing and medical examination, had he been allowed to speak to the press.

He had expected a riotous press-conference, with the networks eager to put their respectively lurid and sensationalist slant on his experiences. He was surprised to find himself interviewed by a single representative of the government-run broadcaster, who had asked a series of anodyne questions – clearly sanctioned by the government official – and switched off her needle after fifteen minutes. Interview over.

That evening he'd tuned into the eight o'clock broadcast. News of the crash-landing, not to mention Sporelli hostilities, had not aired. The latest on the diplomatic crisis between two second circuit worlds, and a lengthy report on the skyball semi-finals, but nothing at all about the brutal Sporelli invasion of Phandra.

He'd checked every hour the following day, with the same result: nothing.

He wondered if the Peacekeepers were planning a strike, and a news black-out was a security ploy.

He was about to leave the house and head down to the Oasis Bar for lunch when his com-screen chimed. He moved through to the lounge and activated the wallscreen. No image showed, but a voice said, "Jeff?"

Maria...

He slumped onto a lounger, glad that she had elected not to show herself. "Activate." He would keep it sound only, too.

"Jeff, are you there?"

"Here," he said, heart thudding.

"I... I heard about what happened, the crash and the rescue. I hope you're okay."

"I'm fine."

"Good." A long pause. He imagined her biting her bottom lip as she considered her next words. "Look, we need to talk."

"Fine. When are you coming home?"

"I... I won't be, Jeff."

"I thought you said..." he began.

"I did. But that was then. Look, we need to talk."

"Fine," he said again, taking a swallow of beer. "We're talking."

"Not like this, for godsake. I mean, we need to meet. There's a lot we have to discuss. I've been thinking."

He thought of what Calla had told him, to meet Maria, talk over their relationship. Be honest with her.

He nodded, more accustomed to being seen when talking over the com-net. He remembered himself and said, "Okay."

"I'll pick you up in... say, an hour?"

"Pick me up?"

"We'll go for a drive into the country..."

He let the silence stretch, then said, "Okay. See you in an hour."

He cut the connection before she could respond. His heart was pounding and his hands, he realised, were clammy with sweat.

He fetched a beer from the cooler, then sat in silence and contemplated the imminent meeting with Maria.

2

HE SHOULD HAVE known not to, but he made to kiss her as he slipped into the passenger seat. She turned her head, offering her cheek instead of her lips, a gesture she had taken to performing increasingly over the years. Like a fool he went through with the action, and kissed her cheek.

She pulled away from the A-frame and drove around the lake.

"Where are we going?" he asked, glancing at her. As ever, he was reminded of the woman he had married, ten years ago, a woman very different to this one.

"Like I said, into the country."

He sat back, staring out at the passing domes and A-frames of this gardened residential area.

"I thought... When I found out about the crash, I feared you'd be badly injured."

Before he could stop himself, he said, "Would you have cared?" and felt an immediate stab of regret.

From the corner of his eye he saw her long fingers tighten on the apex of the wheel. He imagined the compression of her lips, the anger in her brown eyes.

"As a matter of fact, yes. You might not believe it, but I still feel something for you."

"You have a strange way of showing it."

He glanced at her, and he was right: anger flared in her eyes. "Meaning?" she snapped.

"Meaning, why the hell are you running after that bastard Stewart if you feel anything at all for me?"

"Black and white," she said.

He stared at her. "*What?*"

"That's what everything is with you, isn't it, Jeff? Black and white. Right and wrong. Nothing in between. No shades of grey. No moral ambiguity."

"I don't know what the hell you're talking about." He squeezed his eyes shut in impotent frustration. Why was it that whenever they spoke she always twisted his words, or failed to comprehend his meaning?

"No," she smiled. "No, you wouldn't, would you? That's one of the reasons I no longer feel for you what I did, back in the early days."

His stomach turned. "What do you mean?"

"You've changed. You no longer talk, no longer discuss the... the meanings of *things*. Everything's is so clear-cut in your world. Like I said, black and white."

"I haven't changed, Maria. I'm the same person. It's your perception of me that's changed."

She sighed in exasperation and accelerated.

The silence simmered between them.

He said, "Where are we going?"

"The country."

They were heading along the western highway towards Cartwright Park.

He felt a sudden welling of panic. "No. You can't do this. Stop the fucking car and let me out!"

She turned to him, and what he saw in her eyes was shocking: not the hatred of earlier, but something very much like compassion.

"No, Jeff. I'm not stopping the car. You're not getting out until we get there. You need to face this."

He moaned and closed his eyes. He'd rather not see the passing countryside, the rolling hills of the parkland he found so painful. He'd not come this way for years; it was one of the ways he coped.

"Why are you doing this?" He still had his eyes tight shut, willing himself not to weep.

"Because it's necessary, Jeff."

She fell silent, and he kept his eyes shut for the next few minutes until the car slowed, turned, crunched over gravel, and finally came to a stop.

The engine cut out and ticked as it cooled.

He sensed Maria, watching him.

He heard the door crack and the squeak of seat plastic as she climbed out, then the crunch of her boots on gravel. She rounded the car, opened the passenger door, and said, "Get out, Jeff."

He opened his eyes. They were in the car-park next to the picnic area, surrounded by tall pine trees. He averted his eyes from the stand of trees to the right and climbed from the car.

She led him from the car-park to the area of tables and benches, and sat down. He sat across from her, his back to the trees, and regarded her across the slatted timber table-top.

Fortunately, they were alone; fortunately, there were no children playing nearby.

He said, "What do you want?"

He looked up at her, and he was shocked to see tears filming her eyes. He felt a sudden stab of guilt.

She said simply, "To talk, Jeff. Simply to talk." She reached out and gripped his hands and held on tightly, as if preventing his escape. "We never talked about what happened here, Jeff. I wanted to, but you just erased it. As if it never happened."

He nodded, sour reflux blocking his throat. "Self-preservation," he managed.

"Unhealthy," she said. "It's unhealthy to bottle things up. In order to grieve, you need to share the pain, not make it worse by never addressing it."

He said, "How... how could I begin to talk to you, share the pain, when you blamed me?"

She squeezed his hand. "I never –" she began.

He interrupted. "You said... You said, in the hospital... You said, 'Why did you turn away?'"

"I was in shock. I didn't know what I was saying. I don't blame you."

He stared at her, whispered, "I didn't know that, then."

"Oh, Jeff, Jeff." She massaged the back of his hand, pressing urgently with her thumb.

"Do you think," he said, "that it might have come to this, had Ben lived?"

She narrowed her eyes. "This?"

"Our being so far apart, so distant? We would have had a common interest. We would have made the best of things, for Ben."

She smiled sadly. "I don't know. I sometimes think you wanted to get away from us, not long after Ben was born."

A month ago, before meeting the alien called Calla, he might have argued the point. Now he was beyond anger. He said, "You were distant after the birth. You didn't want me. It was as if you just... withdrew your affection. You had Ben, you'd got what you wanted."

"That's not fair!"

"It's what I felt." He stared at her. "Am I wrong?"

"I... I don't know what happened, Jeff. I no longer... Things changed. I didn't feel for you what I'd felt earlier, and I honestly don't know why that was."

"And then what happened here..." He stopped.

Be honest, Jeff, Calla had told him.

"After what happened here..." he said. "Do you know what I felt, mixed up with all the grief and... and the hatred of you for blaming me? I felt that now I could get away from the woman who no longer loved me."

He looked up at her, saw silver tears coursing down her cheeks.

"Maybe we should have split up then," she said. "Instead of playing games, trying to pretend that things were normal."

He felt the tree at his back, a pressing weight, but he could not bring himself to turn around and look at it.

He stared at Maria and said, "Do you know what the worst thing is about losing Ben?"

Biting her bottom lip, she shook her head.

He said, "You spend so much time looking ahead, seeing your child at five, ten, fifteen. You invest emotionally in a future that's out there, a future that's inevitable. You wonder at your relationship with your son when he's twenty, at university or whatever. There are so many possible futures, but the human mind only conjures the very best. And then, something like that happens, and suddenly there is no future, absolutely none at all. And it's impossible, totally and utterly impossible, to express the loss of that future to anyone."

She gripped his hand as if hanging on for dear life, and stared at him through her tears. "Even to me?"

He said, "At the time, yes. It was just too painful to…"

He made a sudden decision and stood up, still gripping her hand. "Jeff?"

"You brought me here. We need to…" He pulled her to her feet. She came around the table and joined him. He took a deep breath and turned to face the stand of pine trees.

He walked across the chipped bark towards the nearest tree, Maria at his side, her arm around him now, and came into its cool shadow.

He fought against the constriction in his throat and said, "I'm sorry, Maria. He was only…" He reached out, touched a bough, only a metre and half from the ground.

He said, "I looked away, for about three seconds. That's all it was, Maria. Three seconds. He was climbing, so happily… I was standing about there, over there, a few metres away. If I hadn't turned away."

Ben had been four, only four years old…

They held each other, her face against his chest, and wept.

"I heard him cry out when he slipped, but by the time I turned, he was already…"

Ben was lying on the floor in a posture so still that it was hard to believe that he wasn't sleeping. He'd known, instantly, that his son was dead, his neck broken, that no amount of resuscitation would restore him to life, even though he and Maria tried ceaselessly, turn and turn about, in mounting desperation, until the medics' copter arrived seven minutes later and eased him aside and confirmed what he knew to be a fact.

If only he'd not looked away, to where Maria was bending over the picnic table, arranging lunch, beautiful in the sunlight.

Then the sudden cry: "Daddy!"

And, later, in the hospital, Maria had said, mired in her own shock and incipient grief, "Why did you look away, Jeff?"

Three seconds, an errant glance, a life extinguished.

Maria led him away from the tree, and they emerged from its enveloping shade into bright sunlight. They walked through the picnic area until they came to the river and paused, side by side, staring at its glittering width in the late afternoon sunlight.

He said, "What now?"

She looked up at him, a question in her eyes.

"You brought me here to talk. We've talked. And now you want to..." He almost said, 'ask my absolution,' but stopped himself. He went on, "Let's remain friends, okay? We've been through too much just to part and never see each other again."

Silently, she nodded.

He said, "Be honest with me. It is Dan Stewart, isn't it?"

She nodded again.

He smiled, reached out and stroked her hair. "I hope you're happy with him, Maria."

"Oh, Jeff."

They held each other, and he looked over her head at the flowing river, and he experienced a strange sense of release, of long-delayed liberation, which at once filled him with exuberance and something almost like despair.

She said, "Come on, I'll drive you back."

He wanted to be alone with his thoughts for a while, and could not face the confines of his A-frame. "No. I'll call a taxi. I just want to stay here a little longer, okay?"

"You sure?"

He smiled. "I'm sure."

They came together again, in an embrace that seemed to him affectionate, and when she pulled away she was smiling. "There's a party at the Governor's place next week. It would be lovely if you could come along."

"I'll try to make it," he lied, and watched her walk away through the trees. She turned, once, to wave, then disappeared into the distance.

He sat on the bank of the river as the sun went down, then lay on his back and stared up at the sweep of the circuit overhead, which would soon be lost to sight as daylight turned to night.

3

HE SAT ON the veranda of his A-frame and stared out across the lake. He was on his fourth beer and he was feeling mellow. At last the long limbo of uncertainty, the time of not knowing for sure whether Maria was or was not conducting an affair behind his back, was over. He had even unburdened himself, and felt better for it, and in doing so had allowed Maria to leave him without the rancour and recriminations he had thought inevitable.

He was sunk in the luxurious lassitude of self-pity, and told himself to snap out of it. He had always despised self-piteous people in the past, and now he was taking the course of least resistance and giving in to the easy emotion.

He sat up. He'd been granted a month's furlough after the medical check up, and at the time had relished the prospect of so much paid leave. He was not so sure about it now, with nothing to do but drink himself stupid, regret decisions made in the past, and dream about how it might have all been very different with Maria.

He'd go over to the spaceport first thing in the morning, buttonhole Kransky in personnel, and report fit and able for duty.

He was about to fetch another beer from the kitchen when the com-screen chimed. He moved to the lounge.

This time an image appeared on the wall, though it was not Maria's. "Accept," he said.

A reptilian face stared out at him. "Jeff?"

"Kranda, what a surprise." He raised the bottle. "Just having a little drink in celebration. Why don't you join me?"

"That might be difficult, Jeff. I'm on Mahkan. What are you celebrating?"

He thought about it. "The end of my marriage, Kranda."

The alien blinked at him. "We Mahkans celebrate the successful completion of gender union," he said. "I thought humans were monogamous for life?"

"In... in theory, yes, that is so. In some cases. Not all. Not in this case. Maria and I have untied the knot."

"And you're celebrating?"

"Yes. Or drowning my sorrows, I don't really know which, Kranda."

"You are, my friend, talking in riddles." She leaned forward. In the background Ellis made out a grey stone wall and a slit window. "I called to say that, once again, I am in your debt."

Ellis shook his head, confused. "You are?"

"You saved my life on Phandra, Jeff."

"Oh... that."

I killed an innocent – well, perhaps not so innocent – Sporelli soldier, he thought. *Instinctively, in order to save the life of Kranda, and maybe even my own... I killed another sentient being.*

He was still trying to work out how he felt about that.

"What about it?" he asked, taking a long mouthful of beer.

"I am in your debt. *Sophan*. I am honour-bound to pay off that debt."

"Kranda," he laughed. "You're nothing of the kind. Humans don't work like that. Forget it, okay? I won't think any the less of you."

"Humans might not work like that, Jeff. But we Mahkans do. I owe you."

He tried not to smile. "Well, if you insist."

"And I know how to pay off the debt, Jeff."

Ellis leaned forward. "Go on."

"I have been monitoring Sporelli movement on Phandra, with the aid of a high orbit observation station. I concentrated on the coast of the D'rayni sea."

"And?"

"And I discovered where the captured Phandrans, the Healers, were taken."

Ellis pulled the bottle from his lips, slopping beer down his shirt. "Calla..." he said.

"I cannot be certain that the Healer you knew is among the prisoners taken to D'rayni, but I suspect it is a high probability."

"And... are the Phandrans in danger?"

"They are in the company of the Sporelli invaders, Jeff."

Ellis climbed unsteadily to his feet and paced up and down before the wallscreen. "Christ! There's no news here about the Sporelli invasion. Nothing. I had hoped the Peacekeepers might have done something by now."

The Mahkan on the screen pulled back her lips in a humourless grimace. "My guess is that your leaders will do nothing for the time being. They are spineless as the faction that at the moment rules my people. However..."

He stopped pacing and faced the alien. "Yes?"

"However, I have been given to understand that, while Mahkan government action might not be forthcoming, the authorities will turn a blind eye to any individuals acting unilaterally."

"Meaning?"

"Meaning that I will shortly be descending to the surface of D'rayni and attempting to liberate Calla, along with as many other Phandrans as possible, from the Sporelli."

"Alone?"

The Mahkan inclined her long head. "Alone."

At the time Ellis had no idea what made him say, "Take me with you, Kranda."

The alien regarded him in silence for perhaps ten seconds. At last she said, "You would be a liability, human."

Ellis said, "You owe me, Kranda! You said so yourself. So, pay the debt. Let me go with you. I owe Calla, for saving my life. I want to pay off *my* debt to *her*." He blinked, then laughed. "And how dare you say I'd be a liability!"

"Well, human, you would. Unless..."

Ellis approached so close to the screen that the Mahkan's great snout was a pixilated blur. "Unless what, lizard?"

"Unless you were equipped with a varnika – what you call an exo-skeleton. And you would have to be armed, of course, unless that goes against your refined human sensibilities?"

He thought of the exo-skeleton Kranda had worn on Phandra, how near-invincible it had made her. And if he were armed, that did not mean he would be compelled to shoot to kill.

"Very well, I agree."

Kranda was silent for a time, thinking. "If you were equipped with a varnika, and armed... We have a saying on Mahkan: two warriors, one brain. I will need to requisition a varnika small enough for your puny frame, but that should be no problem."

"How do we get down there?"

"I'll commandeer a flier, Jeff, and request landing rights at Carrelliville for eight-hundred hours tomorrow, your time."

"And when we get to D'rayni? Have you thought about how we'll go about liberating the Phandrans?" The very thought was enough to sober him.

"That, my friend, will have to wait until we have assessed the situation on the ground. I will see you tomorrow, Jeff."

She cut the connection.

Ellis sat for a while in stunned silence, wondering if what he had talked Kranda into doing had been at all wise. He told himself that he owed it to Calla, after all, for everything she had done for him. He set the half-finished beer aside: any more and in the morning he'd be in no fit state to go anywhere with Kranda.

He slept fitfully that night, dreams of Maria phasing weirdly into images of the tiny Phandran Healer. At one point he came awake suddenly, wondering if the conversation with Kranda had really happened. He even rolled out of bed, his throat parched, and moved to the lounge. He activated the wallscreen, called up the memory, and ordered it to replay the last communiqué.

Kranda stared out at him, saying, "I'll commandeer a flier, Jeff."

He heard his own reply, as ever hating the sound of his recorded voice, and quickly ordered the wallscreen to close down.

So he hadn't been dreaming, and very soon would be touching down on D'rayni soil.

FIFTEEN /// THE HOLDING STATION

I

THE FLIER TOOK off from Carrelliville spaceport a little after six that morning. Ellis sat back in the co-pilot's seat, instinctively reaching for the controls as they powered away from New Earth. He had a pilot's habitual mistrust of other pilots' capabilities, and felt twitchy at not being in command of the ship.

Behind their seats, hanging from the bulkhead like a pair of skeletons in a dungeon, were the Mahkan varnikas. His own was dwarfed by Kranda's, puny by comparison. Equipped with the exo-skeletons and armed with the latest Mahkan weaponry, they would be a forbidding double-act.

He tried not to dwell on what might lie ahead.

He looked through the side-screen at the bright green rolling countryside of New Earth. To the west was the park where he and Maria had parted yesterday. He wondered where she was now, what she might be doing, then quickly closed down that line of thought.

"Won't the Sporelli be able to detect the flier?"

Kranda drew back her lips. "It's shielded. Their early warning systems shouldn't pick up a thing, and therefore their weapons systems will not detect us."

"That's a relief."

"But even if the Sporelli did detect the flier, I am confident that my skill as a pilot will bring us through unscathed."

Ellis glanced through the hatch to the cabin at the rear. "It's big enough," he said. "I think we could easily carry a couple of dozen Phandrans."

"They are small. We'll be able to cram them in like cayl."

Cayl, Ellis thought: *the Mahkan equivalent of sardines?*

Kranda leaned forward and touched a screen. A map appeared, showing the coastline of a world. "D'rayni," she explained. "The circular pulsing mark indicates the present position of the Phandran detainees. It's a holding station, from where I assume the Healers will be sent out to the front line, or thereabouts. It's fringed by forested hills and crags. This coastline of D'rayni is high, wild land, and relatively cold compared with New Earth."

"Where will we come down?"

"Here, approximately ten kilometres from the small town of Panjaluka and the holding station. You'll test-run your varnika there. After that, I'll try to assess whether we should approach Panjaluka by flier or on foot. With the varnikas, the latter should only take fifteen minutes. And then" – Kranda drew back her lips – "then we will assess the situation at the holding station."

Ellis sat back, staring into the indigo of space between the circuits. "And weapons?"

Kranda indicated the racked rifles beside the exo-skeletons. "Take your pick," she said. "Rest assured, they can all be set to stun, to allay your human squeamishness."

Ellis smiled and closed his eyes. "I'm pleased to hear that, Kranda."

He slipped deeper into his couch and slept.

A while later Kranda nudged him with her elbow; it was probably only meant as a light tap, but Kranda's strength was such that it almost knocked him from the couch. "Wake up, Jeff. We're almost there."

He rubbed his face. "How long have I been out?"

"Four hours. I thought you might want to watch our approach."

He stretched and stared through the viewscreen. They had dropped through the cloud cover above D'rayni and were coming in low over the sea. Ahead, an expanse of white cliffs spanned the horizon. Beyond them, grey mountains rose, bleak and forbidding. Many of the peaks were snow-covered.

"Welcome to D'rayni," Kranda said.

"Doesn't look that welcoming."

"The D'rayni are a tough, rugged people," Kranda told him. "Well-used to hostile conditions. In appearance, they're a little like the people known on Old Earth as Neanderthals."

He glanced at her. "You've read up on human history?"

"And that of many other races besides."

"Well, let's hope that the D'rayni put up a fight against the Sporelli." Kranda shrugged. "They're almost technologically equivalent, but the Sporelli outnumber the D'rayni ten to one. Also, the D'rayni are not well equipped for war."

"That doesn't sound promising."

They came in over the coastline and sailed silently between rearing mountain peaks. It looked cold and lifeless out there, in contrast to the verdant New Earth they had left. He judged they were travelling at around Mach three, but the rugged landscape changed little over the next fifteen minutes.

"What always amazes me, Kranda, is the range of worlds that make up the Helix. Ten thousand of the damned things – and the Builders made them all." He shook his head. "It's beyond human comprehension."

Kranda glanced at him and pulled back her lips. "Beyond *human* comprehension, maybe. But my people are Engineers. The Builders had a long, long time to construct the Helix, Jeff: tens and tens of millennia."

"And each world is so very different, in terms of geology, geography, biology," Ellis said. "The logistics of what they did, the research they must have carried out on the original world before they began the transfer of the citizens..."

"More amazing still," Kranda went on, "more amazing than the geological and biological world-building on the surface, is the engineering accomplishment that lies beneath."

"I can't even begin to imagine..."

"One day, Jeff, I will be honoured to take you on a conducted tour."

Ellis laughed. "I'll hold you to that."

The mountain range fell away before them, becoming a chain of rucked, buckled pewter foothills. Beyond he made out a great forested plateau threaded with silver rivers. In the distance, delineating hillsides and valleys, he saw the lights of towns and villages in the cold, grey dawn. There was nowhere like this on New Earth, nowhere this cold and inhospitable; it reminded him of the documentaries he'd seen of Old Earth and the geography of far northern Europe.

Kranda said, "What's that?"

Ellis started. "Where?"

Kranda pointed a taloned finger to the right of the viewscreen. Ellis made out a white streak on the horizon, as if a diamond had scored the leaden sky.

"It's fast," Kranda said. "Too fast." She read something from a screen before her, then looked up. "Look at it go. It must be travelling at Mach ten, at least."

They tracked its progress across the sky before them; in seconds it had travelled half the width of the viewscreen. Kranda read from her screen. "It's moving at a little over Mach eleven, Jeff."

Fear rose suddenly in his throat.

"The thing is," Kranda went on, "the Sporelli don't possess that kind of technology. Fliers, yes. But not hypersonic craft."

He glanced at the Mahkan. "Could it belong to another race, allied to the Sporelli?"

Kranda lifted the side of her lips to reveal a row of sharp incisors. The Mahkan version of a worried frown? "I very much doubt it. There are no races along this circuit of the Helix who are as technologically advanced as the Sporelli, and my flier would have alerted me to any traffic *between* the circuits."

"So?"

"So, though it pains me to admit as much, my people have badly misjudged the Sporelli, if they posses this level of technology."

As they watched, something streaked away from the craft above the far horizon. Two scintillating points of light fell at an acute angle, heading towards the ground.

"What the hell?" Ellis said.

"They can only be..."

The lights impacted with the horizon, bursting with actinic explosions.

"Missiles," Kranda finished.

Ahead, on the horizon, a city burned. Ellis watched as the supersonic craft passed from sight.

"My worry is," Kranda said, "if they have this kind of technology, which we failed to detect, then might they posses that which renders the shuttle's shields useless?"

Ellis said nothing, thinking the question rhetorical.

"Though perhaps I am being overly pessimistic, my friend."

A few minutes later, Kranda called his attention to the screen. The pulsing dot of the holding station and the arrow which denoted their own shuttle were almost one – and in the distance Ellis made out a small town of squat, stone-built dwellings surrounded by forest. Though the sun was up, the cloud cover was such that the town still maintained its street-lighting.

He looked for signs of Sporelli occupancy, but saw none.

"Panjaluka," Kranda said. "I'll bring us down a few kays away, to err on the side of caution."

Minutes later she eased the flier down vertically, with a deftness of touch Ellis found himself admiring. The heat of the flier's engines ignited trees and shrubs, lending the only splash of light to the scene beyond the viewscreen. Even the foliage of the surrounding trees, he noted, appeared to be varying shades of grey.

They bumped down and Kranda cut the engines.

2

BEFORE DONNING THE exo-skeleton, Ellis pulled on a black skin-tight garment like a wetsuit. Then he stood on the deck of the cabin, legs apart and arms splayed, as per Kranda's instructions, as the Mahkan laid the smaller varnika on the floor behind him. Ellis twisted and looked over his shoulder. The exo-skeleton stretched across the deck like some macabre, wasted shadow.

"This is going to feel very strange at first," Kranda said, kneeling behind Ellis and affixing something to his heels. He felt cold metal grip his ankle. Then it was as if a series of hard metal fingers was climbing his legs with a sensation that was almost painful.

He peered over his shoulder and was surprised to see that Kranda was not assisting the varnika's attachment: the device was working by itself, climbing up his thighs, clamping his hips, zipping itself to his body like a swift, sentient cage. Carbon spars and filaments looped themselves around his ribs and braced his neck; something moulded itself around his head like a balaclava.

Kranda said, "Prepare yourself for a sharp –"

He felt a stinging pain as a needle punctured the skin at the base of his skull. "What the hell!"

"– sting." Kranda finished. "Don't be alarmed, Jeff. It's the interface. The sensors anticipate your every action and route the command to the varnika's servo-mechanisms. Don't move for a minute while the smartcore adjusts itself to your autonomic nervous system."

"I'll do my best," he said, wondering at the extent of the varnika's clinical intrusion.

He breathed in and out, feeling the varnika's struts move with him. At the end of the minute he looked down to see a reticulation of carbon filaments encasing his hands like a spidery web. Experimentally he flexed his fingers, forming a fist, and the spars moved with his fingers.

Kranda said, "The varnika will enhance your perceptions, increasing the power of your eyesight and hearing, making your reactions faster. This will be a little disconcerting at first. Expect to feel nauseous for a few minutes. Okay. Now, take a small step, then another. Move towards me slowly. Your balance might be affected to begin with, but don't panic or try too hard to compensate. The varnika will ensure you do not fall."

Ellis took a breath and moved his right foot. He had expected it to be like learning to walk again after a period of convalescence, but the reality was that he experienced no difference with how he moved normally; what he did feel was a disconcerting dizziness and a welling of sickness in his chest. Then, amazingly, he was in Kranda's arms, having made the ten paces across the deck in a couple of seconds.

"Hell, Kranda!"

The Mahkan pulled back her lips. "I recall the first time I used a varnika. It was a liberating experience."

He turned and crossed the deck; his vision blurred, then caught up. He turned and paced back to Kranda, and this time his vision, enhanced by the varnika, kept up. He moved around the deck experimentally, and a minute later realised that the dizziness and nausea had passed.

Kranda fetched four weapons from the rack and handed one to Ellis. "The settings are here. Press this to kill, this to stun. On stun, the charge will render a sentient target comatose for up to a couple of hours."

She passed the second, bulkier weapon to him. "A blaster. This is to take out buildings. The varnika will assess distance, power of charge required. Also, the varnika will increase the accuracy of your shots."

She showed him where to attach the blaster to the exo-skeleton, down the left side of his torso. "The rifle affixes to your right arm, like this." She slapped her own rifle to her right forearm. Filaments wormed from her varnika and secured the weapon.

Ellis held his own rifle to his right arm and watched as the exo-skeleton took possession. He moved his arm, feeling the weapon slip into his grip.

"Very well. We will go outside and you will test the exo-skeleton a little more, and the weapons. Then we will leave the flier here and head for Panjaluka. And don't worry yourself about the cold. The varnika will thermostatically protect you from the ambient temperature."

Ellis smiled. "That's good to know. Wouldn't want to freeze to death out there."

He moved towards the hatch, and it came to him suddenly why he was here: to liberate Calla, and other Phandrans, from the Sporelli. For a split second, the idea seemed impossible.

Then he was out of the hatch and sprinting across the cindered clearing created by the flier, and the notion was no longer quite so fantastic. He stopped suddenly, in a whirlwind of ash, and turned. The flier, its tegument adapting to its background and phasing through a camouflage routine, was two hundred metres away: it shimmered one last time, then vanished. Only by scrutinising where he knew its outline to be did he make out the slight, shimmering demarcation – and that only with the enhanced vision provided by the exo-skeleton.

He turned and reached out, caught hold of a low branch and snapped it from the tree. He stood very still, staring at the branch in his right hand. It was as thick as his ankle, and he had broken it with no effort at all. He wondered why the act had felt so satisfying.

"That's another thing," Kranda's voice sounded, transistorised, in his ear. "The varnika increases muscular strength. And it's equipped with the same shielding facility as the flier, when instructed. We'll appear as blurs in transit, but when we halt, the varnika takes only a nano-second to adapt to its surroundings, and we'll be effectively invisible."

"And I thought we humans were technologically advanced."

A chuckle in his ear-piece. "I'll let you into a little secret, my friend," Kranda said. "These varnikas aren't Mahkan technology, but Builders', bequeathed to us when we became the Helix engineers."

Ellis stared at the spars that covered his hands and arms, and wondered how old the varnika might be. He smiled to himself at the wonder of it, then turned and jogged across the clearing to the tall Mahkan, covering the fifty meters in less than five seconds.

"And now?"

Kranda indicated Ellis's weapons. "We will test them before we set off."

Ellis hitched the blaster into his left hand, then selected a target in the forest – the stump of a tree a hundred metres away. He took aim and fired. A dazzling blast streaked from the muzzle of the blaster, and when his vision compensated for the floating afterimage he was surprised to see that all that remained of the stump was a blasted pit in the ground.

Next he tried the rifle, setting it to stun and firing at a tree trunk fifty metres away. The laser vector streaked out and connected with the tree, leaving no visible trace on the bark.

"Rest assured," Kranda said. "Had that been a Sporelli, she'd now be a twitching wreck."

"I'm amazed I hit the targets," he admitted.

Kranda laughed. "With just a little help from the varnika."

She unclipped the blaster from her left flank and held it up before Ellis. "They can also be used, if we need recourse to such weaponry, as bombs. The blasters are nuclear charged, and when primed will take out a city." She replaced the blaster. "Now, instruct your shield to activate by *thinking* it…" She gave Ellis the numerical code and Ellis repeated it mentally.

"Good," Kranda said. "Now, watch as I do the same."

One second she was towering over him, and the next she was a vague blur, a fractal outline. "This is how we'll appear to each other at all, thanks to the varnikas' visual enhancement. To others, we will be very nearly invisible."

The blur moved. "Let's go. Follow me and keep me in sight at all times."

3

KRANDA TOOK OFF. One second she was before Ellis, and the next she had vanished. He looked up, into the distance, and saw Kranda as a Mahkan-shaped outline between the trees.

He gave chase, sprinting, and soon caught up with the alien.

Trees flashed by like strobing pillars seen from a speeding monotrain, making a whipping sound to his heightened hearing. He had worried about losing his footing at this speed, but his concern proved unfounded. The exo-skeleton compensated and corrected any mis-step he made, smoothing his breakneck passage through the forest.

He trailed Kranda by a couple of metres. In terms of effort expended, he would have judged himself to be moving at a leisurely jog. He guessed, by the blur of foliage to either side, that he was travelling at fifty metres every five seconds.

"Stop!" The order was loud in his ear-piece, and a moment later Kranda came to a halt before him.

He stopped beside the Mahkan, heart hammering. "What?"

Kranda was outlined in a fractal-edged representation of the background vegetation. The Mahkan was crouching. "I heard something – stalking us."

Ellis raised his laser, swinging in a three-sixty sweep of the forest. "I don't see –" he began, then stopped.

He did see something then, through the trees to their right, a swift silver-grey blur of motion he was sure his normal, unaugmented vision would never have caught. "Kranda. Two o'clock, three, and moving."

"I see it."

"Ugly beast."

"A dryll. Carnivorous. The D'rayni's worst enemy and nightmare, back when the locals lived in caves on Old D'rayni."

"Can we outrun it?"

"Probably not. They're fast. They'd chew through our varnikas in seconds and spit out the spars along with our bones."

Ellis glanced at the Mahkan, trying to discern Kranda's face. All he saw was a shimmering fractal pattern in the approximate outline of a lizard's headpiece. "How do you know all this?"

He saw a blur of movement, which he interpreted as Kranda's arm moving to tap something on her exo-skeleton. "I downloaded all the necessary information into my varnika's smartcore before I set off."

"Good move. So what now?"

"Now I do this. Stay here."

Then Kranda was no longer at his side. He watched her blur streak up the incline, dodging through the trees at incredible speed. He almost called out for Kranda not to kill the creature, but stopped himself just in time.

She came to a clearing and a second later the dryll – the size of a lion – emerged from the trees. It snarled, exhibiting a nasty set of sickle-shaped fangs, and approached Kranda warily, low to the ground.

Ellis caught sight of a silver blur as the dryll leapt, then heard a piercing, high-pitched scream.

For a split second he thought Kranda had been injured, then saw the dryll flop through the air and land on its back before the Mahkan.

"Here," Kranda commanded, and Ellis ran up this hillside.

The dryll had three sets of legs and a domed carapace; its long muzzle drooled blood.

"What did you do?"

"Merely a well-judged blow to its larynx," Kranda replied. "Let this be an excellent reminder for us to keep alert."

She took off, a blur through the trees, and Ellis gave chase.

Minutes later Kranda came to a halt on a spur of rock overlooking a broad valley.

At the far end of the valley, five kilometres away, the lighted town of Panjaluka occupied the valley bottom. At this distance, with his enhanced vision, Ellis made out narrow streets between square block buildings constructed from black stone. The architecture was brutalist – in keeping, he thought, with Kranda's description of the natives as resembling Neanderthals.

"What's the local time?" he asked.

"A little before three in the afternoon."

"And the street-lighting's still on. I wonder if they've ever seen the sun?"

A pause while Kranda accessed her smartcore. "Negative. The cloud never dissipates. Not only have they never seen the sun, but they have never beheld the wonder of the Helix."

Ellis thought about it. "If they'd been brought here earlier in their evolution, they might still not know what they're a part of."

"As it is, they are a technological race, here only a thousand years, with written records of their removal to the Helix."

He smiled to himself at the thought of having access to those records, and those of the thousands of other races of the Helix who had documented their respective translocations.

"The holding station is situated to the north of the town," Kranda said, "at the far end of the valley. We will skirt the town to the west, keeping to the moorland."

They set off again, jumping from the spur of rock and entering the forest. They ran side by side. "In my youth," Kranda said, "I hunted with my hive-mother."

He glanced at the blur beside him. "Hunted?" What the word conjured did not sit comfortably with the thought of a civilised, technological race.

"We might be Engineers, my friend, we might be highly sophisticated beings capable of scientific wonders beyond the imaginings of your race, but also we have deep connections to our racial roots. Hunting was, and is, a large part of what it is to be a Mahkan."

"What did you hunt?" he asked as they ran.

"Don't say the word as if it is tainted with poison, human. Hunting, I'll remind you, is an evolutionary necessity for both the hunter and the hunted. One of your greatest thinkers on Old Earth knew that. The survival of the fittest."

Ellis stopped himself from saying that his race had moved on a little from the need to prove Darwin's axiom.

Kranda went on, "We – that is, the Mahkan in their female phases – traditionally hunted coyti and jarl, both carnivorous beasts analogous to your lions and tigers, though twice their size and ten times as dangerous. It was a fine day indeed when a young female Mahkan came back from her first bloody hunt, often lasting ten of your days, with the pelt of a coyti to show for her efforts."

"And your first hunt?"

"I was seven. I went with my hive-mother and we tracked a pair of coyti for two hundred kilometres across the glacial belt. By the end of the hunt, I don't know who was the more exhausted, the coyti or ourselves. We faced each other, we two Mahkans and the pair of coyti, on a glacial ridge, and my mother had the good grace to step back and allow me to prove myself."

He looked at Kranda, or rather at the fractal outline running along beside him, and wished that he could behold the Mahkan's expression.

"Alone?" he asked.

"How else? What would be the joy of being assisted in the kill – I would have felt a deep shame to this day!"

"But the danger..."

"The danger? Fah! What would be the point of the hunt if there were no danger? What would be proved if the coyti were a... a pussycat, you call them?"

"What happened?"

"I, a small girl of seven, exhausted beyond reason, but with joy in my heart, advanced across the ice and attacked the pair of coyti with a kenka blade, and killed them within minutes. My mother bore me home in triumph, bleeding severely from my wounds, but I tell you this – I would not release my grip on the coyti pelts until the time we stepped back into my clan's compound."

"And I," Ellis said, "thought myself brave hurrying past my neighbour's slavering dog, chained up though it was."

Kranda made a sound that might have been laughter, and said, "Humans!"

"Mahkans!" Ellis responded, realising how very alien indeed was his reptilian friend. "And now," he went on, "your race is the Helix's engineers."

"Chosen a thousand years ago by the Builders, to follow on from the Maerl," Kranda said proudly.

"And you consider the Builders wise in their decision-making?"

The Mahkan slowed. "Of course. Why do you ask?"

"Because the Builders also chose my race to undertake an important task, to oversee the reign of peace on the six thousand inhabited worlds of the Helix." He paused, then went on. "I sometimes wonder, considering what I know of my government, if the Builders knew what they were doing."

"And I," said Kranda, "sometimes wonder the same myself."

They came to the valley where the forest petered out and seceded to coarse moorland. They slowed, then halted in the cover of the last of the trees and scanned ahead.

The lights of Panjaluka glittered in the gloom two kilometres away. Now Ellis made out traffic: small grey cars beetling like trilobites along the narrow streets, and the occasional shuffling pedestrian, lagged like boilers against the biting cold.

Of the Sporelli occupying forces there was no sign.

"The run thus far was merely light exercise," Kranda said. "From now on we will be traversing open ground. So we sprint."

She took off, surprising Ellis with her haste, and he sprinted after her.

The sensation was as if he had been caught up in a tornado that bore him in a straight line. The ground was a blur, the wiry moorland shrubs susurrating against the carbon spars protecting his legs. He reckoned that his feet touched the ground every five metres or so, light impacts that sprang him on as far again. He almost cried aloud with exhilaration as he followed Kranda across the open moorland towards the rapidly approaching lights of the D'rayni town.

He thought of Maria, and was surprised to find that for the first time in months he no longer considered her with resentment, nor even jealousy. He was as much to blame for the state of their relationship, he knew, as she was; and yesterday he had gone some way to admitting as much to her.

He smiled as he considered what he was doing here, the sheer absurdity of his actions in relation to his normal, everyday life. What had Maria often accused him of, in her most acerbic moods: apathy and complacency?

They were within a kilometre of the town when Kranda slowed and crouched low to the ground. Ellis came to a halt beside her and did likewise.

"Look."

He peered in the direction the Mahkan was pointing. They were on a slight rise above the town, within sight of the northern edge where Kranda said the holding station was situated.

He made out black Sporelli troop-carriers moving out of the town on the single road that headed towards the distant pass between the enclosing hills. He counted five of them trundling through the grey mist.

Kranda indicated a foursquare building on the edge of town. "The holding station."

"What do we do?"

"We move in, with speed at first, and then when we reach the town itself, with more circumspection. Fortunately it's not a busy place, and the majority of its inhabitants appear to be indoors against the cold."

"Or the Sporelli invasion," Ellis pointed out.

"That too," she said. "Follow me."

They took off and sprinted down the frost-hardened hillside towards the outskirts of town.

The moorland soon gave way to fields planted with rows of round, green vegetables. Occasionally Kranda's steps impacted with the globes. If any locals had been watching they would have beheld the mysterious spectacle of the vegetables detonating spontaneously in a sudden ejecta of shattered foliage. Ellis's own boots crashed through the frosted globes, and it felt as if he were kicking goldfish bowls.

They came to the road and Kranda slowed to a jog. The occasional domed car beetled along, lumpish D'rayni citizens hunched at the controls. If they noticed the disruption of air caused by the varnikas' shields, they gave no indication. Ellis drew alongside Kranda and they jogged along the road. He felt vulnerable; it seemed impossible that the locals could not see him, and every time a vehicle swished past he started involuntarily.

The holding station to the left of the road, a hundred metres away, resembled a warehouse constructed from slabs of black stone. It stood behind a low wall of the same stone topped by a laser barrier, its two blue horizontal vectors the only colour in the vicinity. A timber gate gave access to the yard.

A few seconds later, Kranda halted beside the gate and Ellis stopped beside her.

He looked up at the stave of lasers, bright against the grey sky. "How do we...?"

Kranda interrupted. "Stay here. When I open the gate, slip through."

He was about to ask just how Kranda intended to do that when the Mahkan approached the gate. He made out a blur as she reached up, gripped the top of the gate, hauled herself up and rolled swiftly *through* the lasers. They flickered, and Ellis caught the reek of cloth and what might have been singed flesh.

Seconds later he heard the crunch of boots on the other side and the gate opened minimally. He slipped through and Kranda shouldered the gate shut.

"You okay?" he whispered.

"A little scorched, no more," Kranda replied.

The building before them was grim and foreboding. He wondered if Calla were in there, and how she might react to his unexpected arrival. He smiled to himself. Unexpected? She might already have sensed his presence.

A metal door gave access to the building, with three barred windows on either side.

He felt a strong grip on his upper arm. "Listen!"

A pair of Sporelli soldiers came around the corner of the building, strolling casually, weapons slung over their shoulders. They appeared at ease, chatting to each other and totally oblivious of Kranda and Ellis.

Nevertheless, Ellis felt nervous at the sight of the Sporelli. The pair passed the façade of the building, turned the corner and strode from sight. He let out a relieved breath.

Kranda said, "The token guard. They circle the building every... approximately one minute and thirty seconds. This way."

She moved to the nearest barred window. Ellis followed and peered within, heart thumping at the possibility of finding Calla.

A dozen robed Phandrans huddled around a brazier in the centre of the concrete floor. One or two were lying on their backs, ill or injured, and were being cared for by their fellows. A guard stood before the door, rifle directed negligently at the floor.

Ellis looked desperately for Calla among the seated and standing Phandrans, but could not see her. He feared she might be among the sick.

One Phandran did look up, towards the window. Kranda said, "They know we're here. I just hope they don't inadvertently alert the guard."

Another Phandra glanced their way, and another, then both pointedly looked away and spoke quietly to their fellows.

"What do we do?" Ellis asked.

Kranda gripped his upper arm. Ellis looked to his right, along the front of the building. The two Sporelli guards came into sight and strolled towards them.

"Retreat to the gate," Kranda said.

Ellis ran the intervening ten metres and pressed his back against the gate as the guards strolled by. He told himself to trust in his varnika, but he felt naked as the guards passed a matter of metres away without as much as a sideways glance.

They turned the corner and passed from sight. "I don't think I'll ever get used to being invisible, Kranda."

"I admit it is not a natural state," she said.

He looked back towards the barred window. "And now?"

"The Phandrans are suffering, certainly from the freezing temperature, maybe from more serious ailments." A pause, then: "We get inside and tell them what to do next."

"You make it sound easy."

"We can rescue of all the Phandrans, but they must be prepared."

"Rescue?" Ellis began, then smiled. "The flier, right?"

"I have instructed it to come to us. It will reach here in precisely... four minutes."

"That leaves the slight problem of getting in there."

Kranda said, "That is no problem at all, Jeff. This way."

She shot off towards the entrance, and Ellis joined her.

A minute later the Sporelli guards came into sight again, strolling casually around the corner. Kranda pressed herself to the metal door and Ellis did the same. When the guards had passed by, less than half a metre away – so close, in fact, that he could smell their rank body odour – Kranda surprised him by rapping loudly on the metal at her back. She took Ellis's upper arm and dragged him away from the entrance.

The guards halted, then turned and stared at the door.

The guard within unlocked the door and peered out. He spoke to the pair, who replied in evident mystification.

Kranda acted. She darted forward and the door flew open, as if caught by a gust of non-existent wind, and darted inside. The guard stood back with a brief cry of surprise. Ellis followed, turning sideways and slipping past the guard with centimetres to spare.

All three guards were now engaged in a bemused altercation on the threshold. One stepped back inside, looked around suspiciously, but saw nothing untoward. He reported back to his fellows, then returned inside and bolted the door.

Ellis followed Kranda to the central brazier and the knot of Phandrans gathered there.

A quick glance around the expectant faces of the diminutive aliens, and the four lying on the floor, was enough to confirm that Calla was not among them.

Kranda crouched behind the brazier and Ellis joined her. The Phandrans pointedly looked away, but one woman, red-robed and graceful of movement, came towards them. She knelt beside a shivering Phandran, caressed his forehead, and spoke a few words in her soft, sibilant tongue.

To Ellis's surprise, her words, translated, sounded in his ear-piece. "You are a Mahkan, no? And a human?"

Kranda whispered, "That is so. We are here to help you."

"Your technology is truly miraculous, Mahkan."

"As is your ability to sense us, Phandran," Kranda whispered.

Ellis looked over the brazier at the guard beside the door. He was absorbed in attending to his nails with a pocket-knife.

Kranda was saying, "...your fellows, are they ill?"

"Several of us came down with food poisoning. We are doing our best to ease the pain of the invalids. They will survive."

Ellis said, "A Healer named Calla, was she with you?"

The translated reply came: "We were twenty, to begin with, but the Sporelli moved several of us to where the fighting is intense."

"And Calla?"

The Phandran remained stroking her patient's forehead. She said, "Calla, yes. She was taken from here a day ago."

"And was she well?"

"She was well, human, yes," the Phandran said, and Ellis smiled with relief.

Kranda asked, "Do you know where she was taken?"

"She was taken with six others to a mining complex over one hundred kilometres north-west of here, where the D'rayni were putting up strong resistance. That is all we could gain from the minds of the Sporelli guards."

Strong resistance, which said to Ellis that there was the possibility that Calla might be caught up in the conflict.

The Phandran was saying, "I sense that you have a flying ship, which will aid our escape from here. But the guards?"

"Don't worry yourselves about them," Kranda said. "We'll deal with the guards."

"We – and I speak for all my fellows incarcerated here – would not want the Sporelli killed or even injured. They are innocents, caught up in –"

Kranda said, "We will not kill them, merely render them unconscious. My flier will arrive in a little under two minutes. It will come down in the compound before the building."

"We understand," said the Phandran.

In his ear-piece, Kranda said to Ellis, "I'll stun the guard in here, then deal with the pair outside. When I give the signal, lead the Phandrans outside."

Kranda rose from her kneeling position and streaked towards the door. The guard looked up at the last second, sensing her presence. Ellis heard a quick fizz, saw a burst of white light, and the guard crumpled to the floor with a grunt.

Kranda eased the guard away from the door, opened it and slipped outside.

Seconds later Ellis caught a glimpse of the exterior guards moving towards the open door, exclaiming in alarm when they saw their slumped colleague. They never made it across the threshold. Kranda appeared behind them. Two quick flashes of blinding white light, and they twisted to the ground, unconscious. Kranda dragged them inside and eased the door shut.

Thirty seconds later she said, "The flier approaches. Okay, Jeff, bring them out."

Ellis turned to the Phandrans and began to say, "The ship has landed. Follow me."

But the Phandrans were already moving, some hurrying towards the exit, while the invalids were assisted by their carers. Ellis moved to the Phandran lying beside the brazier, a young woman as slight as a ten year-old human. He knelt and slipped his hands beneath her legs and upper back. She was feather light when he lifted her, assisted by the exo-skeleton. He hurried after the others, bringing up the rear.

The flier's engines had blasted the concrete compound and for a few seconds the radiating heat was the only evidence of its arrival. Kranda issued a command and the ship's cloaking device deactivated and it popped into existence, eliciting a chorus of gasps from the milling Phandrans.

A ramp extruded and Kranda led the way into the ship. The Phandrans followed, looking about them in wide-eyed wonder. Ellis hurried up the ramp, carrying the Phandran, and gently laid her on a couch in the passenger cabin.

Kranda said to the elder Phandran, "I have instructed the flier to take you back to your world. You will be ferried to the mountain retreat of Verlaine. And do not worry about being intercepted. As you saw, the ship can cloak itself."

She gestured to Ellis and they ran down the ramp.

Seconds later the ramp retracted, the engines powered up, and the ship vanished from sight. Ellis stared at where it had been and made out a fuzzy outline like the visual effect of an incipient migraine.

Kranda called out, "We have company!"

Ellis felt his heart kick in panic as the gates swung open to reveal two troop-carriers. He pressed himself against the wall, Kranda beside him, as the blurred outline of the flier rose with a deafening roar of engines.

A dozen Sporelli troops burst into the compound, shouting out loud and firing wildly. One of the soldiers sprinted towards the open door of the warehouse, only to be caught in the downblast as the flier's main drive fired. The Sporelli cavorted in agony as he was instantly incinerated. His comrades cried out and fired into the air, aiming at where they thought the flier might be. Ellis heard the ringing clatter of the bullets as they ricocheted off the ship. The roar of its engines diminished as the flier swept over the warehouse and headed for the coast.

"Kranda?"

"Stay put. Weather the storm, as you humans say. When I say so, follow me."

Ellis pressed himself against the wall and watched the pantomime of consternation play itself out before him.

Half a dozen soldiers clattered into the warehouse, only to emerge seconds later bawling in their ugly tongue that the prisoners had escaped. The other troops scanned the heavens impotently, their expressions torn between rage and bewilderment. The guards Kranda had disabled were dragged from the warehouse and questioned by an irate officer. Groggy, one of the trio shook his head and gestured helplessly.

The officer snapped something to the milling troops, and Ellis's varnika offered up the translation. "Search the place, inside and out! Then go into the town and questions the locals. If the Mahkan had accomplices on the ground..."

The troops split, hurrying to obey his orders.

One of the officer's subordinates said, "Mahkan?"

"Obviously! Only they have such technology. The ship was cloaked. And no doubt the individuals who led the escape were cloaked too." He strode over to the recovering guards, who were slumped in sitting positions against the wall.

"You claim you saw nothing?"

"I..." one of the guards began. "A second before I was hit – I made out a blur of movement."

Ellis looked across at the open gate and the two troops-carriers parked beyond. The same thought must have occurred to Kranda. She said, "Jeff, on three, make for the gate and head to your right, into the hills. One, two... three. Run!"

Ellis took off a fraction of a second after Kranda. Behind him, he heard a startled cry. "Sir! There – I thought I saw..."

Ellis heard the rattle of a ballistic weapon and heard the whine of bullets pass overhead as he sprinted for the gate. Another cry from behind, a barked order, and a dozen troops joined the firing party. Ahead, Kranda exited the compound and disappeared to the right. Ellis felt bullets whistle past his ear, and a second later he was through the gate and heading up the hillside.

Kranda cried out. "Down!" and Ellis didn't ask why. He fell to the ground, watching Kranda as the Mahkan brought his blaster to bear and aimed at the troop-carriers. The first one exploded in a brilliant orange star-burst and a genie of black smoke. She swung and fired again, and the second carrier became a dazzling ball of flame.

The troops ran from the compound, staring at the burning vehicles and firing in random bursts of cathartic anger.

Kranda took off again and Ellis followed, and they didn't stop sprinting until they reached the crest of the hill. There they paused and looked down on Kranda's handiwork.

The double conflagration brightened the pewter grey countryside, the only splash of colour for miles around. Attracted by the commotion, curious locals had begun to gather, only to be screamed at by the enraged Sporelli officer. His troops fired over the crowd's heads, dispersing them at short order.

"Seen enough, Jeff?"

"We have a saying, Kranda. Revenge is sweet."

Kranda grunted. "Obviously a throwback to your more primitive days," she said.

They sprinted down the other side of the hill, entered the forest and headed north-west.

Sixteen /// Pursuit

I

FOR AN HOUR they traversed the high ground, keeping in sight the highway that wound into the foothills towards the mining town of Krajnac. They watched convoys of black Sporelli vehicles snaking along the wide road: troop-carriers, beetle tanks, and vicious-looking rocket-launchers.

Ellis considered the battle that was by all accounts raging north-west of here, and feared for Calla's safety.

At one point they stopped for food. Kranda opened a backpack and passed Ellis a canteen. "A Mahkan speciality, Jeff. It's called keng, the closest you'll get to human beer. Don't worry, its mild."

Only when he began drinking did he realise how thirsty he was. The keng was rich and spicy, not unlike sarsaparilla. He finished half the canteen and accepted a slab of condensed fruit which Kranda told him was similar to apple and good for replacing depleted energy.

As they chewed, sitting side by side while the sky darkened on another short D'rayni day, Kranda said, "I made a mistake back there, Jeff, and I hope we don't live to regret it." She had turned off her varnika's shield so that Ellis could see her, and he did likewise.

"A mistake? You were brilliant. What mistake?"

She chewed, swallowed, and said, "I should have done what my instincts dictated, and not allowed the sentiments of those we rescued to influence me."

"Meaning?"

"I should have killed every last Sporelli down there."

Ellis stopped eating and looked at her. "And you didn't do that because...?"

"Because the Phandrans would have been aghast. I was thinking of them, and not of ourselves." She cast a quick glance at Ellis. "And, truthfully, I was too considerate of your own... hesitancy in these matters."

"But why should we have killed them? We got away, didn't we? What would we have gained by –?"

"They know that we are here!" she snapped. "They will have reported our presence to their commanders. Right now, they are in all likelihood out there, hunting for us. And, Jeff, how do we know that they don't have the technical equipment with which to detect us, despite the varnikas? Heat-seeking devices, thermal imaging..."

Ellis shrugged, uneasily. "It'll be like looking for a needle in a haystack," he began.

Kranda buckled her muzzle. "I know what a needle is, but a haystack?"

He explained the saying, and went on, "We might be anywhere, as far as they know."

"They will deduce that, as we've liberated one set of Phandran prisoners, we would be likely to attempt to liberate others. Therefore we are likely to head for the places where the Sporelli keep their prisoners. That cuts down the range of locations where they will concentrate their search."

Ellis nodded at the logic of her argument. "Okay, I grant that. But it still leaves them with a lot of ground to cover."

Kranda spat on the ground, a surprisingly generous bolus of phlegm that would have filled half a cup. She said, "Also, they know about the flier. That is what I am worried about. What if, this very minute, the Sporelli airforce is alerted to the presence of the flier and attempt to bring it down?"

"I thought you said its cloaking device was –"

Kranda stopped him with, "It's not infallible, Jeff! With the right surveillance technology, weaponry..." She shook her head. "I do not want to think about it. We came here to liberate Calla and the other Phandrans, and now, because we failed to execute a few worthless invaders, we put everything at risk!" She stared at him. "Do you not admit that I am right?"

Ellis looked away, uncomfortably.

"Well?" she pressed.

Ellis considered his words, scuffing a circle in the loam with his boot. "I, along with every other human being on New Earth, was brought up to respect life –"

"As we were on Mahkan, human! You do not have a monopoly on piety!"

He went on, "We were told to believe that killing is bad. Inhuman. We were following the code of the Builders, who abhorred all violence, and they brought us here, after all. They saved us." He closed his eyes, seeing again the Sporelli officer he had killed. "We do everything within our power not to kill others."

Kranda made a hissing sound which Ellis interpreted as disgust. "That is all well and good," she said. "Noble sentiments, easy to follow in the swaddled comfort of one's safe, easy homeworld. But, when different criteria apply, different rules come into play. The equation is simple. The Sporelli invaded Phandra, and then D'rayni. This is wrong. They killed innocent sentients for no other reason than that of gain, self-interest, and the quest for power. That is wrong. Ergo, when we – who are on the side of the right – find ourselves in a life or death situation with the Sporelli, when we have the choice of either killing the evil-doers or risking our own, and others', lives, then we should have no compunction about killing. That is the only acceptable answer. And if you do not agree, then I doubt your sanity, or your honesty."

Ellis looked at Kranda, aware of the Mahkan's genuine rage and bewilderment. He said, "And, if you were in your male phase, Kranda, then would you espouse the same aggressive actions?"

Kranda looked away, staring at the dimming horizon. At last she said, "As a male, I would have been less inclined to kill the Sporelli. But, and this is important, in our male phases we acknowledge our subordinate status to those in their female phase. So I would be *wrong* in opining that the Sporelli should not be killed."

Ellis shook his head and tried not to smile. How utterly *alien* the Mahkan were! He said, "But would you, as a male Mahkan, acknowledge that you would be wrong?"

"Of course not, but the fact is that on our world, the female is always predominant, and right."

This time, Ellis did laugh. "So therefore your predisposition towards aggression is... politically sanctioned. In other words, merely arbitrary." He paused, staring at Kranda. "So how the hell can that be *right*?"

She muttered. "You do not understand our ways, human. You know nothing."

Ellis smiled and said, "Just consider us humans a race of males, Kranda, with no females to put us right, okay? Then you might begin to understand my objection to killing... even when, and I grant you this, it might in the long term be the justifiable option."

Kranda turned her long head towards Ellis and stared at him. "I understand, Jeff. I also know that you are wrong."

Ellis sighed. "I don't know whether I am right or wrong, Kranda. I just know that it feels very wrong to kill. Shall we leave it at that, and agree to disagree?"

Kranda barked what might have been a laugh. "You are a strange creature, Jeff Ellis."

"I could say the same about you, Kranda'vahkan."

He looked up, at the far horizon, and for the first time saw a glow that resembled the embers of a fading sunset. The sun, however, was setting behind their backs. The orange light in the distance could only be one thing: evidence of Sporelli munitions bombarding the mining town.

"And when we reach Krajnac?" he asked.

"We find out where the Healers are being kept, Jeff, and do our very best to rescue Calla and her people. And let us hope that the Sporelli, with what they have learned about us, are not equal to our tactics."

She rose to her full height, towering over Ellis, and commanded her varnika to render her invisible. Transformed into an ever-shifting fractal outline, she took off along the forested hillside.

Smiling to himself, Ellis activated his varnika and followed.

2

ONE HOUR LATER they came to a halt on the edge of an escarpment overlooking a broad plain. The sun had set and the town of Krajnac glowed in the darkness. They watched as a Morse code of tracer stitched the night, hosing in graceful, silent parabolas from Sporelli positions to the south and igniting in the streets of the town itself. Houses were ablaze, entire streets turned into piled rubble and illuminated by the glow of the bombardment.

"But look," Kranda said. "The D'rayni are fighting back." To the west of the town was what Ellis took to be the mine works, a series of buildings and gantries and hulking machinery grouped around the scarred terrain of an open-cast operation. As he watched, bolts of energy spat from one of the buildings, great globes of fire like meteors which flashed across the land and detonated amid the Sporelli positions.

"I surmise that the workers are defending their mine with the only weapon to hand," Kranda said. "The plasma bolts they employ in mining the land."

"It's a pretty effective weapon," Ellis said.

Where the plasma bolts landed, molten fire spread in flowing orange waves, consuming everything in their path. Sporelli tanks and rocket-launchers exploded in silence, the sound only reaching the escarpment seconds later.

"Effective, until the Sporelli bring all their might to bear. It can only be a matter of time before the invaders prevail." She indicated a highway far below, jammed with enemy vehicles heading towards the battle-front.

He scanned the darkened land to the south of the town, searching for an emergency field hospital. Among the block buildings on the outskirts, it might have been anywhere.

Kranda said, "We need to get closer, work out where the injured are being taken."

"Makes sense, Kranda. After you."

They scrambled down the incline, leaping through brush and tangled foliage, until they came to the plain. They were on the edge of farmland, stretching towards the southern extremities of the town. On minor roads and lanes to the east and west, civilian vehicles were fleeing the onslaught.

Ahead, the night-time darkness was alleviated by a constant orange glow, pulsing with each outgoing plasma bolt and incoming Sporelli missile. Even this far south the air was rent with the crump of munitions and the raging crepitation of burning buildings.

They took off at speed, heading through the fields towards the town.

Seconds later Kranda halted. Ellis stopped beside her. The stench of the burning city came to them on the wind, an eye-watering mix of incinerated building materials, charred meat, and something noxiously chemical.

Ellis felt Kranda's hand on his arm. "There. Two o'clock."

Two hundred metres away he made out a Sporelli troop-carrier, an open-backed flat-bed truck transporting what looked like a dozen Sporelli troops. From the agonised screams and cries issuing from the vehicle, Ellis guessed they had come across a makeshift ambulance.

"We should follow it," Kranda ordered, and led the way.

The carrier was barrelling along at speed, forcing D'rayni vehicles off the road in its haste. Even so, Ellis and Kranda kept pace with the ambulance, running through the fields alongside the road.

Half a kilometre away he made out two dozen geodesic domes, the illuminated hemispheres arranged in a circle around a compound. Ambulances entered the compound, unloaded the injured, then sped back to the front line. Judging by the extent of the field hospital, he wondered if the Sporelli anticipated suffering considerable losses in the fight for the Krajnac mine.

They arrived at the domes minutes later, crouched and peered through the hexagonal panes. The dome was a storeroom, piled with containers. They moved on to the next dome, which was evidently a temporary morgue. Dead Sporelli troops, or bits of them, had been piled up without ceremony. The third dome was another charnel house, and only in the fourth did they find what they sought.

Injured Sporelli troops lay on serried cots, some tended by their own medics while others were ministered by Phandran Healers. Six of the diminutive figures moved from patient to patient, caressing, laying on hands, their demeanour calm and unruffled.

None of the six was Calla.

Ellis moved on to the next dome, another casualty ward with the same arrangement of cots, Sporelli medics and Phandrans.

"Well?" Kranda said, at his side.

Ellis shook his head and darted to the next dome. Here, surgeons worked on badly mutilated Sporelli troops, while Phandrans flitted here and there to provide what assistance they could.

They moved from dome to dome around the circle, and Ellis scanned the tiny figures of the Phandrans with increasing desperation. At one point a Phandran stepped out and crossed to a neighbouring dome.

Ellis saw Kranda dart past him and snatch up the Phandran. She returned, murmuring reassuring explanations to the tiny alien.

"We are friends, come to help you. We mean you no harm."

They crouched behind a dome, Kranda deactivating her varnika's shield to reveal herself. Ellis did the same. The Phandran stepped back, eyes wide and staring.

He spoke, hesitantly, and Ellis's translator kicked in. "Who are you?"

"We are friends of the Phandrans," Kranda said. "We have come to take you from here."

The tiny alien's reply surprised Ellis.

"We... we are healing. We cannot cease our ministrations."

"But you're here under duress," Kranda snapped. "The Sporelli killed and maimed hundreds of your own people."

"Regardless, our duty is to heal, no matter who. Our place, for now, is here with the sick and injured."

"We'll get nowhere with him," Ellis said to Kranda. He looked at the Phandran. "I am seeking a Phandran named Calla," he said. "Calla-vahn-villa."

The alien blinked, regarding him. "Calla was with us, but she was taken with others to another medical centre to the east of the town."

Ellis swore to himself.

Kranda said, "Do you know where, exactly?"

"Only that it is a short distance to the east of here," the Healer said.

Suddenly Kranda reached out, gripped the Phandran's stick-thin arm and pulled the shocked alien towards her. Ellis laid a restraining hand on Kranda's arm.

"Now we go," Kranda said. "And be warned: say nothing of our presence to anyone. Understood?"

The alien nodded mutely. Kranda released her grip and dismissed the Phandran. He hurried away and, with a quick backward glance at Kranda, slipped into the neighbouring dome.

They activated their shields and sprinted away from the field hospital, heading east.

Beside him, the Mahkan said, "That, Jeff, I was not expecting."

"Nor was I. But knowing the Phandrans, I'm not at all surprised at their selflessness."

"But working for the enemy?" Kranda spat.

"That is a measure of their... altruism," he said, and hoped that Calla would see sense and agree to leave this world with them. If, of course, they could locate her amidst all the mayhem. "You should not have shown your anger..."

Beside him Kranda grunted, but said nothing.

They came to a highway packed nose-to-tail with slow-moving Sporelli vehicles heading north. Kranda found a gap between a tank and a troop carrier and darted through. Ellis followed her, his heart hammering with apprehension as he slipped between the grumbling vehicles.

On the other side of the road, Kranda said, "See there? A kilometre straight ahead?"

Ellis made out a line of domes similar to the field hospital they had just left, each geodesic illuminating the glow of the distant battle like a glittering gemstone.

They crossed the intervening fields at speed and arrived at the first of the domes a minute later.

This proved to be a far bigger centre of operations than the last one. Troop-carriers came and went with the injured, as well as a constant procession of fliers which landed in the circular clearing, disgorged the dead and dying, then took off again. The air clamoured with the sound of a hundred engines and loud Sporelli commands. Ellis counted fifty domes before giving up, and despaired of ever locating Calla.

They moved from dome to dome around the outside of the vast circle, finding the same scheme of storerooms, wards and operating theatres. As before, Phandrans moved among the injured as if quite content to be pressed into the service of the tyrannical Sporelli.

They arrived back at their starting point, the ground marked by their scuffed footprints. Ellis said, "This is useless. I might have missed her. I'm going into the domes for a closer look."

"Foolish," Kranda counselled. "Amid such chaotic movement, the varnika's processor would struggle with adopting the ambient camouflage. You would run an increased risk of detection, and what would that gain?"

"Okay, okay." He felt impotent, frustrated. "So what do we do?"

Kranda thought about it. "There might be other field hospitals. We need to ascertain this."

"Kidnap another Phandran?"

"Can you think of a better way?"

"Off the top of my head, no."

"In that case..." Kranda fell silent.

"What?" Ellis said. He stared at the disorganised outline of the Mahkan, wishing he could make out Kranda's features.

She said, "We have overlooked the Phandrans working in the compound itself. Look."

Ellis turned and stared through the gap between the nearby domes. As the fliers landed and carriers came to a halt, they were met by emergency teams which included Sporelli medics and Phandran Healers.

Ellis crept closer, Kranda at his side. They crouched between the domes and stared across the clearing.

He scanned the dozen Phandrans, hurrying along beside the stretchered casualties being ferried from the fliers, and dismissed each one in turn: many were male, others too tall...

He started again, desperate to find her, but finally admitted that she was not among the dozen Phandrans meeting the injured as they arrived.

A big flier stood to one side, rotors drooping, its solidity and stillness in complete contrast to the surrounding turmoil.

And beside the flier, huddled in the shadow of its engine cowling, was the tiny figure of a Phandran.

His heart kicked.

He increased his magnification, fearful that he was mistaken – and Calla's calm face leapt into focus and he almost cried out in joy.

He reached out, found Kranda's arm, and gripped it tight. "There!"

"You sure? She looks just like all the others."

Ellis laughed. "I'm sure." He stared across the clearing, recalling their time together fleeing the Sporelli on Phandra. He willed her to look up, to sense his presence among the raging chaos around her.

He said, "Why is she there, Kranda, and not helping the injured in the domes?"

A quick, cold fear gripped him.

A Sporelli officer marched from a dome beside the flier and crossed to Calla, reading something from a screen as he went. He snapped a command, ordering her to move, and uncertainly she made her way to a hatch in the bulging flank of the flier.

A cry rose in his throat. He said to Kranda, "I've got to..."

But even before the intent had fully formed in his mind, he'd leapt from between the domes and sprinted across the clearing.

"Jeff!" He heard Kranda's cry in his ear-piece.

He collided with a Sporelli medic, knocking him off his feet and sending him spinning across the ground. The medic cried out and Ellis regained his balance and ran on. Cries sounded behind him, then shouted commands.

"Calla!" he called.

She turned as she was about to clamber aboard the flier. The Sporelli officer was at her side, gripping her arm.

"Jeff!" she called out. "They are taking me away, to Sporell. Their leader, he is dying. They think..."

The officer stared at Calla then turned suddenly, his eyes focusing on where Ellis had been just a moment earlier. He yelled something, raised his pistol and fired. The bullets missed Ellis by a fraction and Calla cried out in alarm. A soldier within the flier reached out and grabbed Calla, dragging her aboard. She struggled, feebly kicking her feet, but she was no match for the Sporelli soldier. The last Ellis saw of her was the pathetic sight of her bare feet, scrabbling futilely, before the hatch swung shut with a hydraulic sigh.

He barged into the startled Sporelli officer, knocking him off his feet, and made to grab the hatch.

The flier rose, its downdraft battering him, and another shot rang out behind his back. He registered a visual disturbance at his side, felt a strong hand on his arm, and before he knew it he was being dragged away through the chaos of milling Sporelli troops, all attempting to obey the officer's orders and apprehend the insurgents.

"This way!" Kranda cried, and hauled him from the clearing between two domes and out into the open countryside.

Orienting himself, Ellis looked up and saw the flier sweep overhead and disappear into the darkened skies to the south.

Behind them, troops spilled from between the domes and began firing. Ellis looked back, saw a Sporelli with a shoulder-mounted device.

Kranda said, "A heat-detector, Jeff. All we can do now is run."

Ellis kicked, upping the pace, until he was sprinting, imparting volition to the exo-skeleton that carried him across the open fields at ten times the speed he would have normally achieved.

Bullets sang around him, but less numerously now, and minutes later the only sound was the regular rhythm of his breathing and the distant roar of the battle for Krajnac.

"I won't begin to tell you how stupid that was," Kranda said.

"In that case I'm grateful," he said. Then: "I'm sorry. I acted without thinking. I had to do *something*."

"There was little, in the circumstances, we could have done, short of killing the Sporelli and taking the flier."

"Why didn't you suggest this at the time?"

"I considered, and discounted, the action. The Sporelli would have brought us down with ease."

Ellis swore. "So we give up, just like that?" Even as he spoke, some traitorous voice deep within him suggested that that would be the easy option.

"Or we make our way to Sporell, find the ailing dictator, and rescue Calla." Ellis almost laughed, but sensed that Kranda was deadly serious. "We can do that?"

"My flier is on its way back, having safely deposited the

Phandrans. We will gain high ground and rest until it arrives in... in approximately three hours."

"This is crazy!" Ellis cried.

"Nevertheless, human, I have a debt of honour to despatch. I said I would help you rescue the Phandran called Calla, and I will. This way."

They left the fields behind them and headed into the hills.

3

THEY CLIMBED THE escarpment and halted at the top, looking back across the plain they had traversed. The bombardment of Krajnac continued, though the replying plasma bolts were growing less frequent.

Ellis considered Calla, and where the Sporelli were taking her. While she would be away from the dangers of the battlefield, who knew what new dangers she might face on the homeworld of the Sporelli, ministering to the needs of the dying dictator? If she failed to save his life, what then? They were conscienceless killers, as he'd seen for himself.

They sat side by side on a fallen log. Kranda deactivated her shield and pulled rations from her backpack. She passed him an energy bar, which he wolfed down. Until coming to rest five minutes ago, he hadn't realised how hungry and tired he was. His recent exertions were beginning to take their toll. When Kranda's flier arrived, he promised himself, he would snatch a few hours sleep on the flight to Sporell.

He looked at the Mahkan. "Do you really think we can do this?"

She turned her scaled face to regard him. "Fly to Sporell, locate the dictator, and in so doing find Calla? Why not? We came all this way and located her, yes? And but for your foolhardiness we might have devised some means of effecting her rescue."

"I've said I'm sorry, okay? Let's drop it."

"We all make mistakes, Jeff. Next time, before you act unilaterally, think long enough to consult me, yes?"

Ellis nodded and bit off a mouthful of energy bar.

Five minutes later Kranda touched his arm and indicated the night sky above Krajnac. "Look."

He saw nothing untoward at first, just the glow of the flaming town and a high scatter of stars. Then his vision adjusted and he made out half a dozen fliers, fanning out south from Krajnac and heading towards the escarpment.

"They surely cannot have traced us here," Kranda reassured him. "They are merely following the direction we took. But as a precaution I suggest we activate the shields." She did do, and became a vague, dark shape beside him. Ellis commanded his Varnika to do likewise and felt instantly safer.

They retreated further into the tree cover, sat down against a trunk and waited.

Ellis heard the sound of a flier, then through the foliage made out its sequencing lights pass overhead. He tensed, expecting gunfire to rain down at any second. The engine noise passed, diminished, and he breathed a little easier.

Then a second flier roared high above, but this time the growl of its engines remained constant. Ellis judged it to be about fifty metres away. He heard a cacophonous splinter, as if a hundred trees were being felled, followed by a roar of flames. Kranda was on her feet. She tugged Ellis after her. "This way."

They ran, dodging tree trunks both vertical and horizontal. The varnika enhanced his vision, gave him night-sight in which the world appeared in stark contrast: the darkness became darker, and everything else stood out in bold relief. Obstacles before him glowed, and with the assistance of the exo-skeleton he leapt them with an ease his unaugmented self would never have managed.

And his augmented hearing made out the harsh cries of Sporelli soldiers on their trail.

The first gunshot, he thought optimistically, was literally and metaphorically a shot in the dark – surely they could not be seen in the half-light, shielded as they were? The second shot – a laser this time – fizzed by his head and burned a neat hole in the tree trunk before him.

He increased his speed, dodging this way and that through the zigzag obstacle course of the tightly packed forest.

Ahead, Kranda turned and fired. A blazing bolt of light zizzed past Ellis, warming the side of his head.

He wanted to look behind him, to reassure himself that he had put distance between himself and his pursuers, but at the same time fear prevented the action. He ran on, expertly leaping logs and shrubs, dodging between tree trunks. He found a second wind and his breath came easily. Five minutes later he ventured a glance over his shoulder. The forest behind him was clear of Sporelli. He took a breath, relieved, but counselled caution.

They moved on, jogging now, until they came to a ravine that cut through the forest. They stepped out under the stars, and for the first time in a long while they could neither hear the Sporelli bombardment nor see its fiery effects.

Silence filled the night.

Kranda moved a little way down the bank of the ravine and stopped. She was quiet for a few seconds, then said, "My flier has been detected."

Ellis's stomach turned. "What?"

"As it was flying back over the D'rayni coastline, the Sporelli detected its presence. It is being followed, I think by a flier, but..."

Ellis stared at Kranda's outline. She had sounded far from sure. "But...?"

"It's keeping pace with my flier. I have instructed my flier *three times* to take evasive action. And each time the pursuing flier simply matched its manoeuvres." She paused. "Sporelli fliers should not be able to do that."

Ellis recalled the supersonic craft they had seen much earlier in the sky above D'rayni.

Kranda shouted something in her own language, then for his benefit said, "The pursuing craft is firing. My flier should come into view within minutes. I will instruct it to land nearby. With luck, if we can get aboard and I can pilot it..."

"But won't the Sporelli craft simply blast it when it lands?"

"I'm working on the assumption that the Sporelli ship is not a flier but an interworld ship. It is fast, but not that manoeuvrable. I have instructed my ship to take low-level evasive action and then land close by. It is my hope that the Sporelli ship will overshoot, and we'll board the flier and be away before it compensates."

Ellis took a shaky breath. "I hope you're right."

Seconds later something screamed overhead, making him cry out loud. He looked up and made out the fractal shape of the Mahkan flier as it banked steeply overhead. A split second later something appeared above it, a vast ship whose underbelly eclipsed the night sky.

He ducked into the cover of a nearby tree, guessing what was to follow. He looked up and saw the interworld ship bearing down on the Mahkan flier like some mammoth beast. As they watched, a blinding red light lanced from a gunnery nacelle slung beneath the interworld ship. The laser struck Kranda's flier and disabled its visual shield. It wobbled, then listed precariously. A second laser blast speared the night sky, and this one was the *coup de grace*. The flier tipped with spectacular, slow-motion grace, slid out of the sky and hit the ground with a muffled *crump* a hundred metres away.

The resulting explosion lit up the forest with a brilliant orange glare. Ellis covered his ears, but even so the detonation was deafening.

Above, the interworld ship moved away slowly, its task accomplished.

Kranda raised her blaster, then paused. "I am tempted, Jeff, but I fear giving away our exact position."

They watched the Sporelli ship disappear from sight.

"So there we have the answer," Kranda said. "The Sporelli do possess space technology."

Ellis felt his stomach turn. "And with it?" he began.

"The thought does not bear close examination."

He worked to calm his heartbeat and regain his breath. "We need to work out how the hell we're going to get out of here," he said.

"I've already thought about that," the Mahkan replied.

"So have I," Ellis said. "We head for the coast, try to find a boat to cross the sea to Phandra. There, the Phandrans will help us."

"An option," Kranda opined, "but the second best option in the circumstances."

"The second best? So what do you suggest?"

"That we head inland," Kranda said, "to the central mountains."

"Inland?" Ellis gasped, but Kranda was already running down the ravine, calling after her for him to follow.

Wearily, dog-tired now and aching in every limb, he did so.

One hour later, as he jogged side by side with Kranda, the two not having exchanged a word in all that time, he heard the sound he'd been dreading. He looked up, through the tree cover, and made out the running lights of a Sporelli flier.

"We've got company. Bastards have found us. What now?"

"See, ahead. One o'clock, through the tree cover."

He saw the rearing grey summit of a starlit mountain range. "Mountains. Great. I've never been so relieved to see mountains. But... but can you tell me – why the hell are we heading towards it?"

He sensed forbearance in Kranda's reply. "You'll see when we get there, Jeff."

They emerged from the forest and stood on the edge of a glacial ravine. Across it, perhaps a kilometre away, was the slope of the mountain-side.

Ellis looked up, searching for the Sporelli flier. He heard its engines, distant at first but closing in.

"Over there," Kranda said.

The flier came down in the forest at their backs, a couple of hundred metres away. Ellis heard the splintering of trees and then the crackle of burning foliage.

"Now," Kranda said, "with the last of your energy, as fast as you are able, follow me."

"Where to?" he asked desperately.

"See the lateral rent in the second highest peak?" Kranda said. "There."

Ellis took a vast breath. "Could you tell me... please tell me why the hell we're climbing to a cave in a bastard mountain peak? I mean, when we're there, so what?"

"Wait and see, Jeff. Now, hurry. The Sporelli will soon be upon us."

Kranda sprinted away from him.

Ellis took a deep breath and sprinted after her.

He felt terribly exposed as he crossed the glacial ravine, no longer in the cover of the forest and vulnerable as they were to detection by the Sporelli. Starlight illuminated the silver-grey back of the glacier, and ahead the mountain loomed in a dark, thrusting dagger-shape. He felt his boots crunch the ice as he took long, leaping strides, eating up the metres. Ahead, Kranda performed an evasive zigzag manoeuvre.

He took a quick look over his shoulder. The distant forest was a blaze of light where Kranda's flier had crashed and the Sporelli flier had come down, igniting the trees. As yet there was no sign of the troops themselves. He knew better than to feel any relief: they would show themselves before long.

He wondered if Kranda was heading for high ground so that she would be better able to send out a mayday signal. It was the only possible reason he could think of to explain why they were heading towards the mountain peak. He wanted to trust in Kranda, who had served him well so far, but he had to admit that for the first time he was having his doubts.

Something exploded in the ice three metres to his right, sending up a spume of superheated steam. He used the near miss to his advantage, dodging into its ghostly plume and racing up the incline. He judged that in another hundred metres he would reach the face of the mountain where it inclined steeply from the glacier. Kranda was already there, leaping in a switchback course up the grey face of rock. The Mahkan turned just long enough to loose a shot from her blaster, then continued climbing.

Another Sporelli shot slammed into the ice to Ellis's left. He looked over his shoulder briefly. Half a dozen Sporelli troops were crouching in the tree-line, three of them bringing weapons to bear. One of their number had a shoulder-mounted heat-seeker and was instructing his comrades where to fire. Ellis aimed his rifle and fired with little hope of hitting the target.

He made it to the rock face and followed Kranda up the steep incline. He was sure he would never have made the ascent but for the várnika; its speed propelled him from shallow foothold to foothold, where unassisted he would have fallen. He found handholds in the rock without really thinking about it, relying on his augmented vision to locate handy fissures and his extra strength to literally pull him through.

At one point he hung on with one hand and glanced down and across the glacier. Three soldiers were advancing towards the cliff-face, while the others remained in the tree-line, their weapons poised. More explosions rained around them, ricocheting noisily and spraying granite shrapnel in every direction. He winced as shards tore at his arms, drawing black blood in the meagre starlight.

He raised his blaster and aimed at the ground before the advancing troops, fired and opened a melting pit at their feet.

The Sporelli assault only fuelled his flight: adrenalin-powered, augmented by the varnika, he hauled himself after Kranda and caught up with her in minutes.

He looked up, but from this foreshortened angle he was unable to make out their destination, the rent in the peak. "How far?" he gasped.

Kranda came back with, "Fifty metres, perhaps a little more."

The gradient eased off so that he was able to scramble on all fours for twenty or thirty metres. He looked up and made out a dark slash in the grey rock up ahead. He was beginning to think that they might make it to the cave uninjured when he heard the crescendo of a flier's engine. He looked up. A black wedge was rounding the peak, a hundred metres away, and banking straight towards them.

The gradient levelled and became a wide ledge that gave access to the diagonal gash of the cave mouth. Kranda was already crossing towards it, and a few seconds later Ellis pulled himself onto the ledge and sprinted.

Kranda paused long enough to aim her blaster and fire. The bolt streaked towards the flier, winging its flank. The flier wobbled and dropped towards the ledge. Laser fire streaked from the cockpit, striking Kranda. She yelled out and fell to her knees, swore and staggered upright.

"Kranda!" Elis cried.

The Mahkan was up and running again. "I'm okay, Jeff. A superficial burn..."

More laser fire lanced from the flier, striking the rock a matter of centimetres from Ellis's heels. He felt intense heat on his calves and yelled in pain. He slowed, despite the desire to reach the cave, and looked up. The flier was fifty metres away and dropping fast, and the ledge was wide enough for it to land with space to spare.

He followed Kranda into the darkness of the cave. The Mahkan activated a light on his varnika, illuminating the widening tunnel ahead. Ellis sprinted, hearing a grinding impact of the flier on the rocky ledge outside soon followed by harsh Sporelli cries.

He yelled. "They've got us cornered, Kranda!"

She cut him off. "Save your energy for running. Follow me."

There was little else to do, in the circumstances, so Ellis obeyed Kranda's instructions and kept his objections to himself. They were hammering along a narrowing corridor of rock, the clatter of their boots echoing back off the walls. Behind them, Sporelli cries of anticipated victory made his blood run cold.

Kranda came to an abrupt halt and Ellis almost slammed into her. They had come to a dead end. Before them, the corridor terminated in a flat wall of rock.

"Wonderful," Ellis gasped. "Where now?"

He looked behind him, seeing only darkness but hearing the stentorian cries of the pursuing troops.

Kranda laughed. "Are all humans so pessimistic, Jeff?"

"Only when the occasion arises," he said. "Well done on getting us captured, by the way."

"Human, cease your complaints."

Ellis turned at the sound of a footfall just metres away. A flashlight showed in the gloom, dazzling him. The Sporelli soldier called out a single word, which his varnika translated as, "Stop!" He thought about using his weapon but feared provoking return fire.

Instead he raised his hands, despair welling within him.

He was about to step forward and exhort the soldier not to fire when a hand gripped his upper arm and yanked him backwards. He fell, crying out in alarm, seemingly *through* the very surface of the rock that had barred their way.

He hit the ground hard, and when he opened his eyes he was no longer in the rock-enclosed corridor.

He blinked, blinded by a silver light. Kranda had deactivated her shield and was crouching over him. She pulled up the melted material of his trouser leg and inspected his calf, drawing her lips back. "A superficial burn. I will attend to it in time."

Ellis looked around, disbelieving. They were in a perfectly cylindrical silver chamber, three metres wide and three high. Kranda stood and played her hand over a sensor on the wall, and Ellis felt the gut-wrenching sensation of plummeting at speed.

"Where the hell are we?" he asked.

Kranda helped him to his feet. "We are in an access chute," she said, "one of a dozen built into the fabric of every world on the Helix. And now we are descending to the very core of the world."

Torn between laughter and tears of relief, and aware of his extreme tiredness, Ellis reached out and gripped Kranda's hand. "I never doubted you for a second, Mahkan."

Kranda snorted. "Thank you, human," she said.

Seventeen /// In The Spine

I

THEY DROPPED ALMOST eight thousand kilometres in just over ten hours.

Kranda broke out the chamber's medical kit and treated the minor burn on Ellis's left leg, then attended to the burn on her right arm that extended from her shoulder to her wrist. The laser had melted her thermal suit, but the spar of her varnika had taken the brunt of the blast. She covered the wound with synthi-flesh and swallowed a handful of painkillers.

One hour into the descent, Kranda was alerted by her varnika. Its smartcore had integrated with the chamber's security system and its androgynous voice informed her, "*The access security has been breached. You are being followed.*"

She thought: *How far are they behind us?*

"*Approximately one hour.*"

Very well. Keep me updated.

She sat back, considering her options.

For the duration of the descent, Ellis slept. They had deactivated the visual shields on entering the chamber, and now Kranda sat against the curving steel wall of the chamber and stared at the sleeping human.

Ellis had once told her that he was of average height for a human, but he still appeared small in her eyes. Humans possessed little physical strength compared with their Mahkan equivalents, and even their mental fortitude seemed lacking. And yet... and yet Jeff Ellis had saved her life; he had risked his own safety, his life even, and crossed to her stricken shuttle and rescued her. Again, on Phandra, he had contravened his ethos of non-violence and killed the Sporelli soldier and saved her life for a second time.

They had been together, in close contact, for over a day now, but still the human remained alien, his mind-set odd and unknowable to Kranda. She did not understand his stance on violence where violence was merited. She wondered, sometimes, if Ellis himself really knew with certainty what his position was. He had led an easy, cosseted life as a shuttle pilot for the human Peacekeepers, had never had to face the fundamental questions of existence, had never had to fight for survival and so come to some understanding of the value of his own life. When you understood the worth of one's existence, when one faced down a wild coyti and fought it to the death, the encounter taught one something about life and death and the preciousness of existence.

She slept for a few hours, and when she awoke the chamber was slowing in its descent.

The ring of white light that encompassed the chamber – starting at the top when they'd entered the chamber and progressing down as they dropped – had almost reached the bottom.

Kranda gently roused Ellis, watching his confusion as he sat up and rubbed his eyes. "Where the hell...?"

"We have just arrived at the very centre of D'rayni, Jeff."

Ellis looked alarmed. "The Sporelli! They were –"

"We left them on the surface. But... They must have blasted through the barrier and are following."

Ellis ran a hand over his face and through his hair. "I remember the rock wall, the Sporelli entering the cave..." He looked down at the medi-seal on his ankle.

Kranda said, "I've fixed it. You're fine now."

Ellis looked at her arm. "You?"

"This is nothing. I'll be fine."

Ellis shook his head. "The barrier... how did you open the rock?"

"My varnika transmitted the entry code. Unfortunately the Sporelli saw where we went."

"You said we're at the centre of D'rayni?" Ellis sounded awed.

"Almost there," she said, indicating the light that was settling at the foot of the chamber. The plummeting sensation ceased as the chamber gradually slowed, then stopped. Kranda stood, helping Ellis to his feet, and faced the sliding door.

It hissed open to reveal a vista that never failed to stir her sense of wonder.

She glanced at the human, eager to watch his reaction. If she still experienced awe at the sight, then Ellis would be stunned.

Open-mouthed, staring, he stepped out and looked about him. "I don't believe it…" he whispered.

Kranda recalled her first experience of the Helix's spiral spine. She had been brought down by her superior, and he had warned her that she would experience a certain sensory disequilibrium at what she was about to behold. "You will have seen nothing on this scale, Kranda. Your optical apparatus will have little with which to compare what you are about to witness. The central mountains of Mahkana are vast, but the tubular spine of the Helix would contain them with much space to spare."

Now she said, "The spine itself is two hundred kilometres in diameter. The Helix, from the very apex to the bottom, is a little over two hundred million kilometres long."

Ellis staggered forward and stared around him.

He turned a bewildered face towards Kranda. "This… this winds all the way through the middle of every world of the Helix?"

"Through the core of every world and every sea. It is, if you like, the skeleton of the Helix."

Ellis shook his head and whispered something under his breath.

The elevator had deposited them on the inner surface of the spine. To left and right, the white expanse of the floor extended for as far as the eye could see, its curve incremental and indiscernible. So high overhead was the far side of the spine – two hundred kilometres away – that it appeared a milky blur that defied the visual senses; sometimes it appeared illimitably distant, at others it seemed as if she might reach out and touch the surface.

Ellis murmured, "We're like… like ants in a…" He laughed. "I can't think of anything big enough… a drum?" he said. "Ten thousand drums laid end to end without their skins?"

He turned round suddenly and stared at the silver capsule they had just stepped from. "But we were travelling downwards," he said, "and yet we're standing on the bottom of…"

Kranda smiled. "The spine possesses its own gravity field, Jeff. Just before the chamber reached the 'bottom,' it flipped so that we'd not land on our heads."

"I never gave a thought to what was down here," Ellis said.

"You probably wouldn't, unless you were an engineer."

"I always knew the construction of the Helix was a wonder of the universe, but now I can appreciate the true feat of the Builders."

"The walls of the spine are over ten kilometres thick," she said, "and are impenetrable."

Ellis laughed aloud, and the puny sound was lost in the vastness of the spine. "But why *so* big?" he asked.

"It makes engineering sense," she said. "The core has to be so vast, so thick, in order to take the incredible stresses placed on the spine by the rotation of ten thousand worlds. And the hollow chamber of the core has to be of so vast a diameter to be able to contain the colossal machines down here."

"Machines?" he echoed.

Kranda thought about it. How to explain the concepts of Builder technology to someone from a race whose own science and technology was so rudimentary?

She said, "They are… computers which even we, the Mahkan, are only now coming in some small way to understand. We might be the Engineers, the race the Builders chose to look after the structural integrity of the Helix, but there are many things even we do not understand. We maintain the physicality of the structure, attend to the day-to-day engineering problems, but we think that these 'machines,' for want of a better term, integrate and co-ordinate the thousand different systems that function to keep the Helix running." She paused then went on, "In fact, it was a human, one of your own colony founders, who coined a term for the machines when our engineers opened up the core to your ancestors. Friday Olembe called them 'Gaia Machines.'"

Ellis looked around, something almost comically childlike in his apparent eagerness to see one of these colossi. "Where are they?"

"They are stationed at regular intervals along the spine," she said, "one every two worlds. We will pass one on our journey to Sporell."

"The journey?" Ellis said, staring at her. "But how…?"

She gestured across the smooth surface of the core. There was no curve beneath their feet, of course. The decking, for want of a better word, was formed from white tiles five metres square, and Kranda always had the feeling, whenever she came down here, that she was a puny token on a vast game board.

She crossed the tiles towards a ruler-straight slit in the deck, perhaps the width of her leg. As she approached, a silver form flowed from the slit like mercury.

Beside her, Ellis gasped and stepped back. "Kranda?"

She laughed and gestured towards the silver vehicle, now fully formed before them.

"We travel by the mono-car," she said. "If, that is, you still wish to rescue your alien friend?"

Ellis nodded. "Now," he said, "more than ever."

Kranda stared at the small human, a being who had in his short life to date experienced very few of the true hardships of existence, until lately… and now he was still willing to risk his life to save the tiny alien who had saved him.

They might not have *Sophan* ingrained in their cultural psyche, she thought, but the same idea worked on them at an individual level.

She said, "Or I could take you back to New Earth, a slightly longer journey, admittedly."

Ellis smiled. "You don't really think I'd take you up on that, do you, after all Calla did for me?"

"Of course not, human. But I thought I should ask. Come, we shall make our way to Sporell."

They approached the mono-car and Kranda palmed a sensor beside its sliding hatch. They climbed inside, Ellis exhibiting surprise as the padded jade green walls pulsed towards them. Kranda eased him forward. "Don't be worried. This is for our own safety. We'll be reaching speeds in excess of Mach ten."

She steered the human towards the wall and gave instructions. "Find a position comfortable to you and relax. The padding will form itself around you, supporting you. Watch."

She eased herself into the green foam-like substance and sat down facing Ellis. The padding accepted her, flowing around her. Seconds later she was encased in the padding with only her shoulders, arms and head showing.

Smiling uncertainly, Ellis followed suit, laughing in surprise as he was absorbed into the vehicle's walls.

"The Builders thought of everything. Not only does the padding provide safety from the incredible acceleration, it also means that beings of all shapes and sizes – who might succeed the Mahkan as engineers – can use the system with ease."

A pseudopod extruded from the padding beside Kranda's hand. "A simple control column. Pressure either back or forth indicates which direction you wish to travel." She touched the joy-stick once. It retracted quickly from her like the antennae of a slug. "We'll be setting off in a few seconds. I would say 'hold on,' but there really is no need."

On the interior wall to the front of the carriage, the padding had vanished to reveal a strip viewscreen through which could be seen the Helix's spinal core.

The mono-car, with an almost imperceptible humming note, accelerated slowly, the padding absorbing the pressure of their forward momentum. Outside, the view remained the same: it was as if they were not moving at all.

Kranda accessed her varnika's smartcore and said, "Would you believe, Jeff, that we're travelling at over five hundred kilometres per hour, and accelerating?"

"But we've only just set off. It feels as if we're hardly moving." The human peered out. "And... and nothing is changing out there."

She said, "Nothing will change, much, until we approach a Gaia Machine. There's nothing out there with which to judge our passage. Have patience. We should be passing one in little over an hour."

Ellis relaxed. His face, cradled in the cupola of the varnika, looked drawn and tired, for all the sleep he'd had on the descent.

"And when we get to Sporell?" he asked.

"We make our way to the presidential tower, the dictator's residence in Sporelli's capital city. It's approximately one hundred kilometres from the closest access chute." She considered what she knew of the political regime on Sporell. "The system there is a dynastic dictatorship, with power handed down through both the male and female line of a family which has been in power for almost three hundred years. You humans have a term for the political system there: fascism."

"Sounds a delightful place."

"They keep their people subjugated through media propaganda, control of all informational outlets, and by employing a network of paid – and blackmailed – informants. The populace knows nothing about other worlds, other ways of life. And, because of this, they are... satisfied, let's say. Anyway, perhaps in a state where there is no dissent, no opposition, where the dictator – a man in his eighties called Horrescu – has cultivated a personality cult so that he's regarded as something like a deity..."

Ellis nodded. "And President Horrescu has decided to extend his empire."

Kranda considered the offensive on Phandra and D'rayni. "There must come a time when, having ruled with absolute power and no opposition for so long, a dictator's ambitions turn to thoughts of conquest."

Kranda's varnika spoke to her. She cocked her head, listening.

"What?" Ellis asked, straining forward against the padding.

"The Sporelli in pursuit," she said, "have arrived at the core and accessed a mono-carriage."

Ellis stared behind him, as if he might catch sight of the pursuing troops. "What do we do?"

Kranda twisted in her padding and indicated ahead. "Observe."

In the distance – quite how far was impossible to tell in the vast perspective of the spine – was the blurred shape of a looming Gaia Machine.

"When we reach it," she said, "it will provide cover. Then we sit tight and wait."

She reached up, and the control pseudopod obligingly dropped. The mono-car hummed, slowing little by little, and minutes later came to a stop.

2

THEY STEPPED FROM the mono-car and Kranda watched as it was sucked back into the notch along which it had travelled. A second later no evidence of the vehicle remained.

Ellis was staring up in wonder at the architectural immensity of the Gaia Machine. Kranda empathised with the human's reaction to his first experience of beholding one of the Builders' finest artefacts, after the Helix itself. Its grey surface was uneven, deeply fissured with a thousand perpendicular inlets so that it resembled some kind of geological, deep sea formation, a coral reef which rose like a mountain and extended for a kilometre to left and right beside the mono-line. Each fold or fissure in its surface was easily big enough to admit even the bulk of a Mahkan, never mind the slimmer form of a human.

Kranda must have seen a dozen or more Gaia Machines, each one a little different in appearance, but she always felt the same humbling sense of insignificance in their presence. The machines were physically overwhelming, but mentally too they overwhelmed with what they symbolised, working machines many thousands of millennia old which governed the smooth running of ten thousand minutely complex eco-systems, bio-systems, and engineering systems integrated into the one vast precision instrument that was the Helix.

They hurried towards the humming immensity of the edifice, and Ellis reached out and laid a palm against the grey surface.

"It's warm, Kranda, and it pulses..."

"Some of my people," Kranda said, "claim that it lives."

She looked back along the spine, then accessed her varnika's smartcore and asked it to assess how long it might be before the Sporelli troops made an appearance. Seconds later the voice sounded in her ear-piece. *"They will arrive at our current position in between fifty and fifty-eight minutes."*

"Fine," Kranda said to herself.

Ellis looked at her. "What?"

She told him. He looked back the way they had come. "But..." he began, "I might be missing something, but how will they know which direction we took? The mono-cars were set up to go both ways, no?"

Kranda smiled. "That's right. But they're no fools. My guess is that they'll cover both options and send troops in each direction." She laughed to herself at the thought.

Ellis peered at her, and she explained, "One group will run straight into our ambush, and the other will go on round and round the Helix until they reach the pole."

"And then?"

"And then one of my people's engineering survey teams will be alerted and pick them up."

"And the other group...?" Ellis said. "Why don't we just continue until we reach Sporell? We're ahead of them, and will remain ahead."

"And run the possibility of their learning that we're heading for their homeworld? I don't want our presence on Sporell known to the authorities there. When the Sporelli troops show themselves, Jeff, we attack. Agreed?"

She was gratified to see that this time the human had the good grace and common sense not to object. "Very well."

She accessed her varnika. "We have over forty-five minutes before they show themselves." She looked around, assessing the distance from the mono-car line and the best angle of attack. "This way."

They moved around the Gaia Machine until she found a suitable fissure. She slipped into it, then peered out. From its concealment, she had a perfect line of sight along the mono-car line. With the increased magnification provided by her varnika, she would see the approach of the Sporelli car long before its arrival.

She indicated a neighbouring rill in the flank of the Machine. "Conceal yourself in there. We fire when the car draws level with us, understood? I'll give the command."

"We have a phrase for such a rout," Ellis said. "Shooting at sitting ducks."

Kranda repeated the phrase, worked out what it meant, and realised that it was the human's way of voicing his objection. "We could always let the car carry on past us," she said, "and deign not to attack…"

Ellis was staring at her. "Why not?" he said at last. "We could give them an hour and then continue on our way. They'd be ahead of us then, and when we get to Sporell…"

Kranda interrupted. "Because what if they stopped, decided they'd gone far enough, elected to turn back and came across us coming directly at them? No, Jeff, I'd rather we account for them with as little possible risk to ourselves."

She had no intention of admitting that Ellis had a point – that they could easily allow the Sporelli to pass them by… The chances that they would stop and turn back, and so happen upon her and Ellis, were remote.

But then Kranda recalled the image of the dead Phandran villager, murdered through the Sporelli use of the guran, and she told herself that she could take no risks when facing a foe as merciless as the Sporelli. To her way of looking at things, they deserved to die. She had allowed the Sporelli troops at the holding station to live, and had regretted the lapse.

Ellis retreated into his appointed fissure, knelt and activated his varnika's shield. She had no means of knowing whether he had drawn one of his weapons.

3

KRANDA PRESSED HERSELF into her fissure, drew her laser and peered out. She upped her visual magnification and sighted along the mono-car rail. Her varnika reported that the enemy would come into visual range in between thirty seconds and one minute twenty-five seconds.

She tensed, waiting.

Thirty seconds later, she made out a growing irregularity in the distance. She decreased her magnification as it approached, opened communications with Ellis and whispered, "They're on their way. Twenty seconds and counting. On my count of three, we open fire, okay?"

"Okay, Kranda." The human's voice sounded tiny in her ear-piece.

She readied her blaster, feeling the thud of her heart. She was seven again, and hunting coyti with her hive-mother. She felt the same sense of delicious exhilaration, the same awareness of potential danger.

She was in charge of events. Her fate was in her own hands, now.

The mono-car approached. She made out small, pale-blue Sporelli heads through the strip viewscreen at the front of the vehicle.

In a matter of seconds it would be drawing level.

"Okay, Jeff, any second now..."

She had expected the mono-car to continue on past the Gaia Machine, but had failed to consider the possibility that the Sporelli, like herself, possessed a sense of wonder. The mono-car drew to a halt and stopped fifty metres from where Kranda and Ellis were concealed.

Three Sporelli soldiers stepped from the vehicle and walked slowly, in obvious amazement, towards the pulsing Machine. At least six others, Kranda estimated visually, remained within the mono-car.

"Okay," she whispered to Ellis. "After three, you take out the car. I'll take the approaching troops."

She switched her laser to her firing hand and said, "One... two... three!"

She fired, taking out two of the troops instantly but missing the third. He rolled with the athleticism of a gymnast and came up firing.

Kranda ducked back into the cover of the fissure. Ellis had fired, as instructed, but the sound of the returning fire from the Sporelli suggested his shots had failed to destroy the mono-car. Kranda peered from the fissure and made out the vehicle retreating at speed, a scorch mark scored across its flank where Ellis's blaster had merely winged it.

The third Sporelli soldier was on his belly, firing wildly in their approximate direction. She wondered if the soldier with the heat-seeker was still within the mono-car.

She leapt out, saying to Ellis via the com-link, "Stay put. Whatever you do, don't move from here. I'll be back when I've..."

She dodged a lancing laser beam that the sniper had fired towards the Machine. It impacted with the surface, glancing off harmlessly. Kranda roared and bore down on the soldier, firing all the time. Her laser tore him in two at the waist, his torso rolling away surreally while his legs beat a macabre tattoo on the deck.

The retreating mono-car was a hundred metres away and accelerating.

She approached the mono-line and, activated by her presence, a mono-car emerged from the notch. She leapt inside and touched the controls before the padding had time to encapsulate her. There was an agonising delay before the padding cosseted her and the vehicle was allowed to move off.

Seconds later she was in pursuit. She leaned forward, thrusting away the attention of the padding, aimed her blaster and punched a smoking hole in the front viewscreen. The pulse hurtled towards the mono-car in front, missing by a fraction. She grinned to herself – she had almost accounted for the vehicle with an accidental shot. That augured well for a successful outcome.

Not that the retreating Sporelli troops were giving up without a fight. Bright blue laser fire lanced from their mono-car, striking the front end of her vehicle and streaking off into the air. Their second shot was luckier, finding the hole in the viewscreen and missing Kranda's head by centimetres.

She laid down a barrage of return fire, striking the car and ripping through a section of its rear carapace. She aimed for the viewscreen, hitting it on her third attempt. A billow of acrid smoke obscured the view for a split second, and when it cleared she saw that their mono-car was still travelling. She increased her visual magnification, made out blood sprayed across what remained of the rear viewscreen, and knew that she'd accounted for more of the bastards.

But Sporelli troops remained alive in there, or else the mono-car would have come to a halt. In fact it appeared to be accelerating. She fired again, missing the vehicle as it drew away. She reached out, found the pseudopod, and pushed hard; her speed rose with it.

For the next fifteen minutes as the vehicles hurtled along the Helical spine, Kranda and the Sporelli traded fire, occasionally striking their targets but failing – a tribute to Builder technology – to render the cars inoperable.

Then, minutes later, the car ahead slowed and two Sporelli rolled from its protection. At first Kranda thought the soldiers were splitting up in order to attack her – and only then, as the troops climbed to their feet and sprinted towards a silver bullet-shape fifty metres away, did she realise that they had reached the entry to the access chute.

She slowed her own vehicle, leapt and fired, decapitating the first Sporelli soldier. The second dodged his colleague's flailing bulk, flung himself from another laser beam more by fortune than skill, and leapt through the chute's sliding hatch. It snapped shut behind him. Kranda cursed and fired off another shot in frustration, but it merely glanced off the metal and hissed into the air.

She considered, for a brief second, following the soldier to the surface and accounting for him there – the Mahkan hunter in her refusing to be bested. But sense came into play and told her that she would be risking everything against unknown factors if she gave in to the primitive urge.

The fact was that the Sporelli knew about the concealed inspection chutes, and nothing she could do now could alter that.

Best to return to Ellis, continue on to Sporell, and successfully complete what they had set out to do.

She returned to her ravaged mono-car, climbed aboard and set off again.

4

JEFF ELLIS WAS cowering within his fissure, gripping his blaster and peering out fearfully as Kranda crossed from the mono-rail and picked her way through the scattered body parts of the Sporelli. The sight of it didn't affect her in the slightest.

Kranda halted before the human. "Killed them all?" he asked.

She elected not to reply. She reached out, took Ellis's hand, and hauled him to his feet. "Come, we leave here."

They walked to the mono-rail line, and a pristine car flowed up from the deck. They climbed aboard and seconds later were accelerating away from the scene of slaughter, the monolithic Gaia Machine humming to their right.

Ellis said, "You enjoyed that, didn't you?"

She eyed him. "What? The killing? The slaughter? The vanquishing of those out to kill me?" She thought about it, then said, "I will be honest with you, human, and say that yes, I did. It is... it's in my blood. I have killed from an early age; I see no wrong in it, in certain situations. And don't claim, as I've heard certain humans say, that a civilised people is one which has evolved past the urge to kill. My people are highly civilised, if by 'civilised' you mean having laws to protect those who need protecting, if you mean having rights upholding the sanctity of the individual, if you mean having fine arts and literature. But it also happens that we do not always obey the laws of non-violence laid down by the Builders. Now, there might come a time when my people do just that, but until that time arrives... there will be occasions when we need to defend ourselves, and this was one of them."

Ellis said, "They were running away."

She looked past him at the bulk of the Gaia Machine. "They were still a threat," she said. "I didn't want them to escape."

"And were you successful?"

She avoided his gaze and said, "No. One got away."

Ellis just shook his head, his expression impossible to read.

They travelled in silence for a long time. The Gaia Machine passed into their wake and eventually its pervasive thrumming diminished. The gargantuan perspective of the spine reduced the mono-car to a tiny, insignificant speck.

Ellis closed his eyes, his head lolling sideways. A section of the padding extruded to form a cushion.

Kranda said, "There are sedatives available, for extended journeys."

Ellis opened his eyes. "How long before we reach the access chute to Sporell?"

Kranda consulted her varnika. "We should reach the upchute in a little less than ten hours."

"And the sedative?"

Kranda reached out, and a pendant pseudopod descended from the padding above Ellis's head. "Take a little of the fluid in your mouth, and you will sleep. I'll wake you when we arrive."

Ellis moved the tentacle to his mouth and sucked, and a second later his eyes closed.

She asked her varnika how fast they were travelling, and it replied without delay, "*Six thousand kilometres an hour*," it said.

She smiled to himself. They were travelling so fast and yet there was hardly any sensation of movement. The view fore and aft did not change, and the only sound to be heard was the almost subliminal humming of the speeding vehicle.

She considered her return to Mahkan and the unnamed world where a post in Major Lan'malan's team awaited her. She wondered if the routine of duty, after this bout of intensive and non-stop action, might prove monotonous and unrewarding. She smiled at the thought: just a week ago she had been relishing the imminent job of assessing the security of the unnamed world's access chutes, and now she was wondering if the work she had been trained to do for the past twenty years might now seem dull.

First, of course, was the small matter of going among the Sporelli and rescuing the Phandran, which might be the very last action she enjoyed in this life. She banished the thought. The success of the *Sophan* was entirely in her hands, and she would not fail.

She took a mouthful of sedative, then, and in short order was asleep.

5

A GREY, IRON-HARD landscape greeted their emergence from the chute.

They were in a range of hills west of the capital city of Kharmand. Behind them, a slab of rock concealed the entrance to the access chute. Ellis was staring at the rock with an expression of puzzlement. He reached out and touched the cold surface.

He turned to Kranda. "How is it done?" he asked. "We stepped through seconds ago, and now..."

"A substance permeable to matter," she said.

"But only... selected matter?"

"As an engineer, I have embedded biometric codes which access the Builders' artefacts. Don't ask me how the technology works. Even we Mahkan do not understand everything constructed by the Builders."

She moved across the frosted grass and peered down the hillside. She was accustomed to cold, grey worlds – her homeworld being one of them – but whereas Mahkan was a planet of sweeping grandeur and spectacular geography, Sporell was neither. Other than the low hills to the south of Kharmand, the rest of the planet was a flat, featureless place of arable plains extending for thousands of kilometres, the landscape broken only by small towns, villages, and outlying farmsteads.

She indicated the eastern horizon, where a faint glow hung in the sky. "The capital," she said to Ellis. "President Horrescu resides in the presidential tower, looked after by his medics. Not that the people of Sporell know of his illness. According to them he's still their glorious leader, in rude health and leading the invasion of their ignoble neighbours. Look."

The glow above Kharmand intensified, pulsing with polychromatic light. "Up your visual magnification, Jeff."

Kranda ordered her varnika to zoom in on the city, and made out tiny images in the sky above the horizon. She saw a face, presumably that of Horrescu, and lines of propagandising text too small at this distance for her varnika to translate.

"They beam propaganda onto the underside of the cloudscape," she said. "On Sporell, the sun never shines."

Perhaps a kilometre from their position in the hills, a perfectly straight road arrowed from the direction of the capital and vanished towards the western horizon. A convoy of military vehicles chuntered along the road, nose to tail.

"The western coastline is around thirty kilometres in that direction," she said. "The invasion continues. And look."

She pointed to a squadron of fliers heading towards the sea that separated Sporell from Phandra.

Ellis was peering towards the lighted city. "How far away is the capital?" he asked.

"A little over a hundred kilometres. It should take us a couple of hours to get there."

"What's the local time?"

"Four in the afternoon."

Ellis looked around him, then up into the sky. "Four in the afternoon and as dull as dawn," he said.

"We'll follow the road to the capital, keeping a kilometre this side of it. It's unlikely that the Sporelli who followed us guessed where we might be heading, but it's best not to take chances."

They set off, running from the hills to the flat land below, turning towards the capital before they reached the road and keeping it to their right as they ran. It felt good to be active again, after hours cooped up in first the mono-car and then the upchute. Kranda filled her lungs, breathed out easily. The permafrost crunched, compacting beneath her boots.

They came to the outskirts of the city less than two hours later, an ugly industrial sprawl of warehouses, factories and towering residential blocks. Few citizens were about, and those that did brave the sub-zero temperatures wore long padded overcoats as grey as the colourless skies above.

They passed the encircling industrial zone and came to the heart of the city. Here, no expense had been spared in the erection of vast monolithic buildings situated on wide, treeless boulevards. There was something profoundly dispiriting about the scale of the city, as if even the architecture had been pressed into service to suppress the spirit of its citizens.

Kranda came to a halt and pointed. Beyond the brutalist blocks of stone, perhaps a kilometre away, a slim, rearing tower rose as if intent on piercing the cloudscape.

"The presidential tower."

Ellis laid a hand on her arm. "One thing, before we set off again." He hesitated, then said. "Promise me that whatever happens here, we think before we kill, okay? I know it's a brutal regime, and individual soldiers might be sadistic... but we only take life if we're threatened."

She stared at him. "And if the taking of life is necessary to achieve our aim of rescuing your Phandran?"

She could see complex thoughts working themselves out behind the human's eyes. "In that case... then and only then do we act."

She inclined her head. "Very well, Jeff, I agree. However, be assured that I always think before I kill."

Ellis nodded. "Okay, then. Let's go."

They ran down a wide boulevard between the soaring city blocks, individual windows dully lighted in the gloom. Minutes later they came to the centre of the city, the vast ring road which encompassed the dark spike of the presidential tower. A little traffic beetled along the ring road, and pedestrians were even scarcer.

Walking now, they approached the tower.

Eighteen /// The Domain of the Builders

I

MARIA SAW HER last patient of the day, left the lakeside medical complex, and headed for the nearest coffee shop.

She worked four days a week, from nine until three, and she was the first to admit that she had it easy. Compared to her internship at Carrelliville General, ten years ago, this was a sinecure. The reward, she thought, for years of hard work – one of the perks of landing a post with a government body.

She sipped her coffee, stared out across the lake, and realised that she had never felt as happy for a long, long time.

The meeting with Jeff had gone well. She'd felt sick at the thought of the imminent encounter, had almost ended things with him by recording a holo-message telling him all about Dan and her desire to start a new life with him. But Jeff, for all his faults, deserved better than that.

She had expected bitterness and recriminations from him, but he had taken her news with an equanimity which almost earned her respect. Perhaps his experiences of late had changed him, made him reflect on the moribund state of their relationship. She had even, as they'd parted, felt the first stirrings, for a long time, of compassion.

But it was over, done with, and now she was free.

Her wrist-com chimed and she accepted the call. "Dan! What a surprise…" It was the week he should have been spending with his wife; Maria had been counting the days until she next had him all to herself.

"Something's come up. How do you feel about a shuttle trip to the third circuit?"

She laughed. "But I was only just thinking about the perks of the post," she said. "Great. Where to, and when?"

"A place we've never been to before. Unnamed and uninhabited."

"Uninhabited?"

"I'll explain everything when we meet at the spaceport," Dan said. "This is big, Maria." She smiled at the boyish excitement in his voice. "Can you get your things together and meet me at five? That gives you" – he glanced off-screen – "an hour and a half." She wondered if she detected, in that line, criticism of her usual tardiness.

"I'm on my way," she said.

Back at her city centre apartment she packed a case with the usual luggage for a short field-trip, then called a taxi. On the way to the spaceport, a short ride of ten minutes, she wondered what it was that had made Dan so excited. And what, she thought, might his team be doing on an unnamed and uninhabited world?

She passed through the routine identity checks in a few minutes, then joined Dan and the rest of the team in a waiting lounge. A dozen men and women, specialists in various scientific fields, stood around in animated conversation. Something about their collective air of anticipation was unlike the usual pre-field-trip gatherings.

"Director Stewart," Maria greeted him formally, aware of suspicious eyes on her.

He took her to one side, away from the others, and stood before the window overlooking the port and the ships ranked along the tarmac. "Dan, what's going on?"

He said in lowered tones, "You recall my telling you about the tame Mahkan? Well, she's come up with the goods."

She laughed. "The goods?"

"We think we've located the virtual domain of the Builders," he said.

2

SECONDS LATER, BEFORE she could press him for a fuller explanation, a chime rang through the lounge and a female voice invited them to cross the apron and board the waiting shuttle.

"Find a seat up front," he whispered to her as they left the terminal building, "and I'll join you as soon as I can."

She shouldered her bag and followed him across the hot tarmac to the silver arrowhead of the shuttle. For a second she wondered if Jeff might be the pilot, then recalled he was taking a month's furlough.

She climbed the steps and moved down the walkway between the seats, lodging her bag on an aisle seat at the front and taking the window seat for herself. She strapped herself in and stared through the slit-screen, watching the pre-flight activity of a dozen men and women as they scurried round the shuttle then backed off as countdown began.

Ten minutes later the shuttle canted on its gantry, and she fell back in her seat and gripped the arm-rests, closing her eyes as the engines roared in a deafening crescendo and the shuttle blasted from the tarmac.

Only after two minutes, with the ground safely diminished to the aspect of an architect's scale model far below, did she open her eyes and stare out. The lake came into view, and the line of A-frames where she and Jeff had lived for years. The prevailing sense from this high up was that New Earth was a verdant parkland dotted here and there with small townships and settlements, a rural idyll criss-crossed by a few highways and the odd mono-rail.

They climbed, and Carrelliville diminished. Ahead, the sea came into sight, and the resort complex around the Builders' ziggurat. Fifteen minutes later Maria discerned the broad curve of the barrel-shaped world, the far horizon comprising both land and sea, with the stars of deep space beyond.

She pressed her face to the slit-screen and peered up. Far above she made out the filament of the third circuit, their destination.

A voice came over speakers. "Please return to your seats and fasten seat-belts. Transition in fifteen seconds…"

Maria gripped the arms of her seat and closed her eyes. The ion-drive kicked in, pressing her into her seat and boosting the shuttle away from New Earth.

Dan removed her bag from the seat beside her and sat down. She peered between the seats, ensured that no one could observe them, then kissed him. "Now, would you mind telling me what's going on here, Director Stewart?"

He recounted the information from their man liaising with the Mahkan engineers. "I was in conference with Governor Reynolds just this morning," he said, "and he broke the news to me. And something else." He smiled ruefully, looking much younger than his forty-two years. "All along we – *we* being the human authorities – thought we were playing the tame Mahkan, when in fact…"

"Go on."

"Well, Reynolds rather thinks it was the other way around. The tame Mahkan was a plant."

"I don't get it. Why would the Mahkan plant someone in order to give us what we wanted?"

"It's Reynolds' theory that the Mahkan thought it time – for whatever reason – to share this with us, but the Mahkan being the Mahkan, proud and bloody-minded as they are – they couldn't be seen to give us what we wanted. They, or factions within their power-structure, would lose face that way. So they set up the plant and played us along." He shrugged. "Which, to be honest, I don't give a damn about. Just so long as we get what we want."

"The domain of the Builders," she echoed his earlier phrase. "All you have to do now is work out a way to communicate with them – if they want to communicate, that is."

He smiled wryly. "Not a lot to ask, is it?"

She peered through the screen. They were so high now that the entirety of new Earth, from north to south, could be seen far below – along with the seas on either side and the worlds beyond them, stretching away into the hazy distance.

Dan cleared his throat. "I haven't seen you since you met with Jeff..."

She looked at him. Did she detect apprehension in his expression?

He asked, "How did it go?"

She smiled and squeezed his hand. "I told him about us. I told him it was over between me and him."

"And," he asked, "how did he take it?"

"He suspected I was seeing someone, suspected it was you. He took it well, considering. I was dreading meeting him, but he accepted what I said."

Dan sighed. "I wish Sabine was as accommodating."

Maria's heart thumped. "What happened?"

"The agreement we had, that I stay with her one week in four... Well, she isn't happy with it."

"Well, that's tough," Maria said. "I hope you told her that."

Dan looked uneasy. "Of course I did, but... She threatened legal proceedings, threatened to break my... infidelity, as she calls it... to the media. I don't want that."

Maria tried to keep calm and see things from his perspective. "What does she want?" she asked, ice in her heart.

Dan took her hand. "Status quo. Things as they were. I stay with her and see you occasionally. I know, I know... that's not what I want, either. But I think, for the time being, that it'd be wise to play it her way. Trust me on this, Maria. I want rid of her, but I have to play this carefully."

She nodded, a pit of disappointment opening up within her. "Okay," she said in a small voice.

The bitch, she thought.

"We'll wait till we've communicated with the Builders, as I'm confident we will. The story will be so big then that she can blow my damned infidelity to the media and it won't make the slightest splash."

"And," Maria said, "if the Builders aren't willing to play ball?"

He looked into her eyes. "Then I'll just have to face the brick-bats of the media and put a brave face on my depravity," he said.

The shuttle had rotated in transit, so that now they were upside-down in relation to New Earth – but the right way up in relation to the circuit they were approaching. "How long before we land?" she asked.

"Another six hours," Dan said. "Hungry? I'll fetch you a meal."

Maria smiled to herself and settled in for the rest of the voyage.

I

CALLA HUDDLED IN the corner of the flier as it carried her over the sea, away from D'rayni. Two Sporelli soldiers sat opposite, their rifles trained on her, their expressions hostile.

She was still reliving the events of several hours ago, when Jeff Ellis had approached the flier in the medical compound. She had been disbelieving that he had actually managed to find her amidst all the bloodshed and chaos, but somehow he'd located her and attempted to take her from the Sporelli. If only he had come a little earlier, before the officers had selected her to be transported to Sporell.

Frantically, as the big flier had roared into life and lumbered into the night sky, she had probed for Jeff Ellis's signature, fearful that the Sporelli had found and killed him. She had found it with a cry of joy, a tiny, darting thing like a glow-fly far below, growing ever fainter as the flier rose and he ran for his life pursued by Sporelli troops.

And he had not been alone, but accompanied by someone whose signature had been unreadable to her, a big alien who was obviously his accomplice. She wondered if it was this being who had supplied Jeff Ellis with the device that rendered him all but invisible. It cheered her that he was not alone in this venture, and that with the invisibility device he had a chance of eluding the Sporelli.

She wondered, then, if this was what Diviner Tomar had meant when he said that she and the human would be reunited – for brief seconds only, just long enough to exchange a few words before she was dragged into the flier and he had to flee. But no – for hadn't Tomar told her that with the human she would help to bring peace to Phandra?

She shifted her position minimally on the hard deck, making herself a little more comfortable. Across the hold, the guards sat up, their guns twitching. They settled down again when it became obvious that she did not intend to attack them.

She probed, but met with only the opaque, unreadable mush of the Sporelli minds.

She thought back over the hours she had spent tending the Sporelli injured. They had suffered many casualties, mainly with terrible burns. First the Sporelli medics had worked on the injured, treating the injuries and stabilising the patients before handing them on to the Phandran Healers for aftercare. In this, she was proud to say, she and her people had been successful. Perhaps seventy per cent of all the troops she had nursed had pulled through, and her skill had not passed unnoticed by her Sporelli overlords.

Just one hour before she was whisked away from the battle-zone, a Sporelli officer drew her to one side and said in halting Phandran, "Your talents are exceptional, Calla-vahn-villa."

She had stared into his skull-like blue face, his slanting eyes so very alien, and replied, "To heal is our calling. Despite the many differences between our people – the main one being our regard of fellow sentients – there are also many similarities. I heal without consideration of the rectitude of those I treat."

The officer's lips had twitched, and he said, "Would you like to be taken away from here, from the war-zone?"

She looked up at him. "To another world?"

His eyes narrowed. "How did you know that?"

"Because it is destined," she said. "I will travel far, achieve great things. My father told me this, as did Diviner Tomar."

"You will indeed achieve great things. Our leader, President Horrescu, is ill. Our physicians have done all within their power to keep the great man alive as long as they have. You are a... a last resort. You will be taken to the presidential tower on Sporell aboard the next flier out of here."

She had smiled to herself at the thought of leaving this world and visiting another – so Diviner Tomar had been right on that score. And the other – that she would be reunited with Jeff Ellis?

It was as she was being led out to the flier that she'd detected, with a sudden thrill, the mental presence of Jeff Ellis not twenty metres away.

Now she closed her eyes and prayed that he had managed to elude the Sporelli soldiers and that they would, some time soon, meet again.

2

SHE SLEPT FITFULLY, waking with a jolt much later. She sat up and stared out through the window in the sliding door to her right. A grey dawn was seeping from the north, and they were no longer flying over the ocean. A flat, featureless landscape as grey as the dawn spread out far below. If this was Sporell, then it was a bleak and soulless world. She tried to make out if anything lived down there, but she saw nothing – no grass, no trees or shrubs – and her fleeting probes sensed no signs of Sporelli life.

At one point, she did see a long straight road down below, full of black military vehicles heading for the coast, accompanied by the dull, indecipherable emanations of their alien minds. The convoy appeared to be endless, and she thought of the many Sporelli being sent to their deaths, and the many D'rayni who would perish also. All for what? So that a ruler might extend his power to another world?

A ruler...

She would soon – hard though this was to believe – be in the presence of this ruler, this President Horrescu. He would be relying on her to ease his illness, though it was clear from what the officer had said that Sporelli physicians had done all they could.

She was curious as to what kind of man had ordered the invasion of innocent worlds, and the deaths of innocent people, and why he sought to extend his already considerable power. These were concepts alien to her way of thinking. Her people ruled by committee, with every villager having a voice as loud as an Elder;

and her people eschewed violence, knowing that it brought about suffering both to the victim and to the perpetrator.

Perhaps she would have the opportunity to tell President Horrescu this simple fact?

The flier tipped. Through the window she saw a grey town come into view – but a town the like of which she had never seen before. It was vast, and consisted of a hundred mountains that had had their summits planed off and their sides made vertical so that they resembled so many rectangular blocks marching off into the distance. It was not, she thought, natural, and in all her life she had never set eyes on anything as ugly.

The flier came down in a yard surrounded by a high wall. The flier's door was dragged open by a soldier and her guards gestured for her to climb out. The drop was too far for her to negotiate, so the soldier took her arm in a painful grip and pulled her down.

She was marched quickly across the yard, through freezing air, towards a door in a nondescript building like all the others she had seen.

She was hurried along a corridor, which did have the advantage of being slightly warmer than outside, and into a cell.

A table stood in the middle of the room, with a chair on one side of it and two on the other. The guard pushed her towards the big chair. When she sat, her feet dangled a hand's span above the floor.

Two officers entered the room and sat down opposite her. The door closed with a reverberating clang.

She wondered what was happening now; why she was here, and not ministering to the needs of the president.

The officer to her right spoke in halting Phandran, "You were approached by a Mahkan on D'rayni as you were about to leave Erkeles base. What did the Mahkan want with you?"

She stared at the blue-faced Sporelli. "A Mahkan?"

"A Mahkan! An engineer."

She gestured that she did not know what he was talking about. "A Mahkan. I know of no Mahkan. I have never seen a Mahkan in my life."

The Sporelli consulted a screen. "And on Phandra you were in the company of the renegade human." He stared at her, awaiting her reaction.

She said, "And before that I encountered the Sporelli, and saw their handiwork in the dead and injured you left behind you all across my world."

The Sporelli's gaze was like ice. "What did the Mahkan want with you, Phandran? Was he, too, seeking the human?"

Calla gestured again. "I cannot guess the motivations of those who seek me," she said. "Perhaps, like you, they have a sick leader they would like me to assist?"

She considered the line rather humorous, but the Sporelli did not smile.

The translator turned to the second officer and spoke at length – recounting the outcome of their abortive dialogue?

At last the translator turned to her and said, "Have you heard of a device called a guran?"

"A musical instrument?" she ventured.

"A guran reads a subject's mind," he went on. "It elicits the truth, eventually. Sadly, it also leaves the subject dead."

She considered his words, then said evenly, "In that case, I would be of little use to your president, sir."

The two Sporelli conferred again, and she hoped that they considered the president's health more important than learning why she had been approached by the 'Mahkan' on D'rayni.

The Sporelli soldiers stood abruptly and left the cell, snapping orders to the guards outside. They entered, took her arms and escorted her from the cell, back down the corridor and outside. This time, a bulbous black ground vehicle awaited her, and she was bundled into the rear seat. The guards joined her, one on each side, and the car started up and drove at speed from the compound.

They passed through streets devoid of natural life: no trees, no birds, no people – or very few of the latter. Once or twice she saw scurrying figures, dressed in colourless garb, bent against the intense cold.

She peered ahead and saw, rearing into the cold grey sky, a great black spike pierced with lighted windows.

The car passed through a high gate in the wall surrounding the vast tower, approached the building and then, miraculously, dipped underground without losing speed. The car braked and the guards bundled her out, hurrying her through a pair of sliding doors and into a tiny room. They stood still for a minute, their inactivity bewildering Calla, and then the door slid open again. They stepped out and, amazingly, they were no longer in the darkened underground chamber.

The guards tightened their grip on her upper arm and whisked her along a corridor and into a room bustling with men and women in black, blue and grey uniforms.

A silence descended as everyone turned to look at her. Someone spoke, and another laughed in response. A woman approached her with a circle of silver metal and passed it up and down in front of Calla's torso, and another woman moved her hands over her body, patting briskly as if in search of something. This woman spoke to a man, who turned and nodded towards another man who opened the door at the far end of the room.

Through it, Calla made out a large chamber whose far wall was one tall window which looked out over the grey city. The little room, then, must have somehow carried her *up* inside the tower.

Seated on a wheeled chair in the middle of the room, facing the open door, was a man so ancient that Calla doubted he could still be alive.

The guards gripped her arms and propelled her through the door and into the presence of President Horrescu.

3

SO THIS WAS the man, the great leader, who had sent his troops into Phandra and D'rayni, troops who had gone willingly with the belief that they were liberating an oppressed people and bringing them a better life.

This was the man responsible for the deaths of thousands.

Calla stared at him, and all she could feel in her heart was pity.

She felt pity because he was so deluded that he thought the attainment of power was an achievement in itself; and she felt pity because he was in pain and on the verge of death.

Calla looked at President Horrescu, her instinctive probe sliding off his alien mind. She was glad that his mind was shut to her, that she was not privy to his innermost thoughts and emotions.

He reached out, and his thin lips twitched in a feeble smile.

He was thin, but his was not the healthy slightness that comes from exercise and a good diet: his was the emaciation of disease, of some illness that had whittled the flesh from his bones and left him resembling an animated skeleton. He sat stiffly upright, fighting pain; only his bright blue eyes seemed truly alive.

He surprised her by saying in halting Phandran, "Come, child..."

She bridled, remained where she was, and said, "I am not a child. Among my people, I am considered old. In less than one Phandran year, I will be dead."

His eyes widened in surprise. He gestured with a shaking hand to a semi-circle of couches arranged before the floor-to-ceiling window. "If you would kindly propel me..." She approached his mobile seat and gripped the handles, turning the chair and pushing it towards the window. The president was no weight at all, a bag of feathers.

He gestured for Calla to take a seat, and she perched herself on one of the couches.

"Was I mistaken, or did I hear you say that in one year...?"

She said, "In less than one Phandran year... and I do not know how long that is in Sporell years, I will pass from this life, yes."

"One Phandran year," the president informed her, "is a little under two years here on Sporell."

She inclined her head in understanding.

The president asked, "Do you know how old I am, in Phandran years?"

"I could not guess," she said. He seemed ancient. Thirty? More?

"I am almost forty Phandran years old," he said. "Or in our own reckoning, a little under eighty years old." He gestured, his hand trembling. "Which is old, for my people. But then I have had access to the best Sporelli medicines available."

Forty years old, she thought in amazement. He *was* ancient.

"And yet... even the best medicine is sometimes not enough," he said.

He stared at her, at her unlined face, at her still hands folded together on her lap. "But – Calla, isn't it? – Calla, tell me: do you not fear death?"

She stared at him. It was clear, from his question, that *he* did.

She said, "What is to fear? I have led a full life, healing others. I have almost come to the end of my allotted time."

He leaned forward in his carriage, the movement evidently causing him pain; he winced. "Allotted? You *knew*...?"

"Every Phandran lives to the age of approximately ten years," she said, "unless an accident shortens their span."

He shook his head. "To know when one will die... Perhaps, so knowing, you come to fear less the end?"

She made a negative gesture with her right hand. "No. We do not fear death at all, for after this life comes Fahlaine. The realm that follows this life, which every Phandran, and for all I know every other being on the Helix, will attain."

"Even me?"

She stared at him. "Even you. Moral rectitude and goodness are no criteria for admittance into Fahlaine."

"Then what is?"

"Merely that one has lived. In Fahlaine, so our Elders say, one learns of one's mistakes in one's earlier life, and then one repents."

He said, "That is your belief."

She inclined her head. "Of course."

He stared at her. She detected bitterness in his eyes. "I hold no such superstitious belief. There is no glorious afterlife, no Fahlaine. There is only this life."

Into the silence which developed then, Calla said hesitantly, "Is this, then, why you fear your approaching death so much, President Horrescu?"

He smiled at her presumption, and nodded. "Yes, Calla. That is probably why I fear the thought of my death. My extinction. The termination of everything I have ever known, and an end to all my hopes and dreams and ambitions."

"For a man who held... holds... ultimate power, that thought must be very hard." Which is proof, she thought, of the corrupting affect of that power.

He smiled, the gesture appalling on so ravaged a face. "But power brings that which lesser citizens could not dream of," he said. "I might fear death, and stare it in the eye, but I am in no position, even now, to back down and admit defeat."

She nodded her understanding. "Which is why you had me brought from D'rayni, so that I might heal you?"

How to begin to tell him that he was beyond even her considerable powers of Healing? She could ease his pain, prolong his life for a little while, but nothing could undo the disease raging within his wasted frame.

"I had you brought here, Calla, to *extend* my life for a little while, not grant me immortality."

She thought she understood, then, his motivations. "You wish to see the successful end to your campaign on D'rayni? To live long enough to enjoy your great victory?"

He laughed at that. He flung back his head and brayed a hoarse, painful laugh. The effort was punished: he bent double, gasping for breath.

She stood and moved to the president. "Let me…"

She reached out and laid a hand on his chest, easing him back into the carriage. She closed her eyes and concentrated, felt his weak life-force like that of a small animal beneath her palm. She soothed, instilling energy, and worked to ease his pain.

Minutes later his breathing came more easily. He sat up, staring at Calla, then nodded. "Thank you," he whispered.

She resumed her seat and folded her hands on her lap.

The president leaned forward and fixed her with an intense, unsettling stare. "You think I wish to live to savour the puny victory of my army over the feeble D'rayni? We have almost vanquished the lumpen oafs, taken over their world. I will gain little satisfaction from a campaign won so easily."

He had changed in an instant, she thought. From a feeble old man on the cusp of death, he had become the person he might have been years ago, a dictator who showed no mercy, whose every command was obeyed by fearful underlings, who would brook no opposition to his grand schemes.

"You will go on," she said, "to the next world, and the one after that, killing innocents, destroying cities and towns. You will go on and on, from one world to the next. But President Horrescu, even if you had the wherewithal to conquer the likes of the humans and the Mahkan, you will be dead long before that."

He smiled again, that travesty of pleasure on the wreck of his sunken features. "You understand little, Phandran," he said scathingly. "You will keep me alive and free from pain for three further days, and then I will have no further need of your services."

She thought she did understand, then: was the invasion of the neighbouring worlds, the slaughter of innocents, nothing more than a ploy by the president to gain bargaining chips, to hold worlds to ransom so that he might negotiate – with the technologically superior humans or the Mahkan – to have his illness treated?

She said as much to him now, and was surprised by his reaction.

"What? Go grovelling before the humans and the Mahkan, begging for the largess of their medicines?" He shook his head, and the look he bestowed on Calla then was almost pitying. "No, I have no need to go seeking alms from any alien race. In three days my people will have both the means to vanquish any race on the Helix, and I will have a cure for my ills."

He is truly mad, she thought; *his illness, the fear of death, the privilege of untrammelled power, have all tipped the balance of his sanity.*

"How...?" she began.

He waved. "That you will find out in time, Calla. Now, the pain increases." He winced. "Like a knife within me..."

She leaned forwards, placed a soothing hand on his chest, and closed her eyes.

4

OVER THE COURSE of the next two days, as he conducted the business of state, she was constantly at his side, soothing his pain and easing the worst effects of his illness. He was forever in meetings with military officers and civilian officials, issuing orders and overseeing plans, poring over maps of neighbouring worlds with his generals and schemata of the Helix with officers in grey uniforms whose insignia – arrow-shaped craft above a symbol of the Helix – indicated they were members of his space-fleet.

Her presence caused comment at first, doused by the president's barked rebukes, and soon she was ignored. Frequently she was called upon to lay hands on the gasping president, and his aides regarded her with suspicion at first, and then, as her ministrations brought relief to their leader, manifest respect.

She stared at the maps the Sporelli studied, and tried to intuit what they were planning, but their slippery alien minds and harsh language defeated her. They were planning something, something which threatened the safety of the Helix and all the peaceable peoples upon it, and Calla was powerless to comprehend the threat or lift a finger to act against it.

At night she slept in a small room adjacent to the president's, so that she could be on call at all times. In the small hours of her second night on Sporell, she could not sleep and stood by the long window in her room, staring at the lighted city spread far beneath her.

Just as she brought relief to the president's suffering, she thought, she could perform the very opposite. She could use her powers to close down the failing vitality that was keeping the man alive. She could... and she winced at the thought... kill him.

And in so doing, perhaps, avert the catastrophe that was about to befall the Helix...

But she had never killed in all of her ten years, never even taken the life of an insect. It was against everything in which she believed... and it was not an option she could resort to now.

She knew, in her heart, that salvation would come from another direction.

As she stared out into the freezing Sporelli night, at the lights that illuminated this supremely ugly city, she wondered where Jeff Ellis and his Mahkan companion might be now.

Twenty /// In the Presidential Tower

I

ELLIS CROUCHED ON the edge of the ziggurat half a kilometre from the presidential tower. From this elevation he could see over the high wall to the rows of winter cacti which, so Kranda had told him, were the president's favourite plant. The tower rose over the city like an inverted black icicle.

The dull sun was going down and darkness crept over the streets of Kharmand. Ellis was grateful for the warmth generated by his varnika.

There was limited activity on the streets below. Small, blocky ground cars puttered along the wide triumphal boulevards, something ludicrous about the magisterial avenues being used by such rudimentary vehicles. As they watched, propaganda beams lanced into the air and pasted slogans on the underside of the clouds. His varnika translated the bold lettering as, 'President Horrescu leads Sporell towards triumph and prosperity.'

The words alternated with images of the president, a small, thickset man in middle-age. It was easy to see in his dark, deep-set eyes the brutality that his troops on Phandra and D'rayni were making manifest. Ellis looked away from the aerial image: those eyes seemed to be staring directly down at him.

He said, "I wonder if the citizens know how ill the bastard is?"

Kranda grunted. "Everything they tell the populace is a lie. The truth is an unknown commodity, here on Sporell. Even his image is a lie. In reality the president is around eighty years old."

"How the hell did they get themselves into such a situation? The Builders rescued them from themselves, and instructed them in how to form a peaceful, fair society."

"You know the Builders give guidelines only. They don't enforce their views." She barked a laugh. "That would be against their principles."

"So when something like this happens, when one of their saved races goes off the rails and threatens others, they just sit back and let it happen?"

Kranda gave him a quick glance. She said, without a hint of irony, "They handed on the mantle of Peacekeepers to you, the human race. It is for you to uphold the peace so vaunted by the Builders."

"You never know, by now the Peacekeepers might have moved themselves to do something." But, even as he spoke the words, he knew it was a forlorn hope.

Kranda grunted again. "We have a phrase on Mahkan, Jeff. Coyti might turn vegetarian."

"And on New Earth we say 'Pigs might fly.'" Ellis laughed. He looked at the tower. "So..." he asked at last. "Any ideas?"

"We could try to scale the outer wall, but I don't like the look of those." She indicated the small, glowing domes that lined the top of the wall. "My guess is that they're alarms, motion-sensitive."

"Surely someone must use the gate from time to time."

"Unless the arch is purely ceremonial, and for security reasons they have hidden entrances."

"Always assuming, of course, that the president is at home."

"According to my information, he spends most of his time in his official suite, tended by his aides and medics."

Ellis increased the visual magnification and scanned the presidential grounds. Lateral walkways radiated from the tower walls, running between raised beds of spiky silver cactus plants. He looked for any indication of openings on the inner wall's long curve around the tower, but it seemed to be manufactured from one seamless section of dull white, marble-like substance. He wondered if Kranda was right and the tower was accessible via underground passageways.

Kranda barked something in her own tongue. She pointed, and Ellis watched as a convoy of military vehicles trundled along the wide avenue encircling the presidential tower.

Kranda wrinkled her muzzle and gave a snort, which Ellis knew to be a laugh. "And look, riding in the leading open-topped staff-car..."

Ellis switched his enhanced vision to the leading car and saw the thin, imperious figure of a uniformed Sporelli officer staring ahead.

"I see him, but..."

"I came across the coyti while searching for you on Phandra. He was the officer who personally gave the order for the mind-wipe to be used on you."

"Nice man."

"His arrival here is both good news, and bad."

"The bad first."

"I suspect he's here to report our presence on D'rayni... and the discovery of the access chute in the mountain peak. They might be tyrannical, but they're not stupid. They know that we now have access to their planet."

"So they're here to bolster security?"

Kranda thought for a second, then said, "They could not know of our express intentions, but they might surmise we aim to strike at the heart of their empire."

Ellis looked at his alien friend. "And the good news?"

"They're approaching the gated entrance. When they enter, so do we. Come on."

Kranda sprang to her feet and darted towards the drop to the next shoulder of the ziggurat. He followed, a hard knot of apprehension in his gut. The Mahkan vaulted over the low wall and landed with the grace of a gymnast five metres below. Ellis jumped, flexing his legs and landing beside Kranda on a paved terrace.

They ran to the edge of the shoulder and jumped again, landing this time in a cactus garden that Ellis suspected was some good citizen's obsequious attempt to mirror that of his glorious leader.

Kranda paused before another low wall and peered down. Ellis joined him. The street was three metres below them. A gaggle of pedestrians had stopped to watch the military cavalcade, pushing towards the front of the sidewalk. Kranda jumped and Ellis went after her.

They found themselves at the back of the murmuring crowd, over which Ellis watched the convoy as it grumbled towards the gates. Just as he was wondering how they might pass through the press without creating an alarm, a police car drew up and three uniformed thugs climbed out. Their very presence, silent though it was, and the fact that they carried evil-looking carbines, was enough to disperse the crowd.

Kranda touched his arm and whispered, "We follow the last vehicle in the convoy. Once we're inside, move to the left of the gate and we'll take it from there."

The staff car approached the gates and, slowly, they opened to admit the convoy. Kranda took off, crossing the wide avenue with Ellis in her wake.

The last vehicle in the convoy passed by. They gave chase and caught up, tucking themselves in between a troop-carrier and the high wall. Frost scintillated underfoot, and once or twice Ellis almost lost his balance.

The troop-carrier slowed even further as it approached the gates. They hurried along in its shadow as the carrier turned, its tracks grinding with a deafening cacophony. Ellis crept after Kranda into the compound, exhilaration vying with apprehension.

Once inside, he followed Kranda and darted left. He searched for cover. It would have been nice to have had a more substantial bush to duck behind, but the horticultural beds between the radial pathways bore only thorny succulents, half a metre high at most.

Kranda was crouching against the wall. Ellis dropped into a squat beside her, peering over the cactus garden at the convoy drawing up in the square courtyard before the tower.

Troops jumped from the carriers with a crunch of boots and deployed themselves in an enfilade around the tower walls. Kranda commented, "Certainly looks like they're expecting guests…"

"Look," Ellis said, heart kicking with panic.

He indicated a trio of troops being addressed by the officer Kranda had pointed out earlier. The trio carried shoulder-mounted devices, sickeningly familiar from their time on D'rayni.

He looked around again, desperate for cover.

The soldiers with the heat-seeking devices were deploying themselves along the tower wall, checking the settings of the heat-seekers prior to hoisting them onto their shoulders.

Kranda was thinking ahead. "Follow me!"

"Where to?"

But the Mahkan was up and running towards the parked vehicles of the convoy. They came to the squat beetle shape of a tank and ducked behind it.

Ellis said, "Fine. Now the bastards can't see us... but how the hell do we get past them?"

He raised his head above the armour of the tank and glanced towards the tower. Two of the soldiers were concentrating the attention of their heat-seekers on the area directly before the tower's portico'd entrance. The third soldier, twenty metres away, was swinging his device back and forth across the area Ellis and Kranda would be forced to cross if they wished to reach the tower.

"I've thought of that," Kranda said. "We watch him, calculate the duration of his sweeps and time the blind spots. I suspect we'll have long enough to get to the tower's wall, and behind the guards, before his heat-seeker passes this way again. Then we make our way to the entrance. Look."

The grey-haired officer and three of his underlings were standing beneath the portico, the officer engaged in an animated altercation with someone out of sight within the entrance.

Kranda said, "We have a gap of ten seconds when the heat-seeker sweeps away from us. That should give us enough time. When I give the word, follow me."

Ellis watched the soldier with the heat-seeker. He swung it towards the tank, past it and across the courtyard, paused and came back again. Kranda gripped Ellis's arm and squeezed as the soldier panned the device past them. "Now!" she hissed.

She rounded the tank and sprinted across the courtyard with a loud crunch of boots. Ellis winced at the noise and followed Kranda across the frosty concrete towards the tower wall.

They passed within three metres of the soldier, who was swinging the heat-seeker their way again. Ellis ducked and crept past, peering up at the soldier. He was close enough to make out the soldier's determined expression, as if his life depended on successfully following orders. For all Ellis knew, it did.

Seconds later he pressed himself against the tower wall, panting. Kranda tugged him onwards. No time to rest. They crept along the façade, behind the guards, towards the grand portico.

They came to a pair of thick white columns and paused behind them.

The tall, imperious officer was arguing with a uniformed young man who Ellis guessed was a member of the president's security team. Their exchange was too hushed for his varnika to translate, but the outcome was that the officer's argument prevailed and the young security official reluctantly stepped aside to let the officer and aides to pass within.

Kranda waited until the security officer turned and followed them inside, then she gestured to Ellis. Heart pounding, he followed the Mahkan towards the sliding door. They slipped through a second before the door snapped shut.

2

THEY WERE IN a vast marbled foyer, dazzlingly white, whose only decoration – not surprisingly – was a ten-metre-high holographic representation of President Horrescu. The officer and his aides, joined by three uniformed security men, were debating beneath the inscrutable stare of the president's image.

Without warning, Kranda left Ellis and approached them, appearing to Ellis as an eye-watering blur – as if the marble of the foyer were shifting slightly of its own accord. Only when the Mahkan stopped within earshot of the Sporell officers did her image settle into the background, invisible to the naked eye.

Seconds later she returned. "They were expected, but the president's health is failing fast and his security team was unwilling to allow the officer an audience. The officer said he had vital information and it was imperative he see the president in person. It looks as if he's got his wishes…"

With a face like thunder, the young security officer gestured for the older soldier to proceed. The party strode along a corridor leading from the foyer.

"We follow. Where we find the president," Kranda said, "we'll find Calla…"

Ellis smiled at the thought. They followed discreetly, five metres behind the officer and his men. "All that remains, then," he said, "is the small matter of getting her out of here and away."

The Mahkan hissed, "We will address that problem when we come to it."

They hurried down a long, wide corridor hung with images of President Horrescu in various triumphal poses, opening factories, inspecting his troops, addressing massed crowds.

Ahead, the officer and his men, escorted by the trio of security officials, paused before a wide door set into the wall. The group stood around in silence with the patience shown by all races when waiting for an elevator. Ellis swore to himself. "Damn. What now? We can't enter the lift with them."

Kranda gripped his arm and whispered, "See, beyond the elevator..."

A helical staircase occupied a recess a few metres beyond the elevator doors.

"Fine," Ellis hissed, "but how will we know which floor...?"

"Observe. See the light in the lintel above the elevator door. See how, when the cage approaches, it sheds illumination across the corridor?"

The elevator doors opened and the Sporelli officers stepped inside. As soon as the door slid shut, Ellis and Kanda sprinted along the corridor and launched themselves up the spiral staircase. On the way, Ellis noticed, with amusement, that a Sporelli interior decorator had had the notion of painting the handrail in an approximation of the planets and oceans of the Helix itself. Ellis ran his hand over world after world, sea after sea, as he sprinted up the staircase with a rhythm that became tedious with repetition.

Kranda halted as they arrived at the floor above. Ellis peered past her into the corridor. A second later a patch of rising light strobed up the far wall.

They continued their swift corkscrewing ascent.

Ellis laughed, and over her shoulder Kranda barked, "What?"

"Just a thought – we might have to climb all the way to the top."

He wondered what would happen if they met a Sporelli on the way down. The staircase was just wide enough to accept Kranda's bulk. At the speed they were travelling they'd do the hapless Sporelli significant injury and, more worryingly, alert the authorities to their presence.

They came to the second floor, and again the light strobed on upwards.

Ellis wondered how they would have managed the ascent without the aid of the varnikas. Sprinting up one floor might have been possible, even two at a push, but certainly not three... or four... or five... as they were doing now.

He drew a breath, feeling the ease with which his muscles were working, his lungs pumping evenly. He might have been taking a brisk afternoon stroll for all the effort he was exerting.

They passed floors five, six, seven and eight, and still the elevator they were chasing continued its ascent. For all he knew, his earlier quip about ascending to the very summit of the tower might very well come back to haunt him.

He was pumping his limbs with such monotonous regularity now that it came as a shock when Kranda's voice sounded in his earpiece, "Stop!"

Ellis came to a halt, his senses reeling at the sudden cessation of movement.

Kranda was peering into the corridor. The elevator door was opening, its Sporelli cargo stepping out and striding down the corridor. Kranda ducked back as the officers passed. She waited for a count of five, then stepped out.

Ellis followed her, finding himself in a corridor wider and more sumptuous than the one on the ground floor. Which, he reasoned, was to be expected if this was the floor where the all-powerful ruler of Sporell had his living quarters.

Thick carpet cushioned the floor, and hanging on the walls, instead of the hagiographic images of the president in a variety of self-aggrandising poses, were pictures of bleak, snow-covered landscapes.

The officials came to a halt before a door at the very end of the corridor. The young security man palmed a sensor and seconds later the door opened a fraction. He spoke to someone within the room and the door opened to admit the party.

Kranda and Ellis sprinted to join the group and slipped inside after them.

Kranda sidestepped to the left, choosing an area of blank white wall against which to blend – rather than the wall to the right which was adorned with more pictures of icy landscapes. Ellis joined her and looked across the room.

His heart skipped when he saw Calla, and at the very same second she looked up with a fleeting startled expression on her angelic features.

Ellis stared at her thin white face, her startling cobalt eyes. He recalled their time together on Phandra, her selflessness, and he tried to discern in her appearance any sign of hardship or ill-treatment she might have suffered at the hands of the Sporelli.

She seemed, to his relief, as serene and composed as ever.

She sat on a stool beside a shrunken figure in an invalid carriage.

At first glance, Ellis found it hard to credit that this was the robust, thick-set president the propaganda would have the citizens of Sporell believe was the world's glorious leader. He was grey and emaciated, a crooked shell of a man eaten away by some illness the Sporelli, obviously, were unable to remedy.

Only the eyes – the dark, deep-set eyes – were familiar from the propaganda. In their inky depths was some flicker of the man President Horrescu had once been.

Ellis looked at Calla again, finding her own vitality life-affirming. She was looking down at her hands folded demurely on her lap.

The security man addressed the president with stammering deference. Horrescu looked up, something steely in his eyes, and snapped a reply.

Ellis commanded his varnika to translate, and the Sporelli words were rendered intelligible.

"...apologies," the young man said. "Commander Yehn demanded to see you, claiming information vital to your security."

The commander, Yehn, stepped forward. "With all due deference, I have information for your ears only, Mr President." He gestured to the young man and his security aides. "If we could be alone. And the Phandran" – he almost spat – "must be removed."

At this the young security officer bristled. "The Phandran is a Healer, sir, brought here especially..."

President Horrescu looked up, pinning Commander Yehn, then the security officer, with his death's-head gaze. "Mr Jemery, take your team and wait outside. The Phandran remains."

"But, sir –" Jemery began.

"Outside!" the president snapped.

The young official turned on his heel and, his team following, quickly exited the room.

Commander Yehn said, "And the girl…?"

"She is the only thing keeping me alive, Commander. Her powers are remarkable. I need her proximity, if you don't object *too* much?"

"Of course not, sir."

"So… this information vital to security, Commander Yehn? But before we start – a drink?"

"Not, sir, while I am on duty."

The president gestured to Calla, and she slipped off her stool and pushed his invalid carriage towards a vast window that occupied the entirety of the far wall. There, a horse-shoe arrangement of loungers was positioned before the view. Commander Yehn sat down, severely upright, as if even to be seated while on duty was against some code of martial conduct.

Calla perched herself on a lounger beside the president.

"Sir, I reported the pursuit of the human pilot on Phandra –" Yehn began.

"And his subsequent escape," the president put in, with a note of acerbity.

"I would, with deference, term it not so much an escape, as a… rescue, sir, by a Mahkan equipped with an exo-skeleton. He was responsible for the deaths of more than twenty of my men."

"So you mentioned in your original report, Commander. The fact remains, you allowed the human to escape. That was costly. Very costly." He paused, then said slyly, "Are you here to impart the glad tidings that you have managed to apprehend the errant human?"

Commander Yehn said through gritted teeth, "No sir. But we have made a significant discovery."

The president gestured to Calla, who laid a hand on his shoulder and closed her eyes as if in concentration. After a moment, President Horrescu sighed. "Go on, Commander."

"In pursuing the human and the Mahkan, sir, we discovered a great dropshaft in a mountainside on D'rayni. On further inspection, we discovered that the construction gave access to the very core of the world. Not only that, sir, but at the world's core we found a transportation system that…" he smiled as he said this, as if hardly crediting his own words, "that links every world of the Helix. It can only be the work of the Builders, sir, and now the sole province of the Mahkan."

President Horrescu sat forward in his chair. "And you managed to access the transportation system, and its operating methodology?"

Commander Yehn allowed himself a prideful smile. "Yes, sir."

The president sat back, taking in this information. "And do you know if the Mahkan are aware of our discovery?"

"I… I ordered my men to cover their tracks, conceal any evidence of our entry," Commander Yehn said. "However, in pursuing the Mahkan and the human, I lost several of my men."

"In other words, you are trying to tell me that the Mahkan know that we know about the dropshaft?"

Yehn said, "Unfortunately, that is so. However, the immediate benefits of discovering the transportation system are considerable."

President Horrescu considered his words, then said, "There are both advantages, Commander, and disadvantages…"

Ellis glanced at Kranda, wishing he could discern the Mahkan's expression as she listened to the president.

Commander Yehn leaned forward. "Knowledge of the transportation system is to our great advantage, sir. But how in future to go about its utilisation without alerting the Mahkan? They are an advanced race, sir. Their technology surpasses –"

"I am very well aware of the Mahkan, Commander, and their present capabilities!" the president snapped. "But the Mahkan do not worry me in the slightest."

The commander looked non-plussed. "Sir?"

Instead of replying immediately, the president stared at his commander for long seconds. At last he said, "You have proved to be one of my most competent and loyal officers, Commander Yehn. I am blessed to be served by men of your calibre."

"Sir, I am honoured to serve…"

Horrescu swept on, "I have long harboured desires to… let us say… access the potential of the many worlds of the Helix. In my opinion, the resources of the construct are under-utilised. I disagree with the ethos of the Builders, mighty though that race once was. They have long since passed from power, handing the role of Peacekeepers to a feeble and ineffective race." Horrescu leaned forward. "It is my belief, from long study of the natural world, that the strong and the brave outlive the peaceable and the cautious. I use this as my dictum. The Sporell are strong and we are brave."

"Sir!"

"And until only very recently my dreams remained just that – hopeless dreams, without hope of realisation."

"But sir, our advance through D'rayni proceeds well."

"Be quiet, Commander, and listen. We might succeed in taking a few worlds, maybe a dozen... But my ambitions are greater than dominion over a few unsophisticated worlds on this circuit. I look further afield, at the mighty Mahkan themselves."

Ellis listened, aware of the thudding of his heart, and wondered what Kranda was making of this.

The president went on, "Ten years ago, Commander, there came into my hands the wherewithal to achieve my aims. You recall the discovery of the unmarked ship in the northern canton of Krell?"

"Yes, sir."

"What we found when we recovered the crashed ship..." He stopped suddenly, then said, "Commander Yehn, now is not the time to discuss this. Tomorrow, you and your men will escort me to the spacefield. There, I will apprise you of the glory that awaits."

The commander sat very still, his expression stunned. "Yes, sir," he murmured.

Horrescu gestured to Calla. "Enough. Take me to my room. Commander, until tomorrow..."

Commander Yehn sprang to his feet and snapped off a quick salute, a chopping motion at his shoulder. He turned and strode from the room. Calla, with a quick glance in Ellis's direction, stood and propelled the president away from the picture window and through a sliding door.

As the door closed behind her, Ellis felt a hand on his arm.

"Well," Kranda whispered, "the president was right on a couple of points."

"And they were?"

"That the Mahkan are mighty and the human race feeble and ineffective."

"Very funny." Ellis moved to the window. In the night sky, legends boasting of the president's invincible power were alternating with vast images of his younger, healthier self.

The view might have been more spectacular had the city itself been less ugly, but even the elevated sight of so vast and homogenous a metropolis – all hard angles and shades of grey – failed to stir any appreciation in him. Perhaps President Horrescu, knowing no better, found the vista invigorating. His city, his people, sprawling at his feet...

He considered what he'd heard, then turned to Kranda. It was a few seconds before his enhanced vision made out the Mahkan's outline.

"This changes things," Kranda said.

"What Horrescu said about his ambitions?"

"The ship discovered in Krell, and how it makes those ambitions that much more realistic. I can't begin to work out why. I'd like to know where the ship came from." She paused. "I know the plan was to get away with Calla, but we need to know why Horrescu thinks his plans are more realisable now."

For the next fifteen minutes they spoke in lowered tones, then stopped at a sound from across the room. The sliding door to the president's chamber sighed open and Calla slipped out. She paused, looking around the room uncertainly. She tipped her head to one side, concentrating, then redirected her gaze towards the picture window. Her line of sight was out of kilter, like a blind person 'looking' past the intended object.

Ellis wanted to deactivate his varnika's shield so that she could see him. Instead of taking the risk he moved across the room, whispered her name, and reached out. He touched her shoulders and drew her towards him, feeling her elfin slightness against the spars of the exo-skeleton.

He led her to the loungers and they sat down.

"I can sense that you are tired, Jeff. The life of adventure does not suit you."

He smiled. "I think perhaps you're right."

"We'll make a warrior of the human yet," said Kranda. "Are we safe here? The room isn't under surveillance?"

"Many other parts of the tower are," Calla replied, "but not the president's suite. If we keep our voices low, so as not to disturb the president."

"How have they treated you?" Ellis asked.

"Far better than they have treated many of my people," she said. "But then I was chosen for my healing skills, and brought here expressly to extend the president's life."

"He's dying?" Kranda said.

Calla inclined her head. "There is only so much I can do. His condition is terminal. A viral disease which is attacking his internal organs. I ease his pain, make his life liveable."

Ellis said, "Earlier, the president said that he needed your proximity…"

"I exert a certain calmative influence on his nervous system. It works best when I am near him. When the president sleeps, I can withdraw."

"We came here to take you away, Calla," Ellis began.

She looked towards him, alarmed. "That would be… rash, Jeff. And not at all because it would mean the president's premature demise. I know the man is… bad, and though I revere life, I can see that some good might come from his death." She shook her head. "But we need to know why he thinks he can carry out his scheme to invade more worlds of the Helix."

Ellis stared at her. "You can't divine his thoughts?"

"He is… strange. Even your emotions and moods were difficult enough for me to fathom, at first. But the president's mind is a confusing turmoil. He might even be psychotic. I can sense his overweening desire for power, to rule the many peoples of the Helix… but also his fear of death. And I know this is linked in some way to what he discovered in Krell."

"But you don't know what that was?" Kranda asked.

Calla shook her head. "Tomorrow he leaves for the spacefield north of here. You heard what he told his commander. I will be with him for the duration of the journey, when he tells Yehn of his plans."

"Do you know why he needs to go to the spacefield?" Ellis asked.

"I'm sorry, no."

Kranda said, "Might he be taking a ship from there, making a triumphal visit to his invading troops on D'rayni?"

Ellis stared from Calla to the Mahkan's blurred outline. "Or perhaps further afield, Kranda? You saw the Sporelli interworld ship. Maybe that's what he got from the unmarked ship at Krell –

the technological wherewithal to develop an interworld ship. This is what will give him the advantage, and tomorrow he leads an invasion to…"

He stopped, thinking: New Earth… Mahkan?

Kranda gave a short, frustrated grunt. "That doesn't make sense, Jeff. He was going to apprise Commander Yehn of why his schemes were more realisable now. But Yehn already *knew* about the interworld ship…"

"Okay – how about this," Ellis said, hoping that he was wrong. "He did discover the wherewithal to develop interworld ships from the ship at Krell, but he also came across something else."

"Like?"

"Like a weapon or weapons system that he hasn't, so far, felt the need to use against the Phandrans or the D'rayni."

"But against humans or Mahkan…?" Kranda said.

They sat in silence for a while, considering the possibility.

At last Kranda said, "We will be with you, Calla. Or close by." The Mahkan glanced across at Ellis. "We should follow the president to the spacefield, even perhaps attempt to thwart whatever it is he's planning."

Ellis gave a hesitant nod, wondering if the Mahkan could detect his uncertainty. The thought of following Kranda's suggestion filled him with dread.

He said, "We should beam a report of what's happening here to our respective governments."

"As soon as I have time, Jeff, I fully intend to have my varnika do that. Not that they, my people or yours, will move themselves to act with any alacrity…"

Ellis turned to Calla, "Do you know when they're leaving here?"

"An hour after dawn. The spacefield is fifty kilometres north of Kharmand. The president usually travels in convoy, and is always well guarded. Please, be careful, Jeff."

"They will be especially vigilant on the journey to the spacefield," Kranda said. "They suspect, going by the heat-seekers they've deployed, that we are in the city." She fell silent, then said, "We must follow them, with extreme caution."

Ellis reached out and took Calla's hand. "And you," he began, and hesitated. "Take care, too. We'll do all we can to be there for you."

The diminutive Phandran smiled at him. "I survive this, Jeff, and so do you. I told you that we would be reunited, didn't I?"

Kranda said, "If this room is secure, then we will spend the night here and follow you from the tower in the morning."

"The door is locked. The president has no visitors during the night, other than an occasional doctor. However, since I have arrived, he has dispensed with his regular medical team."

"Where do you sleep?" Ellis asked.

She indicated a door next to the president's chamber. "I have a communicating door to his room, should I need to attend to him." She stood. "Will you be comfortable here? What about food, water?"

Kranda said, "We have provisions."

"In that case..." She smiled, moved across the room to the sliding door and slipped through.

He said to Kranda, "I'm surprised you haven't suggested killing the president here and now."

She grunted. "The thought did occur, but I dismissed it. What if Horrescu has confided his plans to others, his ministers, in case of his early demise? What if they are privy to his secrets, and would carry through his plans after his death? No... the president is more valuable to us alive, at present."

She broke out the rations and they ate in silence before attempting to sleep.

I

"Jeff!"

He felt Kranda's hand on his shoulder, shaking him awake.

He sat up with a start, suddenly realising where he was. Images of Maria fled, and he felt irritation that she was still invading his dreams.

Kranda was a vague, crouched shape before him. She whispered, "Dawn. The president is awake. Calla came out to tell us that they will be leaving in thirty minutes. He will take the elevator to a bunker in the bowels of the building, where a car awaits him. Here, eat this."

She passed Ellis a concentrated energy bar and a canister of water. He glanced through the window. A dull dawn showed pale on the horizon. If the previous day was anything to go by, the sun would lose its battle against the cloud cover and the leaden skies would once again mirror the brutalist architecture of the capital city.

He looked in Kranda's direction. "You're enjoying this, aren't you?"

She gave a harsh laugh. "I am a young girl again, hunting coyti. I feel empowered, and I know we are doing the right thing. You?"

He smiled. "I think we're doing the right thing, but I don't mind admitting that I'm..." He hesitated. "Scared, to be honest."

He felt a hand on his arm. "Don't be. Have confidence in me. I will protect you, human."

Ellis laughed. "Okay, okay... I'm that much of a makeweight, hm? And who has saved your life, twice over now?"

"And for that, Jeff, I am truly grateful."

They looked up at a sound from across the room.

The sliding door opened and the president's invalid carriage appeared, steered by Calla. She was wearing one of the grey, lagged coats of Sporelli design, obviously intended for a child; even so, it was a little too big for her. Ellis could not help but smile at the sight of her, bundled up for the harsh cold with only her small face showing through the upturned collar.

She looked in their direction, smiled, and manoeuvred the president from the room.

Beyond the open door, Ellis made out the security team in the corridor, along with Commander Yehn. With Horrescu and Calla, they proceeded towards the elevator.

Ellis followed Kranda from the room. They emerged into the corridor as the president and the others were entering the elevator. Kranda hurried towards the spiral staircase and they descended at speed. Ellis steadied his breathing, listened to the pounding of his heart, and tried to quell the fear growing insidiously within him.

They came to the ground floor and Kranda paused, leaning out into the corridor. A minute later the lift doors parted and Commander Yehn, followed by the young security officer and his aides exited. Calla and the president remained in the lift, presumably continuing down to the basement.

The Sporelli moved along the corridor towards the entrance.

Kranda moved along the corridor after them, Ellis close behind.

The task of following the Sporelli from the building was much easier than gaining admittance the evening before: they simply fell into step behind the last of the departing security men and emerged into the icy dawn.

In the courtyard, the convoy was powered up and ready to go.

Ellis paused beside Kranda beneath the portico. Only the guards with the heat-seekers remained stationed against the wall of the tower, ceaselessly scanning the devices back and forth across the tower grounds.

"We can't make a move while they're there," Kranda said. "I presume they'll be going with the convoy."

The military vehicles moved off one by one, the staff car carrying Commander Yehn leading the way. A sliding door in the wall of the tower opened briefly and an armoured car emerged, its windows darkened: presumably the vehicle carried the president and Calla. It inserted itself into the convoy and slipped from the courtyard.

Only when the last vehicle moved off did the guards with the heat-seekers leave their positions. They unshouldered the devices and sprinted towards the last troop-carrier in line.

Ellis said, "How far away do we follow? The soldiers with the heat-seekers will be scanning –"

Kranda interrupted. "I've thought of that. Follow me."

Ellis followed, wondering at the Mahkan's plan. They passed the last troop-carrier in seconds – the guards were still scrambling aboard, jeered at good-naturedly by their colleagues – and Kranda made a bee-line for a black, beetle-shaped tank.

"What now?" Ellis said as they jogged behind the vehicle.

"Now we climb up and hitch a ride," said the Mahkan.

"Are you mad?"

"If we sit before the engines, Jeff, they will disguise our own heat signatures."

She scrambled aboard the tank, dragging Ellis after her.

They sat side by side, knees drawn up, their backs against the warm metal of the engine cowling. Immediately behind them was a rocket-launcher. The pair of Sporelli troops in the cab seemed to be staring out directly at Ellis and Kranda. He looked away, his flesh crawling, and wondered if a Mahkan exo-skeleton had ever suffered a power failure.

The convoy left the tower and trundled along the encircling boulevard. A dozen or so citizens stopped to watch. A buzz passed through the gathering, as if they had guessed that the armoured car might be carrying their beloved president.

"They live miserable, circumscribed lives under a ruthless dictator, Kranda, and they adulate the man."

The Mahkan touched Ellis's shoulder. "Look into the sky, Jeff. What do you see?"

He looked up and saw a dark, ugly legend, which his varnika translated as, 'Your president has made Sporell secure against outside enemies. Never has our world been so safe!' And the message alternated with an image of the president, smiling and waving to a cheering crowd.

Kranda said, "They know nothing else. From birth they have been fed this lie. They lead humdrum lives, with little heat, food, or amusements, knowing nothing of their relative privations, nothing of how other people on other worlds live – in freedom and with plenty. The word for it is *brainwashed*."

Ellis recalled reading Friday Olembe's account of humankind's arrival on the Helix, and how they encountered the Agstarnians who knew nothing of life on other worlds thanks to the cloud cover which blanketed their skies and hid the Helix from view. They, in their own way, had been as blinkered as the Sporelli were now.

"If they could be made aware of how others lived..." he began.

Kranda said, "Who knows? Perhaps, when we have overcome the president, they will."

Ellis smiled. *A long way to go before that*, he thought.

They had left the centre of the city behind, and with it the vast, monolithic buildings of government. Now they were passing through residential suburbs, row after row of identical grey blocks, ten stories high, their windows lit by wan yellow lights which did little to dispel the prevailing gloom.

The most amazing thing about the city, Ellis thought, was the total absence of colour. He had not noticed it at first, having much else on his mind, but now the fact hit him hard. All he could see, wherever he looked, were graduated monochrome shades from matt black through to dull pewter. There were no trees or plants in sight, not even the colourless cacti so beloved of the president. There were no street-signs or advertisements, and the only paint that adorned the buildings, whether municipal or residential, was battleship grey. He wondered if such a proscription on colour was a psychological ploy of those who ruled, a further tool used to subjugate the masses, or simply the effect of a subdued economy.

Then he looked up, and had the answer. There was colour up there: President Horrescu's face was positively sky blue, his eyes bright, and the red and white Sporell flag fluttered at his shoulder. The people of the planet saw colour, and perhaps hope, when they looked up into the heavens and beheld their leader.

Soon they left the last of the grey dwellings in their wake and passed into the countryside.

If Ellis had been hoping for some relief from the dull tones of the city, he was sadly disabused. Even here, in the flat land surrounding the capital city, a monochrome uniformity prevailed. Field after field was planted with the same dull green vegetable – some kind of cabbage – and even the tractors tending the crops sported the obligatory grey livery.

"Look," Kranda said suddenly.

A troop-carrier was racing past the crawling convoy, and mounted on its roof were the three guards and their heat-seekers. As they passed, they panned the devices across the barren countryside, as if insurgents might be lurking amongst the crops. He wondered how they might react if they discovered the insurgents had been beneath their noses all along.

Then he thought ahead to what might await them at the spacefield, and his amusement gave way to apprehension.

He said, "And if the president is leading an interworld ship to invade Mahkan or New Earth?"

Kranda was silent for a time, before replying, "We board the ship with him, assess if that's what he intends, and perhaps threaten him with the destruction of his precious vessel." Ellis heard her slap the metal of her weapon. "Remember what I told you about our blasters' dual function."

Ellis smiled. Primed, they would become lethal nuclear bombs. "Fine, Kranda. But we'd be calling their bluff. How could we plant the blasters aboard their interworld ship without forfeiting our own lives?"

Kranda reached out and gripped Ellis's arm. She said, "If it came to saving your world by giving your life, Jeff, would you do it?"

She fell silent, leaving time for Ellis to consider her question.

He said, "Would you, Kranda?"

"Undoubtedly," she replied at once. Then, "And you?"

"I... I honestly don't know..."

They fell silent, contemplating the flat farmland on either side. Nothing had changed over the course of the last twenty kilometres: the same crops grew in the fields – did the Sporell eat nothing but cabbage? – and the same ugly grey tractors moved back and forth like clockwork toys.

Kranda touched his arm. "I think we approach the spacefield..."

To their right the fields gave way to acre after acre of flat grey tarmac, graced only by the occasional makeshift building and stationary flier. The field was surrounded by a zigzag cordon of razor-wire and patrolled by guards.

A kilometre further on, Ellis saw the first signs of activity on the spacefield. Fliers came and went, and he wondered if this was part of the war effort. He was answered minutes later when one of the fliers disgorged troops carrying loaded stretchers. He wondered if the casualties considered their sacrifices worthwhile; the depressing thing was that he thought they probably would.

The convoy slowed. Kranda touched his arm. "There…"

Ellis looked across the tarmac and made out the interworld ship. It appeared identical to the one on D'rayni which had accounted for Kranda's flier. For all he knew, it might have been the very same one – a fat, front-loading toad of a thing whose ramp resembled a great waiting tongue.

The convoy slowed to a crawl as it came to the main gate. It turned, and minutes later the tank on which Ellis and Kranda were hitching a lift rattled across the tarmac towards the interworld ship.

Ellis watched, with increasing trepidation, as the convoy came to a halt before the ship. The only vehicle which climbed the ramp was the president's armoured car. Ellis had expected the interworld ship to take the whole convoy but, as he watched, the president's security team boarded the ship on foot, followed by Commander Yehn. The rest of the convoy remained on the tarmac.

Ellis said, "Look."

The troop-carrier bearing the soldiers with the heat-seekers had pulled up before the ship. The three jumped down smartly and deployed themselves at the foot of the ramp.

Kranda lost no time. Hauling Ellis after her, she dived from the tank and sprinted towards the ramp. As he ran he watched, the troops shoulder the bulky heat-seekers and calibrate their settings. He had seconds before they swung the devices in his direction.

But seconds would be sufficient, especially if he increased his pace. He sprinted across the tarmac and up the ramp behind Kranda, passing within a metre of the nearest heat-seeker.

Seconds after he entered, Ellis heard the ramp rise slowly, followed by a deafening *crack* as the great hydraulic hatch sealed itself behind them.

2

THEY WERE IN the cavernous hold of the interworld ship, a stygian chamber stinking of oil and machine parts. The armoured car disgorged its occupants, the president in his invalid carriage propelled by Calla. If she noted their presence, as she hurried with the president towards the elevator, she gave no sign. They were followed by Commander Yehn and the president's security officials.

When the lift door sighed shut on the party, Ellis and Kranda found themselves alone in the yawning hold. Kranda crossed to a ladder welded to the bulkhead. "Safer than the elevator."

She climbed, and Ellis gripped the rungs and pulled himself up after her. A minute later he stepped onto a gallery overlooking the hold. Kranda led the way to a double doorway with a lighted corridor beyond.

Kranda paused before pushing through. "We proceed with caution. They might not be able to detect us now, but who knows what devices the ship might harbour?"

Ellis nodded. "Understood."

Kranda peered through the transparent window set into the swing door, ensured that there was no one beyond, and pushed it open. Ellis followed. They were in a narrow corridor leading to a flight of steps at the far end. As they set off along the corridor, the ship's engines ignited and the vessel vibrated alarmingly. Kranda laughed and called out over the rising din of the engines, "Poor engineering, Jeff!"

They climbed the steps. The interworld ship laboured to take off, turned sluggishly on its axis, and accelerated away from the spacefield.

"If the Sporelli do have a secret weapon," Kranda said, "and it's of the same calibre as this tin can, then we have nothing to worry about."

"Something tells me," Ellis said as he followed the Mahkan up the steps and along another corridor, "that the president wouldn't be as confident as he appeared if he didn't have a…"

Kranda laughed. "A super-weapon?"

Ellis tried to smile. "Something like that."

They came to a bulkhead, and a sealed hatch bearing a Sporelli legend. Kranda said, "An elevator to the bridge." She looked right and left and found what she was looking for. "This way."

Ellis followed the Mahkan up a tight spiral staircase. As they approached the top, Kranda slowed. They passed through a swing door and found themselves on a semi-circular mezzanine overlooking an oval flight-deck. Cautiously Ellis approached the rail and peered down.

The ship's pilot, co-pilot and flight-engineer occupied gimballed seats before a banked control console, above which was a wraparound viewscreen. Through it, the flat landscape of Sporell scrolled, endlessly featureless. They were flying close to the ground, and he wondered in which direction the ship was travelling: towards D'rayni, or the other way – to New Earth and Mahkana?

Behind the pilots were President Horrescu, Calla, Commander Yehn and the security officer. Of the other members of the security team, there was no sign. He found Kranda and murmured, "The others must be elsewhere. We need to be careful."

She touched his arm and led him around the gallery so that they had a better view of the president and Calla. She was standing at his side, staring silently ahead through the viewscreen.

As Ellis watched, Calla looked up briefly, and a slight smile played on her lips as she sensed their presence.

President Horrescu and Commander Yehn were conferring in lowered tones. Ellis upped the volume, but even so he was able to make out only the occasional word. "Duration… rendezvous… our reception…"

He murmured to Kranda, "What are they saying?"

"Something about the reception they'll get when they... meet whoever they're destined to rendezvous with. It wasn't clear."

Down below, the president and his commander fell silent. Yehn saluted and strode from the bridge.

"What now?" Ellis asked.

Kranda considered. At last she said, "Sit tight. Listen. Sooner or later we'll learn something..." She fell silent, then began, "I..."

"Go on."

"If I were alone, or rather if I were to disregard your proscription on killing the Sporelli... then I would find the other members of the security team and eliminate them. That way, we would have only the president and the pilots to deal with."

Logically, coldly, Ellis saw the sense of Kranda's words. At the same time he could not condone the killing of those who were only following orders.

He said, "As a last resort, Kranda. Okay? Only when we've exhausted every other possibility."

"By then, Jeff, it might be too late."

He thought about it. "Once we find out where we're heading, we'll be in a better position to work out what we're going to do."

"I do not agree. By the time we arrive, by the time they make the rendezvous... by then, we might not be in a position to act effectively."

"So you want to go off, find the others and kill them one by one."

"I was about to suggest we do it together, Jeff. But on second thoughts, I rather think your presence might be more of a liability."

He was glad he could not make out the expression of contempt he suspected was on the Mahkan's face. "There is another way we could handle this."

"Which is?"

"We have the element of surprise, agreed? And the invulnerability of near-invisibility. Not to mention superior weaponry..."

"You are stating the obvious."

"What I'm suggesting is that, at some point, we apprehend the president. Threaten him with death if his team attempts to attack us."

The silence that greeted his words was indicative of the Mahkan's disdain. At last she said, "And in so doing we put ourselves at increased risk. It is a problematic scenario, incurring too many unseen and unknown variables. Can you tell me, once we have the president in our custody, how we proceed? We have the golden goose, as the human saying goes, but what do we demand from the Sporelli? That we turn around and go back? That the president divulges his super-weapon and his grand plan?" She snorted with contempt. "The idea is weak, Jeff. Have you considered this: we hold the president and threaten his death, and thereby play to the ambitions of Commander Yehn. He might gladly order our deaths and in so doing consign the president to death – and propel himself into a position of power. As I said, there are too many variables in the scenario for us to be confident of a satisfactory outcome."

"In that case, perhaps we should wait until we learn more about the president's plans?"

"A second-best plan of action, human, but I tell myself that I am here because you saved my life on D'rayni…"

Ellis muttered, "Don't remind me."

He stared through the screen at the landscape rolling by below. They might have been just outside the Sporell capital, so similar was the flat farmland. He scanned the horizon for signs of mountains or even hills, but the viewscreen showed only a perfectly level terrain.

The sun was setting in their wake, and the interworld ship was heading for the planet's nightside, which meant that they could not be heading towards any of the neighbouring worlds. Kranda picked up on this. "Curious. We must be heading north, or south."

"That doesn't make sense. We're heading for a destination somewhere here on Sporell?"

Kranda said, "Krell – where the unmarked space vessel came down – is north of the capital, yes?"

"According to what the president said," Ellis affirmed.

"Perhaps, then, we are making for Krell. Maybe, Jeff, we have yet to pick up this super-weapon."

"Then that might be the opportunity we've been waiting for."

He sat against the bulkhead and drew his thighs to his chest. He rested his forehead on his knees and closed his eyes. He'd slept fitfully in the president's lounge last night, waking often. Now he took the opportunity to doze.

Kranda nudged him awake some time later.

He stared suddenly. "We're there?"

He stared through the viewscreen, and could not believe what he was looking at.

Kranda said, "You've been out an hour, Jeff. Nothing much has happened, other than…"

No longer was the grey monotonous landscape of Sporell displayed. Now, the viewscreen before them was filled by the black velvet immensity of deep space, speckled with a dusting of stars.

3

THERE WAS MOVEMENT on the flight-deck below. Calla pushed the president towards the exit. Kranda whispered, "By my calculations, it is night-time in the capital city. The president will be due his beauty sleep."

Minutes later the swing door to the mezzanine flapped open and Ellis tensed. He relaxed when he made out Calla's slim form hurrying towards them.

She crouched down beside where he and Kranda sat against the bulkhead, staring in their approximate direction.

Ellis reached out and took her hand.

She whispered urgently, "There have been developments, as you can see." She indicated the screen.

"What's happening, Calla?"

"I was with the president when he told Commander Yehn of his plans," she said in a small voice. "Unfortunately my grasp of the Sporelli language is basic, and I did not understand everything."

"But do you know what we're doing out here?" Kranda asked.

"First, Horrescu told Yehn about the ship at Krell. He said that it was… he used an unfamiliar word, but I translated it as 'emissary.' The ship was from far away, but the odd thing was that it was crewed by Sporelli, though only one crew member survived when the ship crash-landed."

Ellis stared at her. "From far away?" He shook his head. "Could there be another Sporelli race on the Helix?"

"That is what I thought, at first. But how could this be? Why would the Builders place one set of Sporelli on one world, and another set on another, distant world?" She gestured, spreading her hands wide. "Then Commander Yehn asked the president something that I did not catch, and Horrescu replied. Suddenly, it all made sense."

"What?" Ellis asked, leaning forward.

"Horrescu explained that the ship at Krell came not from another world on the Helix, but from *beyond* the Helix."

Ellis shook his head. "Beyond the Helix?"

Kranda said, "Did you learn *where* it came from, Calla?"

She frowned. "Horrescu did not say, or if he did then I did not understand. However, I assumed, because it was crewed by Sporelli...'"

Ellis finished for her, incredulously, "That it came from the Sporelli original world, from which they were taken millennia ago?"

"According to Horrescu," Calla said, "his people had been liaising with the emissary ship on its approach to the Helix. He guided it to their world."

Kranda asked, "But do you know *why* the ship came here? Did the president say?"

"That was one of Commander Yehn's questions. And the president replied that they had come here to re-establish contact."

Ellis said in wonder, "They were from the original Sporelli homeworld. Their race survived, established the whereabouts of those Sporelli taken by the Builders, and came here in search..."

Calla inclined her head. "This is what I inferred from Horrescu's explanation, yes."

A silence greeted her words, broken when Kranda asked the obvious question, "And now, the reason we are leaving the Helix?"

For a vertiginous second, Ellis wondered if the interworld ship might be attempting to make the voyage *back* to the original Sporelli world... but that would be impossible; the interworld ship was not equipped with a light-drive capable of taking it to the stars.

Calla stared from Kranda to Ellis, and said, "We have come here to meet a starship that has travelled three hundred light years from the Sporelli homeworld. It is, according to President Horrescu, a vast ship carrying over half a million Sporelli troops. And its mission, he said, is to invade the Helix. The president intends to meet it, and guide it to the Helix, where he will issue an ultimatum to the Builders, or their representatives: submit to the rule of the Sporelli, or face annihilation."

The ugly belch of a klaxon sounded through the ship.

Calla sprang to her feet. "That is the signal for the Sporelli ship's approach. Horrescu said that I must go to him when the signal sounds."

She moved to the swing-door and hurried through.

Ellis climbed to his feet and approached the rail overlooking the flight-deck.

A minute later the president, with Calla, rolled into the chamber and halted before the wrap-around viewscreen. He snapped an order at the pilot and told Calla to push him closer to the viewscreen. Something like insane eagerness showed on the tyrant's ravaged features.

Ellis transferred his attention to the screen, and stared in amazement.

He was accustomed to sleek, aerodynamic interworld ships and shuttles, vessels designed with aesthetics in mind. What appeared before them, hanging in space and filling almost half the screen, was neither sleek nor aesthetically pleasing. It resembled a bloated deep-sea fish, some grotesque bottom-feeder whose appearance was designed to scare off would-be predators.

Ellis whispered to Kranda, "How big is that thing?"

She hesitated, and then said, "According to the pilot's console, it's still twenty kilometres away."

"Vast, then."

"I estimate, no less than ten kilometres from head to tail. But if it contains half a million Sporelli troops, then it would have to be."

Ellis swore, and felt his guts turn to liquid. "What the hell do we do?"

"Jeff, I am out of ideas at the moment. I'll tell you if anything occurs to me. You?"

He shook his head in silence, although the Mahkan would be unable to see the gesture. "I honestly don't know, Kranda." He smiled to himself. "Even killing every Sporelli aboard this ship wouldn't help, now, would it?"

"Do you know something, human? This time, I think I agree with you."

The minutes elapsed, and the Sporelli ship came closer with every second. Soon it filled the screen. Before it, he thought, the interworld ship must resemble a minnow before a whale. All he could make out was excoriated exterior shields, antennae like kilometre-long barbels, and vast lettering in a script which only slightly resembled that which he had seen back on Sporell.

Eventually the viewscreen flashed and the image of the ship was replaced by that of a flight-deck. A blue-faced Sporelli woman in a maroon uniform stared out.

She spoke, and Ellis's varnika responded with, "We [untranslatable] [untranslatable], and then [untranslatable]. Proceed."

President Horrescu replied, evidently more adept at translating this variant on his own tongue. "Understood," the varnika translated. "I look forward to making your acquaintance, Captain."

The woman's face disappeared, to be replaced by the starship. They were even closer now, judging by the size of the ugly Sporelli lettering.

The president barked an order, and the pilot responded. The interworld ship adjusted course, minimally, and a lighted recess set into the hull of the starship swung into view.

Slowly, the interworld ship eased itself into the cavernous hangar.

Twenty-Two /// Virtual Realm

I

MARIA, DAN STEWART and the rest of the liaison team left the shuttle and drove in a ground-effect vehicle across a high, rocky plateau surrounded by a sea of sand.

Maria had expected her party to be first on this hostile, uninhabited world. As they drove north across the flat windswept rock, however, she made out in the distance a collection of domes and what looked like a row of open-ended marquees, the silver fabric dazzling in the sunlight. A reception committee of half a dozen humans and a Mahkan awaited their arrival.

She was still smarting at the fact that Dan's wife, Sabine, had reneged on her word to let her husband see more of her. Their marriage was effectively over, so why couldn't the stupid woman realise this and give in with good grace? Then again, she thought, would *she* so easily give up someone she loved?

They arrived at the domes and marquees strung out in a long semi-circle. Before them, the sand that covered the rest of the plateau was absent in an oval area, revealing a nexus of silver wires like the surface of some vast, futuristic game-board.

Within the domes and marquees, scientists worked at com-terminals and softscreens, and beneath the open tents, other members of the liaison team consulted banks of equipment. Maria made out around a hundred cables snaking out across the rock to the silver grid.

One of the domes bore a red cross, and Maria found it fully equipped with everything she would need to assure the health of the team for the next few days.

She returned outside, into the merciless heat of the sun, and crossed to where Dan was chatting to a tall Mahkan and four humans, one of whom was his deputy, Victor Gonzalez.

Dan introduced her as the resident medic and she shook hands with the three strangers – a woman in the red uniform of the Peacekeepers and two government representatives. She offered her hand to the Mahkan, who merely stared at her with its inscrutable lizard eyes and kept its claws by its side.

She found herself casting covert glances at the Mahkan – Terrell-something, Dan had called it – unable to tell if the alien were in its female or male persona. They looked very much alike whether male or female, apparently: there was a variation in colouration, but the main difference, she'd read, was neurological.

The alien was saying, "To put it crudely, what we have here is a... a terminal interface. The nexus which, millennia ago, the Builders used to access the 'core,' or to put it another way, download their virtual personas into the storage cache."

Maria stared out across the silver nexus, marvelling. She was looking at a Builder artefact that few humans before her had seen.

Gonzalez asked, "And would it be politic to enquire if you, the Mahkan, are in contact with the Builders?"

The alien pulled its lips back, revealing curved incisors, in an expression Maria found impossible to interpret. "That, sir," the Mahkan replied, "I am in no position to answer."

"How did you locate this?" Dan gestured to the nexus. "I presume it was originally covered with sand?"

Terrell-something moved its head in a gesture Maria took to be affirmative. "All I can say is that my people have known about it for centuries."

Dan nodded, and Maria could sense his frustration at the alien's stonewalling.

One of the humans, a government official, said, "Director, if you and Deputy Gonzalez would care to step into the nexus, my team will show you a few salient features. I'm afraid you will have to leave all electrical equipment such as wrist-coms and players behind..."

Dan looked out across the grid. "Lead the way," he said, unfastening his wrist-com and passing it to Maria.

She watched as the government official led Dan, Gonzalez, the Mahkan and the others into the grid. They were obliged to high-step over the silver divides between each square, the effect somewhat comical as the group progressed into the middle of the alien artefact.

Maria returned to the medi-dome and made an inventory of the stocked equipment. The dome was air-conditioned, and a small cooler held a supply of food and drink. She found a beer and dragged a folding chair to the entrance. She sat in the shade, staring out across the barren plateau, and watched the tiny figures of the liaison team pick their slow way across the nexus.

She found herself thinking ahead, to the time when she and Dan could set up home together. She was tired of sharing him with a wife who, Dan had told her, no longer showed him the slightest affection. She felt frustrated that now, when she had finally freed herself from Jeff – when the way was clear for her to enjoy an uninterrupted life with Dan – his frigid wife was proving to be such an unreasonable obstacle.

She swore under her breath and took a long swallow of ice-cold beer.

Members of the liaison team moved back and forth along the margin of the grid, kneeling to take measurements and readings with their softscreens. From time to time they called across to each other, and gathered to pore over their screens and compare results. As often was the case when she sat on the sidelines and observed the doings of the team, she felt excluded.

Her wrist-com chimed. She tapped the access stud, wondering who might be calling her now. The chime continued, and only then did she realise that the sound was a semi-tone lower than her own device.

Dan's wrist-com, on the cooler where she'd left it, flashed an accompaniment to the musical notes.

She was minded to ignore the summons, then thought that it might be from HQ on New Earth.

She crossed to the cooler and picked up the wrist-com.

The display screen flashed the name of the caller: Sabine Lafayette-Stewart.

Her stomach turned as she thumbed the access stud.

The screen flared and a woman's face stared out at her. She had known that Sabine was a few years older than Dan, but this gaunt, white-haired woman looked about sixty.

"And who might you be?" Sabine asked.

Dry-mouthed, she managed to articulate, "I'm Maria, Dr Maria Ellenopoulis." She hesitated, then said, "Dan told you about me."

The woman tilted her head to one side, her expression almost amused. "Told me? About you? Now why should he do that, Dr Ellenopoulis?"

Maria felt dizzy and dropped into the folding chair. She held the wrist-com in a shaking hand and said, "Why are you being so unreasonable?"

The woman blinked. "Unreasonable?" She laughed, shaking her head. "I haven't the faintest idea what you're talking about. Now, if you'd kindly hand me over to Daniel..."

"Unreasonable," Maria said, taking a deep breath, "about us, about me and Dan. Why can't you just agree to what he wants?"

Sudden, pantomime enlightenment dawned on Sabine's face. "Ah... so you must be his latest little fling. Now, I must say that he's chosen well this time: very pretty, and dark, which surprises me. Daniel usually goes for blondes."

Maria felt as if she were about to faint. She had experienced this once before, this sudden feeling of unreality, of being part of something she was unable, or unwilling, to comprehend: three years ago, when she had seen Ben fall from the tree and break his neck.

"Usually?" she echoed.

"Oh, he must have had a dozen women on the side over the past ten years."

"I don't believe you."

"They normally last a month or two, sometimes a little longer, before the attraction begins to pall. How long have you and Daniel...?"

Maria shook her head and found herself saying, "I... Almost a year."

"A year?" Sabine said, laughing. "Well, he must be finding you very beddable. Let me guess," she went on. "Daniel said that he'd told me all about you, am I right? You want him to leave me, and he said that I'd demanded something along the lines of an equal share...? Oh, don't look so shocked, my dear. He's played that little game with his women often in the past. I'm familiar with all his tricks."

"But he loves me..." Maria found herself whispering.

Sabine shook her head. "Of course he'd tell you that. It's what he tells them all, in order to get what he wants. Dr Ellenopoulis, my husband is not a bad man, just... rapacious, you might say. So don't be too hard on him." She smiled, with bitter sweetness. "And if you could tell him that I called, when you see him, my dear..." She cut the connection.

Maria sat staring at the blank screen, the sound of her pulse pounding in her ears.

But Dan had been so convincing when he'd said that Sabine was being a bitch...

She realised that she was crying, tears falling from her cheeks and dripping onto the screen. She flung it across the dome and cuffed the tears from her cheeks.

The bastard, she thought. *The cheating, lying bastard.*

She saw him across the grid, this tall, strong man she thought she'd loved. Her first impulse was to race across the nexus with something heavy in her hand and swing it at his skull.

She heard the sound of an engine and looked up into the searing blue sky. A dark shape was coming in low from the south, and she'd seen sufficient space-going craft to know that this one did not hail from New Earth. As she watched, the ship resolved itself into a long, dark interworld cruiser of Mahkan design.

The ship slowed, banked, and came in to land beside the grid a hundred metres to her left. Led by Dan, the group out on the grid made their hurried way back to the domes.

Maria stood up as if in a trance, at once aware that something major was being played out here with the arrival of the Mahkan, but at the same time concerned only about Dan Stewart's treachery.

A hatch in the side of the cruiser dilated and half a dozen massive, imposing Mahkan stepped out and crossed to the domes. Dan and the others stood, a picture of collective indecision, at the edge of the grid. Dazed, Maria made her way towards them.

Dan was murmuring to Gonzalez, "Well, I think this answers our doubts about whether our tame Mahkan was acting alone..."

Maria stood before him and said, "You bastard."

He flinched. "Maria?"

"You lying, cheating bastard!"

He reached out to her, made to take her upper arm. She lashed out, dashing his hand away. "Don't touch me!"

Beside him, Gonzalez stared at her, wide-eyed.

Dan pleaded, "Maria, not here, okay? Not now. Can't you see...?" And he gestured helplessly towards the approaching phalanx of Mahkan engineers.

She was about to tell him that she didn't care what was happening here, but the words caught in her throat.

Out on the grid, something was moving.

Fifty metres away, in the dead centre of the oval nexus, a shape was rising from the silver spars. She stared, unable at first to work out what was happening. It was as if the spars had come together and were rising from the rock, forming the shape of a domed cylinder, a mere framework at first which, as she watched, became a solid structure as tall as the dome tents and three metres wide.

And, just as the thing solidified out there, the Mahkan delegation arrived before the group and halted.

"Daniel Stewart, Director of the Human-Builder Liaison team?" their leader said in halting English.

Dan cleared his throat. "Yes?"

"You and six of your team will come with us."

Dan said, "Come... where?"

In reply, the Mahkan gestured across the grid to the dome. Maria turned. In the side of the silver dome, an arched hatch had suddenly appeared.

"Where are we going?" Dan asked.

"Follow me," said the Mahkan, then looked directly at Maria. "Dr Ellenopoulis?" it said.

Her heart jumped.

"You, too, will accompany us. Please, remove your wrist-com."

Numbed, she did so, and dropped it to the ground.

The Mahkan and two of its aides led the way across the grid, followed by Dan Stewart, Gonzalez, and four others of the liaison team. Maria brought up the rear, stepping over the silver spars to the waiting dome, unable to believe what was happening.

One by one they stepped into the dome. Around the curved interior of the capsule ran a circular bench, and the Mahkan invited the humans to be seated. Ensuring that she was not sitting beside Dan, Maria took a seat.

Instantly, something embraced her from behind, like a pair of comforting, reassuring arms. She looked down and saw that her midriff was encapsulated in a ring of soft, pinkish rubber-like material. A similar, padded rest prevented her head from moving.

The Mahkan said, "In the padding, please find a..." It spoke a word Maria did not catch. She looked down and saw what looked like a pseudopod wriggle from the substance of the padding. "It is advised that you avail yourself of the sedative. The trip will take several hours."

In a quavering voice, Dan Stewart asked, "Just where the hell are you taking us?"

"We are going to the centre of the Helix," said the Mahkan. "You are, after all, members of the Human-Builder Liaison Team."

But why me, Maria thought?

Beside her, Gonzalez availed himself of the sedative. Within seconds, his eyes closed and his head lolled, supported by the padding.

Maria looked across the circular chamber as the hatch became suddenly, inexplicably solid. She stared at Dan, hating him with an intensity she never knew she possessed.

Suddenly, the pain was too much. She fumbled with her lips for the pseudopod, found it and sucked. The fluid was tasteless. Her vision swam and she slipped into unconsciousness.

2

SHE WOKE SUDDENLY.

The capsule was motionless The others around her were coming to their senses. She wondered how this simultaneous awakening had been achieved, and why her presence had been required by the Mahkan.

Instinctively she glanced at her wrist to check the time on her wrist-com, then realised that she'd left it back on the surface. A Mahkan saw her and said, "You have been asleep for ten hours, Dr Ellenopoulis."

Ten hours...

Across the capsule, Dan caught her eyes and smiled. "I tried to remain awake for the duration of the descent, but lasted only a few hours before I gave in."

She looked away pointedly, ignoring him.

The hatch appeared in the side of the capsule and Maria peered out.

She saw a glimmering white expanse, as pristine as porcelain. Her vision swam, attempting to focus on something out there.

The Mahkan leader gestured for them to exit the capsule and the padding released its grip on them. Maria stood and followed the others from the elevator.

She found herself standing on the surface of a great white plain. It was as if they were in a vast tunnel kilometres wide and illimitable in length, with the perspective diminishing before her and ending in a hazed blur. She looked right and left, and in the distance made out the floor that curved to form the walls of the tunnel.

But if they were standing on the inner surface of a tunnel, then at some point in their descent the capsule must have undergone a half-rotation so that they had come *up* to the surface they were standing upon. Her senses reeled at the thought of it.

"Where are we?" a woman from the liaison team asked.

The Mahkan replied, "We are within the spine of the Helix, eight thousand kilometres beneath the surface of the world."

Gonzalez turned and stared behind him, and something in his awed expression prompted Maria to follow his gaze.

The capsule had miraculously retreated into the surface of the spine, leaving no trace, and beyond where it had stood was a… but Maria had no idea what the thing might have been. It was silver-grey and perhaps a kilometre wide, and rose for kilometres to a jagged point like a mountain of coral or a mammoth termite mound. The surface of the growth was indented laterally, rilled, looking almost organic.

"What," Dan Stewart said, "is that?"

"It is why we have brought you down here," the Mahkan said. "It is, in the parlance of the Builders, a *chansarray*… or you might call it a Gaia Machine."

"A Gaia Machine," Maria echoed, savouring the words.

The Mahkan and his aides set off towards it, and the humans followed. Maria hung back, allowing Dan to get ahead of her.

It was hard to judge the distance of the *chansarray*. Like a mountain, it appeared at first to be closer than it actually was: they walked for ten minutes before they came eventually to its deeply folded surface.

Maria stared up its towering flank, reduced with her companions to the size of ants. While she gazed in wonder, Dan came to her side.

"I can explain," he whispered, desperation in his voice. "Just give me a chance, Maria. I can explain everything."

She stared at him, hoping that her expression conveyed the contempt she felt for him, then looked away and examined the surface of the Gaia Machine.

Gonzalez was saying, "You said that this is the reason we came down here…?"

The Mahkan gestured. "Over time, you and your team will study the *chansarray*. Over time, if the Builders are willing, they might commune with you. In the meantime…"

The Mahkan turned and looked at Maria. "Dr Ellenopoulis, if you would care to step forward."

She stared at the alien, raised a hand to her chest and whispered, "Me?"

"Approach the *chansarray*," said the Mahkan, "approach the surface and do not stop. When you reach the tegument, you will feel a slight resistance at first, but do not be dissuaded. Continue forward..."

"Me?" she asked again. She stared at him, disbelieving. "But why?"

"All will be explained when you enter the *chansarray*," said the Mahkan.

Behind her, Dan Stewart said, "And the rest of us?"

The Mahkan said, "The rest of you have not been... requested."

She could not bring herself to look into Dan's eyes, then, but she heard the hurt incredulity in his voice as he said, "But we're the liaison team. She's merely..."

The Mahkan interrupted. "Dr Ellenopoulis has been requested."

She stepped forward, hesitated. She stopped, then turned and looked back at the people she was leaving. Dan, his expression one of mingled chagrin and envy, just shook his head.

She smiled, and raised her hand in what might have been a gesture of farewell.

She walked towards the Gaia Machine, reached its surface and, despite what the Mahkan had said, halted instinctively as she came up against its flank. She was reminded of tree bark, but expanded a thousand times, and along with the visual impression came the scent of what might have been pepper. She leaned forward, into the tegument, pressing...

And she felt it resist, then ever so slightly give. She pressed forward with greater force, and then she was passing through the surface of the *chansarray*, being absorbed by it. She gave an instinctive cry of panic as it came to her that she would be unable to breathe, but the fact was that she was now part of the skin of the machine... if machine it was... and she was breathing, though darkness had descended on her vision.

She stepped forward, and suddenly she was flooded with light.

She fell forward, as if suddenly released, and stumbled to a halt.

She was on the surface of a world, or at least that was the impression she received. She was standing on a limitless greensward beneath a clear blue sky, a warm wind playing on her face.

"Welcome," someone behind her said.

She whirled to face this person, expecting to see the surface through which she had passed – but the greensward extended forever, occupied by a single figure.

The man, a human, was oddly familiar.

He smiled at her.

"Why...?" she managed at last. "Why have you brought me here? And... and who are you?"

He told her who he was, then said, "And you are here, Dr Ellenopoulis, because we would like to make you an offer."

Twenty-Three /// The Starship

I

As Ellis and Kranda followed the president and his entourage along the corridor of the interworld ship, keeping a safe distance, he found himself thinking about Maria. He recalled their last meeting in the park where Ben had died, and not only did that encounter seem distant in time and space, but the memory of it seemed to belong to someone else – it was as if he were an android, programmed with the memories of the person he had been but unable to access the necessary emotions to appreciate fully what he had experienced.

Oddly, he found himself more worried about the Phandran Healer and her safety. *We are about to be invaded by half a million Sporelli troops*, he mused, *and I'm thinking only of Calla.*

They walked down the ramp of the interworld ship into the hangar of the starship, and the president and his party were met by half a dozen armoured Sporelli soldiers. They were shorter and bulkier than the Sporelli he had encountered so far, as if evolved on a world of far greater gravity. Their body-suits were as ugly as their starship, sharing something of its seemingly aquatic design.

They were also armed with snub-nosed blasters which they held at the ready.

One of their number stepped forward and spoke to the president, his expression unreadable.

The party from the interworld ship were escorted from the hangar. Ellis and Kranda hung back, and the Mahkan whispered, "We follow?"

Ellis wanted to keep Calla in sight. "We might learn something useful."

"Stay close," Kranda said. "We must work on the assumption that these people might possess technology superior to that of their cousins. We cannot take our invulnerability so far for granted."

They followed the Sporelli from the hangar and passed down wide corridors illuminated by low green lighting. The ship appeared ancient, its walls and bulkheads dripping with oil and stained with who knew what noxious substances. As they walked, Ellis wondered how long the ship had been in flight from its homeworld. Even if the Sporelli had achieved near-light speed, it would have taken them hundreds of years to reach the Helix. Which meant that the troops, all half-million of them if the president was to be believed, must have spent the journey in some kind of suspended animation or cryogenic state.

He wondered if the bulk of the troops were still in cold storage.

Kranda leaned close to him and whispered, "We have been assuming all along, Jeff, a worst-case scenario."

"Meaning?"

"Meaning, the president's megalomaniacal plans. He wishes to use the might of this Sporelli force to his own ends – but what about the desires of the newcomers? How easily might they accede to the president's wishes?"

"I understand."

"To use a human phrase, the newcomers hold all the aces. Superior troop numbers, superior technology – and they have, effectively, the most powerful man on Sporell in their custody."

"Don't you think Horrescu will have considered this?"

"I would have thought so, but then who are we to second-guess the thought processes of an alien race? You humans are hard enough to read, and you are a relatively simple race."

"You're so complimentary, Kranda."

"Then again," the Mahkan went on, "perhaps the president is so far gone in his psychotic power-trip that he thinks all Sporelli, no matter how powerful, will bow to him."

"We'll soon find out," Ellis said.

The Mahkan was silent for a while, then said, "The only course of action, as far as I can see, is to prevent the starship's arrival at the Helix."

"That," Ellis whispered, "might be easier said than done."

Up ahead, the Sporelli had slowed. Ellis searched among the crowd for Calla, but both the Phandran and her invalid were lost amid the bulkily armoured troops surrounding them.

They passed through an irising doorway into a vast chamber, and Ellis and Kranda hurried to catch up. The portal was in the process of closing as they squeezed through with moments to spare.

Ellis blinked, wondering where they were.

It appeared that they were no longer aboard a starship, but out in the open under the light of a small orange sun. The tiers of an amphitheatre rose on every side, above which a deep blue sky fitted like a lid. The tiny primary was stationed directly overhead.

"Impressive," the Mahkan whispered at his side.

Ellis looked around him. The amphitheatre was almost empty, perhaps only a few dozen Sporelli dotted about its great curving expanse. He wondered if these people were the engineers and scientists brought from cold sleep to activate the ship at journey's end.

In the centre of the performance space was a long oval table, and at it sat the stern-faced captain and a dozen of her officers.

They rose as the party from the interworld ship entered the amphitheatre. The captain spoke, evidently inviting them to take a place at the table.

Calla manoeuvred the president forward. Commander Yehn and the remaining security officers seated themselves to either side of Horrescu on the squat chairs surrounding the table.

The armoured Sporelli soldiers took up positions in a bellicose cordon around the performance area. Ellis and Kranda moved to the left of the entrance and stationed themselves before a bulkhead perhaps thirty metres from the gathering.

The captain spoke, and as before the varnika's translation facility had difficulty with the archaic form of the language, eight-tenths of what she said being undecipherable.

There was no such problem with the president's replies.

"On behalf of the Sporelli race of the Helix," Horrescu said, "we welcome you, and rejoice that our people have at last been reunited..."

It went on in this vein for some time, the president spouting platitudes and the captain responding with largely unintelligible replies.

As the dialogue progressed, however, the varnika's smartcore reprogrammed itself, and was soon furnishing an almost complete translation of the captain's words.

"Fifty thousand [untranslatable] passed, many of those [untranslatable] in darkness, both literal and metaphorical. We call the time the Sunless Era. Only after much hardship did we rise again, and stories were told of how many of our people were taken by a force more powerful than ourselves. So bizarre were these tales that many disbelieved them... But in time they became a race memory, and, when we achieved star-flight, we looked to distant suns for our captured cousins."

"And you cannot imagine our joy when we made contact with the emissary ship," President Horrescu said. "We never forgot the people we had left, the people we feared dead long, long ago. We prospered, in time, from humble beginnings to the heights we have now attained, the rulers of three worlds on the Helix, and soon to be the rulers of many more."

"You spoke of your triumphs in your last communiqué."

"The Builders were a great race once, but now no more. We think they became extinct... bequeathing, as it were, the playground of the Helix to those it saved. The races number in their hundreds, we think – perhaps even in their thousands, presided over by an ineffectual race known as the humans; another race, the Mahkans, are the Helix's engineers. These are a more worthy foe, more technologically accomplished, more aggressive... But no foe at all beside Sporelli might and ambition."

"You speak of many wonders in this amazing Helix, President Horrescu. Thousands of empty worlds for the taking... Our homeworld, when we left it, was an... [untranslatable] and impoverished place, grossly overpopulated. One of our briefs, on embarking on this mission, was to locate new, habitable worlds where the Sporelli might prosper."

The president gestured. "Look no further than the Helix," he said. "Together, with your resources and my own expertise, we can use the Helix to our own ends."

The captain gave a lop-sided smile. "You paint a picture of riches beyond imagining, guarded only by effete races who would capitulate at the very sight of my armies."

The president gestured. "I do not exaggerate," he said.

"And you, President; what might you gain from our alliance?"

Horrescu hesitated, obviously considering his words, then looked the starship captain in the eye and said, "I am dying, Captain, and I have known this for a year or more. Nothing can keep me alive... Nothing, that is, on Sporell. We might be sophisticated in many ways, but there is only so much that our medicine can..." He faltered, and Ellis upped the magnification and saw the gleam in the tyrant's eyes.

"However," he went on, "the only hope I have is that you, with your sophisticated starship, your drives which propel the ship at speeds as fast as light, might possess a concomitant level of medical expertise. We could reach an agreement, Captain. The ministrations of your best doctors, for my aid in helping you capture the finest worlds the Helix has to offer – for the benefit and advancement of the Sporelli people!"

Kranda leaned towards Ellis and hissed, "The slimy, self-seeking bastard!"

The captain said, "I will have my surgeons examine you, President Horrescu. My people do enjoy advanced medical resources, and it is possible that we might be able to help you."

Horrescu bowed his head. "I would be most grateful," he said.

Beside the president, Commander Yehn leaned towards Horrescu and spoke in a whisper which Ellis's varnika did not pick up.

Horrescu considered what Yehn had said, then looked across the table at the starship captain. "You spoke, in your communiqué, of half a million troops..."

The captain inclined her head. "I commanded a force twice as large as any on our homeworld, President. For twenty years our planet was torn apart by war after war, and only after my forces brought peace to the planet did I turn my sights elsewhere."

Horrescu smiled, skull-like. "War-hardened troops, and half a million of them... Captain, I know the worlds of the Helix where we might meet most resistance, puny though they would be in comparison to your forces. An expeditionary force of ten thousand of your troops, with Commander Yehn as your liaison, would quell all resistance on New Earth and Mahkana."

The captain laughed. "But my dear President Horrescu," she said, "you misjudge me if you think I would risk a single one of my soldiers in battle with the beings of the Helix, no matter how feeble you say they are."

Horrescu's expression faltered. "But then how...?"

"We have weapons on board this ship which will achieve our goals without even a single Sporelli soldier needing to set foot on enemy soil. From orbit we can bombard a world and render it lifeless within six hours."

The president was wide-eyed in wonder. "But, if I may say... if you annihilate a world, render it uninhabitable, then how will our people benefit – ?"

The captain flung back her head and laughed, silencing the president. "But President Horrescu... please forgive me. Thousands of years have passed since your ancestors were taken from Sporell. In that time we have made scientific advances of which you could not even dream." She braced her arms on the table and leaned forward, staring at the president intensely. "President, we have weapons which will rid a world of a specific life-form – Mahkans, humans, whichever – and leave the planet, its flora and fauna, untouched. We have code-bombs and biological agents that will deal death to a billion souls before they even know they are being attacked!"

Horrescu shook his head. "And you say the world would be fit for habitation afterwards?" He sounded shocked.

The captain smiled. "All that would need to be done would be to clean up the corpses from the streets, and then move our people in..."

One of her officers leaned towards her and spoke in hushed tones. She listened, nodded, then addressed Horrescu. "President, we are ready to complete the final approach run to the Helix... Perhaps, as my guest, you would care to be present in the armoury when we fire the first of these weapons... as a display of Sporelli might to whoever might be foolish enough to attempt to oppose us."

Ellis could see the expression on Horrescu's face – greed mingled with awe – as he stammered, "I would be... honoured indeed."

"You might even, President Horrescu, care to select a world to be our first... victim."

Horrescu smiled. "I would have no hesitation in choosing the world of Mahkana," he said. "They are an arrogant race, who think themselves superior, unmatched on the Helix. And, so I am told, they inhabit a vast, cold planet that would make a suitable colony world for our people."

The captain inclined her head. "Mahkana it shall be, then." She spoke hurriedly to one of her officers, who listened intently and tapped her instructions into a screen on the table.

"President, in less than four hours Mahkana will be ours. If you would care to come with me..."

She stopped. One of the armoured soldiers had approached the table and bent to speak in her ear. She stiffened, stared across at the president, and said, "It has come to our notice that your boarding party was accompanied by two beings you chose not to reveal to us. We consider this..."

Whatever the captain said next was lost as Kranda reached out and grabbed Ellis's arm. "That's us, Jeff. We're *persona non grata* at this party. We run."

From across the amphitheatre, half a dozen guards approached cautiously, weapons drawn.

2

ELLIS LEAPT TO his feet and sprinted, diving through the irising portal just as the first Sporelli fired his blaster. The beam missed him by half a metre, scoring a silver rent in the wall above the portal. Ellis tumbled, picked himself up, and ran along the corridor after Kranda.

He glanced over his shoulder. A dozen armoured Sporelli soldiers were tumbling through the exit, the leading pair taking aim and firing. The beams missed by a fraction, scorching the wall to Ellis's right and filling the corridor with blinding light.

Ellis caught up with Kranda. "Back to the ship?" He thought of Calla, in the custody of the starship captain, and his stomach turned in despair.

"What? And have them corner us like coyti?"

"Where, then?"

"This way!"

She turned as she ran and fired off a blast from her laser rifle. All Ellis saw was a bright blue beam lance from head-height beside him. He looked back down the corridor. An advancing Sporelli soldier was flung back, skittling three others.

Ellis increased his pace, Kranda beside him. They passed down grey industrial corridors, their walls stained with the oil and filth of centuries.

"We're outpacing them," Kranda said. "But it's a concern that they're aware of us."

"That's something of an understatement," Ellis panted.

They turned into a corridor and sprinted, came to a T-junction and turned left. Kranda raced ahead, faster than Ellis had ever seen her move before. He increased his pace, saw strip-lighting strobe by like flak. He caught up with Kranda and the Mahkan slowed down.

He looked over his shoulder. They had shaken their pursuers, for the time being.

"And now?"

Kranda grunted. "You forget that we are armed with two very effective nuclear bombs."

Ellis glanced instinctively at where the Mahkan was; he saw only her outline. "Two tiny nuclear devices against a ship this size?" he began.

"Strategically positioned, Jeff, they will prove exponentially effective. If we find the engine-room and plant a blaster within the drive's power-source…"

"And they'll disable the ship before it reaches the Helix, right? Render it inoperable?"

Kranda interrupted. "That will not be enough."

Ellis stared at the Mahkan's outline. "Meaning?"

"I intend the nuclear charges to *destroy* the starship."

Ellis was aware of the thudding of his heart, and an icy fear crawled down his spine. "Kranda…" He marshalled his racing thoughts, "there are at least half a million innocent –"

"Human!" Kranda yelled. "You heard the captain. You heard what she said about her weaponry – you heard what she said about using it!"

"Even so," Ellis said, ineffectually. "Look… there must be some way to disable the ship without killing so many…"

"I cannot gamble with the lives of my people, the future of my world – the future of the very Helix itself. We must *annihilate* this ship. There are no half-measures, no other ways of ensuring the continued existence of the Helix and every race upon it! Now, are you with me, or do I continue alone?"

They had slowed to a fast walk. Ellis was aware of Kranda's stentorian breathing at his side.

He said, "You're not telling me everything."

"What?" It was almost a roar.

"With your engineering expertise, your varnika... I'm pretty damned sure there's a way to disable this ship, render its systems useless. Do you know what I think?"

"As if I give a damn about what you think, human!"

"I think it's because the Sporelli had the audacity to target Mahkana first. That's it, isn't it? You're punishing them for that."

Kranda roared. Ellis saw a blur, felt something grip him by the throat. She lifted him through the air and slammed him against the bulkhead.

"How dare you, human! How dare you accuse me of punishing the Sporelli merely because they elected to target my planet first! Do you think I'd stand idly by – as you would! – if your planet were under threat first?"

She must have commanded her shield to deactivate, then, for she suddenly appeared before Ellis. Her slavering muzzle was centimetres from his face, lips drawn back in rage. She snarled at him. "I am doing what I am doing for the sake of the Helix! Get this into your head – the Sporelli are little more than primitive animals, conscienceless aggressors who deserve to die! They will attack my planet, and then yours and who knows how many others after that, and if we do nothing to stop them, millions of our people will die and nothing will ever be the same again on the Helix!"

She released Ellis, let him slide to the floor, and activated her shield again.

He picked himself up, rubbing his throat.

"Now, Jeff, you can accompany me to the engine-room, or you can make your own damned way back to the interworld ship."

She waited. He said, "Okay. Okay, I'm coming with you..." He wanted to impress upon her that he was accompanying her not because he agreed with what she was doing, but because he feared facing the Sporelli alone.

But he held his tongue and set off alongside Kranda at a jog.

To break the strained silence, he said, "Finding the engine-room might not be that easy. Have you thought of that?"

"You have little faith in me, human," the Mahkan snapped.

"You mean..." he said, "you know where it is?"

"Approximately."

"You're joking, right?"

"In situations such as these, human, I do not joke."

Ellis glanced behind him; there was no sign of the Sporelli. He felt a quick sense of relief, soon tempered by the realisation that they were lost on a vast alien starship.

"How the hell…?" he began.

"On the interworld ship's approach," Kranda explained patiently, "I took the time to observe the starship."

"So?"

"I registered what I assumed were the engine nacelles. The engine-room or drive apparatus chamber cannot be far away."

"And if you're wrong?"

"In that case, we will simply plant the nuclear charges, and hope."

They came to an open elevator and Kranda paused.

"Where now?"

"I'm thinking… Very well, up a level. But not on the elevator – too dangerous, if the Sporelli are monitoring their ship's operating systems. This way."

They came to a recess in the wall and Kranda indicated a column of staples welded to the bulkhead, forming a ladder. She climbed. Ellis looked back along the corridor, then followed.

They were in a low, wide corridor. To one side was a single rail set into the decking, and ten metres further along, a two-seater pod; evidently a means of getting around the vast starship.

Kranda said, "We'll be faster on foot. Again, they might be monitoring their transportation units."

They sprinted along the corridor.

"How far now?"

Kranda considered. "A couple of kilometres, no more."

Ellis yelled, "I hope you've memorised the way back."

"Not me, but my varnika has. When we've planted the charges, sub-voc this code and your varnika will do the rest." She gave him the required code. "Halt," she said.

His heart leaped. "What now?"

They had paused outside a great archway, over which curved a line of bold Sporelli lettering.

Ellis's varnika translated: "*Hibernative Suspension Chamber #1*"

Kranda approached and palmed a sensor beside the sliding door.

She waited a second, but the door refused to open. She raised her laser and fired at the sensor, and the door juddered open fractionally. Grunting, Kranda reached out and hauled the sliding door further open.

Ellis stepped over the threshold, open-mouthed.

They were in a chamber as cavernous as a cathedral. To either side were banked tiers of what looked like aquariums. They stretched to a vanishing point in the distance. He looked up, counting thirty tiers on each side.

He approached a unit and peered through the glass.

A sleeping Sporelli soldier, outfitted in familiar bulky armour, lay like the carven image on a sarcophagus. Kranda said, "I estimate there are fifty thousand in here alone. There must be a further nine of these chambers."

They left the cryogenic chamber, hurried along the corridor and passed another arched entrance. Ellis counted eight more arched entrance-ways giving onto cryogenic chambers.

A kilometre further on they came to a great lateral corridor which Ellis judged ran from one flank of the ship to the other. They stopped, dwarfed by its dimensions. He looked up, making out dim points of light high overhead which dimly illuminated the vast space. A couple of hundred metres wide, he thought, and perhaps as many high.

"What is it?"

"I'm not sure... but I suspect it's an accessway, from when they were building the ship, so that multiple trucks and fliers could negotiate their way across the interior. Look, at the far end: they've begun the process of filling in the space with bulkheads and corridors."

Ellis increased his magnification and made out, perhaps five kilometres away across the ship, what looked like a construction site of half-finished decks and bulkheads.

Kranda went on, "That suggests they were still working on the ship when it took off. Perhaps a ship this size is always a work in progress. It will almost be a tragedy to..."

"Yes?"

"To destroy it," she finished.

Ellis looked at Kranda's outline and swore under his breath.

Kranda grunted. "Strange. I feel nothing for the hundreds and thousands of Sporelli my actions will consign to oblivion. But this is a true engineering wonder…"

Ellis saw her outline as she stopped running and sank onto her haunches. He paused beside her. "Kranda?"

"Silence, Jeff. I need to concentrate."

Ellis looked back the way they had come, expecting to see Sporelli soldiers at any second. The corridors were eerily quiet.

At last Kranda said, "My varnika has infiltrated the ship's communications nexus and is disabling it. This will aid us considerably. The Sporelli will be unable to communicate other than verbally." She laughed. "In other words, they won't be able to coordinate their search for us."

"If your varnika can compromise the Sporelli com system," Ellis said, "then what about – ?"

The Mahkan interrupted. "I instructed it to disable the starship, human! Don't you think that occurred to me?"

"And?"

"And my varnika was unable to break down the smartcore's defences, only the com-nexus. It's still working to compromise the smartcore, but there's no telling how long that might take."

"So in the interim…?"

"Plan, A, human, even though that offends your squeamish sensibilities." Kranda surged upright. "Very well. This way."

They sprinted across the lateral accessway. A low-pitched thrumming filled the air here, which increased in volume as they passed from the accessway into a low-ceilinged corridor. Kranda led the way for a hundred metres, then paused outside a sliding door to their left.

She lasered the sensor beside the door. This time the sliding door did not obligingly open. She forced the muzzle of her laser between the doors and levered. The doors parted enough for her to squeeze her hand inside and, grunting with the strain, force them open.

They ran inside.

The noise here was suddenly deafening. Ellis muted his audio reception and looked around. They were in a cavern, perhaps twice the size of the cryogenic chamber, filled with sloping banks of silver machinery and a labyrinthine system of gargantuan pipes. It was nothing like any engine-room he had ever seen, or even imagined, but then he reminded himself that this was alien technology.

Kranda said, "Follow me," and moved off into the chamber.

They passed bank after bank of thrumming machinery, each one the size of a city block.

Kranda stopped before a domed machine fully twice her height, its silver surface bearing a single rectangular viewscreen. "This room is the fusion reactor chamber," she said, "and I suspect that what we have here is its core."

She led Ellis around the dome so that they were out of sight of anyone entering from the corridor. She deactivated her Varnika and Ellis did the same, allowing Kranda, for the first time since their altercation, to see him. He felt suddenly naked.

Kranda was withdrawing her blaster from its moorings on her left arm. "Now pass me yours," she said.

Ellis stood very still, staring at the Mahkan. He said, "Has your varnika managed to...?"

"No!" Kranda snapped, staring at him with anger in her eyes. "Do you think I'd be going ahead with this if there was another way?"

Ellis restrained himself from answering that.

"We place the blasters together," Kranda said, "timed to go off simultaneously, and this will have a greater effect than if we plant them in two locations." She paused, then went on, "We have to do this, Jeff. There is no other way. The future of the Helix depends on this working."

Ellis said, "Let's get it over with, Kranda, and then work out how to get back for Calla."

"Our original purpose..." Kranda said. "How far we have come since then!"

Ellis grimaced. "How far indeed."

The Mahkan pressed a red stud on her own blaster. "That sets the charge, Jeff. Now the green one..." She thumbed the green stud and Ellis watched as a screen on the butt of the blaster flickered a string of numerals.

Kranda explained. "The timer. I've set it to a little over one hour. That should leave us enough time."

Ellis glanced at her. "You sure? What about finding Calla?"

"She will be with the others, either in the amphitheatre or back aboard the interworld ship."

"What if the captain suspected the president of duplicity when she detected us and ordered their arrest? They might be anywhere by now." The thought sent a shiver of dread down his spine. "I say we set them for a little longer? Two hours?"

Kranda considered this, buckling her muzzle in an ugly gesture. "Very well, I'll increase the setting."

She did so, then said, "Now pass me yours."

Ellis hesitated, and before he could move to pass Kranda his blaster, the Mahkan reached out and snatched it from him. She quickly tapped in the settings.

"The black studs are the primers," she said. "When I press them, the process is underway..." She looked at Ellis. "Believe me, Jeff, there is no other way."

Ellis stared at the Mahkan. "I hope you're right."

Kranda depressed the black stud on the first blaster, then the second.

A series of vents or flanges encircled the dome at head height. Kranda took the first blaster and inserted it into a vent, grimacing as she wedged it tight within the dome.

She moved to her left and slipped the second blaster into the dome.

Then, surprising Ellis, she stood back, closed her eyes, and murmured something to herself.

Ellis said, "A prayer?"

Kranda grunted. "A Mahkan poem – a haiku, I suppose you might call it – which brings good fortune."

"I never had you down as a superstitious type."

"We each have our weaknesses," Kranda said. "Let's get out of here."

They activated their varnikas and Kranda led the way from the engine-room. They sprinted back the way they had come, across the mammoth accessway and along the corridor towards the cryogenic chambers.

Seconds later Kranda said, "Jeff!"

Heart thudding in fear, Ellis fetched up beside her and stared ahead.

He could not believe what he was seeing.

Ahead, two hundred metres away, rank after rank of armoured Sporelli soldiers were filing from the nearest suspension chamber, marching in step and setting up a threatening, thunderous rhythm. As they emerged from the arched entrance, they turned to their left, away from where Ellis and Kranda stood, and marched off into the distance.

Ellis swallowed. "What now?" he managed.

"It would be madness to follow them, even though that route would be the fastest way back. Okay… sub-voc the code *seven-zero-seven-five*, then an over-ride command, *eight-three-five*."

Ellis did as instructed. Kranda explained, "This tells the varnika to take us back to our starting point by the fastest alternative route."

"How the hell does it know that?" Ellis asked.

"My varnika accessed the auxiliary core and uploaded the ship's schemata, then copied it to yours."

In his left ear he heard the tinny, transistorised voice of the varnika saying, "*Retrace your steps, thirty metres, turn right. Ascend to the next level, proceed straight ahead.*"

"Let's go," Kranda said.

Heart hammering, Ellis took off.

3

THEY CLIMBED TO the next level and sprinted along the corridor.

They were above the cryogenic chambers, Ellis judged, in a little-used deck crammed with circuitry, loose wires and humming alien devices. It was as if he had been miniaturised and let loose inside a computer smartcore. Even the stench was redolent of dusty com chips and hot processors.

"Turn left, continue for twenty metres."

He had no idea where he was now, relative to anything. He laughed aloud as he realised that he'd had no real idea where he'd been at the outset, when they left the interworld ship. Somewhere in the great flank of the starship, maybe, two thirds of the way along its length? They'd been running for perhaps an hour since leaving the amphitheatre and had covered only a tiny fraction of the ship's total area.

Something moved up ahead. A silver flicker, there one second, gone the next. They ran towards where it had been, and he saw it again. He was reminded of a pair of scissors, snipping away at something. The thing looked like a cross between a crab and a spider, metallic-silver and faster than either. It was dancing along the ceiling, emitting showers of silver sparks as it repaired circuitry. A robot, he thought; it made sense to have automata tending to the ship's repairs over a journey lasting for centuries.

As he ran he was beset by thoughts of everything that might go wrong. The two imperatives were to find Calla and escape from the starship...

He tried to second-guess the starship captain. What might they have done with the interworld ship's passengers? The most likely scenario was that the president, Calla and the rest had been incarcerated, until such time as the Sporelli troops captured the invisible intruders and assessed their threat. But in a ship ten kilometres long by three wide, the prisoners might be anywhere.

"*Turn left, proceed ten metres, ascend to next level.*"

This level proved to be a narrow, dimly-lit deck even meaner than the previous one, with festoons of wire trailing from the low ceiling and pools of jet fluid on the floor.

"*Ten metres ahead, descend to lower level.*"

They came to a recessed staircase and descended cautiously. Kranda paused at the bottom, assessing the possibility of danger ahead.

She tapped Ellis's arm and hissed, "All clear. After me."

They were in what looked like accommodation quarters, a corridor of plush carpets, painted walls and low lighting. Ellis was increasingly apprehensive. He had felt relatively safe in the more industrial areas of the starship, but here, where at any second a Sporelli might emerge from a cabin...

"How far are we from the interworld ship?"

After a couple of seconds, Kranda replied, "A little more than a kilometre."

"And how long before the big bang?" He judged they'd been running for perhaps thirty minutes, but he couldn't be sure.

Kranda's reply surprised him. "A fraction under one hour."

"One hour! And we're still a kilometre from the ship?"

"That leaves us plenty of time, Jeff. Have faith."

In what? he thought.

"*Thirty metres ahead, descend to the next level, turn left, proceed for fifty metres.*"

They came to a sealed elevator and stopped. Kranda said, "If we drop to the next deck, and there's someone nearby when we exit..."

Ellis's stomach turned. "What's the alternative?" He glanced left and right, fearful.

Kranda consulted her varnika. "It's no good. Any other route would take us over an hour to complete. Okay, we'll take the risk."

She palmed the sensor and they stepped into the elevator.

As they plummeted, a bolus of fear lodged in Ellis's chest like something physical.

The lift door slid open and Kranda peered out. "The way is clear. After me."

They turned left and ran. They were back in a service corridor, similar to the one they had taken on the outward journey: wide, with a monorail track set to one side.

They couldn't be far from the interworld ship.

Then their luck ran out.

Three armoured soldiers appeared around a corner thirty metres ahead. They were fitted with helmets and visors, and Ellis surmised that it was these devices which rendered the varnikas visible.

The troops cried out, shouldered weapons, and fired.

Ellis found himself ducking and returning fire. Beside him, Kranda did the same. One of the three Sporelli yelled and fell backwards, his head a smoking ruin. Another was hit in the chest, knocking him off his feet. As Kranda approached, yelling, she finished him off with a swift blast to the head. The third Sporelli was backing off, but not as fast as Kranda was advancing. The Mahkan lashed out and sent the soldier reeling backwards.

"*Turn right, proceed for fifty metres, then turn left.*"

They did as instructed, sprinted for another hundred metres, came to a T-junction and stumbled into a second contingent of Sporelli soldiers coming from their right. This time there were six of them.

Kranda yelled, "Turn left, Jeff, and *run*!"

"But…" Ellis began.

But Kranda had already turned right, towards the six soldiers, yelling a blood-curdling war-cry as she laid down a barrage of laser fire.

Ellis turned left and ran, knowing that Kranda would have been enraged had he not done so, but at the same time hating himself for running away.

He stopped. He heard a cry behind him, whether Kranda yelling out loud in pain or triumph, he could not tell.

Without thinking, he turned back towards the source of the noise and sprinted.

Seconds later he came across a scene of carnage. Kranda's outline stood amidst a swill of blood and body parts. She had accounted for at least three Sporelli troops, though it was hard to tell as not one of the corpses was whole.

Along the corridor, six more soldiers were advancing, firing as they came.

Ellis dropped into a crouch and fired, accounting for the leading soldier. Kranda barked, "Human, I thought I told you to go!"

"And I ignored you, Mahkan!"

Ahead, six more Sporelli rounded the corner and joined their colleagues.

Kranda let out a blood-curdling yell and sprinted towards them, firing all the while. Ellis remained where he was, picking his shots and trying to avoid winging the blur that was the madly careering Mahkan.

Ellis fired and wept, watching as Kranda was struck at least once by a bright blue laser vector. It seemed to slow her not at all, and the result, when she reached the knot of Sporelli soldiers, was shocking to watch. She hit the soldiers running and they seemed to explode in a burst of body parts and geysering blood.

Ellis advanced warily, staring past the carnage for the first sign of Sporelli back up. Seconds later, it came. While Kranda was still meting out tough justice, fighting hand-to-hand with a particularly stubborn Sporelli, three soldiers appeared further down the corridor. Ellis picked one of them off, but the second dropped to his right knee and fired what looked like a portable rocket launcher.

The ball of fire missed Kranda and exploded through the door of an elevator behind the Mahkan, showering her with molten debris. She roared and returned fire, accounting for the Sporelli with the launcher but coming under fire from another soldier.

Ellis watched, frozen into immobility, as a laser beam struck Kranda in the centre of her chest. She staggered backwards, arms outflung, and Ellis yelled and surged to his feet as he saw, with terrible inevitability, what was about to happen.

Kranda reeled backwards towards the open lift-shaft, teetered on the edge and tumbled from sight.

Ellis surged forward unthinkingly, firing at the Sporelli soldier as he ran. The beam struck the soldier, knocking him backwards.

Ellis stopped dead. An eerie silence filled the corridor. He turned quickly, checking the corridor back and forth. There was not the slightest sign of living opposition, just a battle-scene of flesh, blood and bone.

Weeping, he ran to the lift-shaft and peered down.

"Kranda!"

No reply.

The shaft was pitch black. He summoned the varnika's light-beam and played it down the drop, but the shaft was so deep he could not make out the bottom.

He opened communications and pleaded with Kranda to reply, but all he heard was the fizz of static.

Numbed, Ellis turned and ran.

4

"*Turn left and proceed for seventy metres, then turn right.*"

He careered around the corner, sprinting at full speed. His vision blurred and he realised he was weeping for Kranda.

He ran the hundred metres and was about to follow the machine's instructions and turn right when he suddenly realised where he was. He had passed along this corridor earlier, coming from the interworld ship. To his left was the corridor that led to the amphitheatre. He felt a quick surge of hope.

He turned left and sprinted. He would check the amphitheatre first, and if, as expected, Calla and the others were not there... then he would try the interworld ship in the hope that she had returned.

He came to the portal that gave onto the amphitheatre. He passed through, stopped in his tracks and stared around. The central area was empty, and only two or three Sporelli personnel still occupied the lower tiers. He turned, dived through the portal and sprinted along the corridor. Minutes later, though it seemed to be much longer, he came to the sliding door accessing the hangar. The Sporelli interworld ship squatted on the deck, two guards stationed at the foot of the ramp.

He had the element of surprise on his side. He took aim and fired two shots in quick succession. The guards crumpled silently. He raced across the hangar, sprinted up the ramp and entered the ship, climbing to the flight-deck and pausing on the threshold.

He had harboured the hope that, by some miracle, Kranda had survived the fall... and maybe even made it back to the ship. He opened his com-link to the Mahkan and said, "Kranda? Kranda, do you read?"

The only sound was the hiss of static, and he chose to interpret the lack of response as bad reception within the starship.

Other than the Sporelli flight engineer, bent over a com-terminal, the flight-deck was empty. He backed out, checking the adjacent crew cabins, but drew a blank there too.

He exited the ship, heart pounding with desperation, and ran from the hangar. He had a vague idea, possible only if he could find a Sporelli.

The amphitheatre...

His breath coming in ragged spasms now, he sprinted back along the corridor.

Varnika, he thought, *translation mode*, and he instructed the smartcore to render what he said into Sporelli.

He came to the portal. He passed through, gave no thought to the dangers involved, and leapt up the tiers towards the quietly chatting Sporelli. He grabbed the closest, a small woman who screamed in shrill alarm as he hoisted her from her seat and carried her kicking towards the portal.

He turned. The other Sporelli in the amphitheatre were moving cautiously towards him, one of them drawing a side-arm. He hoisted his laser in his free hand and fired a warning shot, calling out, "Remain where you are, and she lives!"

They halted their advance and Ellis pushed through the portal.

"Your captain," he said to the woman. "Where is she? Take me to her!"

As his words were translated into Sporelli, the woman screamed again, terrified at being abducted by this invisible force.

"Take me to your captain," he said, "and you'll live. If you refuse, I'll kill you."

He heard the varnika translate his words into Sporelli, and they had an immediate effect on the woman. She stiffened with fear and stuttered something. Seconds later he heard the translation, "The next level down... the stateroom. Take the next elevator..."

He carried her across the corridor and entered the lift. They dropped. Seconds later the door swished open. "Where now?"

"Left. Along the corridor, then turn right."

He tightened his grip on her and ran, drawing another alarmed cry from the woman as he followed her directions. A wide door barred the way.

"This it?"

"Yes... the stateroom."

He lashed out at the sensor, but the door failed to respond. Holding the woman around the waist with one arm, he aimed his laser and fired at the mechanism. It turned to slag and the door stuttered open. He pushed through. Three Sporelli guards approached the door, drawing weapons. Ellis fired, accounting for the first two.

The third one rolled and came up firing. The beam missed the woman's head by a fraction and Ellis returned fire. The soldier fell.

He saw Calla, backing into a corner with alarm. Beside her was President Horrescu in his carriage. Next to the cowering tyrant was the starship captain, her face a mask of shock. He wondered, briefly, where Commander Yehn might be.

He considered his options and came to a decision. He flung aside the Sporelli woman, set his laser to stun and fired a brief blast at her torso.

Across the room, the Sporelli captain took a step towards him, squinting in his approximate direction. She spoke, and a second later his varnika translated: "Who... *what*... the hell are you?"

"No time for introductions," he said. He raised his laser and fired.

The woman gasped and fell to the floor, spasming.

He strode across the room, tipped the feebly protesting president from his carriage and held him like a shield. He was as light as a child and felt, in Ellis's grip, sickeningly boneless. "You struggle, Horrescu, and you die. Understood?"

"Who are you?" the tyrant gasped.

Ellis laughed. "Would you believe that I'm a puny human?"

Horrescu began a tirade, but Ellis applied pressure to his neck. The tyrant gasped in pain and fell silent.

"Calla! Follow me. Keep directly behind me at all times, okay?"

Trembling, the Phandran nodded.

With Horrescu dangling listlessly before him, Ellis led the way from the state-room and made for the elevator. He dived inside and slapped the ascent command. A long minute later the elevator door opened and he stepped out and turned right, looking over his shoulder to ensure that Calla was with him.

He hurried along the corridor towards the hangar.

The little party, he thought, would present a strange sight to Sporelli eyes: a tiny, angel-like Phandran following a decrepit, airborne octogenarian.

They came to the hangar doors and pushed through. Ellis led the way across the deck and up the ramp to the flight-deck.

Two Sporelli were seated before the viewscreen, and turned in alarm when he burst into the chamber. A third stood frozen beside a com-console.

Ellis snapped at the president, "Order them to prepare the ship for departure."

The president nodded nervously and relayed the order.

Calla approached him. "Perhaps the president might persuade the Sporelli to cease the attack," she began, then stopped as she apprehended his thoughts.

Ellis smiled. "We'll take him into custody – but the starship will be attacking no one."

He set the president down against the wall, where he slumped to one side with an expression of shocked despair.

Ellis looked around the bridge, trying to discern the disorganised fractal blur that would signify Kranda's return. He saw nothing. He opened communications, and again received only a white-noise of static.

"Kranda..." he said to himself.

The pilot reported, "Ready for take-off."

"Wait!" Ellis snapped.

He asked his varnika, "How long since we planted the blasters?"

"*One hour, fifty seven minutes, three seconds and counting.*"

Less than three minutes before detonation...

He swore. "Okay, get us out of here!"

The interworld ship lifted slowly and swung on its axis.

"There is just one problem..." said the Sporelli pilot.

Ellis stared at the viewscreen. Before the ship, the great hangar door was sealed.

Ellis swore. "Does this thing have weaponry?"

"The very latest –" the pilot began.

"Then use it!"

A dazzling lance of light flashed out from the nose of the ship, striking the riveted panels of the hanger door in blinding actinic starburst. When Ellis's eyes adjusted to the glare, he saw that the metal was blacked and bowed but still intact.

"Again!"

This time the pilot allowed the lasers to play across the hangar doors for a full minute. As Ellis watched, the metal glowed molten then exploded outwards to reveal the welcome vastness of deep space.

"Varnika?"

"Thirty-five seconds, thirty-four..."

"Accelerate!" Ellis yelled at the pilot.

With agonising slowness the ship edged forward through the jagged remnants of the hangar door. When they were free, the ship accelerated.

Ellis staggered as they raced away, staring ahead at the scatter of stars and, centre stage, a sight he had never seen before.

He stepped towards the viewscreen, shaking his head in wonder at the magnificence of the Helix in its entirety, the glittering spiral resplendent in the velvet vastness of deep space, with its ten thousand worlds coiled about the fiery primary.

He had never seen a more beautiful sight in all his life.

Staring at it, as the interworld ship accelerated away from the doomed starship, Ellis felt tears stinging his eyes.

Calla came up to him, raised a hand and found his face. "You are pained," she whispered. "Kranda...?"

He nodded, letting his tears flow now, and reached out for her.

As they headed for the sanctuary of the Helix, Ellis braced himself for the explosion that was now just seconds away.

I

KRANDA SAT UP, trying not to cry out in pain.

Varnika, she thought. *Injury report.*

The calm voice sounded in her ear-piece. "*Fractured left femur, shattered pelvis, five broken ribs, collapsed right lung, dislocated right shoulder...*"

But otherwise, she thought, *I'm fine, hm?*

"*Injuries non-fatal. You will live. I am working to ease the pain.*"

She laughed. "Well, I'm glad to hear that."

Her varnika was as good as its word, flooding her system with analgesics; before long, she could hardly feel a thing, just a spreading, comforting numbness.

She looked about her, ordering the varnika to provide illumination. She was at the bottom of the lift-shaft. Before her was an inspection panel. She lifted her laser and fired. The panel flew open, revealing a lighted corridor beyond.

Okay, I'm attempting to stand up. I'll need your help with this. I want you to walk me forward, supporting my limbs....

"*This is not recommended,*" her varnika replied. "*Remain where you are, preferably in a supine position.*"

I'm afraid that rest is not an option at the moment, my friend. I'm going for upright, despite your recommendations. Here goes.

She hauled herself to her feet, feeling only the spars of her varnika biting into her flesh as they took her weight.

She hitched her rifle into firing position and stepped from the lift-shaft.

2

HERS HAD BEEN an honourable life...

She had served her hive-mother well; she had returned to her birthing place every *yancha* and performed the Ceremony of the Hunt with her siblings. She had distinguished herself in the Mahkan Engineering Corps, graduating a year ahead of time, and then had been appointed to the elite Hakaran squad. For fifteen years she had served the Corps with distinction, travelling to worlds, and *beneath* worlds, she had only ever dreamed of as a cub. Then the human, Jeff Ellis, had saved her life, and she had had an obligation of duty to discharge, a matter of honour to fulfil – twice over – and had performed that duty to the very best of her ability. She had, with Ellis, in all likelihood saved the Helix. Her debt of honour had been discharged. Her people would be proud.

And now her time had come to die.

She limped along, not even the support of her varnika allowing her full mobility. Despite the sedatives, the pain was mounting.

She was in a darkened corridor somewhere towards the outer skin of the ship. She paused, drawing deep breaths, and assessed the situation.

She asked her varnika, *How long before detonation?*

A second later the reply came back, "*Eight minutes, thirty-three seconds and counting.*"

"And how far am I from the interworld ship?"

"*Precisely three point three kilometres.*"

She took a deep breath, then asked, *And how long would it take me to reach the interworld ship?*

The response was a long time coming. *By the most direct route, approximately sixteen minutes, give or take ten seconds.*

She stood tall, facing the inevitable.

She said, *Guide me on the most direct route.*

"*Ahead thirty metres, then turn left, ascend to the next level. There, turn right, proceed for one hundred metres.*"

She followed her varnika's instructions.

It might be impossible, but she had been taught never to lose hope. Sometimes, the impossible happened; sometimes, despite all the odds, if you never gave in, then by force of will you brought about the desired outcome.

She smiled to herself and limped onwards.

As she went, she thought about the human, Jeff Ellis.

Over the course of the past few days she had come to know and understand the man who had saved her life on two occasions. She had seen past his weaknesses, his perverse belief in the sanctity of all life, no matter how undeserving that life, and beheld his unswerving determination to come to the aid of the tiny Phandran, Calla.

With luck, Jeff Ellis would save the Phandran and himself and flee the starship...

She had faith, not only in the human, but in Ellis's varnika. They were hallowed artefacts, and enhanced not only their wearers' strength and sensory capabilities, but their mental faculties. Together, human and varnika, they would survive.

While she, Kranda'vahkan, was destined for other things.

She faced her demise with bravery, knowing that hers had been an honourable life.

3

"*Descend, turn right and proceed for fifty metres.*"

Kranda paused at the top of the stairway, swaying.

She looked down and was shocked by what she saw there. The laser had sliced the flesh and muscle through to the bone of her chest, and beyond, and she had lost a lot of blood. She smiled to herself. Only the spars of the exo-skeleton were holding her shattered body together now.

How far from the interworld ship?

"*Two point four kilometres.*"

She felt a quick surge of hope. *And how long before the detonation?*

"*Three minutes, seventeen seconds.*"

She was about to ask how long it might take her to reach the interworld ship by the optimum route, but stopped herself. She knew in her heart that there was no hope. She would do her best, march onwards…

She stumbled down the stairs, turned left along an arterial corridor and limped on for fifty metres.

Four armoured Sporelli warriors appeared up ahead. They had not been expecting her; they stopped in comic surprise and raised their weapons. Kranda took great delight in lasering them dead, one by one. She heard a sound behind her and turned in time to see a laser beam lance through the air; she ducked, her varnika-enhanced reactions still super-fast, and the beam missed her by centimetres.

Six troops ran towards her, firing as they came. She fired in reply, roaring with anger, and three Sporelli fell dead at her feet. A beam caught the top of her leg, causing a searing pain which the varnika fought to dampen. She shot the soldier who had fired on her, and watched with satisfaction as he died. The others were close now, too close to fend off with laser fire, so she used the laser as a club, along with her right fist, and battered the remaining soldiers to death.

Then she stopped, panting, amid a charnel house of blood, bone and ripped flesh. She grinned to herself. Her mother would be proud.

She walked on.

4

"MAHKAN."

The voice sounded behind her, and she whirled around.

She smiled when she saw the Sporelli soldier standing before her, with what she took to be a miniaturised heat-seeking device balanced on his shoulder.

She said, "Commander Yehn..."

The Sporelli could, she realised, have killed her while her back was turned. Perhaps he possessed a scintilla of honour, after all. Then she reminded herself that this was the very same individual who, back on Phandra, had ordered the guran to be used on defenceless natives.

In his right hand he held a laser pistol, directed at her chest.

Kranda smiled to herself. Commander Yehn really had no idea of the capabilities of her varnika, its lightning speed. He was as good as dead.

The commander said, "Show yourself, Mahkan."

"With pleasure, Commander Yehn." She ordered her varnika to deactivate its shield, and was pleased to behold Yehn's shocked reaction. Shocked, she thought, both by her awesome size and by the extent of her injuries. A lesser being would be dead by now, carrying the wounds she was displaying with pride.

"You know my name?" the commander said.

"I looked upon your handiwork on the world of Phandra," she said. "I watched as you ordered your troops to use whatever force was necessary upon innocent villagers. For that, you will die here today."

The commander sneered. "And you, I presume, will kill me?"

She laughed, a harsh sound in the confines of the corridor. "There is no one else capable of doing the job, Commander."

Swiftly, Yehn raised his pistol and fired. Kranda moved, a little too slowly to escape the beam. It had sliced her ribcage, but not before she had raised her rifle and fired in return.

Her aim was better than the Sporelli's. The beam drilled his chest. He stared at her with something like incredulity as he backed up against the bulkhead and slid into a sitting position. Kranda raised her laser and fired again as he watched, drilling a neat hole in his forehead.

Exultant, she turned and hauled herself along the corridor, following her varnika's calm instructions.

She came to the T-junction she recognised from her arrival aboard the starship. To the left was the amphitheatre, to the right the hangar.

She turned right and limped on, every step an effort now. She knew what she would find when she arrived at the hangar, but she no longer felt disappointed. She had inured herself to the inevitable over the course of the past five minutes, sublimating her anger in a catharsis of destruction.

She came to the sliding hangar door and stepped through.

As she had known it would be, the hangar was empty.

She crossed the deck towards the shattered exit where the stars shone brilliantly through the diaphanous force-seal. She worked to shut out the pain. She looked down, at her upper thigh, and smiled at what she saw. She had walked the last few hundred metres with gouts of blood spouting from a wound the size of her fist, and she had made it to the hangar, her destination.

She came to the lip of the chamber and, wincing with pain, seated herself crossed-legged and stared out.

She smiled. The interworld ship was accelerating away from the starship, dwindling towards the resplendent spiral of the Helix. The sight took her breath away. The Helix was truly miraculous, truly beautiful. She had never looked upon a more wondrous sight in her life, and she gave herself up to the emotion deep within her.

On impulse, she opened the channel between herself and Jeff Ellis, hoping to have one last word with the human.

As expected, there was only static.

Even so, she said, "Jeff Ellis, I have no idea if you'll ever receive this, but... it has been an honour knowing you, human."

She sensed movement behind her and heard footsteps ring across the decking. Let the Sporelli shoot her dead; she would have the final victory.

She asked her varnika, *How long before detonation?*

And the reply came, "*Nine seconds, eight...*"

She looked over her shoulder at the Sporelli advancing across the hangar.

She willed the Sporelli troops not to open fire and kill her, then; she wanted just a few more seconds, to learn for certain that the starship was indeed doomed.

"*Three, two, one... zero.*"

She felt rather than heard a dull thud deep within the ship. The decking beneath her shifted seismically, tilting. A second, bigger explosion bucked the starship; she imagined bulkheads rupturing, decking twisting and folding in the wave-front of the blast. To her right, she could see along the curving flank of the ship, and what she saw caused her heart to leap. Whole sections of the ship were blown outwards in a silent confetti of metal panels and fragmented decking. She looked over her shoulder and saw the advancing troops lose their footing like toy soldiers and tumble across the canted deck. She slid fifty metres and fetched up against the far frame of the hangar entrance.

She lay on her back, looking up at the destruction of the starship as fragments fell away in silent slow-motion. Individual Sporelli tumbled past her, out into the void, and Kranda laughed uproariously and held on.

Finally, another vast explosion detonated deep within the starship, and a searing heat rushed towards her, caught her up, and carried her out into the hard vacuum.

TWENTY-FIVE /// RETURN

I

MARIA ELLENOPOULIS STARED into the familiar face of the man standing before her and said, "Where am I?"

The man smiled. He had a calm and reassuring presence, a gentleness of manner that put her at ease. He wore the red one-piece uniform of the Peacekeepers, but she knew that he could be no real Peacekeeper – or, come to that, a real human.

He said, "You are in the realm of the Builders. This" – he gestured around him at the limitless grassland – "is where the ancient race now reside; though visually it has been *tweaked*, let's say, to accord to your perceptions."

She stared about her. "The Builders live here?" she asked.

"All around you," the man replied.

"I don't see them..."

He laughed. "But you do. You see, don't you, the blades of grass, the trees, the far off birds?"

She stared. "They... they're the *Builders*?"

"It is how their essences are conveyed to your perceptions, yes."

She laughed, then cut short the laugh in case it sounded irreverent. "And you?" she asked. "Are you a Builder?"

"I am merely a human being, Maria, in the employ of the Builders."

She stared at him, then asked, "And why me? Why not... I

don't know... one of the liaison team? Someone more qualified to communicate with the Builders?"

"Oh, that will come, in time," he said. "Now that the Builders have informed your people, via the agency of the Mahkan, of their whereabouts, then in due course the first communications in almost two hundred years can commence."

"And my role in all of this?" she asked.

"You have no role, as such, in the dialogue that will follow. However, the Builders expressly require your... assistance. They have discerned in you the necessary qualities for the duty they have in mind."

"Which is?" she asked, heart pounding.

He gestured to a fallen tree trunk which she was sure had not been there a moment ago. "Shall we sit down, Maria, and I will explain?"

She crossed with him to the fallen log, and sat down.

And she listened as he told her exactly why she was here.

2

CALLA WAS NEARING THE end of the long journey from her valley to the Retreat of Verlaine. The end, she felt in her bones, was approaching. She had originally, before the last great adventure, planned to continue healing in the small towns and villages that nestled in the mountains south of Verlaine – but that had been before recent events.

The ship had brought her back to Phandra, and set her down in the valley near her hut, and she had said a tearful farewell to the human called Jeff Ellis. He had promised to visit her world in the near future, but she doubted that she would see him again; by the time he did venture to Phandra, if indeed he did, she would be long gone to Fahlaine.

She had watched the interworld ship rise into the air, Jeff Ellis standing tall behind the viewscreen, his arm raised in a farewell gesture. She had waited until the ship was out of sight, then turned and made the long climb to her hut.

A surprise had awaited her therein.

An Elder was seated on the crude wooden stool before the hearth.

He smiled as she entered. "Welcome home, Healer Calla-vahn-villa," he said.

She wondered what the Elder wanted with her. She offered him a hot drink, but he declined and said, "I will be brief, Calla. I have a message from Diviner Tomar at Verlaine. You are to make your way there forthwith, and meet with him in the Council chamber."

"But my duties," she began, flustered. "I have people to heal..."

The Elder smiled and shook his head. "You have more than discharged your duties with your exploits of late, Healer Calla. You are required at the Retreat of Verlaine."

So she had taken her leave of the Elder and left her valley for the very last time, and here she was, days later, at the foot of the approach road to the mountainous Retreat.

She looked up at the hallowed edifice where she would spend her last few days, the distant spires and towers resplendent in the light of the setting sun. She was suffused with peace as she made the ascent.

The small door in the great gate of the Retreat opened as she approached, and an awed acolyte – had news of her off-world exploits reached here already? – led her through the foyer, up the steps and through the labyrinthine corridors of the Retreat.

Fifteen minutes later she stood before the hallowed silverwood door, and the acolyte slipped away.

She paused, then pushed open the great door and stepped into the chamber.

Effulgent light from the setting sun flooded down the central aisle through the southern window, dazzling her. When her eyes adjusted, she made out the ranked pews, the ancient tapestries, and she felt peace settle in her heart. She was *home*, at last.

She made the long walk down the aisle towards the circular Council area, where a long time ago, it seemed, she had met with Diviner Tomar and he had told her of her destiny.

She came within a hundred metres of the Council area and stopped in her tracks. Diviner Tomar was seated on the padded circular bench beneath the Southern Window, but he was not alone.

Seated beside him, towering above the diminutive Diviner, was the dark alien she had seen in the chamber on her last visit here. And, as before, she sensed not the slightest emanation from his mind; he was a disturbing blank, a mental lacuna.

The alien was deep in conversation with Diviner Tomar, and only fell silent and looked up when she stepped into the circle of benches.

"Healer Calla," Diviner Tomar said in his hushed voice, "please, be seated."

The alien – similar in form to Jeff Ellis, but of a different colour – was smiling at her, and oddly his gentle smile reminded her of Jeff's.

Heart fluttering, she sat down opposite the pair.

"Healer Calla," said Diviner Tomar, "you have gone far since our last meeting, and achieved much."

She bowed her head. "It was as you predicted, Diviner."

"You have more than exceeded our expectations with your bravery, your commitment to all that is good."

"I did no more than fulfil the destiny you set out for me," she murmured. She glanced quickly at the dark being. He was watching her, a smile playing about his lips.

"But Calla," Diviner Tomar said, "you did not quite *fulfil* your destiny."

She looked up, disturbed. "I failed you in some way?" Her heart sank; she was here to be reprimanded.

The old Diviner laughed gently. "Of course you did not fail me, Healer Calla," he said. "You did not fulfil your destiny because, at our last meeting, I failed to divulge the entirety of that destiny."

She stared at the Diviner, shaking her head in bewilderment. "I don't understand."

"I said you would go far, and achieve much. I said you would pass beyond this world, visit other worlds."

"And I did, Diviner Tomar. I visited D'rayni, and even the terrible world of Sporell."

"And I said you would go even further," Diviner Tomar said, "beyond the Helix, even..."

She smiled as she recollected her flight aboard the interworld ship, the sight of the Helix floating against the backdrop of brilliant stars.

"And that, too, I achieved."

The old Diviner smiled at her, calm, patient, as if smiling at a child. He said, "I meant, Healer Calla, that you would go even further than just the space surrounding the Helix."

She looked down at her hands, knotted in her lap. "Well, in that case I failed," she said, though even as she spoke the words she had some sense that she was being disingenuous.

"You did not fail," Diviner Tomar said, "because that venture, if you decide to take it, is before you."

She looked up, her heart pounding. "Before me...?" she echoed. "But... but I am old, I am near the end. Fahlaine awaits..."

Without warning the dark alien stood up, and the sudden movement, and the fact of his great size as he crossed towards her, made her cower involuntarily in her seat.

He knelt before her, but still looked down. He spoke her language in a deep, rich voice, "The end, Calla, awaits only if that is what you wish. You have another destiny, and one which I would very much like you to take."

She felt dizzy, and fought not to faint. "But I will be dead within the year," she whispered.

He inclined his head in an affirmative. "That is so, if you wish. But, also, if you wish, I have the means to extend your life."

"Extend?" she echoed, disbelieving.

"For five hundred of your years, a thousand, even longer."

"A thousand?" She shook her head. "But why?"

"I could tell you, Calla, but" – he smiled – "it would be far better if I *showed* you."

She was about to ask him what he meant, when suddenly the blankness within his head was no more. He opened his mind to her and she was instantly privy to the exhilarating rush of his thoughts. She gasped as she basked in the wonder revealed there, and understood why the Builders wanted her.

When the human closed his thoughts to her, minutes later, she looked across at Diviner Tomar as if for confirmation. The old man inclined his head, smiling. "It is the destiny I saw for you, Calla, but withheld."

"It is your choice," the human said. He reached out a great, dark hand. "With one touch, I can grant you extended life."

She considered his words, and what it would mean; a new life far, far from here, new experiences she could only guess at; and a postponement, for now, of her reception into Fahlaine.

It was a hard choice, and it took her several minutes to decide.

3

SHE WOKE SEATED in the mouth of the mountain cave.

The icy cold chivvied her flesh, but it was a vital, invigorating cold; a complete contrast to the heat she recalled from her last, living memory.

She was on her homeworld, she realised – which was impossible.

She was dead...

She *should* be dead, immolated in the explosion that destroyed the Sporelli starship, ripped apart by the shrapnel of flying metal, roasted in the resulting sleet of radiation... and, if by some miracle, she had survived that, then surely she should have asphyxiated in the vacuum of deep space.

She raised her hands, and stared at the spars of the varnika encapsulating her limbs. She stared down at her body, which by rights should have been shattered... but, miraculously, she was whole again.

She took a breath, feeling the cold air hit her lungs.

She wondered, then, if this was a trick of her dying mind: if in the nano-seconds before death, her brain had excluded the terrible events occurring all around her and manufactured instead this comforting scenario. In seconds, death would come, extinction, an end to everything.

She sat in the mouth of the cave and waited.

In the distance, notched between two mountain peaks, she made out her hive-mother's manse. The sight of it filled Kranda with a nostalgia that brought tears to her eyes. She was flooded with memories of her earlier life here, the happy times she had spent while growing up.

It was a cruel vision to place before a dying being.

She heard a sound, far below. She cocked her head, listening. She made out the constant soughing of the wind through the peaks, but no other sound. She must have been mistaken.

Seconds later the sound came again, the dislodging of stone, a curse, a panting breath.

She turned her head in the direction of the sound and saw, climbing towards the ledge on which she sat, the improbable figure of a human being.

She stared, incredulity piled on incredulity. A human, at this altitude? They were puny beings, unable to withstand the rigours of such an elevation.

And yet here he was, a dark-skinned human dressed only in a red one-piece uniform, and smiling as he came.

Without a word he sat down, cross-legged, before Kranda, and said in faultless Mahkan, "You have, no doubt, many questions."

Kranda maintained her outward composure, though internally she was in turmoil. She said, at last, "Indeed I have, and my first question is... Am I alive?"

The human smiled. "Take a breath, pinch your flesh, look upon the stark splendour of your world. Do you doubt that you are alive?"

"And my next question is, how? How did I survive the starship explosion?"

"The varnika," said the human, "is a wonderful thing. It has the capabilities of which you are aware, and many others beside. It is also indestructible. Put simply, it recorded your essence, your body, your mind and... for want of a better word, your soul, and over the course of days it rebuilt you."

"And then returned me to the Helix?"

The human smiled. "And then I took a ship out to the wreckage of the Sporelli starship, and retrieved you."

Kranda inclined her head, taking in these incredible facts as if they were no more than everyday items of news. "And this begs the question, human: why? Why did the varnika bring me back to life?"

"Because, Kranda'vahkan, your destiny is not complete. We would like you to work with us."

She let the seconds elapse, absorbing the human's words, and said at last, "And just who are *you*, human?"

He smiled. "I work for the Builders," he said.

Kranda inclined her head. She had guessed as much. The human could only, after all, be in the employ of the Builders.

"Work with you?" she asked, "in what manner?"

The human stood and gestured down the path. "Perhaps you would care to accompany me? We should return to your hive-mother's manse, and along the way I will explain everything."

"That sounds," Kranda said, "a reasonable proposition."

She stood, towering over the human, and side by side they set off along the twisting path through the mountain peaks.

4

A WEEK AFTER arriving back on New Earth, Jeff Ellis visited the grave garden where his son was buried.

He sat on the small mound in the shade of an oak tree. "...and then," he finished, "the ship exploded. You should have seen it go. Bang, and bang, bang... But Kranda never got out. We... we shared a lot during those last few days, and I've never met a braver person."

He would make the trip to Kranda's homeworld soon, and visit her hive-mother, and tell her how her daughter had died a hero's death. Perhaps, at the same time, he would visit Phandra and call in on Calla before she passed away. They had talked a lot on the way back to the Helix, and he had come to understand that from her point of view her passing would not be an occasion to mourn, but to celebrate. Fahlaine awaited her, she had told him, and she looked ahead to the day she left this life with anticipation. Ellis had smiled and said that he understood, though he still found the fact of her pre-ordained death, and the celebratory nature of her approach to it, difficult to accept.

It seemed, when he reflected upon it, a time of death, death, relentless death.

And yet much good had come of the recent events. The threat to the Helix was no more, with the destruction of the Sporelli starship. President Horrescu was in the custody of the Peacekeepers, and the advance of Sporelli troops across Phandra and D'rayni had ground to a halt. Peacekeeping forces, backed up by Mahkan ships, had confronted the Sporelli armies and threatened them with the combined might of their interworld squadrons. The uneasy stand-off had lasted for a day, until the New Earth authorities had prevailed upon ex-President Horrescu to make a broadcast telling his troops that resistance was useless.

Peace, at last, had come to the worlds of Phandra and D'rayni.

He patted the turf of the mound and said, "So I'm taking a few days off. They offered me a month, but I didn't want to be kicking my heels around the house for that long. I'd rather be working..." He laughed to himself. "Though I don't know how I'll adapt to ferrying shuttles back and forth after my recent adventures."

He stood and looked down at his son's grave.

"I've come to say goodbye, Ben, for the time being, at least. And to apologise for not coming before now. It was..." He stopped, then said, "It was just too damned painful, but now..."

He thought about his actions aboard the Sporelli starship, and asked himself if there might have been another way he could have prevented the destruction of Mahkana, and New Earth, without taking the lives of those aboard the ship.

For the life of him, he did not know.

He looked up, suddenly, as he realised that he was not alone. He felt a quick pang of embarrassment at being caught addressing his dead son – or talking to himself, as it must have appeared to the watching stranger.

Then he looked more closely at the man, standing a few metres away and smiling at him.

"I hope you don't mind me saying this," Ellis said, "but you look a hell of a lot like one of the First Four, Friday Olembe."

The man winked at him. "That's because, Jeff Ellis, I am Friday Olembe."

A strange heat passed through his head and he felt suddenly dizzy. He gathered himself. "Now... why don't I believe that?"

The man laughed. He had an easy way with him that was immediately likeable. "Because, to begin with, Olembe died one hundred and seventy years ago, and surely couldn't still be alive, could he? Because ghosts don't exist? Because, when you think about it, why should Friday Olembe seek out Jeff Ellis?"

Ellis managed a smile. "Yes, all those things."

"One day, Jeff, I'll tell you what happened to me, one hundred and seventy years ago. For now, I'll just reassure you that I am indeed, hard though it might be to believe, Friday Olembe. I'm no ghost. And I'm here to make you an offer. Why don't you sit yourself back down and let me tell you something?"

"Before that..." Ellis began, then gathered his thoughts. "The Builders are powerful," he said tentatively, "more powerful than I can even begin to imagine. And yet, they did nothing to stop the approach of the Sporelli starship, the imminent invasion of the Sporelli armies."

Olembe smiled. "They are powerful, yes, more powerful than even *I* can imagine... But there are limits to their powers, Jeff, and limits to their knowledge. There remain only hundreds of their kind, and most of them are in Quiescence, as they call it – the virtual realm as we know it. Physically, perhaps only a dozen go abroad, in various guises – and they use people like myself to monitor events. So, although the Builders are powerful, and have invested me and my colleagues with powers beyond my earlier imagining, there are some events they cannot foresee, and some circumstances they cannot shape, or alter."

Ellis thought about it, then smiled. "Perhaps it's good to know that the Builders aren't... God-like."

Olembe gestured to the hillock, and Ellis did as he was bidden. He sat under the spreading boughs of the oak, and the African climbed the mound and eased himself down beside him.

"It is two hundred years," Olembe said, "since we humans arrived on the Helix. Since then, there have been no new arrivals here. That is not unusual. Centuries, sometimes even millennia, can pass by between arrivals. After all, there are only so many races out there in need of salvation... And we – I speak here of the Builders – we have many ways of gathering those races. Some, like the human race, arrived here under their own steam, so to speak, with a little help from the Builders. Others have had to be sought, brought here physically – and there are many ways we go about that. But however we do it, Jeff, we need ships to transport the Saved. And ships, you will need no telling, require pilots, crew."

Olembe paused, and Ellis just stared at him in silence, aware of what was happening here but unable, just then, to frame an adequate response.

"The Builders are aware of a race on the brink of extinction. We have a world prepared here on the fourth circuit, ten down-spiral from New Earth, called at the moment simply Helix 4721. All that needs to be done is for a starship to travel the five hundred light years to fetch the alien race in question... though I make that sound like an easy operation. I have no doubt that it will not be, that obstacles will have to be overcome, that even on arrival all will not be plain sailing... But all that to one side. I am here today to offer you a period of intensive training, and then a post as one of the starship's pilots. You have," Olembe finished, "no need to tell me straight away; take your time to think it through. However, I think there are a couple of people you should meet who might make that decision a little easier to make."

Ellis stared at the African. "Two people?" he said.

Smiling, Friday Olembe turned and pointed across the grave garden.

Ellis stared, and made out two figures seated on a distant mound beneath a tree. His heart pounded and blood rushed to his head. The pair were a hundred metres away, but even at this distance he could make out that one of them was a Mahkan, the other a Phandran.

He surged to his feet and took a few steps forward, then broke into a run.

He crossed the hundred metres in no time at all, then came to a sudden halt. He stared, open-mouthed, at the people smiling up at him.

"Calla?" he whispered. "Kranda?"

They stood.

He stared at the Mahkan. "Kranda? Is it really you? But..."

The Mahkan pulled back her lips in an attempt at a human smile. "Which other Mahkan would come all this way just to see you, human?" she said.

"But you died! The starship..."

"I died, and the varnika saved me and rebuilt me. And now I live, and perhaps in future, Jeff, you might save my life a few more times?"

Ellis stepped forward and embraced the mighty Mahkan, and Kranda returned the gesture, almost squeezing the breath from his lungs.

He turned to the Phandran, and she murmured, "Friday said I would be working alongside my favourite human being, Jeff, so how could I refuse?"

"But... but I thought you were dying, Calla?"

She smiled up at him. "I was, but no longer, thanks to the Builders."

He stepped forward and hugged her. He released her after a long minute, and held her at arm's length, and through his tears he looked from the Phandran to the Mahkan and said, "You can't begin to imagine how happy I am to see you both again."

"I always knew," said Kranda, "that humans were overly sentimental."

Calla said, "I think I speak for my Mahkan friend, Jeff, when I say that our happiness matches your own."

They turned. Friday Olembe had joined them, and he gestured towards a vehicle parked beyond the perimeter fence. "And now, if you would care to join me, I have a starship I would like you to inspect."

Together they stepped from the shade of the oak and walked from the grave garden.

CODA /// ASCENT

I

JEFF ELLIS HAD one more surprise awaiting him.

At Carrelliville spaceport they boarded a waiting interworld ship and left New Earth. One day later they arrived at their destination, a world named Helix 1, as yet uninhabited, occupying a position at the very end of the Helix's two-hundred-million kilometre spiral.

They hurried from the ship and crossed the snow to a silver dome that rose in the all encompassing whiteness. The filed into the chamber and descended to the central spine of the Helix, spending the ten hours of the journey under sedation.

Ellis woke suddenly, seemingly minutes later, to find that they had arrived. Olembe gestured to the flank of the chamber, where an arched hatch opened. He led the way out, Kranda ducking after him, Calla following and staring about her in wonder, while Ellis brought up the rear.

They were in the vast, porcelain dimensions of the spine, a Gaia Machine looming like a mountain perhaps a kilometre away.

Calla gripped his hand and said, "Where are we, Jeff?"

He tried to view this wonder through her eyes, and recalled his own awed reaction to the spine beneath D'rayni. "The central spine of the Helix, Calla," he murmured.

"And that?" She gestured towards the Gaia Machine.

He told her, then added, "It's the... the heart, I suppose you could say – or maybe even the brains – of the Helix."

Friday Olembe laughed. "I think perhaps both, Jeff," he said.

He led them across the chamber towards a slit in the decking, and Ellis watched Calla as, at their approach, a mono-carriage appeared from the slit like a genie from a lamp. She gasped and stepped back, her grip tightening on his hand.

Olembe gestured to the hatch in the flank of the carriage. "This time, my friends, the journey will last for less than one hour."

"Where are we going?" Kranda asked as they climbed inside and took their seats.

Olembe smiled as he said, "To the very *end* of the Helix, my friends."

They took their seats, and were instantly enveloped in the soft padding.

2

THE PADDING WITHDREW, releasing them, and Olembe led the way from the carriage.

They were standing before a bulkhead constructed of the same material as the floor, a white cliff-face that extended upwards for as far as the eye could see. Olembe stepped forward, touched something in the wall, and Ellis watched as a thick, cylindrical plug withdrew itself with a hiss from the bulkhead and hinged outwards. Revealed was an illuminated corridor. Olembe stepped forward and gestured at them to do the same.

Calla gripping his hand, Ellis entered the bright tunnel and hurried after Olembe.

Seconds later they emerged onto a gallery, crossed to a rail, and looked down.

Beside him, Kranda exclaimed in her own language, and all Ellis could do was laugh in stupefied amazement. Calla whispered, "I do not understand, Jeff. Where are we? What is it?"

Ellis just shook his head, attempting to find the words that would adequately describe what was before them.

Olembe said, "We are at the end of the Helix, my friends. What we see before us is just one level, one deck, of a thousand – and beyond, through the viewscreen, is the star-specked darkness of deep space."

Ellis gripped the rail and stared down on kilometre after kilometre of ranked starships of every conceivable shape and design. "And which is ours?" he asked.

Olembe pointed to the largest ship, a blunt-nosed behemoth directly below where they stood. "We call it the *Phoenix*," he said.

An elevator carried them down to the deck and they crossed to the starship.

"You will be part of a crew of over one hundred personnel of varying specialisms selected from the many races of the Helix," Olembe explained as they approached the *Phoenix*. "Your training will begin shortly, and our estimated time of departure is approximately one year from now."

"*Our*?" Kranda asked. "You mean, you're coming too?"

Olembe smiled. "This is an adventure I wouldn't want to miss out on. Gina Carrelli will be joining us, too."

Ellis smiled. To meet Carrelli, to talk to her and Olembe about their parts in the exploits of the First Four... It was almost too much to take in.

He looked at Olembe and asked. "But what about Joe Hendry and Sissy Kaluchek? Are they still alive?"

Olembe smiled – sadly, it seemed to Ellis. "They were approached by representatives of the Builders, but they declined the offer. They said they had experienced enough adventuring for one lifetime, and wished to settle down. But that seems like a long, long time ago now, Jeff." He laughed. "Come, inspect the ship and meet the rest of the crew."

They stepped into what looked like an ovipositor and were sucked up into the belly of the ship. From there they took an elevator to the flight-deck. Other humans moved about the deck along with Mahkans, a Jantisar, two or three races Ellis did not recognise and even a diminutive Agstarnian. They were all, he thought, smitten by wonder, like children in Aladdin's cave.

And then he saw a familiar, dark-haired figure across the deck, and his heart began a laboured pounding.

He looked at Olembe, who shrugged. "She is, after all, one of the best medics on New Earth," he said.

Calla squeezed his hand. "Go to her," she exhorted.

Ellis nodded, and dry of mouth left Calla's side and made the long walk across the deck towards where Maria was standing, staring through the vast viewscreen, with her back to him.

He cleared his throat and said, "Maria."

She turned quickly, and smiled, and her smile seemed genuine. "Jeff," she said "Friday said you'd been... chosen."

He tried to make sense of the mix of emotions whirling through his head. "I didn't know you'd be here..." He laughed. "I'm sorry, this is something of a..."

"A shock? She smiled, reached out and took his hand. "Welcome aboard, Jeff."

He said, "But... what about Dan?"

She made a bitter face. "History. I'll tell you about him, some day." Then she said, "We'll have plenty of time to talk, in the years ahead."

In silence, side by side, they stared out through the viewscreen at the stars massed beyond the Helix.

At last he said, "Come on, Maria. I'd like to introduce you to my friends."

They turned and crossed the deck to where Calla, Kranda and Friday Olembe were waiting.

ABOUT THE AUTHOR

Eric Brown's first short story was published in *Interzone* in 1987, and he sold his first novel, *Meridian Days*, in 1992. He has won the British Science Fiction Award twice for his short stories and has published forty books: SF novels, collections, books for teenagers and younger children, and he writes a monthly SF review column for the *Guardian*. His latest books include the novels *Engineman* and *The Kings of Eternity*, for Solaris Books.

He is married to the writer and mediaevalist Finn Sinclair and they have a daughter, Freya.
His website can be found at: www.ericbrown.co.uk